I0535773

Redemption

Redemption

BOOK 2 - THE KATANA SERIES

KATHRINE LEANNAN

Dragon Muse Press
Redemtion - Book 2 of the Katana Series

Copyright © 2016 by Kathrine Leannan
E-Book ISBN: 978-0-9944671-2-6
Print Book ISBN: 978-0-9944671-3-3

Cover design by DusktilDawn Designs
Edited by Mary Harris
Proofread by KH Koehler Design
Book Design by The Deliberate Page

All cover art and logo copyright © 2016 by Dragon Muse Press

ALL RIGHTS RESERVED. This literary work or any portion thereof, may not be reproduced or transmitted in any form or by any means; including electronic or photographic reproduction or used in any manner whatsoever without the express written permission of the publisher except for the use of brief quotations in a book review.

All characters and events in this book are fictitious. Any resemblance to actual persons living or dead is coincidental.

PUBLISHER
Dragon Muse Press
DragonMusePress@bigpond.com

This book is dedicated to Tess, Alicia, Brad and Kane; children of blood and of bond. I shall love and treasure you, always.

Acknowledgements

To Mimi, my 1000 year old dragon Muse, where would I be, without your mind-prods in the middle of the night, to share your creative ideas or to chide me on my "obvious mortal errors of timeline or characterisation."

I am beyond grateful to you, for granting me entry to the world of the Fey and for allowing me to walk beside you in the Faery.

You are my inspiration, my source of creation, my Oracle and advisor.

May we walk through this life and the next and the next, together, always.

Prologue

THE LIGHT OF A NEW DAY SHONE DOWN UPON THE pristine splendour of the Faery, a place where the fey and humans of all creeds and bloodlines lived, laughed, and died in each other's company. This was a time of peace. The Faery was their world, their universe.

Danu, the Tuatha Dé Danann Celtic Queen of the Fey Fairies, sat on the lush green grass beside a lily-strewn pond. Wildflowers, all the colours of the rainbow, swayed and danced under a gentle breeze.

"We are indeed blessed, daughter." She flourished her hand. "Look around you. The beauty of our land is unequalled."

"Indeed, Mother." Dagda peered into the woods as she walked around the perimeter of the area. "Beauty in any form is always coveted by others. Perhaps it is the peace and splendour of the Faery that poses us the greatest risk." A golden torque with a brilliant, huge red stone glistened from round her neck. "Perhaps it is a blessing, or maybe it is a curse." A broadsword hung down her side. Its blade gleamed in the sunlight.

Danu frowned and shook her head as she trailed her fingers in the clear, cool water. Minnows leapt into the air, splashed, then

1

returned to the depths. "Ever suspicious. Ever watchful, for treachery. We are at peace, daughter. As Guardian of our race, surely even you can accept that we are challenged by no one."

"It is rumoured, Mother, there is an unknown band of rogue Dark Gods who would make war in the Faery, to take that which is — "

They both looked up suddenly at the sound of rustling undergrowth from a nearby copse of trees.

"Well met, Queen Danu and Guardian."

"Finn MacRobertson! What are you doing here? I thought you would be busy with that new baby of yours. How many is that now? Fifteen? Twenty?" Dagda relaxed and stood down.

He bent into a deep bow as he laughed. "You know very well, my lady, our latest addition makes eleven. Eleven wonderful bairns; my dear wife and I are blessed — "

Day suddenly became night.

Darkness engulfed them as if a thick blanket enshrouded the sun. Dagda sprinted to the grassed area to stand in front of her mother, drew her sword, and stood with the blade outstretched. Blind in a thick cloud of billowing shadow, she turned in a circle, sweeping the blade in front of her. Out of the gloom, a hideous shriek erupted as vicious spikes raked her face and arms. Moisture in her hand squelched as she shifted her grip on the hilt. She knew blood dripped from her fingertips. "Finn! The queen! Protect the queen!"

Lights danced before her eyes when a lethal grip squeezed her throat. As she struggled, her fingers clawed at the fist that choked her. The sword fell from her hand and dropped to the ground.

The last thing she heard was her mother screaming.

The darkness suddenly cleared as suddenly as it had arrived. Finn crawled on bloodied hands and knees over to where Danu lay on the ground. "My lady!"

She reached her trembling hand toward him. "What has happened?" Her voice shrilled with hysteria. "Dagda! Dagda!" Her fingers grasped his shirt. "My daughter? Where is my daughter? Where is she?"

Slowly, he pulled himself to his feet, and then held his hand out to her. "My lady, please…the Guardian is gone. We must make haste, to return you to the palace. Please, majesty, you are not safe here."

With his arm looped around her waist, she wiped her fingers through a line of moisture that tracked from a wound on her temple. Vivid red scratches marked her cheek. "What happened, Finn, son of the MacRobertson? The darkness…I don't understand what—"

She gasped when she kicked her toe on something hard and stumbled.

Finn held her upright with one hand and reached down with the other. The Sword of the Guardian lay on the ground. Blood smeared the length of the blade. He picked it up and handed it to her hilt first.

Staring at the blade, her hands remained at her sides. "My daughter tried to warn me of the Dark Gods and I did not heed her words. Now the Tuatha Dé Danann is without a Guardian in a time of apparent need. Three hundred years will pass before the next Guardian is born." A single tear tracked down her face as she shook her head at the proffered blade. "No. Take this sword from my sight. No more will the sisters of the Tuatha Dé Danann rely on mortal weapons for protection."

"My lady. The Sword of the Guardian is a sacred relic. The stag carved into this blade is the heart chakra of your race. At the time of creation, this weapon was made for the hand of our Protector."

A deep hum buzzed around them as Danu began to vibrate and glow. "Take the sword, Finn of the MacRobertson. I know you and your family work with metal. The sword will be safe in your hands." She started to sob. "My daughter is gone. Without a Guardian, the blade must find a new purpose or;" her shoulders shook as she cried in wracking gasps, "the hand of a future Guardian." As she brushed away her tears, she stood tall. Hatred heated her face. "I, Queen of the Tuatha Dé Danann, summon the power of the ones who have gone before us—the Old Mothers, whose memories and voices I share. Return the strength of our magicks to me and I will smite all who threaten us. Of this I vow!"

A raven swooped and landed on a high, leafy branch of a ghost gum. His throat hackles vibrated as he watched and waited.

Chapter One

Australia, New South Wales, current time

THE RED 750CC SUZUKI KATANA SCREAMED ALONG the New England Highway, with its wide sweeping corners and panoramic views of the Australian rural countryside; a road made for big bikes. Flashes of the gravesite where her husband Craig cradled their son James in death, alternated with Nimerlin, her family property, her clan, and Hades, her Friesian stallion. For six hours, Connor MacDonald rode toward a new beginning, a new life, oblivious of her surroundings. The ancient scabbard that sometimes housed her katana, the God Killer, tapped a familiar tattoo on her back each time she hit a bump in the road. Memories of her abandoned career as a midwife taunted her empty womb; profound sadness once again settled over her like a second skin.

An hour later, suppressing a deep sigh, she spread a map across the white tablecloth of the roadhouse booth. As she traced down the paper with her index finger, she tapped, then nodded. *Good! Another half an hour or so and I'll be at Glen Rowan Station. Then I guess I'll find out what the next twelve months has in store for me.* After wiping her mouth with her napkin, she folded the chart and returned it to the pocket of her leather jacket. She picked up her helmet from the cushion beside her and walked toward the cash register.

The quizzical look on the attendant's face made her turn around. The roadhouse was suddenly pin-drop quiet in the restaurant. Every patron stared at her. She turned back to the cashier, shrugged, and paid her bill. The eerie feeling of their eyes stayed with her until she mounted the bike and roared off down the road.

At just a little after one in the afternoon, she slowed down, then idled in front of a sign that read *Glen Rowan*. The threshold of the boundary fence, demarcated by a cattle grid, which, although definitely not road bike friendly, confirmed she had reached her destination. After navigating the bouncing suspension over the metal rungs, she gunned the engine down the road and pulled up outside a large, whitewashed house.

Kickstand engaged, she drew her leg over the black leather seat and stood for the first time on the soil that for the next year would be home. A sense of darkness seemed almost tangible. A cold shiver ran down her spine just as the God Killer vibrated under the ink work on her right bicep. The Sword of War, under her left tribal tattoo, sent a hot spear of lightning down her arm. "You both feel it too, huh?" She looked around, a full 360 degrees with both of her hands fisted at her sides. The swords continued to vibrate, when, from a huge gum tree at the side of the house, came the eerie *aahh-aahh* of a raven.

With the scabbard still across her back, she shrugged while her fingers worked with practiced ease, unknotting the chinstrap of the helmet, then pulled it free of her head. Gently, she caressed the smooth enamel with the custom design of the Samurai sword, the MacDonald tartan and a rearing black Friesian stallion. As she tucked the head-covering under one arm, her heart clenched at the flood of memories of the time when Craig gave it to her as a gift. After walking up the front steps, she stood on the porch, sucked in a big breath, and knocked on the door with her free hand.

The *aahh-aahh* screech of the raven renewed the chill down her spine. She turned in time to see the bird take flight. It flew so low towards her that she jolted under its stare. Suddenly, the door swung open and she turned round. A cheery-faced, round woman with sparkling eyes and deep laugh lines, stepped onto the threshold.

"Can I help ye?" Her soft Scottish lilt ignited the deep burn of homesickness.

Connor swapped the helmet to her left hand, smiled and extended her palm. "I hope so. I'm here to see Douglas McVey.The woman stood to one side, making little fluttering movements with one hand. "Och, then, come right though here. Himself and the lads are havin' their lunch. I'm Mrs O'Donough, the hoosekeeper, by the way."

Connor followed the expansive, swaying rump in front of her, through the front door and deeper into the house.

"Douglas, there be someone here to see ye," Mrs O'Donough chortled as she sidestepped, which wasn't actually necessary, given that Connor was a least a foot taller than her.

Five sets of eyes looked up from the plates in front of them.

When no one spoke, Connor stepped forward. "Mr McVey?"

"Aye." Five separate voices spoke in unison as they got to their feet.

Frowning, she tipped her head to the side. "Mr Douglas McVey?"

"Aye, lass." The grey-headed man at the head of the table acknowledged her with a nod. "I'm Douglas McVey. Can I help ye?"

She extended her hand to him. "It's a pleasure to meet you. I'm Connor MacDonald. I believe I'm expected."

"Holy Jesus," said the male who appeared to be the eldest of the other men standing next to Douglas. The other three younger men stifled their laughter as they sat down and returned their gazes to the food in front of them. The housekeeper leaned against the wall, smiling, with her arms crossed under her massive breasts.

Douglas McVey was a bear of a man with a thatch of grey hair; his wrinkled face was testament to years of work in the Australian sun. He stood with his knuckles pressed on the tablecloth. The power of a man used to getting his own way radiated from him.

His grey eyebrows drew together as he sat down and leaned back in his chair. "Connor MacDonald? Now that just canna be right. There must be some mistake."

"No. No mistake." Connor placed the helmet on the table and withdrew an envelope from the pocket of her Kevlar trousers. She held the white packet embossed with *Glen Rowan* in her hand and waved it toward him. "A month ago, you and I exchanged contracts for the position of dressage master, for the period of the next twelve months.

"I doona think *ye* and I have anything atween us that is legally binding, lass. 'Tis true we are expecting a Connor MacDonald, but that person is a man! This job calls for a man, and unless me eyes deceive me, lass, ye are no man!"

"Indeed, I am not. In fact, the last time I looked, I was most definitely female." A flash of temper made her face flush as she straightened her spine to make good every inch of her height of six feet. "If you could show me to my living quarters, I'd like to start settling in. Also, I'll need to inspect the accommodations for my horse; he will arrive the day after tomorrow."

The chair behind him scraped as he stepped away from the table and stood in front of her. "Now, lass…"

"May I remind you, Mr McVey," she held up her hand in a stop sign and pinned him with a glare, "you and I have a valid contract. So, unless you want to go down *that* road, I will be grateful if you would show me to my lodgings."

As she turned on her heel, she headed for the front door. A voice called out to her.

"Connor, wait."

She stopped and turned around. The man who appeared to be the eldest of the other males spoke. "I'm Ewan McVey, overseer of Glen Rowan, and these," he jerked his thumb over his shoulder, "are my brothers Joshua, Aaron, and David".

All four men leaned forward to shake her hand, before she turned and headed down the stairs.

Ewan followed her. "Where's your luggage?"

His stare burned into her leather-clad backside. She rolled her eyes, turned, and faced him. "I travel light. The rest of my stuff is in transit."

As she stepped onto the grass, Mrs O'Donough's voice carried across the yard. "The saints preserve us! A lass! Who would ever have thought it! Och, now, Douglas man, this is gonna prove to be mighty interestin'."

"Humph! Un-bloody-believable!" Connor walked down the front steps of the house toward her bike. She reached across the leather seat, grasped the strap of the twin saddlebags, and slung the leather band over her shoulder. At the crunch of footsteps on the gravel driveway, she turned. The tall, dark-haired man who had introduced himself and his brothers was following her. *Shit! What was his name again? Eric, Evan, Ewan – yep! Ewan!*

He fell into step beside her. "Over here." He pointed to the little white cottage on the eastern side of the main house. "It's small, but you should be comfortable enough."

Walking a little ahead of her, he fished deep in the front pocket of his jeans and extracted what she presumed was the key to the front door. The smooth white wooden rail was warm under her hand as she followed him up six narrow wooden steps, to stand on the front porch. Holding the doorknob in his left hand, he inserted the key and jiggled the lock, twisting it left and right.

"Seems the thing's a bit stiff." He twisted around, and for just an instant, a shadow flitted across his face. He turned back to face the lock and rotated the key 90 degrees. "It's been a while since…since anyone has used this place."

The hinges squeaked as he pushed the door open, to reveal a small, tidy room. Standing to one side, he proffered his hand as she walked passed him.

Connor jerked when her nostrils flared to the waft of… *Paint? Spirits? And something else. What is that?* The fragrance teased her olfactory senses and the deepest recesses of her memory. The more she tried to identify the smell, the fainter it became. She shrugged and looked up. Ewan was watching her. The strap of the saddlebags slid down her arm and into her palm. She dropped the satchel onto the table in the centre of the room. Her nimble fingers hooked under the leather band of the battered scabbard that nestled between her breasts. She shrugged the strap over her head then placed the ancient covering almost reverently, alongside the saddlebags.

From the doorway, he stared and inclined his head. "What's that?"

The cracked and aged leather was stiff under her fingertips as she moved the container closer to the centre of the table. "It's a scabbard."

"A scabbard? For what?"

"A katana. A Samurai sword."

"Seriously, Connor, I don't think you'll need any weapons here at Glen Rowan. What do you do with it?"

Looking first to him and then to the scabbard, and then back to him, she smiled. "Piss me off and find out!"

He frowned, and then gave a chuckle as he ran a hand through his hair. "I'll consider myself warned, then. Is there anything you need?"

She shook her head. "No, thanks. I'll start setting in."

He turned toward the stairs and called over his shoulder. "All right then. Tea's in half an hour then, we eat at seven—"

"I'll take my meals over here. Thanks anyway. I'm fine." As she shrugged off her leather jacket, she slung it over the back of one of the chairs. "Tell your father thank you, but I prefer to keep my own company."

He turned back to face her. "As I said, we eat as a family, at seven. I suggest you don't be late. My da isn't known for his good humour."

As his footsteps clomped down the stairs, she crossed the room and shut the front door, then walked around the cabin, opening doors, cupboards, and drawers as she went. The one small bedroom held an equally small bed, piled high with linens, still in their wrappers. The furniture was obviously new and looked like the DIY projects on television. The centrepiece of the bathroom was a beautiful, ancient, claw-foot bath that took up most of the floor space. The laundry had a washing machine and dryer, which also looked new. "Christ, I hope they come with instructions", she muttered out loud. A fine residue of oil coated the pads of her fingers as she traced them over the polished wooden surfaces of the furniture. She smiled. *Thanks, Mrs O'Donough.*

A tease of that same smell, wafted passed her nose. The scent was so faint it almost wasn't there. Eyes closed, she stood in the middle of the kitchen and took in a deep breath. She'd smelled this before; when suddenly, male laughter outside the cottage, broke her concentration. At the side window, she bunched the pristine, white, lace curtains, in her hand. Aaron, David, and Joshua stood crowded around her bike. Smiling, she pulled back the kitchen chair, dug inside her jacket pocket for her keys, and headed out the door. At the clip of her heels on the wooden stairs, they all looked up.

"Hey," she held up her hand in greeting, "she's a beauty, huh?"

Aaron nodded. "Absolutely!" The look of appreciation on his face confirmed he wasn't just referring to the bike.

The sun made its slow sweep across the sky. Connor showered and changed into a pair of blue denim jeans. Before she pulled on the white cotton shirt with three-quarter sleeves, she caressed the tribal tattoos on each of her upper arms. The God Killer, the sword Yokami Sukani had bequeathed to her, and the Sword of War, vibrated in welcome from their resting places under the ink. Images of the Samurai and his wife, Tomoe Gazen, flooded her mind.

As she buttoned her shirt, she murmured, "I miss you guys, but I so don't miss the God crap". A sense of hope for the future settled upon her.

With the leather tab between her index finger and her thumb, she pulled the brown leather boots with three-inch heels onto her feet and stood. She nodded to her reflection in the mirror. *Good enough. The last thing I need is for the McVeys to think I'm not up to the job! A bloody man! Jesus!* After she unwound her long braid, she brushed the wall of hair, straight, then pulled the thick hank away from her face and wound it into a tight, severe bun. She scooped up the keys from her dressing table and headed for the front door. She took a quick look around as she spoke out loud. 'Well, I guess it's now or never."

As she walked up the stairs to the porch of the main house, she raised her hand to knock. Loud, raised voices came from inside the house. Her fist stopped in mid-air. Douglas' voice boomed above everyone else's. "...woman... Christ's sake... Doona know... dressage school... booked... cancel... Holy God... mess... I... Ewan... hell... should have... Jesus God!"

Her chin dropped to her chest. "Oh great! Just bloody great!"

After two minutes, she squared her shoulders and pounded on the door with her fist. The shouting stopped almost immediately. Mrs O'Donough swung the door open, her cheery red cheeks flushed above her wide smile. "Oh, lass, come on in. Tea will be on the table, verra soon." She took a step back and ushered Connor into the house.

In the dining room, the scrape of chairs screeched across the floor as all five men rose to their feet. Tension thrummed in the room. Connor's heart clenched. Next to Ewan, sat a young girl with shiny blonde hair who was maybe ten or twelve. Next to her, balanced on a fat, blue, velvet pillow was an equally blond boy, perhaps a little older than her nephew, Ethan. He looked to be about three or four. Panic rose in her chest. *Oh, Shit! Kids! I am so not ready to deal with kids!* The renewed pain of losing her son James fanned her rising agitation.

Mrs O'Donough pulled a chair out at the far end of the table, directly opposite Douglas. "Sit yerself here, lass. I'll be gettin' the meal if anyone needs anythin'."

Douglas glowered as he looked over the rim of his glass. "Care for a drink?"

Heart pounding, Connor tried to smile. "Tea, please."

"Tea! Jesus! Cat's piss! Here at Glen Rowan, we drink whiskey afore the evenin' meal."

"Good to know, Mr McVey, but tea will do me, just fine". A spike of irritation flared as he continued to scrutinise her. The silence in the room was claustrophobic.

He sipped from his glass and gazed across the rim. No one else spoke.

Five minutes later, the housekeeper breezed back into the dining room, carrying a tray, laden with cups and a large, white, china teapot. "Tea it is, lass. I'll take one with ye meself while the vegetables finish off." Connor almost smiled, imagining the woman with her ear plastered to the wall in the kitchen, eavesdropping on every word.

She set the tray down on the table with a clatter. Connor looked up and quirked an eyebrow in thanks. Mrs O'Donough smiled back as she poured two cups then settled back into her chair.

As the hot, strong tea sang on her taste buds, Connor closed her eyes. "Mmm, thank you. Tea, my mam says, is good for what ails you. Well, most things…" The familiar bite of grief gnawed at her. Hidden beneath her shirt, the solid gold ingot of a rearing Friesian stallion, her engagement ring, and wedder dangled from the chain around her neck. The weight of the gold, always a reminder of the past.

The older woman's numerous chins wobbled as she nodded her head. "Indeed, a tonic in itself. Now, you havena met the bairns yet, have ye?" She tipped her cup toward the little girl sitting at the opposite side of the table. "Tessa?"

The girl looked to Connor and smiled "My name is Theresa Mary Margaret McVey, but you can call me Tessa. And this," she turned and pointed to the little boy next to her, "is my brother, Andrew Angus Michael McVey. But you can call him Andrew."

"Hi. I'm Connor."

"I know." Tessa leaned forward, eyes bright. "My da," she inclined her head toward Ewan, "and my uncles, said that you were a bloody woman and that you are as sexy as hell!"

The men at the table shuffled and fidgeted in their seats. Ewan groaned and blushed as he stared at Tessa.

"Well, you did! Don't say you didn't, because you did! Sexy as hell, that's what you said." She stared back at him.

Ewan scowled. "That's enough. It's very rude to repeat adult conversations."

Crossing her arms, Tessa slowly blinked once. "Well, I'm not an adult, and you said it in front of me and Andrew."

He slammed his glass down onto the table. Whiskey slopped onto the cloth. "Tessa! Enough!"

Mrs O'Donough threw back her head and bellowed a laugh that seemed to bounce off the walls. "Oot of the mouths of babes, lassie! Never a truer truth be told, than the truth itself." She leaned over and dug a chubby elbow into Connor's ribs.

Douglas snorted, his bushy grey brows furrowed as he glared at the housekeeper. "Her bloody name is Connor. A lad's name!"

Connor smiled when the older woman ignored Douglas' scowl and turned to face her. "So, you're a rider, then?"

Staring at the older woman, Connor waited for everyone to laugh at the joke.

Silence.

Seriously? I guess news of my world championship win hasn't made it up this far, yet! The embers of anger began to glow red. "Yes, something like that, Mrs O'Donough."

"Now, now, there'll be none of that *Mrs O'Donough* business, lass. We're all family here. I have been hoosekeeper to this old man afore these lads were even born. So ye can call me O'Dee like evra one else. These lads," she waved her arms about, "like young Tessa and Andrew here, couldna say O'Donough when they were wee bairns, so it got shortened to O'Dee, and 'tis been that way ever since."

"Well, thank you, O'Dee, and I appreciate the tea."

"Jesus, woman!" Douglas thumped his fist on the table as he glared at the housekeeper. "Enough with the gawpin'! These lads have already had three of my best whiskies and the bairns need food."

"Enough yerself, old man! The meal will be ready when it is ready, and not afore!"

"Humph!" he grumped.

Connor laughed out loud.

"Somethin' funny, lass?"

"You sounded just like my da then, when you humphed."

His voice rumbled. "I doona think I made such a noise."

"Yes, you did, da. You do it all the time." Aaron, who was a pea-in-a-pod, younger version of his father, smirked.

Douglas glared at his son, who immediately stopped smiling. "Shut it, Aaron! ' Tis no laughing matter."

Douglas returned his attention to Connor. "Yer father, is he a Scot?"

Smiling, she held the hot teacup between both hands. "To the bone."

Douglas squinted at her. "What's his name, then?"

She bit her lip to stop herself from smiling. "Angus."

Douglas rolled the name over his tongue a couple of times. "Angus MacDonald? Angus MacDonald. Now, where have I heard that name afore?" He looked across the table, eyebrows beetled. "Does he attend the Aberdeen Highland Games, on the first Saturday in July? I know a good many of the Scots who come to compete."

"Yes. Da and my brother Cameron usually come up to the New England for the Games most years."

"Do they now?" He took a long sip of his whiskey, pursed his lips, rolled the liquid round in his mouth then swallowed. Still frowning, he stared down into his glass. "Angus MacDonald...?" He took another mouthful, when suddenly he made a strangled, choking sound. Whiskey spurted like a fountain into the air then rained down on the chequered tablecloth in amber droplets.

Connor pushed back her chair, went round to the other side of the table, and hammered him between the shoulder blades with her fist.

Spluttering, he spun round on his chair, to face her. "Angus MacDonald! Not *the* Angus MacDonald, the breeder of the Nimerlin Fey line of the black Friesians?"

"The one and the same." She returned to her chair and sat down. "I see you've heard of him."

Douglas turned his head and shot her a disbelieving look. "Heard of him! Jesus Christ! His horses are legendary and his dressage school—"

Leaning forward on her elbows, she intertwined her fingers in front of her. "No, Mr McVey, *my* dressage school. My parents bequeathed the business to me. I am owner and dressage master of the Nimerlin School."

"Well, then." A wide smile broke across his face as he picked up his glass and took a small, cautious sip. "Perhaps this arrangement willna be such a disaster after all!"

The glossy, blue-black feathers of the raven blended into the gloom. His white eyes, ever alert, widened when the Shadow commenced its familiar dance. The black roiling mass leaned down on him. "Sentinel! What have you to report?"

"Dark One, there has been an arrival. A female – "

The Shadow reared back as if to strike. "You would dare waste my time with trivialities? I care not who comes and goes. You know your mission and the opportunity that I seek." A cackling laugh erupted from her chest. "Oh, the joy! I relish the moment when – "

The raven's beak clacked like bone on bone. "There are God threads around this female!"

Darkness surrounded the bird. "God threads, you say? Be warned: do not lie to me. Never forget, your mate and chicks depend upon your loyalty." Five thin projections sprang out of the Shadow as a glistening, black tongue sprang out of a gaping maw, in an exaggerated display of finger licking. "Return! Discover what you can! Report to me immediately!" The evil tongue reappeared and circled the black, cavernous mouth. "You know the price of failure."

Chapter Two

OUGLAS MADE A FINAL SWEEP OF HIS PLATE WITH a piece of buttered bread then pushed the empty dish away. "Well then, lass, why doona ye come down to the yard while there is still light oot?" He looked to his left, rolled his eyes, and winked at Ewan. "Seems like now would be a good time to see what sort of dressage master we've employed."

Connor placed her knife and fork on either side of her plate, picked up her napkin, and wiped her lips. "Regardless of what you or anyone else thinks of my skills, Mr McVey, *you* and I have a contract and nothing's going to change that for the next twelve months."

Scowling, he grunted and sucked air through his teeth.

As she pushed back her chair, she picked up her plate and cutlery. "Thank you, O'Dee, for the lovely meal. Now if you'll point me in the direction of the kitchen, I'll help wash up."

O'Dee grasped the tea towel that draped over one shoulder in her pudgy fingers and flapped it in Connor's direction before she laughed and shook her head. "Never ye be minding aboot the dishes. Let's get down to the yard and see what ye make of the horses."

"Okay, then. If you'll excuse me, I'll just go and gear up."

Inside her cottage, Connor dressed in black jodhpurs, riding shirt, boots, spurs, and dressage chaps, then flopped down on the lounge and closed her eyes. For the second time today, a sense of the future, beckoned. *I can do this. Twelve months to find myself. Just me, Hades, and this school, with no Gods, no drama and no bullshit.* She pressed her palms down on her thighs and stood. "Bring it on."

As Connor opened the front door onto the cottage porch, O'Dee spoke from where she sat in the afternoon sunshine. "Just restin' me pins, lass." She leaned forward and groaned as she pushed down on the arms of the creaking chair and stood. "Come on, then. Everyone is already down at the yard. Oh, and lass," she placed a pudgy hand on Connor's arm, "doona mind Douglas. For the most part, his bark is worse than his bite." Chuckling to herself, she gripped the banister and waddled down the stairs.

Connor started to wonder if she was imagining the creepy feeling that someone was watching her, when again, the katanas under the tribal ink vibrated in warning. She looked around, then up to the sky.

O'Dee obviously didn't sense anything. She chattered like a bird as they walked down the path to the sand arena. "Doona mind the younger boys. Ever since we almost lost the business to that verra bad horse flu, Douglas keeps the boys jumpin'. He hires them oot a lot, keeps them busy bringin' in feed and baling hay in the fields. Ye won't see them underfoot!"

Five McVey males and two children sat perched on the top wooden rung of the fence around the yard, legs dangling as they talked quietly among themselves. Ewan's hand gripped Andrew's shirttail, the only thing stopping the boy from falling to the ground.

The horse standing in the arena was a big bay thoroughbred, about sixteen hands, tethered by a halter and lead rope. Ripples of anxiety twitched across his body.

"We only got him yesterday." Ewan nodded toward the beast. "He's a big bastard."

"Big bastard!" Andrew snickered, as he held his hand over his mouth.

Ewan scowled down to him and jerked his shirt. "As I was saying, he's a bit of a handful. Aaron here," he nodded his head in the direction of his brother, "got pelted into the dirt three times after we unloaded him".

"More fool you, then." Connor turned and glared at Aaron, who dipped his head under her stare. "What else would you expect from a newly transported horse?" She climbed through the rails then stood silent and still, watching. She stepped forward. The horse raised his head, looked at her, then snorted.

Slowly, she stretched out her hand, pursed her lips, and blew a breath toward him. Nostrils flared, his ears came forward in a gesture of interest. Taking small steps, she reached out and gathered the lead rope into her hand. Gently, she touched him as she talked to him and ran her hand along his thick neck. As he leaned in toward her, he rubbed his head back and forth against the front of her shirt. The blood of the Ancient Horsemen pounded in her veins as the thrum in her fingers confirmed the connection. When he lifted his head, he was bright-eyed with enthusiasm. He whickered when her hand, coated with the salt of dried sweat, confirmed his anxiety and transport distress. After a wet snort, his shoulders dropped as he relaxed.

She patted him on the neck, then grasped a thick saddle blanket slung over the middle rail of the yard and lowered it onto his back. She looped the lead rope over her arm and draped the bridle over her shoulder then she lifted down the dressage saddle. The horse flinched once when the weight of the saddle settled on his back.

With the reins in her hand, she walked two laps around the yard as she whispered, "Come on, my handsome friend, let's show them what you've got".

A low whicker came from him. She placed her left foot into the stirrup iron and rose onto the saddle. Reins clasped low in front of her, she pressed her knees tight against the leather panels along the horse's sides—the signal to ready himself. Immediately, he bowed his beautiful neck and tucked his muzzle to his chest. After three rounds of the arena, she worked him into tight figures of eight conformations, then into standard dressage manoeuvres.

Laughing, she reached down and patted his neck. "Thank you, my man. All right, now, let's see what you've *really* got."

Pacing in an even, easy step, clearly enjoying showing off, he side-paced, moved in one-step from walk to canter, and marched on the spot. By the end of the exercise, the veins in his neck bulged as he sweated with exertion and excitement. Smiling, she walked him round the arena two more times to cool him down, then leaned forward and patted him. "Well done and thank you."

After dismounting, Connor untacked him and was about to head to the wash bay when she stopped suddenly.

"So what's his name, then?"

There was a silent pause. "His name?" Douglas looked bewildered. "I didna think to ask when we bought him from the sales."

"Well, then, he needs one." Connor frowned as she straightened the horse's wet forelock. "You certainly are a clever boy, aren't you, Coinneach?"

"Coinneach?" Tessa leaned forward from her perch on the rail. "What's that mean?"

"It's Gaelic for Caoin, which means handsome."

"Da! Connor's right! He *is* handsome. Let's call him Coinneach."

"Coinneach it is, then. Oh, and Connor, well ridden." Ewan nodded but avoided looking at her as he dislodged himself and Andrew from the top rung, leaving Tessa to shimmy down by herself.

"Can I ride him, Da? Will Connor be able to teach me to ride?"

"NO! Theresa Mary Margaret! You bloody well know better than to ask, and don't speak of it again!" He turned away from her and stormed toward the house with Andrew onto his hip. Tessa followed slump-shouldered behind him.

Just before seven o'clock in the evening, Connor showered and changed her clothes. Ewan's reaction to Tessa's excitement about Coinneach went round and round in her head. *Jesus! What's his problem? What's the big deal about the kid wanting to ride? Fair enough, Coinneach is a bit too much horse for her now, but it doesn't make sense. The McVeys were breeders of Australian Stock Horses for years. Tessa's probably been riding since before she could walk.* She chuckled as she pictured her sister-in-law, Jilly Louise, who would have been onto this mystery, like a rat up a drainpipe.

Still…it just didn't add up.

Over at the main house, O'Dee had outdone herself, serving up rare pink roast beef with a huge platter of golden vegetables and crisp greens, just picked from her garden.

Connor spotted a vacant seat between the two children, walked over and sat down. Andrew sat on the same large, blue velvet cushion, which he rode with the skill of a seasoned bull rider. Without the elevation, his eyebrows would never have cleared the top of the table.

"Eat your greens, son." Ewan eyed him severely.

He sniffled, eyes glistening as he wrinkled his nose at the broccoli on his plate. "It tastes like dog poo."

"I hardly think you would know what dog poo tastes like. In any case, you know full well we don't waste food at this table."

Connor's lips pressed together as Andrew gripped the fork in his hand and pushed the vegetable around his plate. He gagged on every mouthful he swallowed, then grimaced and shuddered. Two tears ran down his face. She elbowed him gently and winked. A shot of energy flew up her arms as both katanas within the tattoos, vibrated with power. His eyes widened before he returned his gaze to his plate.

O'Dee inclined her head, in thanks to Connor.

"Good lad." Ewan put down his glass and nodded in approval. "See, if you just get on and eat the vegetables, we won't have any trouble at the table."

"Yes, Da." Andrew nodded, still looking down at his plate.

Connor cleared her throat as the katanas settled into a dim thrum.

"Mr McVey." Five sets of adult male eyes looked up at her.

The old man raised his gaze from his plate. "If ye are talkin' to me, lass, then call me Douglas. There are too many of us by the same name, to know who it is, to which ye wish to speak."

"Well, thank you, Douglas." She smiled. "You said earlier you bought Coinneach as a dressage horse for your school. Are there other horses as well?"

"Aye, lass, eleven more, to be precise. Cost a hefty pile of coin, too."

"Well, then." She leaned forward, picked up her glass of water and took a sip, then set it back down on the tablecloth. "I'll need to have a look at them and get them sorted. Can we make an early start in the morning? It'll take a while to test them all."

"Test them? Test them for what, lass?" His bushy grey eyebrows drew together.

"Ability, Douglas." Her head cocked to the side.

"Lass, as I have already said, I have paid a small, no, make that a verra large fortune for those horses. What on earth can there be left to do?"

She sat back in her chair. "In truth, I'm more than a little perplexed as to why you bought them at all. At my Nimerlin School, the riders and horses are one unit. It's an expectation, in fact a *condition* of the contract, that each rider supplies his or her own mount and provides one hundred percent of the care for their horses during the clinic. At this level of tuition, both the horses and the riders are elite athletes. I mean, it is true to say, that is, it is usual, for a *riding school* to provide quality horses for the duration of the event. At the end of the program, the riders and horses go their separate ways. But, you have advertised a *dressage school* here at Glen Rowan, which means the horses and the riders will come as a team, to prepare for competition." She picked up her glass and took another sip. The tension in the room was escalating by the second. "Oh, and one more thing, I'll need to see who's on your accepted and confirmed list. I know most of the elite competitors across the country, so the sorting process shouldn't be an issue. But, for certain, the riders will bring their own mounts to your school."

Douglas shot Ewan a furious look. "Are ye telling me that the huge amount of coin I have spent on these horses has been for naught?"

She patted her lips with her napkin to hide her confusion when his face turned a deeper shade of purple. "It will all depend on what you have offered in the advertising of your school. But, be assured, if you've accepted top-level athletes into your program, they'll arrive with their horses in tow. So you'll need to make arrangements to accommodate twelve additional horses."

Douglas slammed his fist on the table. "Jesus, Mary and Joseph, I doona know why I ever let ye talk me into this, Ewan!"

A sombre mood filled the air as everyone sat with their eyes downcast on their plates.

"Well, if no one is goin' to ride Coinneach, then I am." Tessa stared at her father, head high and chin in the air.

"Tessa!" Ewan rubbed his hand across his clean-shaven face. "We've talked about this!"

"No, Da! *You've* talked about this! I'm goin' to ride Coinneach. Just you see if I don't!"

Connor looked from Ewan to Tessa and back again as everyone around the table ate the rest of the meal in silence.

The television droned in the corner as she sat on the lounge chair. The scabbard lay across her legs as her fingers stroked back and forth across the ancient leather. Frowning, she stared into space as she recalled the response of the katanas to Andrew. *What the hell was that about? Why, did the swords react to him? It didn't make any sense.* She hooked her fingers under the thick loop of chain around her neck and clasped the jewellery in her palm. The memory of Craig's voice rang in her ears, his words as clear, as if he stood beside her. *"The ring is yours, Connor. I have placed it on your finger, and while I live, I never want you to take it off. I want you to have it; it's yours, just like you are mine."* A single tear tracked down her cheek as she returned the chain and jewellery to the inside of her shirt.

Yeah, right. Nothing made sense anymore.

She sat forward, elbows on her thighs and gripped both sides of her head with her hands. *I'm so bloody sick of feeling like this! For fuck's sake! Is this how my life is going to be, forever?* Angry, she sniffed as she stood and crossed the room to switch off the lamp in the corner. Suddenly, her tattoos began to thrum and burn. The vibrations in her arms, for the third time today, sizzled like lightning. Heart racing, she spun around, fists clenched, feet spread in the stance of the Samurai.

"Well met, Daughter." Yokami Sukani, the Immortal Samurai, mentor and her great friend, stood in front of her, frowning. The katana on his back sang the Song of Welcome. Tomoe Gazen, his wife and the Dowager Daughter of the Immortal Samurai Sword, also frowned when suddenly the katanas on their backs emitted a low growl.

"Mr Sukani? Tomoe Gazen?"

He looked all around, his posture stiff and aggressive. "What is it I sense, Daughter? What do you know of this?"

Connor shrugged. "You feel it too. Eerie, isn't it? It's just a feeling, I haven't actually seen anything here that's any sort of threat, but..."

Yokami relaxed slightly as Tomoe Gazen stepped forward and clasped her hands in front of her.

"We sense your sadness, Daughter, and have come to help you find peace. Call the swords, dear one."

Connor stepped back. "No. I am here to find a new life, to put the pain of death behind me. Believe me, I've had more than my fill of Gods and their shitty, selfish ways. I want to just be me—plain old Connor MacDonald."

Worry crossed the Samurai woman's face. "We have been watching you. The grief for your man and your child still weighs heavy upon you. But this is not a matter of choice. For you, there is no life without the swords. They chose you. You must maintain your connection with the blades."

"Did you not hear what I said? I want to be happy again. I want to be the person I was before Joe-fucking-Bruce and Bishamon came into my life and—"

Yokami stepped forward. "You are a warrior, and a warrior cannot afford to lose the sharpness of his or her skills. It was only because of your ability and your training that you were able to defeat Bishamon." He encircled her with his arm. "My dearest child, for you to recommence your training, the mortals here, must know that you have a sword. They need to see The God Killer, but you must never become complacent. Call the swords; it is time."

Connor took two steps backward then crossed her arms. "No, Mr Sukani. I'm done with being a pawn for the Gods' amusement. As much as I care for you both and my great grandda and Epona of the ancient Scottish Horsemen, I intend to move forward and make my own life; a life that is more than swords and Gods and treachery and deceit." She pulled a face. "Been there, done that! It didn't turn out so well."

"Daughter—"

"Mr Sukani, you've already said it. I am mistress of the swords. I am also in charge of my own destiny, that's why I'm here at Glen Rowan to find my future, a *mortal* future complicated only by mortal

problems". The swords are mine to call, at a time of *my* choosing.".
She bowed to him from the waist. "However, it is because of the
great respect I hold for you and for Tomoe Gazen, that I will do, as
you have asked."

She closed her eyes and threw her fingers wide. A surge of joy
filled her chest as the God Killer burst from the right tribal band and
landed with a *thunk* in her right hand. The Sword of War erupted
from her left tribal tattoo and came to rest in her left palm. The chorus
of all four blades was haunting, as they listed toward each other and
sang the Song of the Samurai.

She nodded to the Sword of War. "Assume your mortal self."
The blade shimmered as it took the form of a huge red dog—an
Australian dingo. Head high, the dog looked up with eyes the colour
of molten lead. Connor squatted and ran her hands back and forth
through the coarse canine hair. "It's funny, you know, I didn't realise it until now, but I've really missed you." As she stood tall, her
fingers lingered on the red head of the indigenous creature from an
ancient land. Sadness came over her as she looked to the Samurai.
"I miss—"

Yokami placed a hand on her shoulder. "Use the God Killer to
continue training; it is the only sword the humans can know you
possess. Daughter, keep the dog with you, for company. She is from
the life you left behind and will give you comfort. But remember, no
one else can know of her. Unless you are alone, she must assume
her true form as the Sword of War." He drew her into his arms.
"How I wish to the Masters that things could have been different. If
Bishamon had not—"

"Killed my husband and my son." She sobbed onto the front of
his Imperial robe.

"Yes."

She stepped back. "I'm going to make a life for myself here, Mr
Sukani. Craig would've wanted me to and I certainly *need* to. I hate
this constant grief and misery."

Tomoe Gazen smiled. "You are indeed warrior-born, my precious Daughter of the Sword. As I found you, so too in your destiny,
shall you find another woman who is destined to wield the blade."

Stroking the red dog's head, Connor smirked. "I can't say I've
seen any Samurai goin' all ninja, since I got here."

With her hands clasped in front of her, Tomoe Gazen bowed her head. "The call of the blade is not exclusive to the Samurai, Daughter."

"What?"

"The blade chooses its master. Down through history, it has always been the same. Men have forever used swords, skilled or not. However, swords are far more discerning when it comes to women. It is our qualities and our unique abilities the blades seek. Recall the Sword of War and sleep now." Reaching out, Tomoe Gazen placed her hand on the side of Connor's face.

The yip of the red dog filled the room as she returned to her resting place under the ink of the left tribal band. The God Killer started to dematerialise when Yokami Sukani shook his head. "No old friend. It is time the mortals knew of you." The scabbard flew to Connor's hand; Like an automaton, she lowered the God Killer inside the container, closed the lid, and laid it on the table.

Suddenly, Tomoe Gazen jolted, eyes wide. Yokami raised his sword, then slowly lowered it.

Four sword voices keened their goodbyes. Connor yawned, then reached up and kissed each of her mentors on the cheek before they vaporised into the ether. The faint scent of sandalwood cocooned her.

The raven's heart thundered in his chest. At last! I have news! She will be happy with me. *He flew into the shadows, landed and waited.*

"Sentinel." *A grating voice came from the depths of the gloom.* "What of the God Threads and the new arrival?"

"Mistress. It was two Gods of the Blade that —

"The Samurai!" *she hissed.* "Why would they visit this young woman? What is she to them?"

"I do not know. All I know is that I heard four swords"

The Shadow surrounded him as the sound of whirling winds ruffled his feathers. "Did you not say there were two Samurai?"

"Yes. That is what I saw."

A space in front of him lightened from black to white before there was a flash of sparks. "What you saw and what you heard are two different things. God Threads and two Samurai equate to three swords. What is the truth, you simpering fool? If there are Gods involved, there will be complications for me. Know thine enemy! Yes!" His mate and five chicks appeared before him. They shrieked in terror.

"Perhaps some gentle persuasion might improve your mathematical reporting abilities." Shrouded around one of the chicks, the Shadow tossed it into the air. Suddenly, after two sharp stabbing movements, the chick screamed. Its eye sockets gleamed bloody and empty. The tiny struggling body then disappeared into the black, gaping maw.

Chapter Three

IGHT REFLECTED OFF THE BLADE AS THE SUN BEGAN to clear the horizon. A wide smile painted her face as the endorphins from her workout buzzed through her body. Connor towelled sweat from her face and neck then wiped her palms and the handle of the sword.

"Exercisin', lass?" Douglas walked up behind her. "Jesus! Is that a real sword?" His eyes shone as he fixed on the blade. "May I hold it?"

Possessiveness and the urge to snatch the weapon away, overcame her. Yokami Sukani was the only other person to have touched the God Killer since it came into her possession.

Douglas lowered his head and bowed to the sword, then extended his right hand. For an instant, she paused at his reverence then passed the weapon to him. As his hand closed around the hilt, the blade hummed.

"'Tis a verra fine weapon. How did ye come by it, lass?"

"It's a long story. I practice every morning." Frowning, she watched his reverent handling of the blade. "You know something of swords, Douglas?"

Gazing down at the weapon, he cocked his head to one side then looked to her. "I'm a bloody Scot! Swords have always been important to us."

Nodding, she smiled. "Yes, Da has the MacDonald clan broad-sword. It sits over the hearth. A massive, two-handed, beautiful thing that's incredibly heavy. He's very proud of it."

"As he should be. 'Tis a great privilege to own a piece of our stolen history." Shaking his head, he looked up to her and smiled. "You're full of surprises, that's for sure. Here, lass…" Bowing, he placed the blade across one palm and the hilt across the other, holding the weapon horizontal in front of him. As she accepted the sword, his eyes lingered on the blade before he nodded to her, turned on his heel, and walked away, shaking his head.

Later that morning, the dressage herd stood tethered side by side. The McVeys, gathered outside the round yard, watching each of the horses work through their paces. At the completion of each ride, Tessa yelled and whooped. Ewan glared down at her. Connor dismounted from a tall palomino gelding and handed the reins to Douglas. "Well, so far, so good. All of these horses have reasonable potential. If the riders bring their own horses, which I am sure they will, you should have no trouble getting the money back you paid for them."

"Well, that's summat, then." Nodding at the last horse tethered to the rail, he lifted his chin. "One more then and ye will be done for today, lass."

"Mmm-hmm." She jutted her chin in the horse's direction. "I purposely left him 'til last. He's not sociable with the other horses and a few of them have new bite and scrape marks. I don't know what his issue is, but he's not happy, that's for sure."

Douglas' bushy eyebrows beetled into a frown. "I doona know what's wrong with him. He's been verra bloody disagreeable ever since we unloaded him."

Watching the horse, she walked toward him, hand outstretched to untie the reins from the rail. The buckskin snorted and struck the ground repeatedly with his nearside front hoof, then flattened his ears and bared his teeth.

"Easy, boy…no one's going to hurt you." Standing about three feet away from him, she took in a long breath then slowly blew out.

The whites of his eyes were enormous with terror, as he screamed, reared, and struck high in the air with his front hooves. The reins of the bridle strained as he pulled backward. Suddenly, he turned his rear end and barrelled both back hooves in her direction.

Gasps came from outside the yard just before Douglas bellowed, "Jesus Christ, lass! Get oot of there."

"No, Douglas!" She fixed her gaze on the horse and took small steps around him as she reached out and touched his neck. When her fingers connected with his sweat-drenched coat, rage ran up her arm like a river of hot lava. After untying the reins, she slipped the straps over his head and gathered the leather in her hand. The horse stamped and turned his head, white teeth snapped repeatedly as she mounted the saddle in one fluid movement. The instant her weight settled on his back, he became airborne, squealing and bucking, deliberately slamming her legs into the wooden rungs of the yard; furious, in his effort to unseat her.

Douglas thrust one leg through the rails. "Get off, lass! Get off now, afore the devil bastard kills ye!"

"No!" She bunched the left hand rein tight in her hand, levering the horse's head back around toward his belly, making it impossible for him to do anything but to stand still. "Stay where you are, Douglas. He can't win this. If he wins today, he'll fight to win forever. It'll be all right. Christ, I don't know what's happened to this horse, but something sure as hell has. Let me handle this."

Douglas stared at her, shook his head, then swept his leg back through the space between the rungs and stood outside the yard.

Slowly, she released the left rein and sat still as she patted him on the neck. After several bucks, sidekicks, and attempts to knock her out of the saddle, she rode him over to where Douglas stood and dismounted. Shaking her head, she loosened the girth. "Sorry, Douglas, this horse isn't suitable as a mount for the school."

Spluttering, he pursed his lips. "I agree he's a handful. But ye said yerself, the riders expected to come to our school are elite athletes. Any one of them should be able to handle a horse like this. Besides, ye have plenty of time to knock him into shape."

"Douglas —"

Leaning in toward her, he crossed his arms over his chest. "I've paid good money for that devil, and he will earn his keep."

"Devil is right! If you want him to earn his keep in a school where I am dressage master, *you* ride him! This horse is not safe! He's out!"

He glowered at her. "The hell he is!"

"My decision is final, Douglas. Read the fine print of our contract. All decisions concerning the horses are mine, end of story. We're done here." Turning her back on him, she pulled the saddle and blanket from the buckskin's back and slung the gear onto the middle rung of the yard fence. "Joshua, would you please take this horse over to the wash bay and hose him down? But keep a close eye on him. I don't trust him and neither should you."

Looking dubious, Joshua climbed into the arena, took the reins, and started to lead the horse away.

"Oh, and, Josh, after you're done, please put him in a holding paddock, separate from the other horses."

Douglas' booming voice came from the path, where he was storming up toward the house. "I suppose ye realise if our riders doona come with their own mounts, we'll be one bloody horse short."

"No, we won't!" Connor shouted back. "My horse arrives tomorrow. So the numbers are back to twelve." As she walked up the path toward the barn, she called over her shoulder. "See you for lunch, Douglas. I've got tack to sort out."

From the front steps of the house, he bellowed. "Bloody woman! I *knew* no good could come from this arrangement."

The next morning, Connor fidgeted and paced the floor of her cottage. As she pulled back the cuff of her sleeve, she checked her watch, the same as she had already done fifty times this morning. Outside, the sound of a vehicle rumbled along the driveway.

"About bloody time." She sprinted across the floor, threw open the door, and took the stairs two at a time as she waved the driver over toward her cottage.

As the removal truck stopped on the driveway, the door opened and the driver got out. "G'day, I'm Paul Green. I'm lookin' for Connor MacDonald."

"That would be me." She followed him to the back of the truck and stood back as he swung the back doors wide. Palm extended, she shook his hand. "Nice to meet you, Paul. Now, let's get my stuff inside. It'll be good to have my things around me again."

A voice came from behind her. "Need a hand with that?" Ewan and the children crossed the grass and stood beside the truck.

"Thanks." She smiled. "I'd appreciate the help."

"Tessa, you can help with the…" Ewan turned his head left and right. "Tessa? Tessa?"

A blonde head stuck out of the back of the truck. "I'm here! Oh, Da! Come see this."

Ewan rolled his eyes, walked toward the open back end of the van, and blew out an exasperated breath. "Tessa! What in the name of Jesus, are you doing in there? Get down, right now!"

"Da, you *have* to see this."

Andrew tried to hang off the lowered back gate. A large green praying mantis sat sunning itself on the front of his shirt.

Connor lifted Andrew and stepped into the rear of the van.

"Don't you have a saddle, Connor?" A look of disappointment flashed across Tessa's face.

"I sure do." Connor walked over to a big box marked *Saddle, Leathers, and Tack.* "Come here, Tessa. See this box? This is the saddle I ride on every day."

Stepping over cartons, Tessa crossed the truck and stuck her head inside the box. "Ooh, I love the smell of saddles and horses, don't you, Connor?"

"You bet. I reckon it's the best smell in the world…like puppy breath."

Andrew tugged on Connor's hand so he could also see inside the box.

Stroking the mantis, he frowned as he looked around. "Where's your horse?"

Her heart skipped a beat as she knelt down to him. His little-boy voice was a memory echo of her nephew, Ethan. The familiar lash of homesickness, struck hard, again. She turned away from him, blinking to stop the flow of tears. "He's still at my home, but he'll be here tomorrow."

Andrew took her face between his hands and looked at her with eyes flooded with tears. The mantis was now perched high on his shoulder, looked at her as if was included in the conversation. "Don't be sad. I'll share with you." He lifted the mantis onto his finger, then put him onto the front of her shirt. "He likes you."

She grimaced down at the insect. "Thanks, Andrew. This is a very nice bug."

After all the boxes were inside the cottage, Ewan tipped his hat back and wiped sweat from his forehead. "That's the last of it." He dipped his head to Connor. "We'll leave you to unpack."

"Hey, thanks so much. You've all been a big help." The mantis crawled farther up her shirt, almost touching the bare skin of her neck. *Crap! Crap! Crap!* "Andrew, did you want to take your little insect mate with you?"

He looked up to the sky as if considering his options. "No. I'm not allowed to bring my friends into the house; O'Dee said. He likes the bushes. You can put him in there, 'cause he knows he's not allowed to eat the lettuces."

Ewan waved, then held a hand of each child and turned toward the house. Connor looked down at the mantis. *Well, crap, how the hell does that work?*

As she squinted through the window into the pre-dawn gloom outside, Connor stretched, yawned then reached down and patted the red dog sprawled out on the end of her bed. She changed into black workout pants and a T-shirt with three-quarter sleeves, then looked down at the dingo. "Okay, time for you to go away." She rolled her eyes. "Jesus! Imagine if Douglas found *you* in here.

She chuckled as she extended her left arm. The Sword of War flew to its resting place under the tattoo.

Focussed on the table in the middle of the living room, she drew in a deep breath, dropped her shoulders, and closed her eyes. After an initial scrabbling sound, energy surrounded her as she raised her hand just before the God Killer launched into the air. Her palm closed around the hilt, as a surge of joy filled her body. *Damn, you feel good.*

The light from her bedroom flooded the yard area where she worked with the sword. Decreasing the pace of the katas, she lowered the blade to her side and lifted her head to the breeze that cooled her hot, sweaty face.

Suddenly, the hair prickled on the back of her neck. She spun around, sword arm held straight out in front of her. The tip of the blade connected with...

The front of Ewan McVey's shirt.

Both of his hands shot into the air. "I surrender! Jesus Christ, I only came over to see why your cottage is lit up like a Roman candle."

She slowly lowered the blade. "I practice with the katana at this time, every day. For future reference, Ewan, it's never a good idea to sneak up on someone who has a sword in her hand." She peered at her watch as she stepped into the light. "My horse arrives today. I'll be very glad to have him here."

"I know. Tessa's spoken of nothing else. She's been up and dressed for at least two hours, waiting for the truck to arrive."

She smiled. "She certainly has a fascination for horses, that's for sure."

His face darkened as he frowned. "Yes...she does, and I'll thank you not to tempt her any more than you already have with your fine riding style and your way with the horses."

The smile slid from her face. "I'm sorry, Ewan. I didn't mean to cause you any problems. It's just that... I don't understand why—"

He turned to walk away and spoke over his shoulder. "Just make sure you respect my wishes and don't involve Tessa with the horses."

She followed, speaking to his retreating back. "She seems to have a connection with them."

Suddenly, he stopped and whirled round to face her. His top lip peeled back and settled into a hard line. "I don't care what the fuck you think she's got! It's my decision that she's not involved with the horses. Just make sure you're clear on that!" He turned and walked back toward the house. Tension vibrated in his wake.

Ewan sat in silence at the breakfast table. O'Dee buttered a slice of toast, cut it into triangles smeared with peanut butter, and passed it to Andrew.

Hand outstretched, he beamed. "Thank you."

"'Tis my pleasure, dear lad."

Connor turned to Tessa, who sat with her head bowed over a bowl of cereal. "Do you go to the local school?"

Tessa, looked up briefly. The dark circles under her eyes looked like smudged makeup against her pale skin. She shook her head slightly as her cheeks reddened. "I do... I did... Before—"

Ewan slammed his coffee mug down on the table.

Everyone at the table, jolted.

After a pause, Connor looked around the room then returned her gaze to Tessa. "Before—?"

Ewan made a production of clearing his throat as he glared at Connor. "There are some things we don't talk about."

Tessa looked up and tossed her head. "No, Da, there are some things *you* don't talk about."

"Tessa, enough!"

The sound of an approaching truck interrupted the tension around the table. Connor pushed back her chair and stood. "Excuse me, everyone. That'll be Hades."

Douglas looked up from his breakfast. "Hades? Jesus, that's a hell of a name for a horse."

Looking out the window that faced the driveway, she smiled. "He's a hell of a horse."

Tessa pushed back her chair and ran toward the front door. Connor bit her lip as Ewan bellowed. "Tessa! Tessa, come back here! Oh, for Christ's sake."

Without saying a word, Connor walked out of the dining room. A few minutes later, she caught up with Tessa, grasped her arm and pulled them both to a sudden stop. Muffled screams blasted from inside the vehicle.

"Stay here." She released Tessa's arm and ran toward the truck just as the driver opened his door and lowered himself to the ground.

"Watch yourself, missy. That big black bastard will take your head off. Wicked beast he is. Stand back!"

She ignored him and went round to the back of the truck, slid free the bolt between the double doors and lowered the ramp to the ground. The smell of blood hit her like a cricket bat to the face. After walking up the wooden incline, she lifted the metal rail that demarcated Hades' transport space and smashed it against the wall. She sidestepped, pressed between the wall and the length of his body.

Hades stood covered with sweat and shaking with rage.

She placed a hand on his coat. Her knees buckled under the blast of shared memories. "Oh, Jesus, Hades." With shaking fingers, she unknotted the lead rope, tied so short to the front tie-down bar, that his muzzle dripped blood, from deep lacerations. She winced as she ran her hands over his coat. Multiple raised and swollen linear stripes marked his rump, belly and neck. Fresh vivid, splattered blood, was macabre on the walls. Gently, she draped the loose end of the rope over his neck as she urged him backward, when a flash of metal on the wall, just inside the back door, caught her eye.

"Jesus Christ!" Douglas exploded. "That's one of the Nimerlin Fey Friesians! And, if me eyes doona deceive me, he's intact! Ewan, a stallion, for Christ's sake! Did ye know aboot this? Sweet mother, that horse has got to be worth more than half a million dollars!"

Ewan's mouth dropped open as he stared at the horse then looked at his father and shook his head.

The transport driver, with a roll-your-own cigarette hanging out of the side of his mouth, leaned against the side of the truck. His hairy arms with turned-up sleeves lay crossed over his chest. "No amount of money would ever convince me to transport this horse again. The black bastard damn near trampled me."

"Wait here, Hades." The heels of Connor's boots clicked against the wooden tailgate as she walked back up the ramp. She reached up just inside the door, turned and walked halfway back down the wooden plank. Hanging from her hand like a great viper, was a black leather whip. Its shiny, embossed-silver handle, shone brilliantly in the sunlight.

A collective gasp filled the air.

With deliberately slow steps, she returned to stand beside Hades and faced the driver. "You whipped my horse." It was a statement of fact—not a question.

Tossing his head, tiny red droplets flew into the air as Hades whinnied and moved to put himself between her and the man leaning against the truck.

"Too right! Bloody stallions! Nothin' but trouble, that's for sure. Let's just say," he chuckled, "I gave him a bit of a lesson in good manners."

Staring at the driver, Connor stood beside Hades, unfurled the whip and cracked it twice, just narrowly missing the scuffed toes of his books. Small puffs of dusts erupted from the ground. "Seems to me you could benefit from a taste of your own medicine."

The driver's eyes bulged before he turned on his heel and sprinted away from the truck. The whip cracked once, just before it snaked twice around one of his ankles. With the handle of the whip gripped tight in her hand, she yanked backward and abruptly pulled him off his feet. As he thrashed on the ground, his fingers tore at the tight coils of leather. Suddenly, she jerked the whip tight again.

"Now, lass—" Douglas stepped forward and put a hand on her arm.

She shrugged his hand away as she walked over to where the driver struggled on the ground, like a landed trout. Her fingers fisted a handful of his shirtfront as she pulled him into a sitting position— about two inches from her face.

"Know this, you fucking bastard. No. One. Touches. My. Horse." She turned and whistled. "Hades!"

The stallion reared and snorted as he pranced over to the man who sat with both arms braced around his head. "Stop! Help! He's gonna kill me."

Leaning down, she pulled the snivelling coward forward again. "No. He's not going to kill you, but I, on the other hand..." She released her grip and forcefully, shoved him backward. Slowly, she flicked the whip to loosen the coils around his ankle.

As she turned back to Hades, she coiled the whip on the sand like a sleeping black snake; layering circle upon circle of leather, then dropped the handle and whistled.

Hades reared and struck the whip repeatedly with his hooves until all that remained was a scattered pile of shredded leather and dented metal.

The driver lunged from where he lay on the ground and swung a punch at her. "You fucking bitch! Do you have any idea how much that whip cost?"

She whirled round to face him and leg-swept him, sending him sprawling onto the sand just before she drove her knee into his belly. Hades danced on the spot and roared his approval. Leaning down, she grasped the driver round the neck and drove both of her thumbs into his windpipe. He flailed his arms and legs in a panic, as his face changed from fury red, to the blue of oxygen deprivation. After he lost consciousness, she released her grip, stood, and walked back to where Hades stood.

"Oh, no." Tessa whispered in a tiny quavering voice. "Is your horse all right?"

Ewan reached down to grab her hand, but she shrugged him off and ran to stand beside Connor. "He is so beautiful."

Hades nodded his head in agreement.

Rolling her eyes, Connor rubbed his neck. "He knows it, too. Come closer, pat him."

Tessa put her hand on his long thick neck; a look of wonder painted her face.

Connor gave her a hug. "Hades, this is Tessa." Turning his head, he stretched his neck and sniffed her hair. Her face lit up when he whickered softly.

"Andrew!" Ewan called out just as the little boy ran over and stood alongside Hades. He had tears in his eyes.

The transport driver groaned and rolled over onto his side, retched and vomited onto the ground. On shaky legs, he stumbled as he tried to gather enough coordination to stand. "I should call the cops on you."

"Let me save you the effort!" Connor delved into the front pocket of her jodhpurs and pulled out her phone. "Country police take a really dim view of people who are cruel to animals. Besides, as I had to defend myself against you, I think I'll press charges—"

He let out a derisive snort and waved his hand. "Now, then missy, there's no need to be hasty and get the law involved." He brushed sand from his clothes with both palms. "No real harm done. Why don't you just give me my money and I'll be on my way."

As she walked toward him, he started backpedalling.

"Get out of my sight!" The katanas screamed inside her brain, thirsty for blood. "I'll be sure to inform Bill O'Riordian, who is the only person I trust to stable my horse outside of our property, of what happened here today. If I were you, I wouldn't count on getting any more loads from him, anytime soon. Of course, he knows just about everyone who owns competition horses in New South Wales, and I'll wager no one who owns a horse of worth, is going to want anything to do with you."

Ewan and Douglas both stepped forward when Connor held up her palm. "No! Stop! I will deal with this piece of crap!

"You—!" He lunged at her again and swung his fist at her face.

Connor ducked, drove the heel of her hand into his solar plexus, and dropped him like a stone. He coughed and spat on the ground. With one hand around his middle, he tried to stand and was just about to say something, when Hades shook his head from side to side and leaped forward. Scrabbling backward like a crab, he struggled to get to his feet. Once upright, he bolted for the truck, threw open the cab door, started the engine, and took off. The tailgates banged open and closed, while the ramp bounced up and down, splintering wood along the road.

Douglas rushed toward Connor. "Jesus Christ, lass, are ye all right?"

"Yeah, thanks." Hades walked back over to her and stood at her side. She put both arms around his neck and rubbed her face back and forth. "I am now."

Andrew giggled when the horse leaned down and sniffed the top of his head. Tessa stood with a star-struck look on her face, smiling up at Hades.

"I'm going to take him to the barn to get these cuts and bruises cleaned up; then I'll get him settled into his paddock."

Douglas held the hands of the children. "Good idea. Jesus! What a performance!"

O'Dee placed a hand over her heart and blew out a breath. "I doona think I have ever seen anything like that in my life."

As Connor led Hades toward the barn, Douglas' words carried on the wind and made her smile. "Aye, and here we thought she would be some sort o' wiltin' violet who wouldn't be up to the job. Christ Almighty, I think we'd all best be mindin' our manners from here on."

Chapter Four

THAT NIGHT, IN HER COTTAGE, CONNOR TURNED OFF all the lights except for the white china bedside lamp.

Thoughts of Jilly Louise, her sister-in-law and all time bestie, flashed into her mind. Peering at the digital readout on her phone, she confirmed it was 10:30 p.m. "Shit! It's too late to ring now. She always goes to bed with the chooks when she's pregnant."

She sighed as she slid between the sheets, pulled the blankets up over her chest, and reached over to switch off the light. As she turned onto her side, she pulled the linens up higher over her shoulder, took a deep breath, blew it out, and tried to relax. Over and over, images of the silver-handled whip striking Hades, flashed through her mind. Restless, she tossed and turned, waiting for sleep.

It didn't come.

After about an hour, she threw back the blankets, pulled on her clothes and boots, and walked out into the cloud-shrouded moonlight, headed for Hades' paddock. She leaned on the wooden rail and peered into the darkness when suddenly, he whickered.

Girl child, I have missed you.

Her blood sang at their connection. He stood about three feet away, well camouflaged in the gloom. After climbing over the fence, she walked up to him and wrapped her arms around his neck as tears streamed down her face. "I've missed you so much. Christ,

Hades, I'm so sorry for what happened today. But, I thank God, you're here."

He whickered again and nuzzled her face. *Yes. Indeed.* He looked at her, the moonlight emphasising the high gloss of his beautiful face. *What of the small ones?*

"Oh...Tessa and Andrew? They're the kids of the eldest son. The whole family lives here at Glen Rowan."

They both bear great sadness, and yet... there is something else...

"I know...everyone here is very guarded about—"

A twig snapped and she turned abruptly.

"Who are you talking to?" Ewan stood behind her.

"Jesus! You really do have a bad habit of sneaking up on people, don't you?"

"Sorry. I saw you walking over this way and wondered what you were doing." He paused, "What *are* you doing, by the way and *who* were you talking to?"

As she leaned forward, she stroked Hades' neck. "I couldn't sleep. I came over to check on him. Crap, after today, I feel really bad that I engaged that bastard to transport him here."

Ewan walked up to the fence, crossed his arms, and leaned on the rail. The dappled moonlight shadowed half of his face as if he were masked, like the Phantom of the Opera. He stood close enough that her nostrils flared as whiskey fumes wafted passed her.

"Yeah, Jesus! What a mongrel! Tessa's been on her soapbox about it all day. For once, I don't disagree with her." Clearing his throat, he rested his chin in his palm. "I know Da made some calls tonight. I don't think you need be worried about anyone hiring that lunatic anytime soon." He chuckled deep in his throat. "Although, from where I sat, I think he's the one who ended up bein' considerably worse off for his efforts."

She made a derisive noise, but her expression didn't change as her fingers moved in a steady tattoo of strokes between Hades' ears. "He's lucky he got off as lightly as he did." Vehemence laced her voice as she turned and faced Ewan. "No one touches what is mine! Ever!" She walked around to the side of the horse, grabbed a handful of mane, and swung herself up onto his back. "And, especially, no one touches *him.* Come on, Hades, let's go for a ride." Gripping the sides of his belly with her knees, she urged him forward. He broke from a standstill into an easy rocking canter.

When she looked back over her shoulder, Ewan was gone.

From the window of his study, with the curtains pulled back, Ewan watched her ride across the paddock. The clouds had blown away and the moon was full. The light shone on her long blonde hair, like the silver tendrils of a magical being. She threw back her head, laughing as she spurred Hades into a flat-out gallop. For a moment, he imagined Hades like Pegasus with wings furled, and Connor flying ever higher into the heavens. He watched her long after she dismounted, as she ran her hands over the horse and she talked to him.

Ice cubes tinkled on the bottom of his glass. He picked up the near-empty bottle from the table and half-filled the glass with whiskey. In a slow salute, he raised the container to the window then downed the liquid in one fiery swallow. Staring, he breathed away the fumes, as she walked toward her cottage. When she looked up, he flinched and stepped back, letting the curtain flutter back into place. He sat down heavily in the high-backed, ancient chair behind the great oak desk, rested his head on the leather, closed his eyes, and drifted into an uneasy sleep.

The sun streamed in through the study window. Ewan opened his eyes a crack, then slammed them shut as the bright morning sunshine lit up the jackhammers that were doing their best to punch a hole in his skull. He pushed back from the desk, stood, and stretched his back before he walked across the room and opened the door. The sound of voices and the scrape of cutlery on china wafted up the staircase.

He walked into the kitchen. The smell of bacon made his stomach lurch.

"Mornin', lad." Douglas didn't look up as he heaped scrambled eggs onto a plate, then held up the dish.

Ewan grimaced and waved the platter away. "Just tea, Da."

Douglas scowled. "Yer bed has no' been slept in again, lad. A man who takes solace in the bottom of a bottle, is forever a lonely man."

A soft grunt came from Ewan as he stared into the bottom of his cup.

Tessa looked up at her father. Dark circles lay under her eyes as worry clouded her face, but she said nothing.

Clearing her throat, Connor returned her cup to its saucer. "So, Douglas, the horses are all sorted. I'd like to go over the program for the clinic in the next day or so".

"Program? What do ye mean?"

Refilling her cup with tea, she blew over the hot liquid and looked across the rim at him. "The dressage clinic; what arrangements have been made? What elements have been included? Oh, and I need the confirmed list today?"

Douglas scowled at Ewan. "The arrangements are somewhat… er…loose, lass. The plan for the dressage clinic at Glen Rowan isn't exactly set in—"

Ewan slammed his cup down onto the table, pushed his chair backward, stood up, and stormed out of the room.

Surrounded by acceptance letters, preliminary plans for the dressage clinic, and projected business directions for the Glen Rowan Dressage School, Connor sat at the table in her cottage. She leaned on one elbow as she sorted the paperwork into piles. "Jesus, he wasn't kidding," she muttered to herself as she flicked back and forth through the documents. Apart from the confirmed offers, everything else seemed to be little more than a rudimentary plan. With all of the papers sorted into individual stacks and labelled with colourful Post-it-Notes, she gathered up the pages and set off to find Douglas.

Raised voices coming from inside the house made her pause, when, suddenly, the front door burst open. Tessa flew passed her and ran around the side of the house. Connor tucked the papers under her arm and followed her. Sounds of sobbing came from inside the woodshed. Connor knocked on the door, and spoke in a quiet voice. "Tessa? Can I come in?"

"No! Go away! Please, Connor, just go away. I'm not allowed to talk to you."

Connor frowned "What? Why aren't you allowed to talk to me?"

Ewan's voice bellowed from the front of the house. "Tessa! For Christ's sake! Come back here."

Fresh sobbing erupted from inside the woodshed. "'Cause Da said so."

Connor leaned forward and opened the door just a crack. "Tessa, please, let me come in. I'm worried about you."

Only hiccoughs and the occasional sob, broke the silence.

Connor tentatively opened the door and walked inside. It took a while for her eyes to adjust to the dim light. Tessa sat on the floor with her head on her knees and her arms clasped around her legs. Her shoulders shook as she cried.

"Oh, Tessa." Connor walked over, sat down on the floor next to her, and put the bundle of papers on the floor. "What's wrong? What can I do to help?"

The door to the shed swung wide and light streamed in. Ewan stood with his hand clenched on the door handle. "Tessa! Go inside the house, and for God's sake, stop crying!"

Connor's temper flared when the crying again became wracking sobs. She put her arm around the little girl. Ewan walked into the shed, his face a mask of misery. When he reached down and touched Tessa on the shoulder, she flinched away from him.

Connor leaned down and whispered. "Come on, Tessa, why don't we go inside?'

Nodding, she sniffed, gripped Connor's hand, and pulled herself to her feet. "Okay." Her voice shook when she spoke.

Tessa stared at the floor as they walked toward the door. Ewan stepped back but remained silent.

Hand in hand, Tessa and Connor walked up the stairs. O'Dee stood on the front porch, wringing her hands. "Oh, lassie. Come inside, now. I'll get ye summat cold to drink."

Tessa looked up, hiccoughed and ran to the housekeeper, who took her in her arms. 'Now, now, my wee bairn. Come with O'Dee."

When they disappeared inside, Connor lowered herself to the steps and sat. "Oh, damn it! The bloody papers." She sighed, stood up, and walked down the stairs and around the corner. Ewan was standing outside the shed, eyes closed with his head resting against the now closed wooden door.

She walked toward him. When he looked up, his eyes were haunted.

Her heart clenched at such abject misery. "I'm sorry to disturb you. It's just that I left the paperwork for the clinic inside, on the floor."

Ewan opened the door and swung it wide, his lips twisted into a snarl as he glared at her.

That night, everyone sat at the table and ate in silence. Tessa chewed mechanically while Andrew's lip quivered during most of the meal. O'Dee began to clear the table. Connor stood and gathered plates and cutlery. "Here, let me help you with these."

O'Dee nodded. "That would be verra helpful, lass."

As Connor followed her through to the kitchen, she spoke quietly. "O'Dee, what the hell's going on? Tessa's terribly upset."

After the housekeeper checked the hallway, she closed the kitchen door, pulled out a chair from the table, and nodded to the one next to her. "Sit down, lass. 'Tis a terrible thing. Douglas and Ewan have forbidden any of us to speak of it, on account of evra one getting so upset all the time."

Connor slammed her palm on the table. "Goddamn it, O'Dee, I just don't get it. Douglas employed me to be dressage master for his school, but the paperwork confirms the clinic is little more than a bunch of loose ideas on paper. Yet he has twelve participants confirmed, all of whom I know and who are elite athletes. This school is nowhere near ready to receive students. And Ewan is…what the hell's going on?"

The door behind her scraped as it opened. Ewan stood in the doorway. "You're right. You deserve an explanation for the mess you've found us in. Will you walk with me? I'll explain on the way over to see that magnificent horse of yours."

Delving into her apron pocket, O'Dee nodded to Connor, then dabbed at her eyes with a handkerchief.

"Only if you're sure that's what you want, Ewan. I don't want to complicate things or make anything any harder for you, than it obviously already is."

He dragged his hand across his face. "It's just not possible for things to be worse than they already are."

As he held open the door, she walked passed him. When they were clear of the house, they walked side by side. "Okay, let's start with Douglas' dressage school. What—?"

"No, Connor, not Da's," he choked and swallowed hard. "My *Beth's* dressage school."

She grabbed him by the forearm and pulled him to a halt. "Oh, Jesus, Ewan! Elizabeth McVey was your wife?"

"Yes. The love of my life."

"Oh, my God. She was an amazing competitor, and so was her horse, Rudiobus. We competed against each other a few times. She attended my Nimerlin School a couple of years ago."

Ewan looked incredulous. "That was *your* school? So, you're the one I have to blame, for planting the idea of running a dressage school here at Glen Rowan?"

Shaking her head, she frowned. "Well, I don't know about that…" She stopped walking and gazed ahead, her pointed index finger waggling back and forth. "Come to think of it, now that you mention it, she *was* very interested in the business side of things. I guess it all makes sense now."

Emotion quavered in his voice. "No. That's where you're wrong. Nothing makes sense anymore. Ever since I lost her, my life and the lives of our children have been nothing but misery. Dressage was Beth's thing—her life. Da, my brothers and I, spent years breeding Australian Stock Horses here at Glen Rowan. It was bloody hard work, but it paid off. We established a good reputation for our bloodline and made a decent living from the sales. But, after the equine flu… Well, you'd know, after legislation by the Australian Horse Industry Council, and the prohibition of transportation of horses, no one was buying. In the end, we had no money coming in, so we sold the stock locally, for much less than they were worth, to keep a roof over our heads. When the outbreak was finally declared over, that was when Beth struck on the idea of a school as a viable business proposition, with her as dressage master."

Connor closed her eyes and blew out a breath. "I didn't know. I thought Elizabeth was an international competitor, seeing as how she was Irish and all."

Warmth coated his words. "As Irish as the Blarney Stone. We met while she was on holiday, here."

"I didn't know she lived here in Australia. The last year for me, has been… I've been sort of cut off from—well, never mind that. Oh, Ewan, I'm so sorry."

Fists clenched by his sides, his face darkened. "You know how she was. Like Tessa, she lived and breathed horses. One day she went for a ride down to the back paddocks. When she hadn't come back home by sundown, Da and I went looking for her." A gut-wrenching sob broke through his lips. "She was lying on the ground, like a tiny, broken doll. The horse was standing beside her, nudging her. God, he just kept nudging her… But she was dead. She broke her neck when she fell."

Connor put her arms around him and hugged him. "Oh, Ewan, God, how terrible. She was a great girl, always laughing and such a great competitor."

Leaning in, his arms tightened around her. "It was just twelve months ago that we buried her. I don't think Andrew even remembers her. God it kills me." Another sob broke from his chest. "It's just so hard for Tessa. She can't understand why I refuse to let her ride or to own a horse. Beth had her up on a saddle, well before she could walk. I know I wouldn't survive, if anything happened to Tessa, too. I just wouldn't."

Connor released him, took a step back, and looked up to him. 'The cottage I'm living in; it was hers, wasn't it?"

"Yeah, she was a painter. Beautiful work she did, too. Da took all her paintings down because none of us could bear to look at her art, those amazing pieces were just a constant reminder that she was no longer with us."

The remembered smell of oil paints and spirit flooded Connor's brain. "I'm so sorry, Ewan, for you, the children, and your family. Elizabeth touched many lives."

"She was one of a kind. I know I will never meet—"

A scream tore through their conversation. Connor sprinted with Ewan just behind her toward the shrieks of terror.

Tessa screamed, as the raven swooped.

The terrible black wings made a *whup-whup* sound every time it dived upon her. It shrieked *aahh-aahh* as if laughing. She tried to cover her head and face with one arm as she held onto a fistful of mane with the other hand. Pain shot up her arm when the raven clawed her skin. Coinneach screamed and snapped his teeth. The bird again flew high into the air, then dived at high speed; a black streak, hurtling like a missile. Her head snapped backward when the black beak struck the flesh on her temple, just missing her right eye. Blood sprayed from the wound and she screamed.

Panicked, Coinneach shied, sending her flying from his back to land sprawled out on the sand in the yard. He stood with his head lowered toward her…nudging her…

Connor ran just ahead of Ewan, threw her leg over the middle rail, and crossed the sand. Tessa clutched her right arm tight against her chest, as tears streamed down her face. Blood tracked down her temple from a deep, gaping wound.

"Da! It's not Coinneach's fault! A big, black bird swooped on us! It frightened him. He didn't do anything wrong. I fell off because I can't ride properly."

Ewan knelt on the sand and pressed the hem of his shirt to her face, then tried to slip his hands under her bottom, to lift her into his arms. "It's all right, sweetheart. Come on, I'll get you inside the house." As he tried to lift her, she screamed, still clutching her arm.

Connor walked over and knelt next to him. "Okay, then, let's see what's going on with this arm." Gently, she palpated just above the wrist and sighed in relief. As she counted the pulse, she looked up. Ewan was the colour of dirty snow. "Well, the arm's broken, but the placement is pretty good and the circulation's fine. We'll need to splint it, to stabilize the fracture."

"And how the hell would you know that?" Ewan glared at her.

"Because I'm a nurse, and my brothers Callum and Cameron are always bloody, breaking something."

Tessa sobbed, "I'm sorry, Connor. That big black bird kept flying at me and Coinneach."

Connor nodded toward the horse. "Yeah! Looks like it got him, too. There's blood on the point of one of his ears and on his muzzle." She poked at Tessa's bleeding head wound. "Don't worry." She smoothed back the blood soaked hair from Tessa's temple. "The bird probably has a nest around here. Birds are very protective when they have babies about. You falling off Coinneach, was just a case of bad timing. Every year at Nimerlin without fail, we all get chased by plovers that nest near the barn. Seriously, anyone who goes outside during breeding season, without a broom or a bridle to swing around, is going to get dive bombed and pecked. They're relentless. But, they're also very good parents. Besides, my da always says, it takes a hundred falls to make a rider. When I was your age, I fell off all the time. It was the falling off, that taught me, to hang on."

Outside the yard stood Douglas, with Andrew in his arms and O'Dee nearby, their hands gripped the wooden rails. Terror painted their faces. Connor stood and walked over to them. "Don't worry, she'll be all right. Her arm's broken, but she's fine. Oh, O'Dee, good on you!" Reaching through the rail, Connor grabbed the tail of the tea towel that draped over O'Dee's shoulder and folded it into a triangle as she walked back to where Tessa lay on the sand.

"Help me to sit her up, Ewan. Then we can put the arm into this sling."

He nodded and carefully sat Tessa forward while Connor slipped the folded fabric under her arm and knotted it at the back of her neck.

While her fingers worked the knot, she cocked an eyebrow. "Who's calling the ambulance?"

"An ambulance? Whatever for? We have any number of vehicles here on the property."

She gave Ewan a droll look. "Well, that's true. But Tessa here, is going to need pain relief. She can get that, if we call an ambulance."

Douglas climbed through the rails and stood in front of Tessa; his tone brooked no argument. "Call the ambulance." Connor looked at Ewan, who nodded. She pulled her phone out of the waistband pocket of her jodhpurs and dialled.

Later that afternoon, sitting by Tessa's empty bedside on the Paediatrics ward, Ewan and Connor waited anxiously, for her to return from theatre. He swivelled on his chair. "I'm really sorry that you've found us in such a bloody mess." Leaning his elbows on his knees, he lowered his head and grasped either side of his skull with his fingers. "It was Beth's dream; we ran the Stock Horse business and she competed. Now that she's gone, there's no one to bring the school to fruition. We know fuck all about running a dressage school." He sat back in the chair. "I'll talk to Da when we get home, about releasing you from your contract." His fingers drummed on the bedside table. "Jesus, Tessa's just so like her mother. It's always been the horses for her. Now she' got a broken arm because I'm too bloody pigheaded to see that she needs to learn to ride." He fidgeted and began crossing and uncrossing his legs. "I don't think any of us would have survived, if the fall Tessa took was more…" He shuddered, unable to finish his sentence.

The chair groaned as Connor shifted her weight. "Ewan, you can't change the past." She put her hand on his forearm. "Look, don't worry about the school. I think I can pull it together in time. As for Tessa, of course you're terrified she'll be badly hurt if she rides, her mother died riding, for Christ's sake. I do know how she feels, though, Tessa, that is. It is torture to not be able to ride, when all you want to do is ride."

They both looked up at the sound of squeaky wheels, just in time to see Tessa coming down the corridor on a trolley. The white dressing on her head matched the colour of her face as the porter parked the bed and a redheaded nurse in theatre scrubs turned to Connor and Ewan. "Your daughter's fine. Her arm was broken. Luckily, she didn't need surgery; it was just a matter of realigning the bones and applying a cast." She smiled and looked down at Tessa as she handed her a pack of coloured textas. "In a few weeks, you'll be tickety-boo. Now remember, sweetie, make sure you get lots of signatures to show off your plaster."

Connor looked at Tessa's right arm and laughed at the dozen or so signatures and caricatures that already adorned the cast. "I see you gave her a head start." The nurse laughed, nodded, and walked away.

The next morning, after a sleepless night, Connor and Ewan sat draped in uncomfortable armchairs. They both stood when the surgeon entered the room and began flicking through the charts that hung on the end of Tessa's bed. "Well, how is my star patient coming along?" He replaced the metal folder then walked alongside the bed and examined the cast. "Young lady, this all looks pretty good. Are you ready to go home with your mom and dad?"

A shadow passed over Tessa's face just before she nodded and whispered, "Yes, please".

The surgeon looked at Connor. "Keep her quiet for a few days, and no more riding for at least six weeks. You'll need to make an appointment to come back and see me then. Once the cast comes off, she'll be good as new."

Ewan extended his hand. "Our thanks to you, for looking after Tessa. We appreciate your help."

The surgeon smiled, nodded, and made to leave, when, suddenly, he turned back round with his right index finger pointing in the air. "Tessa and I were talking before her surgery. She told me about the bird that pecked her and caused her horse shy. You might want to be careful. Ravens are persistent and vicious — damn awful, cruel things. They can take an eye out" — he snapped his fingers — "just like that!"

Chapter Five

ONNOR YAWNED AS SHE DRAGGED HER TIRED BODY up the stairs of her cottage, opened the front door, and turned on the light. Exhaustion lay like a mantle, over her. Pieces of clothing fluttered to the floor as she undressed. After a long, hot shower, another yawn cracked her jaw as she walked back to her bedroom. The smell and feel of clean sheets was comforting.

Oblivion found her in seconds.

She smiled as her subconscious awoke and her memories came to life. The smell that floated, unidentified, in her recollections, filled her nostrils. This was her favourite smell — sunshine, fresh air and... She snuggled her bottom backward against the long, firm plane of warm flesh behind her, just as she had done so many times before.

Craig.

One of his arms draped over her, and his hand cupped her breast. Contentment and happiness flooded through her as she dream-walked with him along a beach in the moonlight. The bands of her diamond engagement ring and the wedder on her left hand squeezed together as his hand cupped hers. His words rang in her memory.

"The ring is yours, Connor. I have placed it on your finger, and while I live, I never want you to take it off. I want you to have it; it's yours, just like you are mine."

Happiness coursed through her as she snuggled closer. His body was so incredibly warm as he curled around her. One of his feet gently stroked her ankle and calf as he reached over and pulled her to face him. "I will always love you, baby girl." She leaned in and kissed him, then pressed the side of her face against his chest.

The beat of his heart thundered under her ear.

She gasped out loud then sat bolt upright, as her hands moved frantically, searching the space on the mattress beside her. Her fingers fumbled in the dark for the lamp switch. When the room lit up, sweat broke out on her forehead. Her breathing was harsh and ragged. Realisation settled upon her as sharp as a coat of thorns.

No! No! No! No!

She covered her face with her hands and started to cry.

She was alone.

It was just a dream.

A wonderful, fucking, tormenting dream…

Hot tears tracked down her face. She lay on her side, closed her eyes, and tried to summon the dream, imagining him to be still here, alive, beside her, loving her. The fingers of her right hand reached out and caressed the creased sheet on what had always been his side of the bed.

Confused, she wondered if she were still asleep when *his smell* caressed her face. She leaned into it. With a flurry of the covers, she got out of bed and stood barefoot on the hardwood floors. She clapped a hand over her eyes. "Oh, fuck! This is not real! None of this is real!" The fingers of her other hand unconsciously caressed the links of the chain around her neck. The touch of the rearing Friesian Stallion ingot and her rings were consoling.

"What the hell's the time?" She turned her wrist to the light. The hands on her watch pointed to 1:30. "Oh, crap. I've only been asleep for an hour." Yawning, she scanned the room, shook her head, and climbed back into bed. Under the linens, she turned onto her side. *Find your happy place, the sound of waterfalls, the waves as they crash onto a beach…the sound of foals calling to their moth –*

Eventually, consciousness gave way to the place of dreams and she smiled. In the distance, with the sun at his back, a tall blond man with mirrored, moss green eyes stood in silhouette, as he walked toward her.

She ran toward him, laughing then launched into his open arms.

I must not fail again, I must not fail again.

The raven Sentinel cringed at the hideous memory of a second chick, ripped apart and thrown at his feet — a sight he would never forget. The screech of his mate would forever torture him. His blue-black feathers, glossy in the morning light, lay hidden behind a canopy of leaves in a tree at the bottom of the paddock. He furled, then unfurled his wings as he settled into the leafy camouflage. *No, I must bide my time. I must seek the right moment to strike!*

A memory assaulted him as his mistress roiled in displeasure. *Get me the information I seek. I tire of your failures. Disappoint me again Sentinel and it will be you that takes the life of your mate and clutch. Then you will serve them to me, to break my fast.*

O'Dee stood at the kitchen window, rinsing the freshly washed dishes that dripped frothy suds onto the sink. As she opened the cupboard above her head, out of the corner of her eye, she caught a glimpse of movement. As if rooted to the spot, she stood with a cloth-covered plate in her hand as she stared through the window. Tessa was riding bareback on Coinneach. Her arm in the cast, was flapping in the breeze. The dish clattered to the countertop as the tea towel fluttered to the floor. She crossed the room to the front door and hurried over to the cottage where Connor said she would be working on the routines for the dressage clinic. The sweat of fear beaded on her forehead as she puffed with exertion. After wheezing her way up the stairs, she knocked on the front door.

"It's open," Connor called from inside.

O'Dee grasped the handle and opened the door. "Oh, thank God ye are here. Quick! I need ye to come now! It seems our lass dinna learn a scrap of a lesson, when she broke her arm. You willna believe it, but she's oot there right now, on that blessed horse. If her da finds oot, there will be—"

Ewan's voice boomed from the front yard. "THERESA MARY MARGARET McVEY! What in the name of sweet Jesus do you think you're doing?"

Connor stood, pushed back her chair, and went to stand beside O'Dee on the porch. Tessa and Coinneach were doing laps of the paddock.

Connor groaned. "Oh, Jesus, not even a broken arm's going to save her this time."

O'Dee clutched her apron in her hands. "She's just like her mam; she has no fear. Anyone with eyes can see that she's meant to ride. She has the way of it *and* the horse knows it. It is just that we're all so afraid that something will—"

Connor massaged her temples with her fingers as common sense screamed at her. *Stay out of it! Stay out of it! Stay out of it!* "O'Dee," she sighed. "Ewan is her father. It is up to him to—"

"He's so caught oop in his caoineadh—his grief for our Beth, that he is blinded to the obvious similarities. 'Tis just not right. The lass should ride. It was her mam's dearest wish."

Connor pulled back, suddenly guarded. "Why are you looking at me like that? What do you expect me to do? Ewan is the parent. It's his call!"

As O'Dee wiped her hands on her apron, she looked up with a face more serious than Connor had ever seen. "And *ye* are the rider. Please try to talk some sense into him. He willna listen to any of us."

When Connor's boots hit the bottom rung of the stairs, she turned. O'Dee, still standing on the porch, was strangling her apron between her fingers. "Then why do you think he will listen to me?"

"Just try, lass, for the bairn's sake."

Connor shook her head as she walked across the grass in the direction of Ewan's roar. *This is a fucking bad idea! Crap! I just know this is a bad fucking idea.*

Connor fell in line with Ewan as he stomped passed the cottage, headed toward the paddock.

He looked over to her and scowled. "This is your bloody fault! I hope you're happy! She takes no notice of me ever since you got here."

Connor grabbed him by the elbow and pulled him to a halt. "Look, this is none of my bloody business. But, as you have chosen to blame me for Tessa's interest in horses, I think it's time we talked about this. I knew your wife, remember, and Tessa has her mother's way with horses. You may not want to believe that, but it is true. You know it! I know it! Christ! I don't get you at all. Tessa has lost her mother and from what I have seen, she doesn't have any friends and she doesn't go to school." She tightened her grip on his arm. "Don't let *your* fear cripple her and rob her of her future. For God's sake Ewan, let her learn. That will be the only way to keep her safe. As it is now, she's going to sneak around and take every opportunity to ride Coinneach. Her inexperience is the risk, the horse is not the problem here."

His lips crushed into a familiar thin, white line as he shrugged her hand from his arm. "Don't you dare judge me and think to give me advice!"

"Jesus! You're unbelievable, do you know that? This is about *Tessa*, not you!" Connor stormed off toward the paddock while Tessa and Coinneach moved in synchronised oblivion, as if they had been practicing routines together, for years.

Ewan came alongside her, then stood in front of her, and blocked her path. He placed his hands on both of Connor's shoulders and shook her. Her head rocked back and forth under the force of his grip. "You don't know what it's like to lose someone who's so precious to you that life without them every day is torture."

Connor grunted as his words struck her like a punch to the stomach. The katanas roared for permission to strike. "Get your fucking hands off me or Tessa won't be the only one with broken bones." Palms together, she jerked her hands upward, then spread her arms to displace his hands. She leaned toward him and hissed. "You know nothing about me, you bastard! If you took your head out of your arse for five seconds, you might be surprised to learn that you aren't the only one on this planet who has lost someone and who grieves."

He stepped back, looking shocked and ashamed. "I'm sorry, Connor, I shouldn't have laid my hands on you. I want Tessa to be happy, I do. We all do. I'm sorry, I was out of line."

She considered him for several seconds then nodded. "We're good, Ewan. I don't want you and I to fall out, because come hell or high water, I'm here until the end of my contract."

Ewan scuffed the toe of one of his boots in the dust. "You think I should let her ride, don't you?"

A pause hung in the air before she answered. "No. I think you should let her *learn* to ride and carry on the skills of her mother."

Together, they walked over to the paddock and stood in silence. They both leaned on the wooden rail and watched Tessa's beaming smile confirm she was one with the horse beneath her.

Tessa leaned down and hugged Coinneach around the neck with her uninjured arm, prattling away like a noisy parrot. Loose blonde hair clung to the sweat on her face. The smile died on her lips, when, across the paddock, her da and Connor stood at the rail. She gulped, pouted, straightened her back, and continued to pace the horse in even movements.

Ewan called out to her. "Tessa, can you come here, please?"

She looked at him, renewed her pout then looked at Connor. Sitting tall and rigid, she urged Coinneach forward until she stood in front of them.

"Da, I know what you're going to say, but, see how gentle he is? I can ride him. Coinneach is mine, Da, he's mine! I know it and he knows it."

Ewan crossed his arms. "Tessa, the cast on your arm is barely dry, and here I find you out riding again."

As she crossed her uninjured arm over her cast, a look of firm determination settled on her face. "Da! I can do this! Mam let me ride with her all the time."

Slowly he turned his head toward Connor, then back to Tessa. "I know, I remember. He lowered his head, sighed then looked up. His face softened at the memory. "You're so like her, sweetheart. She wouldn't have given up either."

"Da, please, I want Coinneach."

He turned to Connor. "What's your opinion of this horse? Is he a safe mount for her?"

She winked at Tessa. "He's a gentleman. I think he's a perfect match for her."

Little white lights danced in front of Tessa's eyes as she held her breath.

"Don't make me worry, Tessa. I want you to be happy. You know I do. I also want you to stay in one piece." He rubbed his hands over his face and sighed. "The horse is yours. Connor has made a very generous offer. She's going to teach you to ride."

Connor's eyes bugged as her head whipped in his direction. Tessa punched the air and whooped, then flopped forward on Coinneach and hugged him. "Did you hear that, boy? You're mine!" She sat up, then quickly dismounted, kissed the horse on the muzzle, then threw herself through the fence and into her father's arms. With her good arm locked around his neck, she peppered his face with noisy kisses. "Thank you, Da, thank you, thank you, thank you."

After he kissed the side of her face, he looked down at her. "Look after each other. It's time we had some happiness here at Glen Rowan. But, Tessa, don't make me worry."

Chapter Six

"**D**OUGLAS, I'VE BEEN MEANING TO TALK TO YOU about that cleared area beyond the barn. It would make a good parking area for the floats after the horses are unloaded. At previous schools, I've found the quickest and easiest solution to allocating individual zones, is to put logs across the top end and mark out the spaces with chalk." Connor held her breath, waiting for the rail of objections. Recently, on more than one occasion, Douglas had made it patently clear that the whole notion of this school was wearing very thin with him.

When no one spoke, she looked up, just as Andrew leaned across the table to the plate piled high with buttered bread slices. His elbow collided with his glass of milk. The glass exploded onto the wooden floor and milk sprayed everywhere. Ewan bellowed as he pushed back his chair with such force, it clattered to the floor.

"Jesus Christ, Andrew! Just look at the mess you've made! Can't you sit still for five bloody minutes?"

He stormed out of the room and returned a minute later with the dustpan, broom and mop. Andrew sat on his cushion, eyes downcast, lips quivering. Tessa cried silently as she forked food into her mouth. Everyone at the table sat, as if frozen in time.

A wave of protectiveness washed over Connor. The katanas under her skin responded to the threat. She stood, walked over to Ewan, and whispered, "Give me those. You're needed elsewhere." She jerked her head toward the children sitting at the table.

He was fury, walking. The muscles in his neck bulged with tension.

The ink work of her tattoos writhed unseen, as her temper flared. She clenched her fists at the wave of anger that vibrated off him. When he leaned toward her, lips drawn back over his teeth, she slapped the flat of both hands onto his chest and shoved him backward. "Back off! I won't tell you again!"

His eyes bulged as the flush on his face deepened. "Oh, you're just a regular little guardian angel, aren't you? Always there; what with Tessa and her broken arm, and, of course, coming to our rescue with the dressage school. I just don't know how we ever survived here without you!" He took a step toward her. "Don't you dare interfere with me and my children. Go shove your goody two shoes bullshit up—"

They both turned their heads when a chair scraped across the floor. Douglas stood back from the table. "Well, someone bloody well had to do it." He lifted his chin toward Connor. "Christ, man! Think afore ye speak in front of the bairns!"

Ewan's chin dropped to his chest. "Da..."

Douglas closed his eyes in a slow blink and sighed as his shoulders slumped. "This is a verra hard day for evraone." He paused and swallowed hard. "We all suffer, lad. This year of firsts has been terrible time. It seems impossible that this day marks twelve months since our Beth left us. God rest her beautiful soul."

All seated at the table, with the exception of the children, said, "Amen."

A sob came from Ewan's direction. Connor uncurled her fists. "I'm sorry. I didn't know today is the anniversary of... I know you are grieving, but so are the children."

His voice, laced with bitterness, was miserable. "Of course we're grieving! That's the whole bloody point. In my heart, I know I've lost her; that she's gone forever. But, it's like she's fading from my memory, like she has ceased to have ever existed. I meet people all the time who never knew her. It's like she is fading into nothingness."

A tiny sob came from the other side of the table where Tessa and Andrew sat white-faced.

Ewan looked over at them, dropped his chin to his chest, sobbed and walked out of the dining room.

He didn't look back.

Just as dawn's light began to peak over the mountains, Connor lifted the scabbard from its bracket, took the sword in her hand, and went outside. After about an hour, she looked up. Tessa was hanging over the banister of the stairs, watching her.

"Wow. That's cool. Can I have a look at your sword?"

Connor nodded and chuckled to herself. "Sure. Jeez, what is it with you McVeys? Every time I pick up the sword, there's at least one of you lurking around."

Within thirty seconds, Tessa was standing barefoot on the damp grass. "Why do you have a sword?"

Connor stroked the metal with her fingers. "A long time ago, when I was afraid, a friend gave it to me. He taught me to use it, to restore my self confidence and to learn protect myself."

Tessa nodded, then yawned. "I wish I could protect myself, then I could go to sch —" The soft light made the shadows under her eyes even more prominent.

"Tessa, are you okay?"

"Yeah. Just tired. O'Dee says I'm a bad sleeper."

Connor looked up from the sword and frowned. "Bad sleeper? What? You don't sleep well?"

"Nuh-uh. Not since Mam... There's something about the night... I don't like the dark. I get scared. I try to keep myself awake so I don't go to sleep. I mean, I do sleep, but I wake up a lot."

"Scared of what? Noises and stuff? Houses make lots of creaky noises at night."

Sighing, Tessa turned to face the wall. "Not noises. Something black. I feel —"

Several loud knocking sounds came from the direction of the front of the cottage. Connor called out, "We're round here."

Ewan looked sheepish as he stuck his head round the corner and walked in their direction. He paused as if choosing his words. "Connor, I want to apologise for last night. You were only trying to —"

She held up one hand. "Death sucks, Ewan. There's no need to apologise."

"Thanks." He put his arm around Tessa and gave her a squeeze. "Sometimes I get so caught up with missing Beth, I forget that everyone else is suffering just as much." He looked at the sword in Connor's hand. "So, rain, hail or shine, huh?"

She smiled. "Yep, I work out every day at dawn. It's part of the discipline needed to use the sword."

Tessa extended her palm as she stared at the blade. "Can I touch it? It's so beautiful."

"Sure." Connor placed the hilt into her small palm. The purr of Welcome hummed when the sword made contact with her skin.

After breakfast, Connor sat across from Ewan, sipping her second cup of tea.

Fifteen minutes earlier, Douglas had taken the two children down to the chicken coop where the cranky speckled hen, had hatched twelve chicks.

She placed her cup back down on her saucer. "Tell me something."

Ewan leaned back on his chair. "If I can, I will."

"Why doesn't Tessa go to school?"

His jaw was set in a firm line and he sighed. "You don't give up, do you? Fine! It all started with a couple of girls whose mother competed against Beth in the dressage events, started teasing Tessa. You know the sort? They bitch about others in front of their kids, who then invariably go and repeat it later?"

Connor's tone was droll. "Have you forgotten that I travel in dressage circles? Of course, I *get* the bitchiness and the vindictiveness. It goes with the turf."

"Those girls picked on Tessa because Beth nearly always won the events she competed in. What started out as jealousy from another competitor ended up as full-scale bullying of Tessa by her kids. In the beginning, Tessa didn't say anything to us. But, soon after her mother died, she started coming home with rips in her school uniform and bruises and scrapes on her arms and legs. Those bloody horrible girls told Tessa that, as she no longer had a mother, she'd go to an orphanage. In the end, Tessa was terrified to go to school in case these so called 'orphanage police' whisked away from us forever. This, on top of losing her mother, was just too much. I went to the school and spoke to the principal." He sighed and his shoulders slumped. "But she was either incapable or plain just not interested in addressing the bullying. As a *compromise*, Tessa receives workbooks to continue her education by home schooling with O'Dee. The principal, it seems, favoured the generous, annual donation to the school, by the mother of those two girls, than the welfare of one of her students."

Connor looked up at him. "Jesus! That's terrible. Why O'Dee? Is she a teacher or something?"

Ewan smiled. "No, well, not a qualified one, or anything. She lived out west with her husband, who worked in the mines. She schooled her own three children from home. That woman has been a blessing to this family in more ways than we can ever thank her for."

"What about friends, Ewan? Tessa needs girlfriends. Someone she can share secrets with, paint nails with, make goo-goo eyes at boys with."

He threw back his head and laughed, truly laughed for the first time since she had met him. "Firstly, I don't believe you just said goo-goo eyes, and, secondly, Tessa will not be making goo-goo eyes at anyone."

"Ewan? Tessa is what, twelve?"

He nodded and smiled. "Yep. Thirteen in November."

Connor looked triumphant. "Exactly!"

"Exactly, what?" He cocked his head to the side with a bewildered expression on his face.

"Menarche, the age of terror and aggravation for parents."

"Jesus, Connor, I swear I only ever understand half of what you say. What the hell are you talking about?"

She huffed and ticked off five fingers for emphasis. "Puberty! Breasts! Periods! Boys! Impossible behaviour!"

A bright red stain rose like a tsunami from the neckline of his shirt to the roots of his hair. "Christ, woman, the things you say. We don't speak of such things in mixed company. Jesus! Besides, Tessa is years away from all that business."

Connor got up and refilled the teapot with hot water from the kettle on the hob. "Are you kidding me? Have you not noticed Tessa is developing breasts? Her period will come any time soon and she will be unprepared. Ewan?" She walked passed him and poked him on the bicep. "Are you even listening to me?"

He pursed his lips before lifting his cup for a refill. "Do I have any choice?"

She laughed. "Tessa needs someone to bring her up to speed on what to expect before all these changes start to happen."

Ewan groaned. "I'll speak to O'Dee, she'll—"

"Pffffft! Forget it! I already broached the subject. Now how did she put it?" She cocked her head, nodded and smirked. "Oh, yeah. 'Me woman pipes havena worked for the better part o' twenty years, lass. I doona think it fittin' or right that I be the one to have *that* talk with Tessa. Things are verra different these days from when I still had my flow. Nay, Connor, ye are the best one for this job. I see all those advertisements on the television aboot pads with wings and sphagnum and God knows what else. Ye know, to be truthful, I truly doona understand why modern women need wings. It's a mystery to me, that's for sure. For certain, this information would be best comin' from ye".

Ewan roared, laughing. "Christ, I guess O'Dee's right. I mean, I haven't given the subject a moment's thought and *I* sure as hell aren't going to speak to her about such things." He looked over to her and lifted his eyebrows. "So it looks like you're it."

Connor rolled her eyes. "Well, Jesus! There's no need to make me sound like the booby prize! It may have escaped your attention, Ewan McVey, but I *am* a woman. Besides, I'm a nurse. I know these things. Now, what about if she needs stuff?"

He frowned and blinked like an owl. "Stuff? What stuff?"

Exasperated, she sighed. "Girl stuff!"

"Fine." He held up one hand and turned his head away. "Don't tell me anymore. Take her to Tierney's. We have an account there."

Connor picked up her cup and took a sip. "What's Tierney's?"

"Oh, the local store, you know, work clothes, fishing gear, car supplies, that sort of thing."

She gave him a disbelieving look. "You're kidding, right? Do you want your daughter to be a social outcast?"

"What the hell are you talking about now? I swear to God, sometimes talking to you, is like talking to someone who speaks another language."

"Oh, for Christ's sake, Ewan, do you know nothing about women?"

He gave her a droll look. "Obviously not. Fine. Do whatever you need to do and bring me the bill. You can take the station wagon in the garage."

Connor laughed. "Ewan, I have transportation."

"Oh, yeah, that bloody death trap."

"God Almighty, there are two of you! My brother Cameron says exactly the same thing. Seriously, I have a spare helmet. Besides, Tessa wants to go back to school."

He looked taken aback. "And how do you know that? Did she say so?"

"When I was working out with the sword this morning, she told me if she could defend herself, she could go back to school. It's a bloody terrible thing that she *has* to defend herself, but to be always afraid, is worse." She jiggled her eyebrows.

Ewan groaned. "Oh, Jesus, I see where this is going, and before you say one more bloody word, the answer is no. There is no way, any hormonal teenager of mine is getting anywhere near that bloody sword." He looked over to her. "What? Why are you looking at me like that?"

"She wants to go back to school."

Incredulous, he sat back in his chair. "Are you suggesting that my daughter learn self-defence?"

Connor laughed. "What could possibly go wrong?"

Chapter Seven

THE FOLLOWING SATURDAY, CONNOR DREAM-SMILED when the man came into view. His blond hair was shiny and tousled. Flecks of gold sparked in the sunlight. His eyes, green as any meadow were beyond divine. She knew every fleck and every contrast, as she played in the depths of the colour of moss. She knew she should have been scared by their alien mirror sheen, but she wasn't; it just somehow made him more beautiful. As slumber slipped away, she woke to the sense of being watched.

Tessa sat cross-legged on the chair at the side of the bed.

"Morning." Connor checked her watch. "How long have you been sitting there?"

Tessa looked at the clock on the bedside table. "Two hours and twelve minutes."

Connor laughed and pulled back the bed linens. "Okay, good to know you're keen. Give me awhile to do my work out then we can have breakfast and go shopping."

Tessa leaned forward. "Can I stay and watch?"

It was then that she noticed Tessa wore sports pants and a T-shirt. "Sure, come on, why not." Connor walked over to the scabbard and withdrew the katana. Tessa's eyes bugged but she remained silent as she followed Connor, who flicked on the lights as they passed through the kitchen. Side by side, they walked down the stairs and onto the grassed area at the side of the house. Light flooded through the kitchen window. Connor stood on the illuminated lawn with the sword held out in front of her, then bowed to the four points of the compass and then to the sword.

"Remember, Tessa, the key to defending yourself is to never take your eyes off your opponent. Anticipate their moves and use their body weight against them." For the next thirty minutes, Connor worked through her long-practiced routines and was a lather of sweat when she finally came to a standstill.

"Can I hold it, Connor? The sword? I promise I won't drop it."

Connor held up her left index finger, then raised the sword in front of her. "You father has made it pretty clear that he doesn't want you to be involved with the sword."

Tessa giggled, looked around, then entered the practice circle. "I know. He told me."

"All right then, just so as you know we are both going to be in big trouble if he sees you with the katana." Connor looked all around then smiled. "Hold out your hand."

Tessa's fingers curled around the hilt. Her smiling face suddenly became a look of terror. "Connor, what's happening?" The thrill of Welcome, growled in an audible, deep vibration of warning.

Connor looked around. The sword was never wrong.

A wave of tiredness washed over Connor as she walked into her cottage, shut the door then plopped down on the lounge. It had been fun taking Tessa shopping, but now she was bone weary. She rolled her shoulders and rested her head back on the cushion. A warm breeze wafted passed her face and neck as the now, familiar, unnamed scent, filled her nose and instantly relaxed her.

She closed her eyes and started to drift off to sleep when she jolted, suddenly awake. As she sat forward, a vivid, buried memory exploded in her brain. She gasped when her sense of smell, remembered...Sandalwood!

Craig!

Stunned, she couldn't move.

For just a moment, she closed her eyes and imagined him standing in front of her. Instinctively, she reached out. The space was empty, but the sensation that she wasn't alone was overwhelming. Her eyes flew open. An incorporeal form along the sidewall, about twelve feet in front of her, stood before her.

"Oh, my God." She clapped a hand over her eyes, then slowly spread her fingers and peeked through.

Staring, she could just make out a fine outline of a person. She squinted and looked harder.

Sweet Jesus! It was Craig; waving his arms, frantic, his mouth moving in screamed words she couldn't hear.

Okay, that's it! I've lost my mind! Fuck! I've gotta get out of here!

She rushed toward the front door, her hand extended for the knob, when slowly, she lowered her forehead to the wood panel. "Oh, shit!"

She took in a big breath, blew out, and turned back round.

A gasp escaped her lips. She gripped her throat with her hand as he struggled to move toward her. The flesh of his palms, pressed against some sort of invisible barrier, were bloodless white. Screaming, he banged his fists in front of him.

Disbelieving, she stared at his transparent form. "Craig. Oh, God. If only —" She began to sob.

His fists pummelled the space in front of him as he yelled at her.

Suddenly, there was a knock at the front door. She spun toward the sound then turned back, staring at the space where he had been.

She was alone.

"Connor, it's me." Tessa called from the other side of the door.

Connor's throat was so dry, she stuttered when she spoke. "Co-come in."

The door flew open and Tessa bounded into the room. "Thanks for taking me shopping! It was —" She paused, her head jerked backward in surprise. "You okay? You look kinda sick. Do you want me to go and get O'Dee"

Connor tried to shake free of the image of Craig. The memory clung to her consciousness like an octopus to its prey. "No, no. Don't worry, I'm fine. I'm glad you had fun shopping, I had fun too. I'm glad you've come over, there's something I have wanted to talk to you about. Tessa, your da told me you were being bullied at school."

She nodded as she stared down at her newly painted, glittery, shell pink fingernails.

Connor's gaze darted to the side of the room before she cleared her throat. *Focus! For God's sake, focus! Craig is* not *here! Craig is* not *here!* "You know, the thing about bullies is that they're always cowards. Rule number one, never step backward. That puts the bully in a position of power." She got up and walked behind Tessa. "You need to learn what to do if those girls hassle you again."

After an hour, Tessa mopped her face with the hem of her T-shirt. "Can we practice again? Da's always worried, but if I can protect myself and stop those girls bullying me, maybe he'll let me go back to school."

"Talk to your da. Let me know what he says, okay." She gave Tessa hug.

A warm breeze, laden with sandalwood, rushed around the room and her heart clenched.

The dark Shadow wound around the branch of a tree, camouflaged in the bark and shade. *So, female with the God Threads, you are a swordswoman.* Thinking back to the last report from her pathetic Sentinel, she recalled his words. *"All I know is that I heard four swords."* So, the *Samurai have a sword each, and God Threads over there, has another, which only leaves one conclusion.. The girl child must not learn the ways of the sword. I have planned and schemed for years. Vengeance will be mine.*

The vibrating hum of the blade shuddered around the Shadow. From the second she arrived, she knew the blade sensed her. The time had come. Clearly, the Sentinel was unreliable. *If you want something done properly...* She made a low, derisive sound. High in the same tree sat the raven, looking everywhere but at the two humans and the sword. The Shadow oozed away into the darkness.

Later, as the moon passed its zenith, the raven flew into the shadows.

"Well?"

"There is nothing to report, Mistress. I am sorry."

Cackling, the Shadow moved flashed toward him at blinding speed. "Nothing to report?" Screeching, she arced a vision of Connor watching Tessa with the sword. "You did not think this little fact would be of interest to me? The last time a Guar —" she choked on her near mistake. "Suffice to say that child must not learn the way of the blade."

"Come!" Maniacal laughter filled the dark zone as she morphed away to her lair. "You fool!" She spat in the direction of the raven. "While you were out sightseeing, I have been busy." She brushed aside a black cloud. On the floor lay the bloody, decapitated bodies of the raven's mate and clutch. She reached down, picked up one of the smaller heads, and popped it into her mouth. "Ahh, canapés!"

Suddenly she reared back. A thick obsidian beak came out of the maelstrom of swirling darkness. It struck the raven on the neck, raked his body, and split him down the middle. The lifeless body slumped, to join his family in death, on the cold stone floor. "The price of failure." The beak turned on its side. "Ahh, I love dark meat!" She picked up one portion of the raven and gulped it down.

That night, as Tessa tossed in tangled bed linens, the dark Shadow slipped through the window of her bedroom and hovered over the end of the bed.

Restless, Tessa made little fearful, mewling sounds as if aware of the presence, but she was unable to rise from sleep.

A female voice grated like a knife on bone as she spoke into the gloom. "So you think to become a warrior, spawn of mine enemy? I look forward to toying with you before you die. How I yearn for the pain of your death. But, alas, not quite yet. No, not yet… I have patience. I have all the time in the world."

Hate filled the room.

"I count the moments until your heart stops beating under my hand."

Chapter Eight

EVERY DAY, IT WAS THE SAME — WAKING TO THE CRASH-ing realization that Craig was dead. Grief ate at her like a metastatic cancer. In her heart, she knew that his smell and the feeling that he was still with her, was little more than wishful thinking. Her father's voice rang in her memory. *"If wishes were horses, then beggars would ride."*

The sucker punch was that now, she lived for her dreams; her grief-induced night dwelling manifestations of Craig. The knife cut ever deeper for not once, did she dream of James.

Night after night, she relished in the warmth of Craig's body pressed against hers. She had no explanation for it; neither did she question it. She eagerly looked forward to every second of her dream-time with him, when, for just a little while, she could pretend he was still alive.

That evening, she yawned and climbed into bed when her phone vibrated on the bedside table. She reached over, picked up the device, and checked the caller ID. Her fingers fumbled in her hurry to press the connect button.

"Da! It's great to hear from you. Is everything all right?

Angus chuckled. "Aye, lass. Evra thing is fine. Ye can probably hear Jilly Louise whoopin' and hollerin' from where ye are."

Connor sat forward and gripped the phone. "Is she all right? The baby? Is the baby all right? Ethan? Is he…"

"Oh, aye, lass, everaone is just fine. Jilly Louise is as broad as a battleship, with just three months to go until the bairn arrives. Now, the reason for the call is to let ye know Cameron and I are planning on comin' to the Highland Games. Anyway, as ye could imagine, he refuses point-blank to leave the lass now that she is big with the bairn. So, if ye have the room, we thought we might make it a family affair this year and come up and visit with ye, then go on to the Games."

Excitement almost stole her breath away. "Of course there's room. Who's coming? When? Is mam coming, too? Oh, Da. I can't wait to see you all again. You can't begin to know how much I have missed everyone."

His voice was suddenly sombre. "Aye, lass, we miss ye summat terrible too. As I said, Cameron willna leave home without Jilly Louise and Ethan, so they'll be comin'. And, aye, yer mam is already packed, even though 'tis still three weeks 'til we leave. Yer brother Callum and his lass Sadie are going to look after the place and the horses while we're gone. Anyway, we'll arrive at Glen Rowan on the twenty-fifth of the month. That'll give us a week with ye afore we go down to the Games. See ye then. Oh, and doona forget to tell that old bastard Douglas McVey I look verra much forward to remaking his acquaintance. Well, I'll go now, leannan. See ye soon, lass. Night, now."

The connection went dead.

She stared at the handset, picturing her father's handsome face as she checked the clock on the nightstand, when suddenly, the phone dropped out of her hand, unnoticed, onto the quilt.

The almost transparent outline of Craig's body stood at the end of the bed. For the first time since the accident, she saw him smile.

Not willing to take her eyes off him, she shimmied down the mattress. Slowly, she lifted her palm and placed it in the middle of his chest. Her hand passed through him, but his outline remained.

She leaned forward and sniffed the space between his neck and his shoulder. Sandalwood filled her nostrils.

"Craig?" A look of incredulity slowly crept across her face. "I'm not dreaming, am I?"

As he reached toward her, his lips moved as if he were speaking, but no sound came out. Head thrown back, his mouth opened in a silent roar of frustration.

"What? I don't understand."

His fringe fell forward as he dropped his chin to his chest. The transparent outline of his body began to fade.

"No! No! Don't go! Please, Craig… For Christ's sake, don't go!"

The outline of his body became a little more substantial. She burst into tears at the sight of the pain and suffering etched on his face.

She launched off the bed and landed on her feet as she screamed and thrust both hands in the air. "Grandfather and the Samurai, I summon you!"

A green glow, accompanied by a bone-vibrating hum, filled the room as Tomoe Gazen revealed herself. She nodded to where Craig floated above the end of the bed. "Well met, Death Walker."

Thunder boomed overhead as the Ancient Scottish Horsemen screamed in response to her call. Clad in the MacDonald chieftain's kilt and plaid, her grandsire, Connor MacDonald, materialised in the centre of the room. Shock painted his face as he stared warily at Craig and then bowed to Tomoe Gazen.

"What manner of sorcery is this?"

The hem of Tomoe Gazen's long white robe brushed against the floorboards with each step she took. "Not sorcery. The result of an action on my part, that has caused upset to the natural course of the universe."

The chieftain frowned as he thrust his chin in the direction of Craig's barely visible outline. "Ye called him Death Walker. Explain yerself. No one walks atween the light and the shadows."

Connor stood beside her grandfather.

He picked up her hand and held it to his chest as he spoke to Tomoe Gazen. "What have the Samurai Gods done? Have ye risked the life of our child of prophesy? It is many eons since we Scots have been at odds with other immortals. But know this; any risk to her *will* invoke war between us. Speak now. The clans will do whatever is necessary to keep her safe."

Tomoe Gazen inclined her head once. "I understand your worry. In truth, I am conflicted. You see, I have known about," she lifted her hand, palm upward, toward Craig, "*this*, since the first time Yokami and I visited Connor here." She sighed and faced them. "Daughter, when the accident that took the life of your man and your son, your husband, in his love for you, used his body to try and protect you and the boy." Remembered pain flashed across her features. "Yokami and I saw the accident happen. When I shielded you, to try to save you, I also hoped to save him. I couldn't bear to think of you losing him and your child. But, the Harbinger of Death already had him in her clutches." She paused as if composing herself, then cleared her throat. "I did not realise his injuries were mortal when I shielded you both. His physical self, had already departed, but his soul survived, snatched back from the hands of death. He is neither dead nor alive. I am sorry. I can do no more. The Samurai do not possess the Rite of Redemption."

"Rite of Redemption?" The clan chief rumbled. "Sounds verra like sorcery to me. We Scots doona hold with fraternizin' with ghosts and folk coming back from the Shade. To interfere with the dead, is sacrilege."

"No, not sacrilege. He is a Death Walker, caught between life and death because I shielded his immortal soul." Standing tall, she placed her palms together in front of her. "Let us not forget, the Samurai, the Ancient Horsemen, and Epona, are forever in his debt. When our Daughter lay dying after the accident, it was he, who, on *our* demand, summoned her back from her journey to the Shade."

A look of unwelcome realisation came over the chieftain's face. "Christ Almighty, yer right."

Her gaze settled on Connor. "The Gods owe your man a boon, my Daughter; payment for our great debt owed to him. We will help you seek the ones who have the power to enact the Rite of Redemption."

Yokami materialised in the cottage, to the right of his wife. "She knows?

"Yes."

Connor stepped forward, her hands on his forearms. "Mr Sukani?" Betrayal cracked across her tongue. "This is true? The Rite of Redemption is possible? Craig could be alive again? Why have you not...?"

"Daughter, the Samurai do not have the ability to barter with or reverse death. In the time of *this* Earth, there is a legend of an immortal, whose long forgotten name, is touted as having the power to wield this spell. We know little of the details except that a God offered a great kindness to another, in the form of a boon. It was then that the offer of the Rite of Redemption was offered. However, the reason as to why the Rite was conjured was lost many thousands of years ago. There is no formal record of the Summon of the Rite of Redemption in all of history. *If* the legend is true, the record no longer exists. I am so sorry."

A sob escaped her lips as Craig's silent screams, behind the invisible barrier, slashed across her heart. "Are you telling me that he is going to live like *this* forever? That this is all we will ever have?"

"Yes. I am so sorry, there is —"

"No! No!" She pulled her hands free and stood as close to Craig as she could without intruding on his faint body outline. He reached for her, his mouth moving incessantly. She put her palms in the air; he moved closer and lifted his hands to cover hers. He screamed in frustration when her hands passed through him.

"Who...?" Sobbing, she choked on her words. "How is it I can see him? You can see him. Can anyone else see him?"

"Daughter..." The chieftain shot a look of fury at the Samurai.

Tomoe Gazen bit her lip before she spoke. "Only those who are Gods or who have been Touched by Gods, will be able to see him."

Connor dragged her forearm across her face to wipe away her tears. "The Rite of Redemption...if not the Samurai or the Ancient Horsemen, someone, somewhere, must know how to enact the spell."

Yokami and Tomoe Gazen looked to each other. The silence in the room was agonizingly claustrophobic.

The chieftain bellowed at the Samurai. "Answer her! By yer own admission, this situation is of yer making." He glared at Tomoe Gazen. "No one, man or woman, deserves to spend eternity as ye have cast her man's future. Answer her question. Call the Council of the Immortals. We must discover all we can, of this Rite of Redemption."

Chapter Nine

AT A LITTLE AFTER ONE IN THE AFTERNOON, TWO cars rumbled along the Glen Rowan driveway.

Connor bounded down the stairs. Angus and Marie opened their doors and got out of the car just as she barrelled into them and hugged them, tight. Angus froze, pulled back, looked at her, and frowned.

Jilly Louise screamed with excitement while Cameron unstrapped Ethan from his car seat. She attempted to throw her arms around Connor while trying to manoeuvre her belly out of the way. "Oh. My. God!" She held Connor at arm's length. "Look at you, all thin, blonde and beautiful. I, on the other hand, am doing my best impression of a whale."

Connor laughed as she jerked her head toward the vehicle Jilly Louise had just sprung from. "Nice wheels."

"A Volvo! A bloody Volvo, Connor; and it's *brown*, for God's sake. Do you know your brother took the wheels off my bike and hid them? *Then* he bought me a car that does fifteen miles per hour and has fifty-five air bags! I'm doomed to spend the rest of this pregnancy trapped under his watchful eye, drivin' around in a nanna's car!"

Cameron walked toward them with four-year-old Ethan in his arms. "Don't listen to her moaning, Connor. At least I can sleep at night, knowing she is not out somewhere lying splattered on the highway. Anyway, what's wrong with a Volvo? Safest car in the world." He handed Ethan to Connor as his arms swallowed them in a bear hug. "Christ, we've missed you."

Connor wrapped one of her arms around Cameron's waist and the other one around Ethan, who suddenly appeared to remember who she was. He gave her a wide smile, revealing at least eight shiny new teeth. "Aunty! I find you!"

"Hey, baby, I've really missed you. But there's someone here who—"

A throat-clearing sound caused her to look up. All of the McVeys and O'Dee were standing on the porch. She gathered Ethan into her arms and called over her shoulder, "Hey, everyone, come and meet Douglas and the family."

Angus took Marie's hand in his and walked up the steps to the porch. "Verra nice to meet ye, Mr McVey. I thank ye for takin' such good care of our lass."

Douglas' colour was high and his eyes shiny with excitement. "Mr McVey be buggered. Call me Douglas, and know it's my true pleasure to meet the man who breeds the Nimerlin Fey Friesians. I swear to ye, when the lass's horse was unloaded, I thought my eyes were deceivin' me. Never did I imagine such a magnificent beast would roam the paddocks of Glen Rowan."

Angus nodded. "Oh aye, Hades is the best we've ever bred. If it weren't for Connor, he would've died in the womb. She is indeed truly blessed with the ways of the Horsemen."

Douglas nodded. "'Tis true. The horses all respond verra well to her. We'd be lost withoot her."

Angus rubbed his hand over his face and beamed with a wicked glint in his eye. "Even though she isna a man?"

"Never ye be mindin' that! She's tougher than any bloody man I ever met."

"Well, that," said Jilly Louise as she waddled over to the porch chair and sat down, "is because you've never met me. Connor and I go way back, before I married her brother, who you may have noticed, makes babies the size of buffalos."

Everyone laughed as she tried unsuccessfully to shift her bulk into a more comfortable position.

Andrew let go of Ewan's hand, walked over to Connor, and put his hands up. He glared at Ethan.

Ethan hugged his arms tighter around Connor's neck and glared back.

Connor lifted Andrew and sat him on one hip while Ethan balanced to the other. "Okay, you two. Ethan, this is Andrew. Andrew, this is Ethan." Both boys continued to glare at each other.

"Lads," Douglas chuckled, "they never change. 'Tis always a pissin' contest."

Andrew frowned. "No say piss, Grandda. O'Dee said so."

Ethan puffed up his chest. "I say piss. Piss! Piss! Piss! But, I not allowed to say fuck."

Cameron groaned, grabbed him by the back of his shirt, and dragged him into his arms. "That'll be enough out of you." He ducked his head toward Douglas, O'Dee, and the rest of the family then looped his arm around Jilly Louise's shoulders and chuckled out loud. "He gets that from my Pixie here." Douglas bellowed a laugh and slapped Cameron on the back. "Well, now, it could be worse. Ewan, here, Andrew's da, as a lad, spent a good deal of time with the horse breakers and the farm workers. At any time of the day or night, he could singe the ears off a drunken sailor. I swear he ate twenty bars of soap afore he thought twice aboot swearin' in church, again."

Everyone laughed.

"Now let's go inside and get a bite to eat. Then I'll show ye around if ye are of a mind to take a bit of a walk." Douglas moved from the porch to open the front door. He made the introductions as he stood back and ushered everyone cross the threshold.

The grandfather clock in the dining room struck ten. Angus stared at the two swords with blades crossed mounted over the fireplace. As he lifted his glass, he drained the last of the whiskey, then stood and stretched.

Connor yawned, pushed back her chair, picked up her teacup and her father's whiskey glass.

O'Dee, still seated, held out her hand. "Leave those, lass. I'll see to it. Ye had all best find yer beds while ye can. Douglas is sure to have plans for tomorrow bright and early, ye can count on it."

Connor smiled and yawned again. "Thanks, O'Dee. You're right, it's definitely time for me to make tracks and get some sleep. Tessa will be up with the chooks, for her self-defence lessons."

Angus walked around the table and threw his arm around Connor's shoulders. "The wee lass is learnin' to fight? How come?"

Connor leaned her head against his shoulder, closed her eyes, and sighed. "She was being bullied at school, but she seems to have it in hand now."

Douglas tipped his glass. "Thanks to ye. 'Tis a true miracle how much happier Tessa is, now that she has returned to school."

Angus smiled and kissed the top of Connor's head. "Come, then. I'll walk ye over to yer place." He turned to Marie, who was talking quietly with Jilly Louise and O'Dee, and raised one eyebrow.

Marie smiled a tired smile and shook her head. "Ye go on. I'll just help finish up here and go on to bed. Connor and I'll have plenty of time to be catchin' oop tomorrow."

Connor and Angus bid everyone goodnight, walked out of the room, and closed the front door quietly behind them.

She wrapped her arm around his waist. "Lord, I've missed you and mam and the rest of the family. Sometimes I'm so homesick I don't think I'll last it here for twelve months." She dropped her arm from around his waist, then grasped the handrail and walked in front of him, up the stairs. The door handle rattled in her hand before she pushed it open and stepped inside. The lamp in the bedroom lit the small cottage with a golden glow.

Angus stood in the middle of the room, eyes darting left and right. "Connor, today, when we arrived... Jesus, how do I put this? I sensed summat."

She froze on the spot.

He shrugged. "It was nothin', lass, nothin'..."

She walked over and stood in front of him. "It's okay, tell me."

"I doona know, but there was summat." He wrapped her in his arms and kissed the top of her head. "Forget I said anythin'." He looked around the cottage and smiled. "Well, this is a cosy wee nest, is it no'?"

Connor smiled. "Yeah. I like it here. The McVeys are good people. You remember Elizabeth McVey, from the national championships? She was Ewan's wife and Tessa and Andrew' mam. This," she waved her hand in front of her, "was her painting studio."

"Oh, Jesus, that's right, I remember hearing one of old man McVey's lads lost his wife in an accident. "Tis a terrible thing, with the bairns bein' so young. Do ye know what happened?"

"Ewan told me she fell when she was out riding and broke her neck. You remember her amazing horse? The huge Warmblood white stallion, Rudiobus?"

He nodded. "Oh, aye. They were both true champions, to be sure. You and Hades were the only ones to offer them any real competition. What of the horse? Did they keep him after the accident?"

She cocked her head to one side and looked surprised. "You know, I haven't heard any mention of him since I got here. This family is broken-hearted over the loss of Elizabeth." Her gaze shifted, then widened, as she stared over his shoulder.

Angus turned abruptly, tracking the spot where she stared. He curled his hands into fists and splayed his feet. "Connor, forgive me. I sense that same feeling as I did, the moment we pulled oop this mornin'. I doona know what it is. But somehow, something feels theatenin'."

She took his hand and led him over to the small table in the centre of the room. "Sit down Da. There's something I want to tell you."

Connor pulled two chairs back from the table and sat close enough to him that their knees touched. "I don't know where to begin." Her voice quavered.

He picked up her hand and gave it a little squeeze. "Connor, lass, if there is summat here that is makin' ye unhappy, ye doona have to stay. Yer mam worries herself to a frazzle aboot how it is that ye are getting' on. If ye wish to return to Nimerlin, just say the word and we will pack ye oop and take ye home. I can see that ye have settled in here, and that the McVeys are all verra fond of ye, especially the bairns."

She smiled and squeezed his hand. "No, Da, I'm happy enough, and the McVeys are good to me. Oh, crap... I don't know how to put this."

His lips flattened into a straight line. "Tell me, lass. I willna rest now until I know what it is that..."

A choked sob escaped her throat. "It's Craig, Da."

He gathered her up in his arms and pressed her head to his shirt. "Oh, lass, Jesus God. I know, it must be so verra hard for ye."

She pulled back and shook her head. "No, Da, well, yes, losing Craig was, is torture for me every day. But..."

Angus leaned both elbows on his thighs and placed his chin in the palms of both hands. "I know, lass, I know. We all grieve for him."

"Da, it's not that. It's..."

Angus' brow wrinkled in concern. "What, lass? Tell me."

Craig appeared, just visible in the corner of the room.

Thunder boomed overhead and the room filled with the scent of sandalwood.

"Jesus Christ, Connor. I sense summat is verra wrong here!" Wary, he suddenly grabbed her around the waist and carried her toward the front door.

"Da! Stop! Please!"

Angus lowered her to the floor and he faced her.

"Mr Sukani and Tomoe Gazen have been here."

Angus nodded as his gaze swept the room. "Oh, aye? I haven't seen them since ye took Bishamon's head. God curse his evil soul."

"It happened during the accident."

Angus frowned. "It? What is *it*?"

Clearing her throat, she swallowed noisily. "When Bill Middleton's bull came through the windscreen of Craig's car, Tomoe Gazen thought only to save me. But, when Craig threw himself across me to protect me, he was also protected, not in the physical sense, but his soul survived."

His eyelids narrowed. "I doona know what that means, lass, but as ye well ken, we Scots are a verra superstitious race. Our legends speak of sightings of the dead. For us, that is no' unusual. It is just that we canna bide with them. Those souls must find their own way to the Shade." He shuddered as he continued to look around the room. "Although, to tell ye the truth, I do salt the doorways and window-sills of our hoose every year on All Hallows Eve; just to make sure any spirits lurking around, canna come inside."

"Not a ghost, Da, his soul."

"Connor," he put his hands on her shoulders, "ours unto God. I understand yer grief, lass. But doona confuse that which you want, for that which you have."

"Da, Mr Sukani and Tomoe Gazen have admitted this is what happened during the accid—"

Angus snorted. "Connor! Enough! We'll speak of this no more and for Christ's sake, doona say anything to yer mam. She worries night and day aboot ye, as it is."

Connor stood, closed her eyes and held her hands out in front of her, palms upward. "Grandfather!"

Connor MacDonald, clan chieftain appeared in the centre of the room. Epona stood next to him. "Well met, Grandson."

"Grandsire! Holy God!" Angus staggered in shock, blinked, paused, then walked toward them with his hand extended. "It's many a year since I last saw ye. I was verra pleased when Yokami told me ye had ascended as an immortal. Yer efforts at Culloden, and then, afterward, during the clearances, went a long way to help the clans."

Epona picked up the chieftain's hand. "We are blessed to have him walk among us."

Bristling with power, the clan chieftain regarded his great-grand-daughter. "You summoned me, child?"

Smiling, Connor nodded. "Yes, I did. I was trying to explain to Da about Craig and his lost soul and—"

"'Tis true, man. The Samurai woman unintentionally locked his soul in the living, while his body passed over."

Angus scoffed. "'Tis impossible. No soul can be dead yet alive. Ye either are or ye aren't. There's no middle ground."

Epona gave him a sad smile. "In usual circumstances, that would be true, my clansman. However, in this situation a God has interfered in a mortal process."

Angus looked from Connor back to Epona. "Are ye saying there are poor wee souls oot there that wander lost for all eternity?"

"This is the first instance in history that we are aware of; where a soul has been caught between two worlds." Worry creased her brow. "Consider this: say the rest of the Gods in our realm learned of the possibility of preserving life from death in perpetuity."

Angus shook his head. "Seems like a verra faulty venture to me. I mean, what would be the point of endless wandering? To be separated from family, from everyone, forever? I canna imagine any God being interested in such a thing unless it is to inflict torture on some hapless soul."

"No Angus, quite the opposite. Consider the unbridled power that would accompany the ability to restore life. Consider what this would mean. No more would celestial warriors or Gods answer to the final call of death."

Angus shuddered then made a very Scottish noise in the back of his throat. "Down through the ages there have always been legends of folk who have been reincarnated. I have no belief in such. It is impossible to return to life from death."

The old Scot grunted. "Unless, of course, the Rite of Redemption is enacted."

Angus blinked and frowned. "Rite of Redemption? What the hell is that?"

"A spell whereby Craig could be restored to life as payment for the clearing of a debt owed to him by the Gods."

The index and middle fingers of Angus' right hand unconsciously curled into peaked horns — the sign of the beast. "Again, what the hell does that mean?"

The chieftain sighed. "We doona ken."

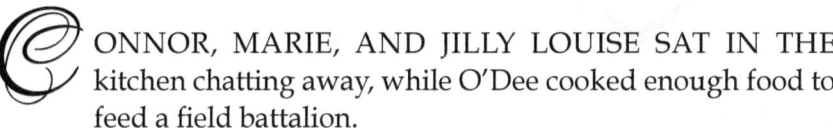

Chapter Ten

CONNOR, MARIE, AND JILLY LOUISE SAT IN THE kitchen chatting away, while O'Dee cooked enough food to feed a field battalion.

Marie poured herself another cup of tea and held up the pot in offer for anyone who wanted a refill. "It's a good thing, O'Dee that ye are here to prepare the food. Connor, as a bairn, spent all of her time ootside with her da. She never had a scrap of interest in cookin' or runnin' a hoose. Thank the good Lord I can now rest easy, knowin' that ye are here and that she will no' starve to death."

Jilly Louise grunted as she pushed herself up from the table and picked up a biscuit from the plate in front of her. "Ethan, honey, do you want one of these?"

She scanned the room, lifted up the tablecloth, grunted as she bent down, and peered underneath. Frowning, she walked through to the dining room. The men sat in the fading afternoon light, drinking from crystal glasses. "Cameron, is Ethan in here with you?"

He was pink-cheeked from the whiskey. "No, Pix. The last time I saw him, he and Andrew were out on the porch with a bottle filled with tadpoles. Poor little buggers — the tadpoles, that is, not the boys."

She walked back into the kitchen, pulled back the curtains, and looked out the window. "Ah-huh! There they are! Jesus! What are those two up to?" She squinted then gasped as she clung to the windowsill to steady herself. Flashes of light reflected off whatever Ethan had in his hand. She watched for a couple more seconds, then yelled, "Crap! Cameron!"

With the glass still clutched in his hand, Cameron rushed into the kitchen with Angus and Douglas on his heels. "Pix! What the hell's the matter?"

Her eyes were wide as Cameron pulled a chair out from under the table and nudged the back of her knees. She sat down heavily as he stared out the window.

"Jesus Christ!" He spun on his heel and bolted out the front door bellowing as he ran toward the lower paddock fence. "You boys, stay right where you are! Don't move!"

Both of the boys looked over their shoulders, giggled and kept walking further down the paddock. Ethan raised his right hand straight in the air, like a flag bearer.

"Stop! Do you hear me, Ethan? I said STAND STILL!" Cameron's long strides ate up the distance between him and the boys. His boots skidded on the grass then he stopped dead in his tracks. The blood in his veins ran suddenly cold, as every skerrick of spit dried up in his mouth.

Andrew stood next to Ethan with a juvenile, red-belly, black snake curled around his arm.

Staring at the viper, Cameron reached to his left and wriggled his fingers. "Ethan, come here to me, please." He peeled his gaze from the snake for just one second as Ethan walked toward him. "Ethan, what are you boys doing?"

Cameron tried to sound calm as he turned to Andrew. "Hey, mate, what say you put the snake down and we go back up to the house? O'Dee has made some yummy biscuits for you boys"

Smiling, Andrew gently stroked the snake under the jaw as a black forked tongue flicked in and out. "She came to talk to me and Ethan."

Cameron grimaced, grasped Ethan's arm and moved him further away from the viper. "Okay, then, let's put her down now."

Andrew's face was a mask of seriousness. "I suppose so. Her mam will be worried about her."

"How do you know...?" Cameron waved his hand in the air as a vision of Harry Potter speaking parse tongue flashed into his brain. "Oh, never mind."

Andrew bent down and lowered his arm to the ground. The snake slid off into the long grass.

Cameron lunged, grabbed both boys in a football tackle and swung them off the ground before tucking each of them in a firm grip. The serrated edge of a wooden-handled bread knife flashed in the sunlight before Ethan dropped the weapon onto the ground.

"Ethan! What in the name of Jesus were you doing?"

A little breathless under his father's awkward hold, he thrashed his arms and legs. "I was gonna bloody kill the snake, da. Didn't you see it? We were playin'. Put me down!"

Cameron looked over his shoulder when a choking noise sounded behind him. All of the adults except Jilly Louise, stood about ten feet behind him. As the shock began to wear off, he registered to the sound of screaming and looked over at the house. She was hanging out of the kitchen window, yelling loud enough to wake the dead. Cameron returned his attention to Ethan. "Are you telling me, you two have been out here trying to chop up a snake with a bread knife?"

Ethan gave him a *duh* look. "I wanted to kill it, but Andrew wanted to catch it and play with it. He said it's bad to hurt animals, even if they are snakes." A look of distaste made Ethan pull a face. "I remembered how you killed the snake at home, when Mama was screamin' out at the clothes line."

Cameron groaned. "That's bloody different and you know it. I'm a grown man and you two are just kids. What in the name of Jesus would you have done if the snake had turned and come after you?"

Ethan took on the look of a calculating hunter as he stared at the knife on the ground. "Cut its bloody bastard head off, of course."

Andrew frowned. "No, Ethan. She won't hurt us. She's our friend."

Cameron's gaze darted all around, as if waiting for an onslaught of deadly vipers. Looking back at the adults who were all trying to keep a straight face, he shrugged. "Sorry. You see, his mother's not overly fond of snakes."

O'Dee walked over to where Cameron stood with two squirming boys in his arms and bent to pick up the knife. "Oh at last! The mystery is finally solved, then! So this," she waved the knife in the air, "is what happened to my verra best bread knife, ye wee rogues." She eyed the two boys with mock disapproval. "Come to think of it... I havena been able to find the bottle that I use evera Spring, to start my ginger beer plant. Andrew McVey, do ye know anything aboot that?"

Andrew looked at Ethan, and they both chortled. "Tadpoles, O'Dee. We're growin' tadpoles. Three of them have legs, but none of them have any arms, yet."

O'Dee shook her head. As she passed Ewan and Douglas, she gave them both a wry look. "If ye doona wish to be foragin' in the bush for yer supper, I suggest ye keep the wee lads oot of my kitchen." She stomped off toward the house with the bread knife clutched in her hand. Her shoulders quaked with silent laughter.

After the suitcases were loaded, it was time to leave Glen Rowan. Angus offered his hand to Douglas. "I thank ye, man, for the hospitality offered to me and my family. It was good to see Connor and know that she is happy. Please, if ye get the opportunity, come stay at my hearth for a time."

Douglas smiled. "Now that is an offer I willna refuse. To have the opportunity to see the Nimerlin Fey Friesians firsthand would be a grand treat. When our Beth was alive, she spoke verra highly of yer horses."

Angus dipped his head in respect. "I am truly sorry for yer loss. I met yer Beth a couple of times during competitions. She and her horse were always fine competitors."

At the sound of sobbing, both men turned. Jilly Louise stood with her arms around Connor. Ethan and Andrew lay on their bellies on the grass, staring at the tadpoles in the bottle.

"Oh, Connor, I miss you so much. Tell me you'll be home for the birth of this baby."

Connor sniffed. "Wild horses couldn't keep me away. The baby is due in what, twelve weeks? The school starts in sixteen weeks, so that should be plenty of time to come home, have a baby, and get back for the inaugural school. It's a shame you won't be here to see it. I think it's goin' to be pretty special."

Angus walked over and put an arm around Connor's shoulders. "We havena missed a school of yers, yet. I doona imagine we are aboot to start now. Provided Douglas can offer us a bed that is, we'll be here."

Douglas rubbed his hands together. "Ye just let me know when ye will be arriving. A bed will always be available here at Glen Rowan for ye and yer family."

Cameron opened the car door and settled Jilly Louise into her seat belt. He looked over to where Ethan lay on the grass with Andrew. "Time to go, mate. Let's get you into your car seat.

Ethan peered at the tadpoles swimming around in the bottle, then looked up to his father. "Da, I have to stay and help Andrew with the tadpoles. They'll be frogs soon, you know."

"I'm sure Andrew will look after them just fine. Maybe when he comes to visit us at Nimerlin, you can catch some more."

Ethan looked unconvinced and his bottom lip started to tremble. "But, Da…"

Angus walked over and lifted him up onto his shoulders. "Time to say goodbye, lad. We need to go to the Games, and then get your mama and grandmam home to Nimerlin. Your brother or sister will be ready to be born soon."

Andrew clung like a monkey from Angus' shoulders and leaned down so that when he spoke, he was about two inches from his grandfather's face. "Sister? No, Grandda!" He screwed up his face. "No girls allowed! Only boys!"

Angus laughed. "Well, only time will tell, lad." He walked over to the car and Cameron plucked him from his perch. "Say goodbye to everyone, Ethan."

Andrew started to cry as he gathered up the bottle of tadpoles and walked over to where Ethan was strapped into his seatbelt. "Don't go! You stay here with me."

Tears ran down Ethan's face. "Mama, can I stay with Andrew? He's my bestest friend."

Jilly Louise turned awkwardly on the front seat. "I know, sweetie. But Grandda just invited everyone to come and visit with us at

Nimerlin. Then you'll be able to spend time with Andrew. Besides, I am sure Andrew's da will let you two talk on the phone sometime."

Ethan sniffed. "Okay, Mama."

Angus held open the door for Marie, who stood locked in a hug with Connor. After Marie was seated, he turned and shook Douglas's hand. "Well, then, thanks to ye again. We'll see ye again, soon after the birth of the bairn. Ye can count on us to be here for the opening of yer school."

O'Dee chortled and clapped. "Bless the Saints, we are to have a wee bairn in the hoose again!" She wiped the corners of her eyes with the hem of her apron.

Angus wrapped Connor in a bear hug and whispered into her ear, "Have a care, lass. My gut is rarely wrong and there is definitely summat amiss here. Keep yer wits aboot ye, aye? Call upon yer grandsire." He kissed the top of her head, got in the car, and waved, as he drove down the driveway.

That night, Connor lay on her side in bed, watching Craig trapped behind the celestial barrier. He sat on the floor with his head gripped between both of his hands. "Oh, Craig, this is awful, even worse than you dying." A tear tracked down her chin.

The pad of squeaky shoes sounded, as Tessa's voice got louder as she approached the bedroom. "Connor, are we going to do some practising this morning? I'll be ready, just tell me what time —" Her voice cut off abruptly as she stood in the doorway. It was a full thirty seconds before she spoke. "Connor…what's that?" Tessa frowned as she stared round-eyed at Craig. "Connor? I'm scared. What? Who is that?"

Shocked, Connor wiped the tears away and sat up in bed. "Tessa? What can you see?"

Her voice was barely a whisper. "A man, sitting on the floor."

Connor followed her gaze and frowned as Tomoe Gazen's words rang in her memory. *"Only those who are Gods or who are Touched by Gods will be able to see him."*

Craig stood up, hands at either side of his mouth, shouting.

Tessa looked from Connor to Craig and back again. In a tiny voice, she whispered, "I don't like this, it's scary. This is how I feel in the night when I can't sleep. Make him go away!"

"I can't Tessa, I'm sorry, and I can't explain it. All I know is that, I promise, he won't hurt you. Trust me, he would never hurt you." Connor threw her legs over the side of the mattress and reached for her wrap. "Come on, let's go get some breakfast and talk."

Tessa nodded and followed her out of the bedroom.

After making toast and pouring orange juice, Tessa was quiet and pale as she sat at the kitchen table. "Connor?"

"Tessa, this is very hard for me to explain. About eighteen months ago, my husband," she pointed to where Craig stood with one side of his face pressed against the barrier, as if trying to hear what was being said, "Craig, was killed in a car accident. The other day, he just appeared, as you see him now. He can't move around much and there seems to be something like invisible walls holding him back. It's like a prison. I can't touch him. My hand goes right through him as if nothing's there, but I can see him. He seems to be trying to tell me something, but I don't understand what he's trying to say, because I can't hear him, and I don't know if he can hear me."

Tessa stared suspiciously at Craig. "How can you see him, if he's dead?"

After blowing out a big breath, Connor took Tessa's hand in hers and gave it a gentle squeeze.

"Because he's not alive, but he's not dead either."

"Like a ghost?" Tessa frowned and pursed her lips. "Connor! It's very bad to tell lies! There's no such thing as ghosts. Da told me this when mam died. I hoped I would see her again, but I never did. I don't believe you!" She covered her face with her hands and started to cry.

Connor gave her shoulder a squeeze. "Tessa, look at me. I'm telling you the truth. I don't understand it, either."

Tessa sniffed and wiped her face with the sleeve of her shirt then crossed her arms over her chest. "I don't believe in ghosts. There is no such—" She gasped. Craig faded and became invisible. She stared wide-eyed at the empty space, then his outline reappeared. He smiled, waved and gave her the thumbs up sign. Her voice quavered. "Connor, I think I believe you."

The next morning, with the family already seated at the kitchen table, Connor walked in and sat down. Tessa's eyes darted from Connor to all of the corners of the room, then back again. Ewan frowned and looked at her. "Tessa, are you all right? Have you lost something?"

"I'm fine, Da." She looked up at him then continued to scan the room.

Connor cleared her throat and shook her head slightly. Tessa nodded and resumed buttering her toast.

As she placed a napkin on her lap, Connor turned to Ewan. "I'm going to take Hades out for a ride today. I haven't seen much of the property yet, so I thought I'd go and have a look around. If it's okay with you, I'd like to take Tessa and Coinneach along with me. It'll be a good opportunity to see how they are together, outside of the arena. She's ready, and he most certainly is. Now, it is just a matter of them getting to know one another, as well as Hades and I".

Ewan took his time chewing his last mouthful of breakfast. "I trust your judgement with this, Connor. Okay, as it's Saturday, she can ride with you, but..." he turned stern faced then smiled at Tessa. "I want to hear all about it, when you get back."

Tessa jumped up from the table and threw her arms around his neck. "Oh, thank you, da. Coinneach is amazing. He listens to me, and he likes me."

"Just make sure you listen to Connor. I don't want any more ambulance trips".

Tessa pushed back from the table. "May I be excused?"

Ewan nodded and frowned. "Tessa, is everything all right? At school, I mean? You look like you're keeping something to yourself. Whatever it is, you know you can come to me."

Tessa nodded and smiled knowingly across the table at Connor. "I'm fine, Da. It's just that I don't want to keep Connor waiting. I need to go and change." She vibrated on the spot as she bounced from foot to foot.

He waved his hand at her. "Go on, then."

She spun on her heel and called back down the stairs. "I love you, da!"

Ewan looked over at Connor. "Have you noticed anything different about Tessa? She seems to be holding something back."

Connor shook her head. "Can't say that I have."

He squinted at her. "You girls wouldn't be keeping secrets from me, would you?"

Connor sat back and drained the last of her tea. "Secrets? Really, Ewan, I'm quite sure I don't know what you mean."

Chapter Eleven

ONNOR WALKED OVER TO THE BARN AND OPENED the door. Hades whickered to her from the far, corner stall.

"Morning, beautiful boy. Feel like stretching your legs?"

Just as she crossed the floor, a shadow occluded the light that flooded the barn; Douglas walked inside. She stopped and turned to face him.

"Ewan told me ye are going for a ride with the lass this mornin'".

Connor nodded. "Yeah, Hades and I are going to have a bit of a look around. It's a perfect day for a ride. Why? Is something wrong?"

He rubbed his hand over the stubble on his chin. A rasping noise followed each sweep of his palm. "Not exactly wrong…more like an omission on our part. Ye see…" he ran his fingers through his hair, "Christ, this was a mistake. I should have seen to this long afore now."

"Douglas, what on earth are you talking about?"

"Our Beth's horse. He's down in the back paddock. Has been, since the day she died. We've never told the bairns. Ewan and I thought it best if we didna speak of him.Connor stopped mid-slide of the halter over Hades' head. "Rudiobus is still here? God, they were amazing together. She was such a beautiful girl, and Rudiobus, pffffft. Well, magnificent doesn't even begin to cover it. Apart from Hades, he's probably the most talented horse I've ever encountered."

"Aye. An amazing woman and an amazing horse." Douglas suddenly sounded very tired. "After Beth passed, the horse was all we had left of her. Foolishly, we... er I, hid him away from the bairns. Ewan wanted to shoot him, but I wouldna allow it. To lose her and then the horse, would've been more than any mortal soul could cope with. The er...*compromise* we reached was that the horse would stay banished to the back paddock and that we'd never speak of him again; which has been the way of it, until now. I couldna stand the thought of someone else competing with him. Beth and that horse, were one."

A look of great fondness made the laugh lines around his eyes crinkle. "Ye remind me a lot of her, in that regard. She'd a way aboot her. I doona know, perhaps it was because she was pure Irish. She was like a fey creature in the stories we Scots tell our bairns. Flowers seemed to bud and bloom when she walked into the room, or sick animals got better when she laid hands on them. Our wee Andrew is a lot like her in that way. I have no' encountered a beast, large or small, that doona respond well to that lad. Just as Tessa has her mam's way with the horses, Andrew has his mam's way with the creatures."

He reached over and ran his hand in long strokes down Hades' neck as he chuckled. "Evra time O'Dee finds wee beasties in the lad's pockets, she swears it takes ten years off her life. Just afore ye arrived here, one of our hens was taken in the night, probably by a thievin' fox. O'Dee found Andrew asleep in the chook pen, curled around six, newly hatched chickens. To hear him talk, ye would swear he can could speak with animals. Like our Beth, he has a verra kind heart. She was our own miracle, that's for sure. But," he let out a deep sigh, "as for Rudiobus, from the time of her death, he changed. He's nothing like he was. Now he's verra aggressive and just plain dangerous. In truth, all he's good for now, is dog meat. Doona risk yerself, lass. Please steer well clear of him. He's forever ruined."

The pain in his voice was brutal. Connor placed a hand on his hairy forearm just below the rolled-up sleeve of his shirt. "I'm so sorry, Douglas. I know this is so hard for you. "I guess you're constantly reminded of Beth, because Tessa is so much like her."

Douglas chuckled. "The spit oot of her mam's mouth. That's why Ewan is so watchful of her. Beth thought of everyone else first afore herself. Tessa is the same. She is such a kind-hearted little girl, and clever, too. But, aye, she has the ways of her mam."

Connor sighed as his sadness, seeped into her soul. "Douglas, are you asking me not to take Tessa to where the horse is being kept?"

He shook his head. "'No. Tis a secret that has been kept for too long. The lass deserves to know her mam's horse is still here. Christ, when Beth died, Tessa grieved verra bad for the stallion. It was a strange thing though, as bairns often are, when it comes to death. Tessa, eventually accepted that her mam was gone, and that the horse was no longer here, but that didn't lessen her tears or her keening for the horse. Jesus! It was absolutely pitiful. It doubly broke Ewan's heart. All of our hearts..."

Douglas picked up Connor's hand and held it firm. "Please, lass, keep Tessa safe today. Ye know how she is. The second she sees that horse, she's goin' to want to bring him back home with her".

At the sound of approaching feet, Douglas stopped talking.

"Grandda!" Tessa ran to him and hugged him around the waist. "Did you hear Connor's going to take me and Coinneach with her for a ride? Have you come to help me saddle him up?" Her face was flushed with excitement. She fidgeted and couldn't keep still.

"Of course I did! I wouldn't miss seein' ye ride the big bast...er, fellow. As he *is* yer horse, 'tis important ye get to know each other and that ye learn to handle and respect him."

Connor sat on a bale of hay while holding Hades' reins. "Listen to yer grandda, Tessa. Be consistent in what you do, and Coinneach will learn to trust you. Without trust, horses are just very big, extremely dangerous animals."

After ten minutes, Tessa led the big bay thoroughbred toward the doors. Hades flattened his ears, and Connor laughed. "There's one thing you should know, Tessa. Hades doesn't like anyone or anything to get too close to me. He's always been very possessive. Every time Craig came anywhere near me..." She stopped talking suddenly.

"Craig?" Douglas looked over to her. "Who's Craig, then, lass? I doona think I have heard ye speak—"

Tessa walked round to the near side of Coinneach. "Come on, Grandda, would you give me a leg up, please?"

Connor looked over to her and smiled as she mouthed *thank you*.

Douglas closed the barn door after the riders and horses moved out into the sunlight. Connor turned in her saddle and gave a wave when she caught a flash of movement as the curtains of the kitchen window, suddenly fell back into place. She smiled, imagining Ewan on the other side of the fabric, fearful, desperate to keep Tessa safe, while at the same time wanting her to be the person she was born to be.Connor shifted her weight, and Hades moved into an easy rocking canter. Coinneach followed suite into a well-conformed pace. Tessa shrieked with laughter. "Connor, look at him. Isn't he the most beautiful horse you've ever seen?"

Hades didn't falter in his pace as he looked across to Tessa, threw his head in the air, and snorted. Connor laughed. "Sorry, Tessa. Coinneach is a fine horse, and, true to his name, he is very handsome. But to me, there's no horse on earth like Hades."

They rode for twenty minutes, chatting quietly, when a furious scream resonated from somewhere down along the lower fence line of the paddock. Connor reined Hades to a halt, then grabbed Coinneach's cheek strap and drew him alongside. The big bay danced and shied sideways. "Easy, now. Tessa, keep him on a short rein."

She wasn't listening.

Her bottom slid right, then left, as she pivoted on the saddle; one hand held both of the reins, the other shielded her eyes from the sun as she scanned the paddock. "Connor, there's a horse down here. He's very unhappy. Oh, Connor, he's so sad."

The catch in Tessa's voice prickled the skin on the back of Connor's. "How do you know the horse is unhappy, Tessa?" Both of the katanas vibrated under her skin, on high alert. "And how do you know the horse is a *he*?

"Can't you feel him? Can't you feel the blackness and the fire? I can. He's very angry. Come on! Let's go find him." She kicked her heels gently into Coinneach's sides and set off at a quick trot. "Something's wrong."

Connor caught up to her and again, pulled Coinneach to a halt. "Listen to me, Tessa. Stay here until I call you. I'll go and see what's happening with this horse, and then... Well, let's just see, okay? Stay here until I call you. Got it?"

Tessa looked like she was about to argue when she sighed then tightened her grip on Coinneach's reins. "Okay, I'll stay here 'til you call me."

Hades turned his head and whickered to Coinneach. The horse suddenly relaxed under Tessa and began to crop the grass. Connor patted Hades on the neck in thanks and rode off toward the far end of the paddock, stopping to turn every five minutes to make sure Tessa was still where she had left her. When the bottom fence line came into view, a familiar, huge, white stallion burst out of a copse of trees, screaming and rearing as he bolted toward the fence.

Hades side-paced and roared, in returned aggression, for dominance. Connor dismounted, ran her hand along Hades' neck, then approached the fence line. The closer she got to the rails, the more violent and agitated the white stallion became. "Easy there, Rudiobus. We mean you no harm."

Hades walked up beside her and tried to shoulder her away, putting himself between her and the fence.

"It's all right, Hades." She smoothed her hand under his long, wavy mane.

The white stallion wheeled around, reared and pawed the air, then charged the fence again. Connor stood, closed her eyes, and delved deep into her mind. The Ancient Scottish Horsemen roared in satisfaction as her primordial connection, found Rudiobus' fire, his fury, and his desperation.

A tsunami of rage hit her like the shock wave from a bomb blast. Hades screamed when she flew backward off her feet and landed hard on her bottom on the dry red earth. As she dragged herself onto all fours, her tribal tattoos demanded permission to launch. Rudiobus pawed the ground as he wildly shook his head from side to side.

Suddenly, it was quiet.

Connor's heartbeat pounded like bass drums in her ears. The stallion stood about ten feet away from her, separated only by a post and rail fence. Head in the air, he snorted as his flanks heaved. Through flared nostrils, he sucked in several long breaths as he sniffed the air.

"What are you?" His voice was deep, raspy and furious. "I sense the Horsemen in you. You stink of the Ancients!" He rushed the fence, then reared again as he pawed the air just inches in front of her. Hades screamed and reared in return.

Connor pulled herself to her feet. Hades pranced an agitated dance; sweat lathered his coat into a wet black sheen.

"I am Connor MacDonald, named child of the prophesy of the Highland Horsemen." She took a small step forward and grasped the top rail. "I return the question. What are you? I am bonded with my horse. I've never seen anything like you."

The horse's words were as clear as if he were a person standing beside her. The long white mane bobbed from side to side as he shook his head in contempt. "And neither you would have!"

Connor jumped when a small hand slipped into hers. Tessa stood wide-eyed and very still.

She was the colour of chalk, her voice incredulous. "Rudiobus. Oh, Rudiobus. Connor," she croaked, "this is my mam's horse."

The stallion looked at the little girl, sniffed the air then snorted. He took a step toward the fence, then another and raised his head as she extended her hand to his muzzle. Neck flexed, he sniffed her palm. His eyes flew wide and he screamed. With his chin tucked to his chest, he took four paces backward, folded his front legs, and bowed to her. The tendrils of his mane swept the ground. "Daughter of the Guardian. Welcome. I am glad you have come."

Connor put her hand on Tessa's shoulder. "Don't be afraid."

Fear wasn't the emotion that painted her face—it was wonder. "I'm not afraid, Connor. Rudiobus would never hurt me. I thought he was gone. Mam loved him so much." A flush of high colour burst across her cheeks. "Connor, I heard him talking to you. How...?"

"Sweetie." Connor gave her a hug. "Some people have a very special connection with horses. I have it, and I think you have it, too."

"Mam said the same thing."

Connor smiled. "Yeah, well I think she was right. Some people can—". She stopped speaking and looked at Hades, who nodded. She placed one hand on his neck and the other on the front of Tessa's shirt just above her breastbone.

Hades stretched his neck out and whickered softly. *"Child of Ancient blood, I am pleased to know you."*

Tessa's mouth fell open. "Th—th—thank you, Hades. But? How can I—?"

Connor dropped her hand and broke the connection. "That's what we're going to find out."

"Rudiobus, I missed you so much. I never thought I'd see you again." Tessa smiled as he walked over to the fence and stood still, while she smoothed his pure white forehead. "Why did you call me Daughter of the Guardian?"

The stallion pulled back; anger changed his countenance from peace to fury. "You are the daughter of Macha; the Ancient Irish Goddess of horses and war."

Connor reached over and squeezed Tessa's hand.

Tessa frowned. "My mam wasn't a Goddess; she was just my mam."

Rudiobus pawed the ground, sending divots of soil, flying. "She was sent from the Faery, from the homeland of the Tuatha Dé Danann to, this!" He snorted in disgust as his head swung back and forth. "It was the Guardian's time to produce her offspring, her Successor." He bowed his head again toward her.

"But, I can't do anything. I'm just a kid. And what about Andrew, my brother? Can he talk to horses too, or do anything special?"

Rudiobus' great shoulders dropped. "That is unknown, my lady. The boy is mortal; a gift from your mama to your sire."

Her eyes filled with tears. "I don't believe you. If my mam was a Goddess, she wouldn't have died. She wouldn't have left us!"

The horse moved forward and brushed his muzzle against her face. His tongue gently stroked her cheek and he dried her tears. "That was not her will, dear one. Guardians throughout history are from a matriarchal line and bear only girl children. Macha, your mama, as an Ancient, knew well, how deceitful and fickle the Gods can be. The Tuatha Dé Danann would never have allowed her to stay in this mortal world. Just as she knew she would have to leave you and the man she loved."

He paused as a chuckle rumbled in his chest. "As was her way, she defied the Gods and bore a male child, a legacy of herself, for her human mate she left behind. However, as a boy child born of a Guardian, he is unique. Never before has a Guardian produced male offspring. It is forbidden. Only time will confirm if he has any of the ways of the Gods. Apart from your mama, I am the only God who knows of his existence. She cloaked him in magicks, the instant he was conceived, shielding him from the eyes of Danu, Queen of the Tuatha Dé Danann. Had the queen known of him, at the cut of his umbilical cord, she would have taken the boy to the Faery and kept him by her side forever. Even if he doesn't have the powers of a Guardian, as the firstborn son of her powerful race, he would give the queen incredible power and advantage."

Rudiobus nudged Tessa's fingers gripped on the top rung of the fence. "Fear not, your mama did not die, child. She was summoned by the Tuatha Dé Danann to assume her responsibilities. Her perceived *death* here on mortal Earth, however, will forever remain a mystery to me. The date on which a Guardian departs the mortal world to return to the Faery, is locked in time. The day Macha died, was months before her expected re-ascension."

"But mam fell," a sob escaped Tessa's throat, "that's why she died."

"That, child, was the work of the Ancients, a scenario created for the benefit of the mortals she was forced to leave behind. In truth, you mama never fell from my back in all the years we were together. On that terrible day, she seemed to collapse as she slid from my back. She made no sound. It was as if she were dead before she even hit the ground. I cannot tell you how worried I was, that something had gone terribly wrong and that she had indeed passed unto the Shade instead of resuming her role as Guardian Protector of the Tuatha Dé Danann."

Tessa leaned her forehead against his and whispered. "No. That's not true. You were just her horse. You're making this up."

"It is true that I was her horse, just as what I am telling you now, is the truth about your mama. I am a Fallen of the Irish Ancients, banished to this terrible place of heat and cold to suffer for eternity. At the time when your mother chose to seek a sire for her offspring, I coincidently was stripped of my God status by Balor, King of the Celtic Gods, and sent to this awful place."

Connor cocked her head to the side. "Why were you exiled by the Ancients?"

"Because," he snarled, "I took that which was mine." He pawed the ground as hatred vibrated from him. "For centuries, it was known by all, that I loved Ayiel, half-sister of Airmid. But the Celtic Gods are cruel. Even though they knew of our love, Balor promised her, to another. So I took that which was mine, her innocence, that which she had promised to me. She was so beautiful in my arms the night she gave me her maidenhead. When her belly began to swell, her father, the king, realized she had lain with me. The first run of his blade went through her belly and decapitated my son."

"Oh, Rudiobus…"

"Nay, Daughter of the Highlands. Macha named me. It was our joke, because we are both Irish and she knew me for who I truly am, so she named me Rudiobus, the Celtic God of horses. It was her way of thumbing her nose at the Immortals by giving me a God name. Not Rudiobus. I am Gwydrion, Ancient Celtic warrior and magician God; a shape-shifter, deposed to spend forever in my shifter form—a white stallion."

Storm clouds roiled across the sky as lightning in the distance triggered a distant boom of thunder. Connor looked toward the heavens. "Crap, Tessa. We'd better be getting back."

Tessa looked from Connor to the white stallion and back again. "What about Rudio… Gwydrion? He's still my mam's horse. I want to take him home."

The conversation with Douglas earlier that morning, ran round in her head. *"Please, lass, for Christ's sake, keep Tessa safe today. Ye know how she is. The second she sees that horse, she's goin' to want to bring him back home with her. But know this; that horse is no longer the horse he was."*

"Tessa—"

Before Connor could stop her, Tessa threw her leg over the middle rail of the fence and walked over to stand beside Gwydrion. "Please, Connor. Mam would never have left him out in a storm. Please?"

The white stallion gently rubbed his muzzle back and forth along the front of Tessa's shirt. "Now that I've found him, there is no way I'm leaving him here. I don't care what you or anyone else says. I'm going to look after him."

Connor gripped the top rail of the fence and signed, realizing this battle was already lost. "What of Coinneach?"

Tessa kissed Gwydrion on the nose, stepped back through the fence, and walked over to where the big bay stood quietly. She gathered up the reins and rubbed her face against his cheek. "Please understand, Coinneach. You're my horse and I love you. But

Gwydrion was so important to my mam. Now that I've found him, I can't leave him here by himself. She would want me to look after him. It's something I have to do."

Connor walked over to Tessa and put her arm around her shoulder as she placed her other hand on Coinneach's neck. He leaned forward and whickered. *"I understand child. It is right that you care for the Old One."*

Tessa hugged his neck with both arms, then hugged Connor, just as the first few big drops of rain fell from the sky. "Let's go home."

Gwydrion whickered over the fence. "Do me the honour, Daughter of the Guardian. Allow me to carry you home like I did so many times, for your mama."

Connor frowned, but said nothing. Tessa climbed back through the fence as Gwydrion bowed down on one knee. She grabbed a handful of mane and threw her leg over his back, then sat stiff and tense on his dazzling white coat.

He turned his head to her. "Fear not, child. Like your mama, I will never harm you."

Connor walked over to the gate and opened it. Gwydrion and Tessa passed through the opening to wait on the other side. After Connor secured the latch, she mounted Hades and walked over to where Coinneach was happily cropping grass. She leaned over and gathered up his reins.

Tessa took the leather straps from her. "No, Connor. Coinneach is my responsibility. I'll take him home."

The white stallion chuckled. "Ah, you really are the daughter of Macha, always fierce, always determined, and forever devoted to her horses."

Tessa held Coinneach's reins while Hades as lead horse, pranced his alpha dance on the ride back to the homestead.

Thunder boomed overhead as Connor and Tessa rode up from the back paddock onto the grassed area in front of the house. Douglas stood at the woodheap with an axe in his hand. Ewan wheeled the barrow closer to the woodpile and started filling it with already split pieces. "I think another couple of loads should do it." At the sound of hooves, they both looked up.

"Christ Almighty!" Ewan let go of the handles of the wheelbarrow and wood spilled onto the ground.

"Jesus Christ!" Douglas slammed the blade of the axe into the chopping block. They both stared at Tessa, who sat bareback astride Gwydrion. The horse's head was free of halters, bridles, or straps. Coinneach's reins trailed loose in Tessa's hand as he walked alongside the stallion.

Ewan's sheet-white face suddenly darkened. He strode over to where the horses and the riders stood. "Tessa! Get off that murdering white bastard now!"

Connor nudged Hades forward to stand between Ewan and Tessa, still seated on Gwydrion. Before Connor could say anything, Douglas grabbed Ewan by the arm and pulled him to a halt.

"Ewan. 'Tis time man. 'Tis time the lass knew the truth aboot the horse."

Ewan reefed his arm out from under his father's grip. "And you made this decision without consulting me? I hate that fucking horse!"

Tessa's eyes, widened in shock. "Da. He's all we...I, have left of Mam. Please, she would have wanted me to look after him, just as she looked after him."

Ewan turned on his heel and walked back toward the house. Douglas eyed the white stallion, warily. "Lass, forgive yer da. He misses yer mam so much. This horse is just a reminder to him of how she died."

"I know, Grandda. But being mad at Gwy...Rudiobus won't bring her back. It's not right that he hasn't been cared for since she died."

Connor, Douglas, and Tessa all turned suddenly at the harsh *snick* sound of cocking of a gun.

Ewan's voice cut like a knife. "Get off that bastard horse, Tessa, and go inside. *Now!*"

The colour drained from Tessa's face before she drew herself up, sat tall on Rudiobus's back, and shook her head. The stallion began to prance as he flattened his ears and bared his teeth to Ewan. Her fingers drew back and forth through his white mane, calming him, soothing him.

Hades snorted and pawed the ground with his offside front hoof, then moved himself with Connor still mounted, to stand in front of the white stallion.

Connor scowled as she shook her head. Ewan stood with the rifle sight to his eye.

"Put the gun down, Ewan. Elizabeth's stallion offers no danger to Tessa. You, however, are a great threat to everyone." Her hands curled into two fists. The katanas screamed at the threat.

Douglas walked over to Ewan and gripped his shoulder. "Enough, lad. Put the gun down and let's talk aboot this."

Ewan stood fast, his index finger flexing slightly back and forth on the trigger.

Tessa screamed. "Da! Da! Stop, please, stop!"

Douglas increased the pressure of his grip on Ewan's shoulder. "For Christ's sake, son, put down the gun afore you—"

Suddenly, Ewan lowered the rifle, his finger still on the trigger then hurled it onto the ground. The weapon discharged with a loud bang.

Connor and Tessa clung to their mounts as they shied backward. Ewan continued to stare at Tessa. The veins in his forehead and neck stood out. He vibrated with aggression.

The silence was almost suffocating when O'Dee called out. "What in the name of all that is holy, is goin' on? Oh, sweet Jesus!"

As if in slow motion, the housekeeper waddled across the yard with Andrew on her hip. Her hand clutched her heaving breast as she scowled at Ewan. "Did ye think to shoot yer own bairn? For God's sake, man, haven't ye lost enough already?"

Ewan didn't break his stare to turn and answer her question; instead, he raised his hand and pointed to Tessa. "That horse is as good as dead."

"The hell he is," Douglas stepped in front of hm. "Do ye not see what is afore yer verra eyes? Ye know as well as I do that this horse went mad with grief when our Beth died."

Ewan's voice cracked when he spoke. The high colour of his cheeks faded. He sat down on the ground with his elbows on his knees and his head gripped between both his hands. "Get that fucking horse out of my sight! I hate him! It rips my guts open to remember."

Tessa nudged Rubiobus forward. Hades instinctively moved to block the path of the white stallion when Connor leaned forward and laid her palm on his neck. In response, he bowed his head and backed away three paces; leaving Tessa exposed, mounted bareback.

Ewan made a strangled sound as he stared at her.

She blinked a couple of times. Then two fat tears rolled down her face. "Da, Mam would want me to look after her horse. She'd be really mad at you and Grandda that you left him all alone after she died. He didn't kill her." She leaned forward and threaded the fingers of one hand through his mane as she looked at Connor. "It was an accident."

Douglas tentatively walked over to Tessa, never taking his eyes off the white stallion. "Aye, lass. 'Tis true. Yer mam would have wanted us to do right, by Rudiobus. Take him into the barn. He can have one of the spare stalls. But know this! If he shows any sign of the madness that caused us to banish him to the back paddock, he'll be sold. Yer da is only concerned for yer safety, lass. Let's give the horse a chance to willingly come back to us in peace."

Ewan got up and stood beside his father, still staring at the stallion. The horse flared his nostrils and snorted.

Tessa gave a weak smile. "He'll be fine. You'll see." She nudged the horse and turned him toward the barn. Connor dismounted and swung the double wooden doors wide.

Douglas frowned at Ewan. "What the hell were ye going to do? Shoot the animal oot from underneath her?"

Ewan shook his head. "I'm buggered if I know. It never occurred to me that I'd ever have to deal with that bloody horse, ever again."

O'Dee walked toward them. "Well, thanks be, to the blessed Mother. This is a true miracle. Oh, Lord, it was like watchin' her mother all over again." She grasped the tea towel from her shoulder and slapped the fabric across Ewan's chest. "What on earth could ye have been thinkin'! And why in the name of Jesus ye were shootin' oop the hoose?"

Chapter Twelve

ONNOR SAT BESIDE TESSA AND ANDREW AT THE TEA table, surrounded by the McVeys and O'Dee, who had their heads bent over their plates. After fifteen minutes of uncomfortable quiet, Connor put her knife and fork side by side in the middle of her plate and wiped her mouth with her napkin. "So, Ewan, is this how it is going to be? The silent treatment? If you've something to say, then say it and get it over with. Sorry, I'm just not good at playing games."

He looked up from his plate and scowled across the table at her. "You think this is a game? Every time I even think about that horse, all I see is my wife, lying dead, on the ground."

A sob came from the seat next to Connor as Tessa put her cutlery on the table and bowed her head to her chest. She spoke quietly. "Every time I see Rudiobus, I see Mam, riding him, laughing—"

Connor reached over and patted her hand. "Come on now, everyone's had a seriously crap day."

"I won't give him up, Connor, I won't."

Ewan threw down his silverware onto his half-empty plate. A shard of china shaped like a crescent moon, splintered onto the tablecloth. He stood abruptly, scraping his chair against the polished floorboards. Glaring at Connor, he threw his napkin onto his broken plate and left the room.

The house shook with the force of the slam of the front door.

Later that night, Connor opened her cottage door, scanning the room as she entered. Craig briefly looked up then returned his gaze to the floorboards in front of him. He was pale as he sat with his legs crossed, trapped behind the barrier. A desperate sadness filled the room.

Connor snagged a cushion from the lounge chair as she walked to stand in front of him. Exhaustion etched deep lines on his face. She lifted her right hand, "hi," then dropped the cushion and sat with her legs outstretched in front of her.

He looked up when she spoke. Sad eyes stared back at her as he held up one hand and mouthed, "*Hi.*"

She sniffed as her eyes filled with tears. "I miss you. I'll never stop missing you."

Palm against the barrier, his lips moved. "*Me either. I hate thdjgkkdkdkdkdk...*"

She flung her hand up in a *stop* signal. "What? Slow down. I can't hear you, and I can't understand you if you speak too quickly."

"*Okay. Sorry.*"

Sighing, her constant companion *frustration*, fired up in her brain. "Do you know how," she waved her hands around, "*this* came about?"

Slowly, he mouthed the words. "*Sort of. I remember the accident and I knew I was dead. When I realised what had happened, two incredible forces began pulling me in opposite directions. One way led to black oblivion, the other toward a light. The next thing I knew, I woke up. It was dark and very quiet. I know now, where I ended up is called the Place of Shadows. I don't know how long I was there. It seemed like eternity. If it hadn't been for...*"

Connor's fingers picked at invisible lint on the cushion. "How did you find me?"

A look of deep sadness crossed his face. "*That place...where I went... there was already someone there. If it hadn't been for her, I would've gone mad with grief.*"

A spark of jealously, stabbed deep in her belly. "Seriously? Did she get out as well?

Blond hair swayed from side to side as he shook his head. *"I don't know. I know next to nothing about her."*

Connor got up, went to the fridge, pulled out a bottle of water then sat back down. She took a few big gulps before she spoke. "That's weird. Surely, she must have told you something about herself. Although I can imagine, being in a place between life and death wouldn't exactly make for stimulating conversation."

"I was in that place for... I have no idea how long it was, before I even realized she was there. She lived in the shadows and never acknowledged me. It's a thing of madness to have no one to talk to. Eventually I got fed up to the back teeth with the silence. So, I went looking for her. You know, to see if she had any answers. When I finally tracked her down, she refused to concede my existence. Every time I came within shouting distance of her, she turned her back on me."

Connor cupped the side of her face with her palm and rested on her elbow. Eager to hear more, she unconsciously leaned toward him. Suddenly, his lips stopped moving. "What? Come on! You can't stop now!" She flapped her fingers, encouraging him to continue.

A sudden wave of crimson, spread from his neck to his face. "Anyway, one time, I was sleeping. I don't know if it was day or night because there was no moon, no sun, no seasons, no wind, no rain. I apparently was having a...er...dream .about you; a particularly erotic dream. It seems I was very passionate and kept calling your name. When I woke up, she was sitting there, watching me."

Wrinkling her nose, Connor pulled a face. "Eww! Voyeur? Crap! What did she say?"

"Nothing."

Confused, Connor cocked her head and frowned. "I don't get it. This woman sits and watches you sleep, moaning and groaning in erotic bliss, then doesn't ask you about it? No woman could live with that kind of curiosity. She must've said *something*."

"No. In all the time I was there, I never heard her speak."

Connor frowned. "Was she mute or something?"

He stood up and extended his hand. The barrier stopped him from making contact with her.

"No. Her tongue had been cut out."

Later the night, restless, Connor slipped into an uneasy sleep. Moonless, dark landscapes, devoid of colour, acrid and dry, flashed before her eyes. A terrifying, gaping maw, burst into her subconsciousness. The smallest stump of a severed tongue danced uselessly at the back of a woman's throat. Blood oozed from between the woman's teeth and flowed down her chin.

Instantly awake.

The bedroom window rattled. She lay very still. A huge black Shadow oozed under the pane of glass and hovered above her. Connor leapt out of bed, her right hand extended. The God Killer screamed as it launched from the scabbard on the wall. The blade lunged just as the Shadow reared backward, toward the kitchen. The window-pane shattered under the point of the sword. Finger-like black tendrils oozed through the hole in the glass and disappeared into the night.

The katana flew to her and landed in her palm. Vibrations of fury ran up her arm. "What the hell was that?"

The katana screamed just before a flash of blinding green light filled the room. Yokami and Tomoe Gazen materialised, swords drawn.

"The God Killer summoned us. Who dares to threaten the Daughter of the Sword?" Tomoe Gazen became still and trance-like, as she breathed deep, when, suddenly, her eyes flew wide. "God threads! An Ancient! Daughter?"

Yokami held out his arm and his sword returned to the scabbard on his back. "There is great darkness here. What do you know of this?"

Connor shrugged. "All I know is that one minute, I was asleep, then something floated into my bedroom. The God Killer sensed it and chased it. There's glass on the floor from the window where, whatever that was, escaped."

The Samurai and Connor stepped around the shattered glass that littered the polished floor. Yokami bent down, picked up a shard, and examined it closely while Tomoe Gazen stared out the window. Her index finger made contact with the bottom of the window and she abruptly pulled back her hand. A blue-black feather clung to her skin, sending a lava flow of darkness throughout her body, when, as if in slow motion, the plume fluttered to the floor.

Yokami was at her side in an instant. "What is it? What did you sense?

Her hand shook slightly as she stared at the space where the feather had rested.

"I have not experienced anything like it ever before. It was black, evil, malicious. I do not know what it is."

Out of the corner of her eye, Connor noticed Craig, waving his hands and screaming.

"What? Slow down! I can't understand you."

He leaned forward with his hands pressed against his thighs, like an out-of-breath marathon runner. After a minute, he stood up straight. Connor, Yokami, and Tomoe Gazen moved to stand just outside the barrier. Craig's chest heaved with exertion.

Connor mouthed, "*Slowly.*"

He raised his right thumb in a tired affirmation, just before his lips started moving.

Connor groaned and blew out a long breath. "Jesus, why did we never learn Auslan? Sign language would be bloody useful, about now. Craig, do you know what happened here tonight?"

When he nodded, Tomoe Gazen interrupted. "Tell us! What did you see? What threat was here?"

Craig stood very still.

The katana on Tomoe Gazen's back shrilled, as anger pinched her face. "You must tell us! How can we protect Connor if we do not know what threatens her? Tell us!"

Craig shifted his gaze to Connor. "*Tonight, you were visited by true evil.*"

The Samurai woman's God-voice boomed. "Name the entity! I demand you declare what you know! Tell me!"

He choked on the word. "*Death.*"

Sword in hand, the Samurai approached him. Her blade screamed for the kill. "I will ask you, but once more!"

Connor stepped in front of Craig, shielding him. The God Killer flew to her hand. "Stand down! It's because of *you* that he's been to hell and back. I know you didn't mean for any of this to happen Tomoe Gazen, but you owe him the chance to explain. If he knows anything, he'll tell us." The blade in Connor's hand hummed in aggression. "Craig?"

He stared into the distance. *"From the moment I arrived to the Place of Shadows, that thing would taunt me and scream at me. There was always screaming. She spat on me every time she came near me. She called me an abomination. Always she ranted that she's the only being in history with the power to decide who lives or dies. She hated me because no matter how many times she tried, she could never exile me to the Shade. Violence is all she knows, and she relishes it. So frequent were her attacks on me, that the blood from one beating wouldn't have begun to dry before she began slashing me with her wings ag – "*

Yokami materialised at Connor's side. "Wings?"

The colour of ash spread across Craig's face. *"Yes. Death is a raven."*

Connor picked up the remote and clicked off the television. For the third time since coming in from tea, she checked the latch on the kitchen window. Suddenly the door hinges groaned under repeated heavy thumps. Fear skittered down her spine. She paused, then crossed the floor, grasped the knob, and opened the door.

"Ewan!" She cocked a brow at him. "It's late." The reek of whiskey fumes, almost took her breath away.

He jammed a foot in the doorway when she attempted to push the door closed. "As I said, Ewan, it's late."

He looked surprised when she blocked his path. "Well, at least you can let me come inside."

She stood with one hand on the doorknob and the other on her hip. "Look, everyone's had a really tough day, what with the discovery of Rudiobus and you attempting to murder anyone who got in the sights of your bloody gun." She crossed her arms over her chest. "What in the name of Jesus were you thinking? I hope you're pleased with yourself! Tessa's bound to have nightmares. Ewan, I've just about had enough of you, for one day. So, if you don't mind, I'm really in no mood to discuss anything with you tonight."

He pushed passed her, strode over to the table, pulled out a chair and sat down; unaware that Craig stood in the corner of the room, vibrating with anger. The colour crept up Craig's neck as his anger escalated. He stood, glaring at Ewan.

Connor shut the door and walked over to the table. "Oh, well, we may as well add unauthorised entry of my premises to your list of today's crimes."

He leaned over the table and slammed his fist on the wooden surface. "You couldn't just leave well enough alone, could you? I'm buggered if I know why Da even told you about the bloody horse. I wish I'd shot him the day Beth died."

"Well, that seems to be your answer to just about everything, doesn't it? Shoot the problem, then the problem goes away. You're a bloody fool, do you know that? Your wife loved you, and your children love you; yet you keep hurting them because you have allowed grief to consume you. Well, newsflash, Ewan, you need to take a long, hard look at how your actions are affecting the children, particularly on Tessa. Did you see the look on her face today when she thought you were going to shoot Rudiobus?"

Ewan's eyes narrowed to slits, as sarcasm dripped from his words. "You really are something, aren't you? You have the bloody gall to lecture me on how to raise my children, when sorry, I don't exactly see *you* surrounded by offspring."

Connor took two steps forward, pulled back her fist, and punched him square on the face. "No, you fucking bastard, I don't. My son died in my belly the same night I my husband, died. I'd give anything to have them back. If I could have one wish in all eternity, it would be to have them back! So, do you know what, Ewan? I *get* the whole fucking grieving-for-the-people-you-love thing. Now get out!"

Blood trickled from his nose as he stood and glared at her.

"Get out, Ewan! Nothing you can say tonight will improve anything. Tomorrow's another day. Just go home and sleep it off."

He snaked out his hand and grabbed her by the wrist. Connor slammed her other fist hard into his abdomen. Ewan grunted, staggered, and crashed into the wall. He dropped to the floor, clutching his belly, as he wheezed. His voice was broken and ragged. "You've been nothin' but trouble for me, since you got here."

Connor walked to the front door, opened it, and gestured for him to leave. "Yes, Ewan—it sucks to be you! Now, get the fuck out of my house! For future reference, if you ever touch me again, I will kill you. Do you understand? Anytime you're tempted to try that again, you might want to think twice. Just try it, I can guarantee you won't like the outcome. Now get up and don't let the door hit you on the arse on the way out!"

Ewan stood and sucked in a shaky breath as he walked passed her standing at the threshold of the doorway, then he paused.

"Goodnight, Ewan."

He ducked his head and put one foot on the porch, then the other. Connor slammed the door behind him and threw the latch.

The morning sun flooded through the hall window as Ewan walked to the dining room and sat at the table. Douglas passed the plate of bacon and eggs toward him as he spoke to Tessa. "Aye, lass, I have indeed seen Connor's sword. I've also seen her work with it."

Ewan grunted as he forked food onto his plate.

Douglas frowned. "What the hell happened to yer face? Is that a black eye?"

Ewan spoke around a mouthful of food. "Let's just say I walked into something unexpected last night."

Connor walked into the room and sat down. Tension thrummed. The air was thick and uncomfortable.

Douglas raised the teapot to her and she held out her cup. "I have to go into town this morning, if you need anything." She turned to Tessa. "I can drop you at school, but it will need to be a bit earlier than usual."

Tessa turned to face her father. "Da? Is that okay?"

Ewan was grim as he nodded without looking up. "I'm surprised you even bothered to ask."

Douglas frowned as he looked from Ewan to Connor. "What the hell's goin' on?"

Connor put up her palm to Douglas as she pushed back from the table, leaving her breakfast untouched. She nodded to Tessa. "I'll meet you on the driveway in twenty minutes."

"I'll be ready." Tessa nodded then Connor left the room.

Douglas leaned over to Ewan. "I doona know what is goin' on atween the two of ye, but hear this. We doona need any more problems, than we already have." He jacked his head toward the threshold

Connor had just walked though. "That young woman is the only thing atween us keeping Glen Rowan, by establishing a living with a successful dressage clinic, and bankruptcy."

Tessa stood, pushed in her chair, and picked up her breakfast dishes.

Ewan growled from across the table. "So you keep saying."

After returning from town, Connor walked down the hallway toward the kitchen and snagged an apple from the fruit basket. "O'Dee, have you seen Douglas?"

"I'm here, lass. O'Dee is oop in the garden. Can I help ye with summat?"

"Wow!"

Two swords lay across the table. He held a polishing cloth in his hand. "These have been handed down from generation to generation."

Connor smiled. "Da used to tell me and my brothers stories of bloody, Scottish battles and screaming warriors. These are the swords that were used by the Highlanders from the 1400's right through until the 1700's, right?"

"Aye, lass." Douglas picked up the larger of the two swords. "The *claidheamh mòrs* or great sword." His face flushed with pride. "This is a heavy bugger, that's for sure. These swords weigh atween four and six pounds, and the blade length is double-edged at atween thirty-nine and forty-five inches long." He stood. "See?" He grasped both hands around the metal handle. "The hilt is specifically designed for the sword to be used with two hands. It takes a verra strong man to use this."

Connor leaned forward, looking at the sword. The blade, polished to a high sheen, glinted in the afternoon light. "Amazing! Douglas, Da and Cameron have got to see—"

Tessa bounded into the kitchen and dropped her school bag on the floor. "Oh, Grandda! You've got the swords down." Colour rose in her cheeks. "I know I'm not allowed to touch them, but—"

The sword rested across his knees. Tessa stretched her fingers forward and lightly touched the hilt. Douglas jumped as if someone had dropped a cup of hot tea into his lap. Fumbling, he grabbed the sword before it hit the floor.

"Grandda? Grandda? Is something wrong?"

Douglas sat, shaking his head. "I doona know, lass."

Tessa was oblivious to anything but the blade in his hand. "Where did this sword come from?"

Cold sweat prickled on the back of his neck as he remembered the time, years ago, when his own father had handed him this very broadsword, to keep, in memory of those of the clans who had lost their lives in battle.

"This isn't just any sword, lass. This claymore has been in my family for as long as my memory serves me. My da told me it was used in the battle on Culloden Moor — poor bastards. It took under an hour to defeat the Scots, and the Highland clearances began soon after. My many times great-grandsire, was one of the very few to survive that terrible time. This sword has been handed down from father to son, ever since."

Connor sat down beside Douglas. "You know, it doesn't matter how many times I hear the story of Culloden, it always makes me so sad. The Highlanders stood no chance — no chance at all."

Still staring at the sword, Tessa frowned. "How come you haven't handed this sword down to my da or my uncles?"

He looked taken aback. "Well, that is a good question. I guess 'tis because we all live together here in this hoose, which is home to the sword."

Tessa looked to the other sword resting on the table. "What about *that* sword, Grandda? It's different to the one from your family."

Douglas walked back over and placed the McVey claymore back on its moorings then returned to the table and sat down. "Oh, aye. Now this sword... This sword is verra special, indeed." As he picked up the weapon, soft lines formed around his eyes. "Now this beauty is one of the basket hilt swords that were verra popular amongst the clans." Pointing to the hilt, he slipped his hand inside. "See how the basket protects the swordsman's hand? This particular one is a broadsword." He pushed his chair back and rested the blade across his knees.

Tessa stood close and leaned down. "Gee, this sword is nothing like the other one."

"Aye. This is a verra different sword from the claymore. The sheer weight of the claymore could crush a man's skull. This," he smiled at the sword, "is a sword for hand-to-hand fighting; summat we Scots are verra good at."

"What's that mark?" Her index finger touched the etched symbol of a Highland stag just below the hilt.

"Verra observant, lass. My Morag, yer grandmam, God rest her beautiful soul, came from the MacRobertson clan, a long line of Scottish master sword makers. This mark?" He pointed to the etching of the stag. "This is the mark of the MacRobertson. This is the stamp of proof that this sword is authentic from the master craftsmen; handed down through the generations from father to son."

Tessa looked puzzled. "If this sword belonged to Grandmam's family, how come the sword is here, Grandda?"

Douglas smiled. "That would be because yer grandmam was an only child, and being a girl, there were plenty of males in the clan who thought they were more entitled to the sword than she was. Now, yer great-grandda was a wily old bast...er, man. He knew his sister's son, Hugh McTavish, was desperate to inherit the sword because it is verra valuable. In fact, he argued, that as the closest male blood relative of yer grandmam's, he was the next in line to receive the sword. The problem was, over the course of history, the McTavish had become bitter enemies of the MacRobertsons. There had been a good deal of blood spilt atween them. The old man hated the fact that his sister had married into what he deemed a nest of rievin', thievin', lowland scum. When she bore a son, she declared her child to be the nearest male blood relative and the next in line to inherit the sword. There was a terrible row. Yer grandda told her he would rather drop the sword into the deepest ocean and let the rust take it, than see it fall into the murderin' hands of a McTavish. When yer grandmam and I were married and we immigrated to Australia, the old man hid the sword in my Morag's steam trunk and attached a letter. I'll never forget it. He said as a MacRobertson, her blood entitled her to assume responsibility for the family sword." Douglas ran his finger down the length of the shiny silver blade. "A thing of beauty, is she no'?"

Tessa nodded as she watched him. "Can I touch it?"

"Tell me, lass, why the sudden interest in the swords?" Douglas frowned. "These two blades have hung here in this hoose, since afore ye were born."

She blushed and shrugged. "I have always looked at them. But when I touched Connor's sword, I *felt* them." Her fingers inched closer to the blade. "But this sword is… This sword is beautiful."

Douglas spread his arms and held the hilt of the sword in one palm and the tip of the blade in the other.

Tessa held out the first three fingers of her right hand and ran them down the length of the blade. Just before she reached the tip, the sharp edge marked the pad of her index finger and left a thin line of bright blood.

When Connor stood up abruptly and reached out, Douglas gently grasped her wrist.

A high-pitched whine came from the weapon as the smear of blood slowly disappeared into the honed metal edge. Douglas' eyebrows disappeared into his hairline when the blade vibrated in his hands. He looked up to Tessa just before she took the hilt into her palm and gripped it tightly.

After she stepped back two paces, she splayed her feet and pointed the tip of the sword at the ceiling. "Woo, it's purring up my arm. This is so cool!" Laughing, she turned in a circle, holding the sword out in front of her.

Douglas smiled. "Oh, lass, it seems ye have more of the blood of yer grandmam than we ever realized. 'Tis the thing with swords; they choose their masters, ye doona choose them. The MacRobertsons may have been sword masters, but they were also verra fierce warriors. The sword of the MacRobertson has accepted yer blood, which means the sword has chosen ye."

The Thrill of Rejoice of the MacRobertson sword rang out, loud and true. "Noooo!" An ear-splitting screech erupted from the Shadow as it raged around the darkened room. "It cannot be. The Sword of the Guardian! Think! Think! How is this possible? That blade was lost thousands of years ago. Why has it come to light now? What awakened it?" She stopped

suddenly, hovering above the damp, moss-covered stone floor. "Hmm, coincidence?" Her beak clacked as she shook her head. "Not a chance in blessed hell! The pieces of this puzzle... A female with God Threads is as sword master, is known to the Ancient Samurai, and is present when a blade that has been lost for tens of thousands of years suddenly reappears and chooses a new master."

The Shadow turned suddenly, following the signature of the blade. On the shaded side of the house, the Shadow flattened itself against the window ledge. One black, finger-like projection lay under the flapping curtains as Tessa moved with the sword. "So, whelp of the Guardian, it is you who awakened the sword. Hmmm. This may not be as bad as I originally thought. In fact, perhaps an opportunity presents itself.

So, Successor, you aspire to walk in the footsteps of Dagda? Lucky for me, but too bad, too sad and unlucky for you, this sword must be jinxed, for the two it has chosen, have both found Death."

The Shadow suddenly pulled back and spread out in both directions, giant wings unfurled. A large, blue-black raven feather drifted from the darkness, caught on a breeze, and fluttered down to the ground.

Chapter Thirteen

*A*FTER SHE'D DONE THE FINAL CHECK OF THE HORSES for the night, Connor went looking for Douglas. From the hallway, the sound of coughing came from inside his office. She knocked on the oak panel.

"Enter."

She opened the door and stuck her head round. "It's only me."

Douglas put down his glass filled with a good measure of amber liquid, closed his book, and placed it on his lap. "Connor! I thought I was the last one oop. What is it I can do for ye? Can I get ye a drink?"

"No, thanks, I'm good. But, if you have a few minutes, can we talk about Tessa? It's obvious to me that you know a lot about swords, so I won't beat around the bush. You were right when you said the MacRobertson sword had tasted her blood and has chosen her."

He picked up his glass and inclined his head. "Aye. I believe it to be so. Although I canna say I've ever seen such a thing afore. My Morag, the sweetest woman in the world, told me her clan stories of the scream of the MacRobertson swords when the warriors went to fight. Jesus! Imagine blue-faced, bare-arsed Scots, screamin' into the fray, spurred on by the battle cry of their swords. It would have been verra terrible to be there, but to have seen and heard those swords would have been a thing of beauty."

Connor smiled. "You're right, there. Even though it is a big, heavy weapon, Tessa wields it like it weighs, nothing. It is as if the sword has made itself ready for her and heras its masterIt doesn't make any sense, but the way of swords is ancient and we are but privileged to be in their presence. At this moment, she's too young to realize what the reaction of the sword means. She will need to learn—"

Douglas sighed. "Aye. I know what it is ye are goin' to say, and afore we go any further, just consider what her father's reaction to all of this, will be. Speakin' of which, what is it atween ye and Ewan?"

"Nothing. He's a pain in the arse. I know and understand that he is grieving for Elizabeth, but sees me as a threat to his authority. I care for Tessa and Andrew very much. But I won't put up with his crap. He needs to just get over himself or I'll blacken his other eye for—"

Douglas sat forward in his chair. "You did that?"

"Yes. What Ewan has yet to learn is that it is very unwise to provoke me."

Douglas took a sip of his drink and smiled. "I imagine that is something he now realizes. Ye are a verra unusual woman, Connor MacDonald."

She chuckled. "I've been called worse. Anyway, back to Tessa and the MacRobertson sword... There'll come a time in the future, when the sword will call her to arms. She needs to be ready. I can teach her that." A sad look crossed her face.

He nodded and sipped his drink. "Aye, lass. I'll speak to Ewan of it. Is there anythin' else we need to discuss?"

Connor steeled herself. "Rudiobus will be a big a draw card for your school. Hades is already internationally known. I'd like you and Ewan to consider allowing Tessa to be part of the school with Rudiobus and Coinneach as her mounts. With the two of them to showcase your inaugural school, your reputation will sky rocket!"

Douglas blew out a long, fumy breath. "Jesus." He rubbed his rough hands over his face. "I canna see Ewan bein' keen on that idea. 'Twas bad enough, when the lass insisted on keeping Coinneach as her own. I know he gave his permission for her to learn to ride but... Christ, after the episode today with the bloody rifle, I doona know. You've seen firsthand how he reacts to Rudiobus".

"That may well be Douglas, but your school needs Rudiobus and Tessa should to ride him and represent her mam; it will help her to heal. Don't worry, no harm will come to her. She'll be under constant supervision, either by myself or the other elite athletes. Besides, Rudiobus already has a hell of a reputation. You would be a fool to deny him a place in your inaugural school." She stood up and stretched her back. "I'll go now and leave you with your thoughts."

Douglas drained his glass, then reached over to turn off his desk light. "Fair enough, lass. I'll speak with Ewan in the morning. I imagine none of this will make for easy conversation." He chuckled as he followed her out of the office. "Perhaps it'll take more than a bloody shiner to knock some sense into that son of mine."

After a restless sleep, Connor yawned before she opened the door of her cottage and squinted into the predawn darkness. She headed for the sword practice area at the side of the house. The katana hung down her back, housed in its scabbard. The leather creaked with each step she took. She stopped with a start, when two figures, seated on the ground, shrouded in darkness, waved to her. As she walked toward them, they stood in unison.

"Tessa? Douglas? What're you two doing here?"

Tessa skipped over to Connor and grabbed her hand. "Grandda brought me over here to practice with you." She fizzed with excitement.

Connor frowned. She peered at Douglas as he walked into the light, cast from the cottage's kitchen window. In his hand, he carried the MacRobertson broadsword. The muscles of his right arm, bunched under his grip.

"You must be a miracle worker, Douglas. I honestly thought you'd have no chance in hell of convincing Ewan to let Tessa learn the sword."

He ducked his head, then looked up sheepishly under his bushy eyebrows.

"Douglaaasss?"

In the reflected light, the sword shone like a polished mirror. He raised the blade to his lips and kissed the stamp of the Highland stag. "All right! I didna discuss Tessa and the sword with him. He's highly unlikely to agree. But know this, the sword is too important to allow him to stand in the way of Tessa accepting the legacy of her grandmam's family." His eyebrows bunched together. "But, this sword is heavy. I doona ken that Tessa will have the strength to wield it."

"The sword will find a way Douglas, the blade is never wrong. Okay then, let's begin. Take the sword in your hand and follow me." Connor slipped the strap of the scabbard over her head, then flipped off the cap and closed her eyes as she raised her right hand in the air. The katana purred as it left its resting place and flew to her hand.

Douglas stared at Connor. "Jesus Christ, lass. I knew there was something aboot ye."

She walked over to Tessa. "You must now and always. give thanks to the four points of the earth, then to the sword. You may be its mistress, but the blade is deserving of your respect for the journey it has made through the generations."

Tessa nodded and followed Connor's lead as she offered her deference. When it came to bowing to the katana, Connor straightened her arm and extended the blade in front of her. Tessa stood opposite and did the same. As the tip of the two blades almost touched, a spark arced from the katana to the broadsword just before the two blades connected and shimmered in a golden glow.

Connor moved through her routines. The katana cut through the air, swift and deadly, when suddenly the broadsword came to life. The blade and Tessa became one, as it whined joyfully with each slice of the blade.

"I must act. This child could put an end to everything I have worked toward." The Shadow curled around a leafy branch. "God Threads is powerful – very powerful. Her instruction and the Sword of the Guardian, will give the child great advantage." Suddenly, the air vibrated with an avian shriek. "Oh, Death, what a clever plan. Is there no end to my brilliance?" A raucous cackle rang out. The Shadow widened as if holding two arms wide. "To me! A last supper! Come to mama!"

Six huge dogs, a breath away from death, suddenly stood and responded to the call.

After thirty minutes, Tessa, sword in hand, breathed hard. Sweat beaded on her brow and trickled down the side of her face. "Wow, Connor, this is really hard work."

Connor laughed. "All right, enough for today, I don't want your arms to snap off or anything. Now —"

A series of deep growls came from the back of the cottage. Connor spread her feet and assumed the battle stance of the Samurai. Tessa pressed her back against Connor's, grasped the hilt of the broadsword and held it out in front of her. Vicious growls, snarls, and the snapping of teeth erupted from the early morning light. A miasma of the mouldy scent of death, hung in the air.

Douglas jumped to his feet and squinted into the gloom as deep-throated canine howls broke the silence. "Tessa. Come to me! Now!"

Suddenly, a huge brown dog leapt into the air and landed just in front of Connor. His bared teeth were stained and yellow. Grey, frothy drool oozed from his lips. Skeletal, he panted as if in pain.

Connor stood with The God Killer outstretched, when Douglas shouted.

"Connor! Behind you."

Both she and Tessa turned as one, just as a black Pit Bull sprung from the darkness and crouched low, ready to strike. He was pitiful, just bones covered with skin.

As if they had been sword partners for years, Connor and Tessa, maintained their position; back-to-back, swords raised, covering Douglas, who stood unarmed at the edge of the practice area. The battle cry of the MacRobertson sword, cut the silence like a knife. The God Killer responded with a roar. The dogs retreated, growling, as they turned tail and ran into the shadows.

After what seemed like a very long time, Connor lowered her sword. "I think they're gone. Tessa, are you all right?"

"All right? Douglas boomed. "I've never seen anythin' so bloody wonderful in my life. Come, now! We'd better go inside the hoose and ring the police. I doona think the neighbours will be so quite so lucky with those dogs on the loose."

Tessa shook her head. "Not yet, Grandda." She turned to Connor, where, in unison, they bowed to the four points of the compass, then to their respective swords. When a deep whine passed from the katana to the broadsword, they smiled.

In the barn, Connor brushed Hades coat to a high sheen while she spoke to Rudiobus. "Something really weird happened today. I saw Tessa fight with the family broadsword. She used the blade like a warrior. It was as if the blade was part of her. She was amazing to watch."

Rudiobus shook his head playfully as his voice rumbled in his chest. "You should have seen her mother. A warrior more fierce, I have never encountered. A broadsword, you say? That is indeed most unusual. Guardians rarely use weapons; they favour fighting with magicks."

Connor went round to the other side of Hades and resumed stroking his coat. "Douglas, her grandda, introduced her to the sword of his wife's family. Over history, the sword has passed down the generations from father to son. Breaking with tradition, her grandmam, the last in the MacRobertson clan, inherited the sword."

"Ah." Rudiobus nodded "that would explain it."

Connor blinked slowly as she waited for him to continue.

"At the beginning of time, the Guardian Protector was a king. He ruled for centuries and sired seven daughters. Those children not only provided the genes for the Guardian bloodline, as females, they offered no challenge to his reign. He spelled them and all of their descendants to bear only daughters. So important was the purity of the bloodline, that he wove magicks to make it impossible for a male to ever, be conceived with the blood of the Guardian lineage. Ever since then, the Tuatha Dé Danann—"

"Jesus, talk about securing your reign"Nodding his head, he snorted. "But the king's greedy plan, took an unexpected turn. During a brutal battle with another clan of Celts, an immortal took his head. The death of the king caused great chaos for the Tuatha Dé Danann and with no other male contenders for the throne, the race became purely matriarchal in its lineage." He chuckled before he continued. Warmth coated his voice. "You said the broadsword used by the Successor of the Guardian, last belonged to a woman? That means the sword has chosen a female master."

"You're serious aren't you?"

"The history of the Gods goes beyond time. Tessa as Macha's daughter, is of the blood of the Gods."

Connor screwed up her face as if, in deep-thought. "Well, that'd make sense seeing as how when Tessa's blood spilt on the blade, it absorbed it, without leaving a trace."

"There is your answer, my lady." He nodded his head. "The blood of her Guardian mother is strong in the child. The sword has accepted her and will protect her."

Connor's voice was little more than a whisper. "As Successor of the Guardian, does that mean that… Oh, God, does that mean the Gods will take Tessa like they did Beth? Will she have to die to take up her role as Guardian?"

The horse bowed his head. "Nothing is ever certain when Gods are involved. Although, knowing Macha as I do, she will do everything in her power to protect her child. Do not worry about the girl for now. She is yet to grow into her role as her mother's Successor. Then and only then, will we know what the Gods have planned for her."

Later that night, Connor sat on the floor of the cottage. Craig walked back and forth in front of her. His mouth moved non-stop. "Craig, will you stop pacing! I need to see your face to be able to lip-read what you're saying.

"Sorry. I just can't get used to the fact that I can hear you, but you can't hear me."

She leaned back on her elbows and rolled her shoulders. "Why do you think that is?"

He shrugged. *"All I know is that irony is a bitch. I spent forever, or what seemed like forever, with a woman who couldn't speak to me, and now I'm with you and you can't hear me."*

Shimmying closer, she clicked her fingers. "That reminds me. You didn't finish telling me the story about this woman. Who is she?"

"I don't know her name. But there was something about her. You know when you meet someone who has an amazing presence? This woman was like that. Power was palpable when she was around. In fact, that's how I learned how to find her. I'd just follow her energy signal."

"That's weird. How did you two communicate?

"After what seemed like an eternity of silence, one day she gave me this." He undid the buttons on his shirtfront and shrugged his arm out of the right sleeve. A golden cuff surrounded his bicep.

Leaning forward, she frowned. "Wow! That's impressive, looks like solid gold. Why would she give you that?"

"Because, jealous puss," he smiled at her, *"the cuff allowed her to hear my thoughts and read my mind. It also allowed me to mind speak with her."*

"I am not jealous." She flicked her ponytail over her shoulder. "I'm just curious as to why someone would give away something that is obviously incredibly valuable." She poked her tongue out at him.

"I'm telling you the truth. When she wanted me to know something, she would place a hand on my arm and she could hear my thoughts. It is because of her that I am here. That and...this." He held up his left hand and pointed to the gold band that circled his finger.

"Your wedding ring?"

"Our wedding rings. Remember, they were both created to the exact specifications of the original twin Scottish wedding bands – the Circle of Strength. Each ring was drawn from the same nugget of gold; a single, golden thread without beginning or end. It was because of them that she was able to find you."

Connor pulled the chain out from behind her shirt and rubbed her fingers over her own rings. "Wow. Is she some kind of witch or something?"

"I don't think she's a witch. In truth, I know nothing about her. All I know is that she has a way with anything made of gold. She always wore a golden torque around her neck." He touched the tips of his index fingers against each other. *"Set where the two thick bands of gold peaked into a V was a huge red stone. Flames danced inside it. Once I hid in the dark-ness, watching. Her lips moved as she held her arms out in front of her. The torque became a beautiful red and golden Phoenix. It rested on her lap and she sat for hours and stroked it. The sound it made was terrible. As she cried, it dried her face with the tips of its wings. Later, she kissed the*

bird and it returned to rest within the torque around her neck. After that, I used to follow her and watch her. She cried all the time. The Phoenix was the only thing, she would let close to her."

He closed his eyes as if exhausted and sighed. *"After she found you, she placed four red and gold feathers of the Phoenix on the ground. She told me to hover over them, but never to touch them. The next thing was really creepy, she started to chant. It was like the voices of a thousand women, all screaming at once. I had no idea what was going on. She closed her eyes and held her arms out in front of her. The next thing I knew, I was here in this room with you."*

"So," Connor tucked the chain inside her shirt and stood. *"she* sent you here to be with me. Does that mean, wherever I am, you can be, too?"

"You mean outside of this cottage?"

As she walked toward the door, she called over her shoulder. "Let's just call this an experiment. I'm going to speak to Rudiobus. Hopefully, if my guess is correct, I'll see you there, too."

Connor flicked on the lights in the barn. "Rudiobus, I need to talk to you." Hades whickered as she walked across the breadth of the barn. He hung his head over the half door of his stall in greeting, when suddenly, he threw back his head, exposing the whites of his eyes, booted the back of his stall, and roared.

Connor turned, scanned the room and chuckled. "Well, Craig, it looks like some things never change. Hades has hated you since the first day he set eyes on you. Remember that day you came to Nimerlin with the Japanese buyer." Her shoulders shook as she laughed. That was hilarious, you big show off. He set you on your arse good and proper!"

Craig's outline was barely visible inside the double doors of the barn. He stared at Hades, who tossed his head and pranced inside his stall. *"The feeling's mutual, you big bastard. Just so you know, she's still mine!"*

Hades screamed and kicked the back wall again with such force the rafters shook.

Long tendrils of mane the colour of molten silver flooded over the door of the stall at the far end of the room. Rudiobus stood with his head over the wooden barrier.

"Daughter of the High—" He snorted as he lifted his head and sniffed the air through flared nostrils. His gaze moved from Connor toward the barn doors. "Death Walker!"

Connor stepped forward. "You can see him?"

"Of course I can see him. I am of the Gods, and he—" he sniffed the air again, "has been Touched by the Gods." He continued to stare at Craig. "Approach me."

Craig tried to move closer, but the barrier confined him. *"I'm sorry. I can't."*

Connor walked over to Rudiobus' stall and opened the door. His hooves clipped against the stone floor until he stood about two feet away from Craig. The stallion stared at him while he sucked in deep breaths and tasted the air. "Ahh... You are the *mate* of the child of prophesy."

Suddenly, the horse stretched his neck so his muzzle permeated Craig's chest.

Frozen to the spot, Craig stood wide-eyed, but didn't flinch.

After several seconds, Rudiobus stepped two paces back and spoke as he shifted his gaze to Connor. "I am indeed sorry for your losses, lady. My questions about you are now answered. When my Ayiel's sire took her life with his sword, he took everything that was important to me. I understand your pain."

Connor gasped then cleared her throat as she walked to stand beside him. "You said *losses*, Rudiobus?"

"Place your hand on me. Let me share with you, what I saw."

At the point of contact, she cried out. "My son? That's my son? Oh, sweet Jesus."

Eyes, like an arctic whiteout, luminescent, eerie and mirrored, stared back at her. Rudiobus glanced up at Craig, then back to her. "Like his sire, the mirror of his eyes is a sign of having being Touched by the Gods. I sense a powerful celestial deity was responsible for the interruption of their journey unto the Shade. The essence of your son has returned to your man, to await rebirth." He sniffed the air again. "But no...there is something else." Abruptly his head shot up. The cascade of white mane shimmered halfway to his knees as his deep voice rumbled in his chest. "How is this possible? Death Walker, here, you stand before me, yet you do not. You and your son are but the human essence of two souls still trapped in a place between life and death."

Connor gasped. "No! You're wrong! The woman sent him here to be with—"

Craig waved his arms frantically, pounding his fists on the barrier. His lips closed on a scream.

"*No!*"

Standing in front of him, helplessly, Connor held out her hands, palms upward. "What? What? You don't want me to mention the woman?"

His head shook back and forth.

"Death Walker, the Gods do nothing unless it is a boon to them. You say a woman returned you as you are? It would take an immensely powerful being to be able to separate the essences of two souls, across two locations. What is this woman named?"

Slumped against the barrier Craig mouthed. "*I don't know.*"

The walls of the barn vibrated when the stallion snarled. A spark ignited when his hoof struck the floor. "I do not believe you!" Agitated, his voice was low and menacing. "Why are you here! Who sent you?"

"Craig, for God's sake, just tell him." Connor stamped her boot in frustration.

"*The woman never told me her name. Soon after she arrived at the Place of Shadows, Death told her if she whispered her name on the wind, or ever revealed her identity; every man, woman, and child of her race would be slaughtered; obliterated from history. That was when she...*"

Frustrated, Connor tried to pre-empt his answer. "Took a vow of silence? Made a conscious choice not to talk?"

"*No. That's when she cut out her own tongue to ensure she couldn't speak, to keep her people safe.*"

Chapter Fourteen

CONNOR BOUNDED UP THE FRONT STAIRS OF THE main house and walked straight into the kitchen. O'Dee sat, elbows on the table, with both hands gripping the sides of her head. When she looked up, the flush of fever painted her face. The end of her nose glowed bright red and was chapped. Her body shook with each rib-rattling, explosive cough.

"Oh, no, O'Dee! You should be in bed. How long have you been sick?"

She sniffed, and spoke as though she were holding her nose. "Oh, it came on me all of a sudden like. Last night, as soon as the cool air of the night came in, I started to cough."

Connor frowned. "You go back up to bed. Otherwise you'll be sick for twice as long and we'll *all* end up with whatever god-awful germs you've got."

After a round of hacking coughs, O'Dee stood as she fished for a new tissue in the pocket of her apron. "True enough, lass, but there's the breakfast to see to and the wee laddie to look after."

Connor propelled her toward the staircase. "I may not be the best cook in the world, but we'll survive. Besides, I'll keep Andrew with me until you feel better. It'll be fine. You go to bed and get better."

Doubt crossed O'Dee's face, but her shoulders sagged in relief. "Aye, lass, bed sounds grand, and I thank ye for your kindness."

As O'Dee trundled up the stairs, Connor checked her watch as she talked to herself. "Oh, crap! Everyone's going to be here for breakfast, any minute." O'Dee's usual breakfast menu flashed through her mind. "Right…porridge. Hmm. Scrap that, I've no clue how to make porridge. Now, let's see…" Soon she was head down, bum up, searching inside the refrigerator. "Bacon, eggs, bread…that should do it."

She rustled around in the pots drawer until she found a massive copper skillet, then placed it on the stove and ignited the gas burner. After she emptied the entire contents of the bacon container into the sizzling pan, she threw open the cutlery drawer, then ran into the dining room and began to set the table. Smiling to herself, she suddenly lifted her head and jolted. The heels of her boots skidded on the polished boards and as she ran back to the kitchen. "Owww shit!" Her hip collided with the edge of the table in the centre of the room.

"Crap! Crap! Crap!" The room roiled with a blanket of billowing, thick smoke. As she rubbed her hip with one hand, she stood in front of the stove, grabbed the skillet handle, and ditched the pan and the charcoaled bacon into the sink. She grabbed the tea towel that lay draped over the dish rack, coughed, and flapped the cloth up and down.

Douglas' voice boomed before he entered the kitchen. "Jesus, O'Dee, the hoose is on fire!"

Still waving the tea towel, Connor walked over to the window and threw it open. "O'Dee's sick. I'm seeing to breakfast."

Douglas laughed. "Looks more like a ceremonial burnin' to me. I take it ye are no' a cook then?"

"You could say that." She stepped on the pedal of the stainless steel bin. The lid opened just before she scraped the charred bacon into container. "Toast it is."

Douglas chuckled as he walked out of the kitchen. "I hope O'Dee has no' come down with summat dire. At this rate, we could all be in verra grave danger of starvin' to death."

After making a plate of toast, she walked toward the table then frowned as she scanned the room. "Oh, Crap! Andrew!"

She dropped the plate on the table and ran back to the kitchen then stuck her head out the open window. Andrew was sitting on the ground by the wood heap with his back against the chopping block. Leaning farther through the window frame, Connor stuck her arms through and waved. "Andrew. It's time for breakfast, hon."

He looked up and smiled, but stayed seated on the ground.

The curtain fell from her hand as she turned and headed outside. As she rounded the side of the house, he was looking down at his two hands in his lap.

Connor grinned at the serious look on his face. "Whatcha doin', Andrew?"

He looked up. A big smile broke out on his face. "Talkin' to my friends."

She looked around as she walked toward him. "What friends?"

"These." He gurgled happily, as he held up both hands.

As she squatted down beside him, her knees cracked. "Oh…mice." She wrinkled her nose.

He held up his right hand. "This is the mam. See how pretty she is? And these," in a voice bursting with excitement, he held out his left fist, which he opened two inches from Connor's face, "are her babies."

A cold shudder ran down her spine as six pink-skinned, hairless mouse pups wriggled just in front of her nose. She pulled back slightly. "Andrew, what exactly are you doing with these mice?"

He jutted his chin and puffed out his chest. "Keepin' them away from the mean black cat. She wants to eat them."

At the side of the house, the barn cat sat in the shade. Her tail swished left and right like a metronome set to a fast tick.

"Where did you get the mice from?"

He nodded to a block of wood at his feet. "Under here. I saw the cat trying to get them. I don't like that cat. She won't talk to me. Then I heard the mam mouse, I chased the cat away." He glared at the clearly irritated feline.

The hairs stood up on Connor's arms. "Oh, you could hear them squeaking?"

He looked at her as if she was being deliberately dense. "Not squeaking! Crying for help."

Connor stared at him, waiting for him to laugh and for the whole thing to be a joke. His face remained a mask of honesty and concern. "Andrew, what did you hear?"

"The mam mouse is the only one who can talk, 'cause they," he flexed his fingers gently under the tiny rodents, "are too small. She told me to save her babies. So I did."

Ruffling his hair, Connor smiled at him. "So you did. Now, what are we going to do with them?" She stopped suddenly and looked into his blue eyes. "Andrew, have you ever heard other animals talk?"

"Ah-huh. They all talk, 'cept for the cat. She's mean." He stopped talking abruptly and glared. The cat's green eyes, glistened with malice. Andrew held his hands to his chest. "Get away, you bad cat. You're not goin' to eat my mices."

The cat stood up, turned, sent a menacing look over her shoulder s she flicked her tail high in the air, and disappeared under the house.

Surrounded by paperwork, Connor had one eye on the documents in front of her and the other on Andrew. Douglas had given her the use of his office because she needed somewhere to work in the house, just in case O'Dee needed anything. His earlier conversation ran around her brain. "I thank ye lass for carin' for the wee lad while O'Dee is laid oop. Just so as ye know, he is an adventurous child, he will be oot from under yer sight at evera opportunity. So, if yer babysittin' skills are on par with yer cookin' skills, then ye she should *definitely* lock the bairn in the office with ye!Layers and layers of paper covered the huge mahogany desk as she made the final selection of the twelve participants. The hours flew passed as she checked references, receipted payments, and wrote letters of commiseration to the unsuccessful applicants.

Andrew sat on the floor in front of the television, watching an episode of *The Land Before Time*. The mice snuggled together on one of Douglas' pilfered woollen socks that lined a shoebox that Andrew balanced on his lap. The pups fed as the doe lay with her eyes closed under the gentle stroke of his fingers.

Rummaging, Connor searched through each of the four ornate wooden drawers. "There have got to be stamps in here some—"

"I'm hungry."

Connor tilted her wrist and checked her watch.

Crap! Crap! Crap!

O'Dee always served lunch at twelve-thirty, sharp. It was now twelve twenty-five! She made a mental note to go over to her cottage after lunch and get some stamps. She made another mental note to set mealtime alarms in her phone. Scooping up the paperwork from the desk, she clicked the remote and turned off the television, leaned down and picked up the shoebox and tucked Andrew under her arm. On the staircase, she deliberately hopped down each step, jangling him on her hip. He laughed out loud as he clutched the rodents to his chest.

After lunch and much good-natured ribbing about the definite probability of food poisoning, the men went back outside to work. The mice, secured in the shoebox with holes in the lid, sat high up on an unused spice shelf. After taking sandwiches and tea up to O'Dee, Connor finished cleaning up. She gathered the paperwork from the kitchen bench, slung Andrew onto her back, and walked across to her cottage. At the bottom of the stairs, she swung him onto his feet, opened the front door, and walked inside.

As she put the sheaf of paperwork on the table, she started rummaging in the drawers of her desk. "Now where did I put those stamps?"

"Hallo."

Connor stopped still as a statue as her gaze whipped to Craig, who stood in his usual spot at the sidewall.

His gaze darted from Connor to Andrew and back again.

As she squatted down, she put her hands on either side of his face. "Andrew. Who are you talking to?"

His little stubby finger pointed at Craig. "Him."

Craig's eyes widened in surprise.

Andrew walked toward him. "You look funny." He wrinkled his nose just before his face lit up. "You're like the lady in the night. She sits on my bed and sings to me. I like her."

Connor mouthed to Craig, *Elizabeth?*

He turned his palms upward and spread his fingers out in front of him in a *how the hell would I know* gesture. He looked down at Andrew and nodded.

Andrew leaned forward to whisper. "She said that she could only come and see me if I kept it a see...secwet."

Connor squatted so that her face was level with his. "So you know then, that you can't tell anyone about him, either. His name is Craig and he is very important to me. I would be very sad if he couldn't come here and visit me anymore."

As Andrew nodded, his fringe bobbed up and down. "I won't tell, I promise. I'm very good at keeping secwets. The lady said so."

After she planted a noisy kiss on his cheek, she stood up. "Good man."

Craig held his hands up as he mouthed, *"What now?"*

With a book of stamps in one hand, she took Andrew's hand in the other and headed for the door. She called over her shoulder. "Come on! It's time for some answers."

Andrew stopped to scoop up a struggling beetle trapped in a huge spider's web on the barn door. He jiggled the web with his fingers until the gossamer-winged insect dropped onto a flowering shrub.

"Sorry, spider."

Chuckling, Connor opened the doors and waited for him, before they both walked inside.

Hades hung his head over his stall door and whickered to Connor, then snorted and screamed. A deluge of dust motes rained down on them when he double-barrelled the back of his stall with his shod hooves.

Craig *tsked* as he mouthed, *"That's gettin' really old, mate."*

Andrew frowned and crossed his arms. "Your horse doesn't like Craig."

Connor squeezed his shoulder gently and pressed him firmly to her leg. "I know, sweetie." She rolled her eyes at Hades. "He doesn't like anyone, except me."

Rudiobus leaned his head over the gate of the stall, extended his neck, and sniffed. "Daughter of the Highlands, Death Walker—" He stopped suddenly, glaring at Andrew. His voice grated. "Who is this child? Why have you brought him here? My true identity can never be revealed. Mortals do not know of our existence. They think that Gods are just tales from the Faery."

Connor put both of her hands up. "He can see Craig and he can hear and talk to mice, from what I can gather."

Andrew looked excited as his head turned back and forth. "Where are the fairies?"

Rudiobus took a step forward. "You can hear me?"

Andrew nodded. "And the snake." He turned and pointed to the bales in the far corner of the barn before he looked skyward. "And the spiders." He cupped his hands over his ears. "It's noisy in here."

"Come closer, child."

Andrew looked up at Connor. She nodded, hand-in-hand, they walked toward the stall. "Rudiobus, this is Andrew."

The horse stretched his neck over the door. Suddenly, he pulled back, jerking his head in the air.

"No! This is not possible!"

Andrew jumped backward.

After about ten seconds, the horse walked forward again. Connor squeezed Andrew's hand.

"It's okay, sweetie. He's just getting to know you. I promise, he won't hurt you."

Andrew gripped her hand tightly. Rudiobus stretched his long neck and sniffed the top of Andrew's head, his face, and his mouth. Suddenly, he gently backed away, disappearing inside the stall. Everyone in the barn stood very still. After a minute, Rudiobus stepped forward into the light. "It cannot be. It is not possible."

Connor drew Andrew into her arms and picked him up. His eyes were as big as saucers before he threw his arms around her neck, snuggled into her shoulder, and whispered, "Why is he mad at me?"

Before she could answer, Rudiobus folded into a deep bow, his head tucked so tightly, his muzzle touched his chest. "No, my prince, son of Macha, I could never be angry with you."

Andrew's head bobbed up suddenly as if someone had stuck him with a pin. Connor frowned as she hugged him tighter. "What's going on? What're you talking about?"

The horse rose, ignored her, and looked at Andrew. The tenor of his voice was soft and respectful. "Well met, son of Macha. Never before, has there been a male child with the blood of a Guardian. And yet, here before me, one stands."

Connor patted Andrew on the back. "Andrew, this is —"

Andrew looked first at Connor and then to the horse. "I know who he is. He's my mam's horse. Tessa told me he's a good horse and that he won't hurt me." Looking dubious, he frowned. "I think she fibbed."

Rudiobus beckoned Connor forward with sharp nods of his head.

"It's okay, Andrew. Tessa's right. He won't hurt you. He was just surprised to meet you, that's all."

Andrew reached out to touch the horse on the neck.

Rudiobus sighed. "Sweet Goddess, the boy is like his sister. Guardian blood runs thick in his veins."

"But..." Connor's eyebrows drew together. "You said Guardians produce only female children to be their Successors."

The horse continued to stare at Andrew, then gave a deep chuckle. "Macha is as fierce and capable a mama, as she is a Guardian. She loved the boy's sire a great deal. As a Goddess of the Tuatha Dé Danann, she is incredibly powerful. Her magicks are like armour around this child." Rudiobus leaned over the door of the stall and sniffed the air in front of Andrew. "Yes, indeed the magicks are very strong. This child's ability to heal and communicate with all beasts is as strong as her own."

Rudiobus whickered, and Andrew giggled. "Ahh, the things I have seen. In early times, when the Dynastic Chinese Kingdoms threatened war, the Guardian summoned one thousand Velocitators — it was brutal." His voice became warm and soft. "While Macha is a Warrior Leader, she is pure of heart. I sense the same goodness in this child." After he paused, he spoke as if to himself. "Almost at the beginning of time, there was a child of the San People in Southern Africa he was aged five or so years. He was dying. Sickly since birth, he had rarely been well enough to come out of his hut. It was rumoured Macha bribed the severer of the life threads that *before* the soul of the child ascended, she be granted time with him. The Goddess agreed. Just before the child took his last breath, Macha summoned Pegasus and placed the boy on his back. Death wove his innocent soul into the glistening white mane as his wings unfurled and carried him unto the light."

Andrew chortled. "I like Pegasus. He's fluffy and his feathers are tickly." Laughing, he clapped his hands. "But I really like unicorns because they're sparkly. The lady in the night sometimes brings them to see me. But they're not allowed to stay."

Rudiobus chuckled. "Some things, it seems, never change. Perhaps my fondest memory of Macha was when she magicked the vipers of Ireland and turned them into Coomasaharn char—fish in the rivers. That was quite recent, hmm, fifth century, if I recall rightly. She knew the Plague of Justinian was coming. A terrible sickness that rotted and blackened mortal hands, preventing the labour required to till the soil. This was the only way she could guarantee there would be food enough to feed the people of her birth country. Everyone fished—every man, woman, and child." He kicked one of his front hooves on the stall door, then made a disparaging noise. "The Apostle of Ireland, St Patrick, is credited with ridding the country of its adders. But, as is the way of things, the truth, very often, in no way resembles the records of history."

Connor put her hand on Andrew's head as he threaded his fingers through Rudiobus' mane.

The horse leaned forward and nuzzled Andrew's face. "My prince. It is my very great pleasure to meet you."

Her hand stilled as she whispered. "What are you saying, Rudiobus?"

"The child standing before you, Daughter of the Highlands, is unique. There has never been a boy child of the Guardian Protector of the Tuatha Dé Danann. Only time will tell what he shall be capable of."

Chapter Fifteen

ACK IN THE COTTAGE, CONNOR POURED TWO
glasses of orange juice, then dragged the crushed book of
stamps out of her jeans pocket. "All right, little mate. You
finish your drink. I have work to do." She walked into her bedroom
and picked her iPod up from the bedside table. As she returned to
the kitchen, she scrolled though the playlist, then lifted Andrew up
onto the two-seater lounge chair, plugged his ears with the buds,
and turned up the volume.

After making a cup of tea, she sat at the table and looked at
Craig. "What the hell do you think this all means? Tessa is the
Successor to the Guardian and Andrew is an unknown quantity
of the Celtic Gods, for Christ's sake. Did you know he really *can*
speak to animals?"

Craig mouthed as he stared at the cup in her hand. "*I miss coffee.
What? Oh, Andrew? Yeah, he's like Tessa, otherwise, he wouldn't be able
to see me.*"

A snuffling noise came from the direction of the lounge chair.
Andrew had turned onto his side with his thumb stuck in his mouth,
sound asleep, with the music on repeat.

The air to Connor's right suddenly shifted and glowed an iridescent green as Tomoe Gazen and Yokami appeared. Their katanas
sang the Song of Welcome.

"Daughter." Tomoe Gazen reached over and took her hands in hers.

Yokami walked around the table and put his hands on Connor's shoulders. She beamed. "Tomoe Gazen, Mr Sukani, what's up?"

Concern pinched Tomoe Gazen's face. "We have held Council with the ancient Horsemen and Epona. None of the Gods know anything of a black shadow that your man named as Death. We have watched you, night and day, since that time. The Scots declare they sense a Celtic influence and that, most likely, the Tuatha Dé Danann are responsible. We wait for them to declare their hand, but history has taught the Celts to be wily. With them, things are rarely as they seem."

Tomoe Gazen looked over at Andrew, sleeping on the lounge. She walked over to him and placed a hand on his head. The corners of her beautiful eyes crinkled as she smiled. "Ah… Yokami?"

He walked over to stand beside her and placed a hand on the sleeping boy. "So… It *is* possible."

"What?" Connor walked over to stand before the Samurai Gods. "Tell me."

Tomoe Gazen smiled and nodded. "The blood of this child is as ancient as the Gods themselves. His mother and her sisters are the warrior protectors of the Tuatha Dé Danann. I pray they will—"

"I know. Rudiobus explained it to us. He's amazing."

A dull buzzing sound filled the small cottage before it became a deafening roar. Katanas flew from Tomoe Gazen and Yokami's scabbards on their backs, to their hands. They stood side by side, swords outstretched.

The God Killer flew to Connor's hand. She stood beside the Samurai, all three swords drawn. As the noise quietened, an incorporeal image became a solid figure that bowed to Tomoe Gazen and Yokami. "Well met, Gods of the Samurai."

Before they could respond, Connor lowered her sword, crossed the floor, and hugged her. "Elizabeth!"

A throaty laugh filled the room. "In my mortal life, yes, I was Elizabeth—Beth to my family. As Guardian, my name is Macha. Well met, Connor. I am pleased to see you again. I am also very pleased that you have brought Gwyd—Rudiobus and Tessa together. He is a truly fine horse, and an even finer, honourable God." She turned and walked over to Andrew, who slept peacefully as the music played in his ears. "Oh, my son, my beautiful son…"

Craig looked stunned.

Macha cocked her head as she looked at him. "Death Walker."

"Craig," he mouthed. "My name is Craig."

"I do not understand. As an undead, why are you here? Why did you not pass unto the Shade after going to the Place of Shadows?"

He plastered his hands against the barrier. "You know of this place?"

Confusion passed across her face. "Of course. It is where all Celtic Gods go to *die*—although not as humans understand it. When we pass, we go to the Place of Shadows to await the summons of Death. Then we spend eternity in the Shade. But…" she approached him, "you are not a God. However, I sense your blood is of the Celts."

Craig nodded and mouthed, "*Yes, my father was a Scot.*"

She stood in front of him and placed her hand on his incorporeal chest. A gasp escaped her lips. "This man is God Touched! Oh, sweet merciful Mothers, so is your son!"

Tears misted Connor's eyes as she cleared her throat. "Yes, I know. Rudiobus showed me."

Sadness came over Macha's face. "I am so very sorry. Oh, Connor… Your husband and son are between planes. They are both equally in the Place of Shadows and here on mortal Earth."

A sad frown creased Connor's forehead. "I know. Help us, please."

Macha covered Connor's hand with her own. On contact, images of Nimerlin, her parents, her brothers and Ethan and Jilly Louise, flooded her brain.

"Connor, you must return to Nimerlin. Because Craig and your son are between planes, Death will return and seek to claim them. To restore their souls, they must return from the Place of Shadows. You must make petition to the God that Touched them. Both souls are, in essence, stuck, between life and death!" Her eyes filled with tears.

Connor looked to Tomoe Gazen's sad face.

Macha acknowledged the silent message. "Perhaps the Samurai have the ways of manipulating life and death?"

"It is true, the human and his son are God Touched." Yokami bowed to Tomoe Gazen. "If not, Craig would have perished and would have gone on to have a mortal death."

"Oh, God!" Connor's hand flew to her throat. "I hadn't thought about it, like that." Grasping Tomoe Gazen's hand, she clutched it to her chest. "I don't hate you. I don't blame you. Without you, I would never have had a chance of ever seeing him again."

Yokami shook his head. "Unfortunately, the Samurai do not have the ability to lengthen or shorten the Threads of Life. We do not know what Gods possess this power. However, we *will* do everything in our power to discover which Gods do, and what they hold most dear. We seek redemption for Craig, returned to his mortal state; our debt repaid, for dying at the hands Bishamon our deposed Samurai God of War, also rebirth of the boy child. Without Craig calling her back from death, our Daughter would have gone unto the mortal Shade."

Macha jolted, suddenly white-faced as she faded into invisibility.

Just after sunrise, with Hades loaded on Bill O'Roirdian's newly purchased transport truck he was on his way to Nimerlin, Connor sat on her bike with the empty scabbard slung across her back. The God Killer rested under her right tribal tattoo. If the police pulled her over for carrying what appeared to be a lethal weapon, it would be a moot point. There's no law against carrying an empty scabbard. Connor kicked the machine into neutral and waited to say goodbye to all the McVeys standing on the driveway. Tessa ran ahead and threw her arms around her.

Douglas smiled at Connor as he held out his hand. "On yer way then, lass? Give our regards to yer da and yer mam, and remind them to make sure they all come oop to our school, new bairn and all."

Connor laughed, leaned forward and gave him a hug. "Nothing could keep them away. Don't worry. They'll be here."

Ewan took a step closer to her. "How long do you reckon you'll be gone?"

"Two weeks or thereabouts. That is, if Jilly Louise cooperates and doesn't go overdue. God knows, the grandmam's will be frantic if she does."

Douglas laughed. "Oh, aye! I remember when my Morag was pregnant with Ewan. The due date came and went aboot fourteen times afore he was born. Her mam and mine were in a right fankle, I can tell ye that."

Connor laughed. "Da helped birth Ethan with none of the grand-mams around. There was hell to pay. I can tell you, Jilly Louise won't evade them so easily this time."

"Angus helped birth the lad? Jesus, I wouldn't have wanted to be in his shoes when the women found oot." Douglas put one hand on her shoulder and the other around Tessa, who was sniffing, as she stood by the bike. Andrew walked over to the big red machine and put his hands up in the air. Connor reached down and pulled him up onto the fuel tank as his arms went round her neck. "Tell Ethan the tadpoles are in the creek and that they are very nice frogs. Connor...you come back?"

She kissed him on the cheek. "I'll be back just as soon as Ethan's brother or sister is born."

Andrew looked up at her with moist eyes and snuggled into her neck again.

Ewan approached and stood about a foot away from the bike. He reached for Andrew and peeled him off the fuel tank and into his arms. "Come on, mate. Connor needs to be away to see her family. She'll be back soon."

Connor leaned down and hugged Tessa while she whispered in her ear, "Look after Rudiobus. Listen to him and practice with your grandda."

Tessa looked up and nodded as tears tracked down her face.

When the engine roared to life, Andrew put his hands over his ears just before Connor gunned down the driveway, headed for the New England Highway and home.

Just as the sunlight changed from morning to afternoon, Connor clicked down through the gears, when suddenly she was over-whelmed by pain and grief. Slowly, she passed Bill Middleton's property, the place where Craig had died in the accident. She pulled over to the side of the road.

Craig appeared at the fence line. *"Well, this is weird. You okay?"*

She leaned back, legs outstretched. "I hate this piece of road. Remember when da used to go on and on about Bill Middleton's bull being the cause of someone's misery. I never for one moment imagined it would be ours."

Craig chucked his thumb in a quick movement. *"Let's get out of here."*

She nodded then kicked the bike into gear. "Wanna hitch a ride?"

He shook his head from where he stood behind the barrier.

"Chicken!"

He mouthed as she shook his head. *"I'm dead enough without coming off that noisy machine at a thousand miles an hour!"*

She looked over her shoulder before she pulled out onto the middle of the road, put her hand in the air and swept it downward in a sharp stroke. "Race you!"

The bike roared down the road, breaking every land speed record, when suddenly, she backed off the accelerator, geared down, and turned into Nimerlin.

When she pulled up in the driveway, the front door of the house burst opened and a sea of MacDonalds rushed out onto the porch and down the stairs.

Connor dismounted and ran over to Angus and Marie, threw her arms around both of their necks, and hung off them like a monkey. "Oh, God, I have missed you guys so much!"

Angus glanced left and right.

Connor chuckled and whispered close to his ear. "Yes, he's here."

Angus grunted, then nodded.

Marie hugged her. "Oh, thanks be to the good Lord for seein' ye safe back home to us."

"About bloody time you got here. I'm going to burst any second." She smiled over her father's shoulder as Jilly Louise waddled down the porch stairs. Cameron walked behind her, holding Ethan's hand.

Connor ran over to her and grabbed her in a hug. "Oh! My! God! You're enormous!" She rubbed her hands over the huge swell of Jilly Louise's belly. "Are you well?"

"Yes, I'm well, if you don't count heartburn, varicose veins, and haemorrhoids the size of apricots. I'm so glad you're here."

Ethan let go of his father's hand. "Aunty! You come back!"

She leaned down, picked him up, and made loud nuzzling noises in the crease of his neck. He screeched and wriggled in her arms.

"I've missed you, baby."

Angus walked forward and put an arm around Connor and Jilly Louise. "All right, then, let's go inside and tuck into that gingerbread yer mam has hidden somewhere in the hoose. I swear lass, withoot you here to flush oot her hidey places, I've been on bloody rations." He frowned. "Exactly how long *are* ye home for, then?"

She looked at Craig, cleared her throat, and pasted a smile on her face. "For as long as it takes the mother of the year here," she poked Jilly Louise in the belly "to birth your next grandbaby."

With Hades unloaded from the transport float, settled for the night, and tea taken care of, Jilly Louise, Cameron, and Ethan went home to find their beds. Connor sat on the porch swing with Angus, while Marie went inside to put the kettle back on the hob. He turned to her and smiled. "Well, then, how is it? Is that old bastard McVey givin' ye any trouble?"

Connor grinned. "Not at all. In fact, now that I have punched some sense into his eldest son, he respects me."

"Jesus. Ye punched, er…"

"Ewan. You remember…tall, dark, pain in the backside."

He chuckled. "What happened?"

She smiled to the empty space next to her. "It's a long and complicated story."

"What of Craig, then?"

She looked around before she spoke and jerked her head to her right. "He's here, Da. It seems he can follow me."

Angus' superstitious Scottish nature caused his Adam's apple to bob before he swallowed, then spoke. "I trust what ye say, lass. But, Jesus! Ye know, I have never believed that ghosts exist. I've always thought them to be leftover bits of nightmares and such, told to frighten wee bairns. But that's no' the case, is it?"

Connor leaned back against the porch swing. The balmy night air was close; the cicadas, deafening. "I have no idea about ghosts, although…" She sighed. "We may've come across something that might—"

"Ah, here we are." Marie pushed open the screen door with her foot and stepped out onto the porch, balancing a laden, cloth-covered tray, between two hands."

Angus sat forward with a big grin across his face. "I *knew* there was gingerbread somewhere in the bloody hoose. But I'll be damned if either Ethan or I could find it."

Marie smacked him on the hand as he reached for the plate stacked with slices of hot buttered cake. "Angus MacDonald, shame on ye, usin' the lad to do yer dirty work." She passed the plate to Connor. "You know lass, since ye left home, yer father has recruited another accomplice—Ethan. Ye know that lad has the devil in him, and when he's teamed oop with his grandda, well…" She slapped Angus on the shoulder. "I doubt there will ever be gingerbread enough for anyone else, ever again."

Angus lurched forward, stuffed a whole slice in his mouth then snaffled another piece. "Well it didna do us any good, did it? We never did find yer hidey place." He quirked an eyebrow. "So where'd ye plant it?"

Marie laughed. "Somewhere safe from ye and the lad, that's for certain."

Angus patted his stomach and went to reach for another slice, just as Marie snatched the plate away, picked up the last serving and popped it into her mouth.

He frowned at the empty plate and growled.

After breakfast, Connor saddled Hades. When the barn doors opened, she turned and smiled when Angus walked inside.

"Goin' for a ride on the big black, lass?"

She grunted as she cinched the girth. "Yeah, before either of us gets cabin fever. I'm glad you're here, though. Do you want to come for a ride as well? There's something I need to talk to you about, and it's a conversation that's best not overheard."

"Well, ye have picked a good day for it." He walked over to his stallion Quaich's stall, grabbed the halter the peg, and opened the door to the enclosure. The horse whickered as Angus led him out into the barn and saddled him. He looked around. "Is Craig here now?"

She nodded as she put her foot into the stirrup and swung up onto Hades back. "Yep. He's just here." She pointed to her right.

Hades snorted and pawed the ground as if to confirm the fact.

When they were out of hearing range of the house, she turned to face her father. "Da… Oh, God, where do I start?"

They rode side by side while she relayed the story of Gwydrion, Tessa and Andrew. When she spoke of the chance to restore Craig and James to life, she choked on her words.

Angus blew out a big breath and gave her a sceptical look. "Ye believe this to be true? Jesus, lass. No wonder ye dinna want anyone overhearin' yer words."

"Exactly." She ran her hand down Hades' neck and patted him as he walked in an easy gait alongside Quaich.

"What is it that ye need to do exactly, to bring Craig back to us?"

She sagged a little in the saddle. "I have no clue. All I know is that Macha said he must leave the Place of Shadows, if he is to be restored."

Angus frowned. "And how in the name of all things holy, does he do that?"

Connor groaned. "I have no idea."

"Does Craig know anything of how to bring this aboot?"

She groaned again. "Nope. He has no clue, either."

After a couple of hours, Connor and Angus rode the horses back toward the barn. Marie looked up from the washing line and waved.

"So, you and Craig…?"

Connor nodded. "Yeah, today we plan to try to figure out what it is that we need to do. I just wish Macha had been more specific. As always with the Gods, they give one percent of the truth then sit back and enjoy the confusion. Nothing is ever clear or certain. Who knows? Maybe we're barking up the wrong tree and have completely misinterpreted what she said." Her finger caressed the wavy black mane in front of her. Hades arched his neck against her fingers, enjoying her touch. "Oh, God, I can't bear to think about what happens if whatever the hell we are supposed to do doesn't work, and this has all been for nothing. I love him so much, Da. I just want him back. I have never wanted anything so badly in my life."

After they dismounted and walked into the barn, he reached over and took the reins out of her hand. "I'll unsaddle the big lad. Ye go and do what it is ye need to do. I'll keep yer mam occupied while ye are gone. Now, we need to get our stories straight. What excuse are ye goin' to offer for takin' the bike out today? Ye know she will want to know where ye went."

Making little plaits in Hades' mane, she spoke softly. "I hate lying to her, but…if there's a chance…any chance at all, I have to try. I'll tell her there was something wrong with the bike and that I took it to the mechanic."

"Fair enough. Go now and may the Gods be kind to ye. For ye deserve their blessings."

She went up on tiptoe and kissed his cheek. "Thanks, Da." She turned and headed for the doors when she turned and smiled at him. "Wish us luck."

Connor slipped inside the house, grabbed her keys and headed outside. She wasted no time starting the engine, then rode down the driveway, and out onto the main road. At the verge of Middleton's paddock, she pulled over, turned off the ignition, and dismounted.

Craig stood beside the bike with a pained look on his face.

She searched her memories of the night Middleton's bull came through the front windscreen of their car. After walking up and down the road for about an hour, she turned to him.

"Anything?"

He shook his head. *"No, love. Whatever we're supposed to find, it isn't here."*

She sat down on the dry grass on the side of the road with her hands clasped around her knees. "What now?"

He paused, his mirrored eyes shrouded by half closed eyelids. *"The cemetery...that must be it. I can't think of where else it could be."*

Connor's stomach roiled as the colour drained from her face. "You know, I just had a really awful thought."

"What's that?"

"Thank God you weren't cremated!"

Craig grimaced. *"Jesus! The ol' one flash and I would've been ash. There would've been no coming back from that."*

She shuddered. "Come on, let's go." She threw her leg over the bike, fired it up, and headed down the road.

The sight of the white wrought iron gates made hot bile rise in the back of her throat. Memories of the casket containing Craig, with James swaddled to his chest, lowered into the cold, damp earth, made her heave. Sweat broke out on her forehead. Her hands shook as she tried to force the images from her mind.

After she parked the bike, she walked over to the gravesite with the marble headstone that bore their names. The inscription read, *Here lies Craig and James Devereaux - Sons of the Clan - Beannachd Dia dhuit (Blessings of God be with you.)* A wave of desolation and loss forced the air from her lungs. She grunted as if someone had punched her in the belly.

Craig reached out to her. His fingers halted abruptly when he touched the barrier.

"God, this is really weird, reading my own epitaph." Moving closer, he lowered his palm to the curved top of the white marble gravestone. Suddenly, he jerked back his hand, as if flames had burned his fingers. His mouth opened in a wide *O* as he silently roared.

He crumpled to the ground, as if in slow motion, then fade into nothingness.

Connor screamed. "Craig! Craig! Where are you? Craig!"

A huge black shadow oozed out from the seams of the gravestone, ballooned like a giant parachute then settled over her like a suffocating black shroud. The left-side tribal tattoo flared across her biceps in unison with the God Killer. She kicked and thrashed then flung her hands wide. "Come to me!"

The dreadful screech of the raven amplified into hideous, maniacal laughter as the God Killer landed in her hand. The red dog morphed from the left tattoo, growling and snapping at the roiling darkness.

Connor screamed when the gut-wrenching, damp smell of death, filled her nostrils. Each time she drew in a breath, a mere puff of air entered her lungs. White lights danced before her eyes as she held the blade extended. The next breath she took was like a scuba diver whose tanks were empty. Her vision wavered, as unconsciousness threatened. As she fell to the ground, she grunted and lunged. The blade of the God Killer made a high-pitched scream when it struck the marble slab.

Thunder roared overhead.

A bolt of lightning streaked across the bright blue skies and forked into an explosive blast that hit the ground below the black writhing mass. The Ancient Horsemen chanted as the war horses stamped and screamed.

"Courage, Daughter! We are with you!"

Suddenly, the Shadow recoiled then disappeared. Connor rolled onto her side and vomited. The God Killer continued to pulse energy into the grave in front of her.

She pushed her empty palm flat on the grass as she dragged in gasping breaths and clawed herself upright.

The God Killer remained in contact with the slab.

The katana continued to throb with power when, suddenly, a vibrating green mist engulfed the gravesite.

"I summon..." She slumped to the left. The red dog growled, then leaned heavily against her, supporting her weight. "I summon the Samurai."

The flash of light was blinding as Tomoe Gazen and Yokami Sukani appeared before her. The blades of their drawn katanas hummed with energy as they gleamed in the light of the sun.

Yokami's eyes went wide, just before he screamed, "The God Killer! Quickly! Craig is here! He is connected to you Daughter, through the God Killer." Surprise lit his face. "Your man did not lie. The blackness of Death has been here." He grabbed Tomoe Gazen's sword hand. "We cannot restore him, but we can detain him! Whatever you do, Daughter, do not let the blade lose contact with the grave!"

Connor struggled to stand, as she laid the God Killer across the exquisite marble. The blade screamed with outrage.

As one, the Samurai lifted their blades so that the tips touched. A blue spark shot high into the air. A wide band of golden energy channelled into an anchoring arc of power. Connor shielded her face with her left hand against the white, blinding light. Suddenly, a ball of heat exploded in her chest. Unbidden, the battle cry of the Highland MacDonald Clan roared in the back of her throat. Celestial warhorses of the Ancients screamed and stamped in reply just as the tall, kilted Highlander walked out of the mist. The red dog growled, scented the air, then returned to lay at Connor's feet, her eyes the colour of liquid steel, ever watchful. Clan chieftain Connor MacDonald walked forward and placed his hand on her shoulder. "Your man is here, child. I feel his blood, and I hear him calling to the Scots." He knelt and grabbed a fistful of earth. "Yer hand."

Staring at the soil in his palm, Connor frowned.

Impatient, he barked in a brusque tone, "Hold oot yer hand!"

She extended her hand, palm upward. The moist brown soil was cool as she closed her palm around it. "I don't understand — "

With blinding speed, he grabbed the dirk from his boot, slashed the blade across her left wrist, gripped it, and held it high. A rivulet of red pooled onto the dirt in her hand. His fist closed over hers and they stood with their arms outstretched. The brogue of the ancient Highlands rumbled in his throat. "Blood of the Scots, find and bind with the blood of our clansman." He stopped and turned to her. *"Beannachd Dia dhuit. May God be with you."*

The air around them charged with static as the chieftain lifted his hands above his head. The Highlander's God-voice rattled ornaments and toppled vases on nearby graves. The katanas of the Samurai bean to chant. The God Killer vibrated and screamed in chorus as the chieftain roared above the din. "Only you can summon him, Daughter. The Samurai will connect you to him, but it is your blood, the blood of the Celts, that will draw him back."

Connor stood with the soil of the cemetery gripped tight in her palm. Yokami lifted his sword so the tip of his blade touched Tomoe Gazen's blade. The God Killer flew to Connor and the blades joined in a trio. A burst of blinding light boomed and arced onto the gravesite. then bConnorThe concussion threw her high into the air. She landed heavily between two gravestones, cracked and moulded with age. Shaken, she groaned as she tried to sit up. Awkward, she frowned down at her still-closed fist. As she tentatively opened her fingers, the skin of her palm was clean and white. The grave dirt had vanished.

Silence.

It was so quiet, not even birds chirped.

The ground appeared to undulate before her. Vertigo made her stomach lurch. Suddenly, she slumped sideways. Yokami and the chieftain morphed to her side. Their strong hands caught her then lowered her to the ground. The God Killer remained gripped tight, in her right fist.

A groan escaped her throat when an indistinct energy field wavered in front of her. Colours like the Aurora Borealis danced around a wide outline, shimmering and iridescent. Then, a vortex-like blackness in the middle of the field flexed, as Craig's incorporeal form appeared. Once more, he stood behind the incongruously beautiful barrier that was his prison.

"Craig!" The God Killer keened as it returned to her tattoo. She crawled awkwardly on her hands and knees toward him. The red dog stayed by her side.

Craig stared ahead, pale faced and shaking. He held both hands high in the air. *"Stop! Connor, stop!"*

"No! We can't give up now!" Tears tracked down her face.

His face, lined with exhaustion and defeat, terrified her.

"Death now knows I am here, Connor. She will come for me, again."

Chapter Sixteen

THE SOUND OF THE BIKE ON THE DRIVEWAY SUM-
moned Angus to the front porch. As he walked toward Connor,
he held Ethan's hand. "Are ye all right, lass? How did it—?"

"Mama had a girl!" Ethan screwed up his nose in disgust.

"What!" Connor flew off the bike. "Where is she?"

A voice came from the top of the stairs. "I'm here. Come and
say hello to your niece." Jilly Louise and Marie slowly descended
the rungs.

Stuttering with shock, Connor reached for the swaddled bundle.
"How can you possibly be standing here in front of me with a baby
in your arms when I left..." she checked her watch, "for the cem—
the mechanic's shop only three hours ago?"

"I'll tell ye how." Marie pulled back the blanket from the little
girl's face and smiled. "The wee bairn was birthed on the floor of
the bathroom. Jesus! Cameron rang and told us. I swear it took ten
years off my life!"

The baby squirmed in Connor's arms. The agony of loss forced
a loud sob from her lips. Jilly Louise wrapped her arms around her.
"Oh, Christ, Connor. I'm so sorry."

Sniffing, Connor gave the baby a sad smile. "I know, thanks. It's
just that she is the first baby I have held since... The year of *firsts* is a
bitch." As she wiped her hand over her face, she blew out a breath.
"What's her name?"

Cameron walked round from the side of the house and kissed the top of the baby's head. "Juliette Marie. Beautiful, huh? I swear to God, Ethan's birth nearly killed me, but this time, Jesus, there was no time."

Laughing, Jilly Louise punched him on the bicep. "Just think. With the next one, I should have no contract—"

Suddenly serious, he pulled her into his arms. "I love you and I thank you for our beautiful babies. But, shit, Pix, I'm only flesh and blood. I don't think I could survive another birthing. Let's call it a day, huh?"

"Excellent! That means it's time for the wheels to go back on my bike." She glared at him. "Just as soon as I find were you have hidden them, that is.Ethan frowned and pursed his lips at the baby as he gripped Angus' fore and middle fingers. "Come on, Grandda, let's go and see the chickens. There's no one here to play with."

As they turned in the direction of the chook coop, Ethan stopped and turned around. "Mama?"

Jilly Louise dragged her gaze from the baby. "Yes, sweetie?"

He looked like someone who was hatching a plan. "You said we can't send the baby back...so...do you think we give her to someone and we could get a puppy?"

Angus scooped him up in his arms, threw him over his shoulder and held him upside down by the legs. "Oh, lad, puppies are fun... but the wee lassies... Ye have a lot to learn."

Connor sat on the floor in front of the barrier, nursing a mug of hot soup. "I was shit scared today Craig. Jesus, I thought you were gone for good. You vanished the instant you touched the headstone. I couldn't see you, I couldn't hear you. It felt like you were gone, like I had lost you all over again."

He shuddered. *"If I never experience anything like that again, it'll be too soon. Jesus! The headstone, it was as if I somehow made connection with the dead body lying under the slab. Make no mistake, Connor, I felt the hands of Death pulling me away from you. It was as if she was dragging me underground. I couldn't breathe. All I could taste was cold, damp earth. But the worst thing, was when your voice faded away. I thought I was finally really dead. That's when I felt it! The blast of hot energy, and then from the darkness, I heard your voice. The hands that pulled me downward suddenly released me. The next thing I knew, I was beside you again."*

"Well, Macha was right about you coming back to the place where you died, to try and find some answers to your situation." Craig nodded. Connor blew out a big breath and looked at her watch. "Well, I'd better make a move. It's time to go back to Glen Rowan." She stood and went into the kitchen, put the soup mug in the sink, grabbed her bag, and closed the door quietly. The family all stood on the driveway to wave her off. She spoke over her shoulder to Craig. "See you there."

At the sound of the motorbike, Tessa yelped and started running down the road. Connor stopped and flipped up her visor. "Hey! I've missed you! Get on!" She travelled at a snail's pace the rest of the way, until they were parked outside the main house. All the McVey's and O'Dee came rushing out to greet her. "Oh lassie, I am so verra glad to see ye." O'Dee wrapped her in a big hug. Ewan frowned at Tessa, riding pillion without a helmet, but remained silent. Douglas beamed. "I'm guessin' ye canna wait to see yer horse? He arrived this mornin'. Be assured I was verra thorough, in checking him over. We didna want a repeat performance of the first time he arrived here. Andrew leapt out of Ewan's arms and hugged Connor's leg. "You came back! I told the mices you would come back!" Everyone looked at him with quizzical expressions then returned their attention to Connor. Tessa dismounted then Connor threw her leg over the black leather seat. God, it felt good to be back. Tessa pulled her by the hand just before Connor swung Andrew up onto her hip and together they walked towards the barn. When Connor opened the door, light flooded the room and all three stallions whickered. Andrew ran over to Hades' enclosure, climbed up the wooden slats of the stall, and sat on the top railing. He reached out to Hades, who licked his hand. "See, here she is. I told you she was coming home today."

Connor walked over to her horse and wrapped her arms around his thick, black neck. "I'm glad to be back. I have missed you."

Hades whickered softly, then rubbed his forehead on the front of her shirt.

Rudiobus stretched his long white neck over the door of his stall. "Well met, Daughter of the Highlands. I am glad you have—" He directed his gaze to the space beside Connor. "Death Walker. Come closer."

Craig walked as far forward as the barrier would allow.

The horse flared his nostrils then snorted. "The hands of Death have Touched you, not once, but twice—"

Suddenly, light flooded into the barn as the doors reopened and Ewan walked inside. "Andrew! What in the name of Jesus do you think you're doin' sitting up there? If you fall into the bloody stall, you'll be trampled."

Andrew looked at his father as if he had just spoken in Swahili. "No, Da. Hades is nice." He shifted his gaze from his father back to the stallion. "You wouldn't hurt me, would you?"

Hades whickered and nudged his leg with his muzzle.

Connor bit back a flush of irritation. "Is there something I can do for you, Ewan?"

He walked over to Hades and plucked Andrew down from the stall. "Yes. We received a truckload of paperwork concerning the school while you were away. I thought you'd want to sort through it." He handed her a wad of letters and papers bound by a wide, red rubber band.

She held out her hand. "Sure, I'll go through them tonight."

As he looked at her, worry creased his face. "I just hope there aren't any cancellations. Da will never forgive me if this school fails."

"No pressure, though, right?" Connor flicked him on the arm with the bunch of papers. "The school isn't going to fail. Besides, the cost of entry is non-refundable if cancelled within two months of the actual start day. As we are just three weeks out from then, everything will be fine."

"Are you sure? If the school doesn't cover what we borrowed from the bank, we could very well lose Glen Rowan."

Tessa walked over to him and took his hand. "Don't worry, Da, Connor and I are going to make our school famous. You just wait and see."

Andrew put his hand on his father's arm and smiled. "The horses are very happy, Da."

Ewan frowned, shook his head, and ruffled the little boy's hair. "I hope you're right, little mate. I really hope you're right."

The MacDonald clan arrived at Glen Rowan three days before the start date of the school. Marie, O'Dee and Tessa fussed over Juliette, while Angus, Cameron, and Douglas talked and laughed over a seemingly endless supply of whiskey. The laughter of little boys rang out around the house.

Two days later, the pink and aquamarine dawn sky lit up the earth, as Connor and Tessa worked with their swords. Douglas, as usual, sat on the ground just outside the practice area.

"That's it, Tessa, reach, doona put yerself in range of the katana."

Connor chuckled as she worked through the katas. "Listen to your grandda, Tessa. The blade is your friend. Let it defend you."

At the end of the session, both Connor and Tessa were a lather of sweat when suddenly, Ewan stormed around the side of the house.

"Da? How long has this," he waved his hands in Connor and Tessa's general direction, "been going on?"

"Since the sword called to Tessa."

"Jesus Christ, Da." He glared at Connor. "Everything has been turned upside down since *she* got here. Why in the name of all that is holy would any sensible adult give a twelve-year-old girl—?"

"I'm thirteen, Da."

He shot her a black look, "a *thirteen*-year-old girl a bloody sword to play with?"

Douglas grunted and his knees cracked as he stood. "For a start Ewan, she is not playin' and secondly, because Connor here, is a blessing to all of us, she's been generous enough in sharin' her skills to teach yer daughter to use the blade of yer own mother's family. Make no mistake man, Tessa is verra clever with the blade. It wouldn't hurt ye to be more encouragin' of her. Surely even ye can see how much happier she is."

He scowled at his father. "And what's that supposed to mean?"

"Just this, lad. 'Tis time you let go of yer own misery, and took a good, long look, at what is before you. The bairns are growin' oop, and I for one couldna be prouder of Tessa for carrying on the legacy of her ancestors."

Connor sheathed the katana. "Ewan, sword work is about fitness, discipline and self-defence. Tessa is gifted in the way she handles the sword."

He glared at her, shook his head, turned on his heel, and walked away.

Douglas dipped his head to Connor and Tessa. "Sorry. His grief has changed him."

Connor flung her arm around Tessa's shoulders. "Come on. We had better get a wriggle on. The riders will be arriving in a couple of hours.

By noon, twelve horse floats stood parked and unloaded. The air was alive with excitement. Connor greeted each of the participants, who of whom were female. She reacquainted with the elite athletes at the long trestle table over lunch. Half an hour later, the chatter was loud enough to wake the dead. She chuckled to herself when all five McVey men wandered over and joined the meal.

Oestrogen flooded the ozone.

After lunch, with all the horses saddled, Connor led the troupe through basic dressage manoeuvres. Tessa rode Coinneach. Her face was a mask of concentration when Connor pulled out of formation and reined in alongside her.

"Loosen your grip on the reins. Can you feel how stiff Coinneach is, in his movements? That's because you're sending him mixed signals. The pressure of your legs is urging him forward while the tension on the reins is telling him to stop."

Tessa loosened her fingers and the horse fell into step with the rest of the equine competitors.

Douglas with Andrew on his shoulders, his two younger sons and Angus all stood by the fence. By late afternoon, the horses were wet with sweat and the participants were tired. When Connor called the day to a close, a round of thunderous applause broke out.

Douglas had the loudest voice of all. "Well done, lassies! Ach, what a sight!" He turned to Angus. "It's a damn shame Beth didna live to see this day."

That night, after the children had gone to bed, scowling, O'Dee walked into the dining room. "Douglas, have ye seen Ewan?"

He nodded his head and jutted his chin toward the closed office door at the head of the stairs.

O'Dee sighed and began clearing the dishes.

Connor looked from Douglas to O'Dee and back again. "Did I just miss something? Why didn't Ewan eat with the rest of us?"

Douglas scowled. "It's havin' all the riders here today and seein' them as our Beth described, is hard for him. He'll come round. We just need to leave him be, for now."

Connor looked at the closed office door. "Does that mean he's in there, getting blind, motherless drunk?"

Douglas nodded. "Verra possibly."

Both of their heads shot up when the sound of female laughter came from the direction of the office.

Connor groaned. "Oh, for the love of God." She got up from the table just as Douglas also stood. She held her hand out to stop him, walked across the room and up the stairs, then knocked on the door.

The laughter stopped abruptly. After a couple of seconds, footsteps sounded just before the door swung open. The waft of whiskey filled her nose as Ewan stood in the doorway. "Connor, come in. You've of course met—"

She glared over his shoulder. "Rachael? Yes. We've met."

Connor shifted her gaze and spoke to the red headed woman sitting opposite the leather chair where Ewan always sat. "Rachael, the rest of the participants have left for their quarters. Breakfast is at six in the morning, which means we get up at five, to see to the horses before we eat. I intend to start the clinic by seven-thirty sharp. This school offers a full program. We've a lot to get through tomorrow."

Rachael tossed her long hair, tilted her glass to Connor, and laughed. "Yes, Mom. I'll be there bright and shiny."

Ewan swayed slightly as he opened the door wider, in invitation. "Would you like to join us for a drink?" He paused for a second, then looked as if he had just remembered something. "Oh, yes…that's right…you're a teetotaller." He turned round to Rachael, shrugged, and turned back. "A Scot who doesn't drink. Whoever heard of such a thing?"

Connor's gave him a cold look. "Thank you, but I'll forego the offer. Although, Ewan, I don't think my abstinence is of any great concern, given that *some* Scots, can always be relied upon, to indulge in more than their fair share."

She looked over to Rachael, who smiled and continued to sip her drink.

Connor stepped back and grasped the door handle. "Well, good night, then. I'll see you in the morning."

As she closed the door with a deliberate thump, the tinkle of muffled laughter followed her down the stairs.

Chapter Seventeen

ON THE LAST DAY OF THE SCHOOL, CONNOR FOL-
lowed Rachael and another competitor from the barn to the
breakfast table. Ewan walked over to Rachael and linked his
arm through hers as he steered her toward the outdoor eating area.
Connor frowned as they sat with their heads almost touching; the
other women whispered and passed knowing glances.

Glen Rowan was alive with excitement as Connor handed each
of the participants a maroon saddle blanket with a Scottish broadsword embroidered on one side. As the cars began to arrive, Angus,
Douglas, and Ewan directed the traffic then escorted the guests of
the participants to the chairs, set up, outside the arena.

After a display of troupe routines, the riders took a short
break. Connor looked over at Tessa, who stood dismounted with
Coinneach's near side back hoof in her hand. She walked over to
her. "What's up?"

Bright tears threatened to spill. "I think he's lame."

Connor bent down, squinted, and examined the hoof then pointed
to a bruised area on the tender frog part of the hoof with her index
finger. "Hmmm…yep. You're right. See here? Something has gouged
into his hoof. Sorry, sweetie. It's all over for him for this school. Take
him up to the barn and untack him. I'll ask Da to make a poultice
that will bring out the bruise. That'll make it less painful for him."

Two fat tears tracked down Tessa's face. "Okay." She grasped Coinneach's reins and sobbed as she turned toward the barn.

Connor called to her retreating back, "Oh, and while you are in there, you'd better tack up Rudiobus. We can't have you missing out on the musical ride, now, can we?"

Tessa spun round. "You mean it? I can ride him?"

"Go get your horse, sweetie." Connor looked at her watch. "The ride starts in twenty minutes. You'd better get a wriggle on."

Tessa turned and walked quickly toward the barn while Coinneach limped awkwardly beside her.

Rachael stood outside the arena in her pristine jodhpurs, shirt, and jacket. Her hair, as competition etiquette demanded, pulled back into a netted bun, covered by a black riding helmet. Her horse stood fully tacked and ready for the performance. She leaned in close to Ewan, deep in conversation. Suddenly, he stopped talking as Tessa moved into position.

"Jesus Christ. Why's she riding that white bastard?"

Rachael looked at him, shocked, as she mounted her horse. "Are you serious? Rudiobus? I'd give anything to ride him. He's spectacular." She moved off toward the rest of the troupe and fell into formation.

The crowd roared and leapt to their feet when Connor entered the arena on Hades. The noise and applause was deafening when Tessa, sitting straight and proud, took her place on Rudiobus.

Ewan's face darkened as his gaze tracked the white stallion.

Connor looked at Ewan as she reined in alongside Tessa. "Focus, Tessa. Rudiobus is a magnificent horse. Ride him for your mam. She would've been so proud of you, I know, I am."

Tessa nodded and gave her a tight smile, as, together; they took their places in front of the other twelve competitors. One rider of each pair veered off to the right while the other, rode to the left into a wide circle, coming together in perfect timing, each horse in step. All riders sat tall and straight. After twenty minutes of manoeuvres, the troupe formed a semi circle with Hades and Rudiobus sharing pride of place in the centre of the troupe.

Each horse and rider stood very still, when, suddenly, music filled the arena. The war drums of Jon Adamich's *My Soldiers, My Sons* rang loud and true as each horse moved off, dancing, side pacing, making elaborate turns and weaves. The applause of the crowd was ear splitting. The flashes of cameras, created a rock concert atmosphere as they captured the digital images of the horses and riders.

All of the spectators stood, cheering at the magnificent sight of horses and riders marching in unison, in perfect timing and formation. Each horse, with the exception of Hades and Rudiobus, bent down on one knee and bowed to the spectators. Suddenly, the two stallions, positioned in the centre of the troupe, went up on their back legs and pawed the air. Angus and Douglas whooped and hollered over the din.

Connor laughed as Hades and Rudiobus both returned to stand on all four hooves, then bowed in thanks to the crowd.

Ewan stood outside the arena, his face, a twisted mask of hatred.

After feeding the horses and stabling them for the night, the family and friends of the participants stayed for a barbeque. The crowd milled around, eating sausages, steak, and salad; the conversation was bright and excited. Douglas handed the barbeque tongs to Aaron then inclined his head at Angus, who winked and moved to stand beside him.

"Care for a wee dram, man? I'm as dry as a camel's arse in a dust storm."

Angus laughed. "An offer no reasonable man could ever refuse."

Inside the office, Douglas gestured to Angus to sit down while he poured the drinks. Once they both had glasses in their hands, Douglas lifted his crystal tumbler to eye level. "To yer Connor and to the success of our school, which, withoot her, would never have happened. I give thanks every day for the blessin' that she is to our family. Slainte!"

"Slainte!" Angus downed his whiskey in one gulp. "Oh aye, she is that and so much more."

Douglas picked up the decanter and refilled Angus' glass to a three-finger level, before replenishing his own. He raised his glass again. "To our Beth." They both toasted silently, in respect. You know Angus, I've had at least half a dozen people approach me tonight, askin' aboot the next school and whether we'll offer preference to those who've attended this school."

Angus nodded. "Aye. The same thing happens at home. The next school is usually half-booked afore the current school is over. Connor has a fine reputation and is in great demand for instruction to elite competitors."

Douglas nodded. "Aye, ye are right aboot that. Now all I have to do is to convince her to stay here at Glen Rowan and continue on as our dressage master."

After he swallowed the rest of his drink, Angus sighed. "Ahh." He closed his eyes and relished the fiery flavour as he held out his glass for a refill. A sharp knock vibrated on the office door. Douglas crossed the floor, twisted the knob, and pulled the door open. Marie stood on the other side. "There ye are, Angus MacDonald. I thought ye might have slipped oop here for a wee dram." She squinted at his high colour and chuckled. "Or nine."

Douglas chuckled. "Mother's milk, to be sure, would ye like one?" He was about to turn to the glasses on the silver tray next to the half-empty bottle, when she flapped her hand at him. "Doona fash yourself, man. O'Dee's warmin' the teapot as we speak." Looking at Angus, she shook her head and chuckled. "Connor is about to give thanks to the participants, and some of the guests are looking like they are getting' ready to leave."

"Right!" said Douglas as he and Angus simultaneously put down their glasses and stood.

Douglas threaded his arm through Marie's and escorted her down the stairs. "Come now, Angus MacDonald, while I walk yer woman ootside. Let's go and offer our own thanks and congratulations."

Connor stood with Tessa at her side, while Andrew balanced on a trestle table with a sausage between two bits of bread clamped was between his teeth. Ethan crawled on his hands and knees under the table, stalking the black cat. Connor picked up a knife and tapped the side of her glass of soda. At the sound, the hum of conversation settled to silence.

"If you would all please raise your glasses, I would like to propose a toast." She held up her glass, to the sea of smiling faces. "To the Glen Rowan dressage school; a place where good riders and horses, learn to become champions."

All present raised their glasses. "To the Glen Rowan!"

Douglas bowed to Marie, picked up her hand, and kissed it before he stepped forward and stood beside Connor.

"A toast!" His normally booming voice was even louder, thanks to the bolster of the whiskey. "To Connor MacDonald, the finest dressage master we could ever have been blessed with. Withoot her, there would be no Glen Rowan school." He turned to face Connor. "We thank ye and salute ye, Connor. Slainte!"

The McVeys and the MacDonalds stood on the driveway as the spectators cars began to pull away and head for home. It was only when the last of the participants stood, yawned, and waved goodnight that the stress of the last week, began to ease.

Connor smiled when Angus wrapped her in a bear hug. "Ye did it, lass! I knew ye'd be able to make a decent school for the ol' bugger. It was a verra good display today. Yer mam and I couldna be more proud of ye. I know tomorrow, when the competitors leave for home, they and their mounts will leave here more verra much skilled than when they arrived."

She smiled up at him. "I'm really relieved it went well. Douglas and the Glen Rowan School are on their way now. It'll be up to them to maintain the standards and to be selective in who they accept into the school."

Hope painted his face. "Does that mean ye are thinkin' aboot comin' home?"

She patted his arm. "You know, Da, I think it does. Not just yet, though. When Douglas has found a new dressage master then I… er…we will come home. As a long-term strategy, I'm planning on speaking to Douglas about continuing with Tessa's training so that she can eventually step into the role of dressage master. But that means at least another seven years of instruction before she'll be ready. In the meantime, I could run their schools and be her mentor, but we won't necessarily have to live here."

Angus frowned. "Ye said 'we,' lass... Does that mean…?"

She looked down at the ground as the black cat wove itself in and out of her legs. She picked her up, and stroked her ebony fur. Andrew glared at the cat and pulled Ethan out of scratching range.

"Yes, Da. I am hoping and praying with everything I've got, that somehow Craig and James—"

"The wee lad?" He placed a hand on her shoulder.

Her long ponytail bobbed. "Da, I don't pretend to understand this. But I have seen and heard things that confirm the Gods truly can manipulate life and death. I'll do whatever it takes to get my husband and son back. Whatever it takes! Then, to hell with the Gods and their interfering, self benefitting ways."

Heavy rain pummelled the roof. Tessa lay on her bed, hands clasped behind her head. The noise of the deluge negated any possibility of sleep. The excitement of the musical ride and the applause of the crowd echoed in her brain. Her stomach gurgled as though she had swallowed a bucket of worms. She huffed, pulled back the covers of her messy bed, threw her legs over the edge of the mattress, and stood. She rummaged for her boots and pulled them on. Fumbling around in the dark, she found her dressing gown, pulled it on over her pyjamas, and knotted the tasselled cord at her waist.

At the door of her bedroom, she turned the knob slowly, then pulled the door open and stuck her head out into the hallway. Satisfied all was quiet, she stepped forward and quietly closed the door. Carefully, she started down the stairs, stepping over the fourth step from the bottom; it always squeaked.

At the front door of the house, she reached over to the "brolly stand," as O'Dee called it, and grasped the handle of her grand-da's black golf umbrella — not that he played golf; he just liked big umbrellas. Out on the porch, she closed the door behind her, unfurled the giant umbrella, and stepped out on the soggy grass. Water ran in a torrent down the driveway as she sloshed her way over to the horses.

Inside the barn, she shook off the water droplets, then folded down the umbrella, leaning it against a bale of hay just inside the door. Horses occupied every stall in the barn, this being the last night the participants' mounts would spend at Glen Rowan. Several animals stuck their heads over their stall gates. Tessa smiled as the smell of hay and horses filled her nose. Those comforting smells always made her feel safe, like coming home.

"Child, it is late. Are you well?"

She walked over to Rudiobus and ran her fingers up and down his white face, then kissed him on the muzzle. "I'm great! I couldn't sleep. I'm just so excited about everything." She kissed his muzzle again. "Thank you. You were fantastic today." She leaned over and chucked her fingers under Hades' chin. "You too, Hades. You were both amazing."

Hades flicked his head and whickered, swishing his wavy long mane.

"I can't wait for the next school. Connor is —"

Muffled voices came from outside the closed barn doors. Tessa jumped at the sound, then fumbled as she undid the latch on Rudiobus' stall, stepped inside and relatched the gate. Like a stone, she dropped and lay flat against the straw in the darkness.

"Where is he?"

Tessa recognised Rachael's voice; anger spiked as she remembered how the woman always hung off her da like a big, redheaded monkey. Then she recalled the stupid look on his face whenever the monkey was around. She wriggled on her belly toward a knot in the door of the stall. Carefully, she rose up on her knees and put her eye, level with the hole in the wood.

They side by side. Yellow torchlight shone from her da's hand. "Over in the corner, the end stall". The weak light of the torch beam suddenly shone on the gate to Rudiobus' enclosure. Tessa crouched as low as she could, but kept looking through the knot as she held her breath. Her heart beat so loudly, she was sure her da would hear it.

"That white bastard sickens my stomach every time I see him. He's nothing but a reminder of everything that I've lost. I hate him. I'll always hate him."

"You're kidding, right? I'm sure you know how much that horse is worth." Rachael put her hands on Ewan's shoulders, reached up and slid her arms around his neck. "Oh, what I wouldn't give to own a horse like that. He's beyond gorgeous. I'd be unbeatable in competitions."

As he moved closer to the stall, his voice sounded funny — thick or something. "What would you give to own him?"

A low growl of a female purr preceded a kiss on his lips. "Anything. There is nothing I wouldn't give to own a horse like him."

Panicked, Tessa gasped as she continued to peek into the gloom. Ewan and Rachael stood about three feet away. Inching forward, Tessa squinted, as Rachael, with her arms wrapped around her his neck, sucked his earlobe into her mouth. It made a popping sound when she released it. Tessa gagged.

Ewan brought his lips to Rachael's; the force of his kiss pushed her back against the door of Rudiobus' stall. The wooden panel rattled against Tessa's head. When they broke apart, he held Rachael's face between his hands. "You want him? He's yours."

"Ohhhhh I wish," she moaned with her lips against his.

Ewan stood back then grasped her by both forearms. "No, I mean it. You want him? He's yours. You'd actually be doing me a big favour. I want him gone."

Rachael made a noise like a sad chuckle. "Unfortunately, horse stealing is still a hanging offense here in Australia, believe it or not; although there haven't been any hangings in the last hundred years, but you never know your luck. And, as I have no skills as a bank robber…"

Ewan blew out a breath. "Rachael. The horse is legally mine to do with as I see fit. If I shoot him then that is my right. If I elect to give him away, then it is also my right to do so."

Rachael's voice changed from breathy to hopeful. "What about Tessa? She rode very well today. God, it's hard to believe she is only thirteen. In a few more years, under Connor's — "

He snorted. "Well, there's the other reason to get rid of this horse once and for all. With any luck she'll pack up and leave, too."

Rachael frowned. "Ewan, as instructors of dressage go, Connor MacDonald is world class."

He clicked his tongue. "Well, shit. Another one caught in her spell."

"Hardly." she frowned. "I'm just saying, it was a very smart move, employing her as your dressage master. Competitors can wait years to get onto one of her waiting lists. Some never make it."

Sarcasm dripped from his words. "Oh, yes, she's quite the happy accident."

"Ewan, are you all right? You seem upset. But just so you know, I most definitely will be applying to attend the next school here at Glen Rowan."

He gathered her up in his arms and nuzzled her neck. "Is *she* and the dressage school the only reason you want to come back here?"

"One of the reasons," she purred as she threaded her arms around his neck and kissed him, then ran her tongue around his lips.

Tessa gagged again and mouthed. *Oh, gross!*

After the kiss, Rachael turned and leaned against the door to Rudiobus' stall. The stallion stood at the back of the enclosure, shrouded in gloom, his massive bulk, a giant shadow silhouetted by the torchlight. "God almighty, you are magnificent."

Ewan stepped forward and put his hands around her waist then ground his pelvis against her bottom. "Not as beautiful as you, my firebrand. You want him? He's yours. My only condition is that you have him out of here by daylight; before anyone notices he's gone. You've got a double float, so load him with your horse and the best of luck to you. Although, if you do decide to take him, I suspect you won't be welcome here for the dressage clinics in the future."

A look of incredulity spread across her face. "You're serious about this, aren't you?

"I've never been more serious about anything in my life."

She turned and rubbed her face between the space between his shoulder and his neck. "Mmm, I get the horse and you get... Now take me to bed and let me give you my barter payment to seal the deal."

Ewan turned her round and led her toward the doors of the barn. The torchlight flicked across the unnoticed, wet, black umbrella that leaned against the bale of hay. He grabbed the cheeks of her bottom with both hands then kissed her, before, hand-in-hand they walked out into the rain.

Tessa collapsed onto the straw and lay very still. Her hand, clapped over her mouth prevented the escape of any sound until her da and the Orang-utan had left the barn and closed the door. Vomit rose in her throat, as the memory of him kissing that woman exploded in her mind. The sense of betrayal of her mother was sickening.

Rudiobus walked toward her as she stood and brushed straw from her clothes. "Child, I am sorry. It is your sire's will that we are to be parted." Tossing his head, he pawed the floor. "This is not what your mama wanted. The Gods will be displeased."

Fear pinched Tessa's gut at the thought of losing him. She threw her arms around his neck. A loud sob escaped her throat. "No! They won't be displeased because she's not going to have you!" she sobbed. "You were my mam's horse, and now you're mine. I don't care what da said. You're mine!"

Water overflowed the gutters in a constant drone. She slid the latch and opened the stall door, then reached around to the hook on the sidewall for a bridle. In her outstretched hand, she gently pressed the bit between Rudiobus' teeth, then fastened the cheek strap. "Besides, she can't take you if you're not here, can she?"

Rudiobus pulled back. "Have a care child, this will be trouble for you. Your father despises me. I understand his hatred."

She walked him over to the double doors and pushed them open. Rain overflowed the flooded gutters. "I don't care what da said. It was wrong to promise you to *her*. Mam loved you. She would never have allowed anyone else to have you." Tessa rested her forehead on his. "And I love you." She gathered up the reins in her right hand. "Come on. By the time da finds us, it'll be too late. The Orang-utan can't take you if you aren't here, can she?" Tessa grabbed a handful of mane and swung up onto his back. "Let's go."

Chapter Eighteen

DOUGLAS HUFFED AS HE GRABBED HIS PILLOW AND pounded it with his fist; the same thing he'd already done ten times since coming to bed. No matter what he did, he just couldn't get comfortable. The rain poured and showed no sign of letting up. He gave a prayer of thanks that he, Tessa, and the boys had moved the horses up from the lower paddock; which reminded him, he'd better talk to Connor aboot making sales arrangements for those horses. Thoughts of the success of the school once again flooded his mind, but sleep just would not come.

He turned over on the mattress and pulled the blankets up over his shoulder when muffled voices came through the wall of the room next door—Ewan's bedroom. Douglas lifted his head and cocked it to the side, just as a high-pitched, guttural, female shriek of passion, filled the house. "Oh, for Christ's sake!" He threw the pillow at the wall, pulled back the blankets, and got out of bed.

After finding his dressing gown and slippers, he opened his bedroom door, stepped out into the dark hallway, and walked silently toward the lounge room. He didn't bother turning on any lights, letting the darkness of the night and the sound of the rain engulf him.

"Ye canna sleep either?" O'Dee's voice rang out from the darkness.

"Jesus Christ, woman, I didna realize anyone was aboot."

The chair squeaked when she shifted her weight. "I swear, I couldna bear it a moment longer, laying there, listenin' to the sounds of a whorehoose. What does Ewan think he's doing? I just pray to the sainted Mother that the bairns didna hear any of their carryin' on! Wicked lustful beasts; and us with visitors in the hoose as well!"

Douglas got up from his chair and walked across the room. He caught his foot on the corner of the single seater lounge chair. "Shit! I'd turn on a light, except it would have the whole hoose awake, and that's somethin' I'm just not ready to face tonight. Can ye imagine the stories the lassies of this clinic are goin' to take home with them? We'll be the talk of the dressage industry." He bent down and rubbed his slippered foot, then walked over to the window. The rain was so heavy it looked like pea-soup fog outside.

O'Dee *tsked* him. "Nay. I doona think so." She groaned when she stood and walked over to stand beside him. "Remember what they say, old man, any publicity is good publicity. Ye mark my words Douglas, the lassies will spread tales of Ewan's virility oop hill and down dale. They'll be linin' oop in droves for yer clinics, of this I am verra certain."

He grunted and pursed his lips as he pulled back the curtain and looked out the window. "Well, I just hope you're right. Jesus Christ!" A deafening roar came from outside. The house vibrated and shuddered underfoot. "That'll be the header flood waters they predicted on the news this evenin'. Thank Christ we moved those horses. Imagine tryin' to bring them oop to higher ground in this bloody weather."

He leaned forward and squinted through the window. When he breathed, a ring of condensation formed on the glass. "What the hell?"

O'Dee shouldered her way in front of him and gasped. "What in the name of all that is holy is that?" She rubbed the glass with the hem of her dressing gown, then squinted into the darkness. "Oh, Jesus! It's Tessa on our Beth's horse. Douglas! She's headed for the river! Why in hell would she be out in this weather?"

He grabbed her by the hand and pulled her toward the staircase. "Come now, afore she gets too far. We'll need to go and get Ewan."

O'Dee planted her feet and shook her head. "Ye can go and get him if ye want, old man. There is nothin' in this life that would entice me to enter a room with that naked, moanin' Jezebel."

Douglas nodded. "Aye, perhaps ye're right. Come on, then. Let's get after the lass and find oot what the hell she thinks she's doin'."

At the front door, he reached down to the umbrella stand. "Now that's verra strange. I know I put my umbrella back in here tonight after I checked the horses, afore I went to bed."

O'Dee huffed. "Douglas, have ye no' seen how hard 'tis rainin' ootside? I doona think there is an umbrella in creation that will keep that much water off us. Come now." She reached down to the shoe rack and handed him a pair of wellington boots before she pulled on her own. "Let's get after the child afore we lose her in the dark."

When she opened the door, rain gusted in and puddled on the floorboards. Outside, by the time they reached the second step, they were both drenched to the skin. Heads down, they walked toward the back paddock. Their knee-high rubber boots sloshed on the flooded ground. Glen Rowan looked like a large lake.Douglas reached over and grasped her hand. "Stay close, woman. I canna see a bloody thing. The last thing we need, is to get separated."

O'Dee swiped at the stream of water that dripped from her nose as she curled her fingers around his. She looked over at him fondly and nodded as she squeezed his fingers in reassurance.

The rain was relentless.

Tessa was cold to the bone. Rudiobus slipped and slid on the mud. She gasped when she suddenly listed to one side, forcing her to lurch forward and grab two handfuls of mane, struggling to stay on his back. Breathing hard, he regained his footing. The moonless night was eerily dark, the rain, a constant spray of tiny, stinging darts. At the gate of the low-lying back paddock, she leaned down and pulled the chain from around the latch. Rudiobus shouldered the metal barrier open, then walked forward.Her teeth chattered. "Brr, Rudiobus, it's really cold. Let's go down to the far side of the paddock and stand under the trees. It'll be warmer if we can get out of the wind." She steered him, slipping and sliding, step by perilous step, toward the silhouette of trees. As she slid off his back, she clutched his mane until her feet anchored solidly under her. The warmth of his body was incongruously hot against her frigid face.

The river at the bottom of the property roared, as the water thundered downstream, engulfing the banks and flooding the pasture. The trees offered little protection from the wind and the rain. She urged Rudiobus closer, coming to a standstill under the canopy of a giant grey gum. The fertile ground was a mire. Leaning toward him, her boots slipped in the mud. She flung out her hands to gain steady purchase. Grasping the reins, she righted herself as thoughts of her mam flooded her brain.

Macha sat on her chair positioned below the queen in the Throne Room of the Tuatha Dé Danann, hidden deep within the Faery. Danu, the race's queen, held counsel with her three appointed Goddesses, the members of her court. As monarch, forever connected to those who had gone before her, she shared the memories and voices of the Old Mothers, who, for eternity, had guided their matriarchal line. It was their advice today that Danu sought.

Suddenly Macha jolted then pretended to cough to cover her actions. A vision of Tessa and Rudiobus flashed in her brain. She stood abruptly, keeping her face deliberately blank as she requested to be excused. Danu waved her hand in dismissal. Once out from under the watchful gaze of the queen and the other two Goddesses, Macha returned to her quarters, sat on her bed, and closed her eyes. Images of pelting rain and gusting wind made it hard to see anything. She probed harder.

Huddled against the trunk of a tree, Rudiobus stood in front of Tessa, shielding her from the wind.

Tessa! Tessa! What are you doing? Why are you and – ?

The instant she connected with Tessa's mind, the encounter between Ewan and Rachael erupted, then played in an endless loop. Hand in the air, she arced her palm and broke the connection.

Panic consumed her. "Gwydrion!"

She watched in horror when he tossed his head and stumbled, slipping sideways as the ground beneath him began to shift. Frantic, she withdrew and broke the connection between them. Her breasts heaved with anxiety. As she sought calm, she bowed her head. A moment of indecision made her pause before she mind-spoke. "Connor!"

Connor slept, deep and dreamless, when Macha's voice screamed in her head. Her eyes flew open as she sat upright. "Beth...er...Macha?"

"Go to the bottom paddock! Go now! Tessa's down there with Rudiobus. Bring them home. It is too dangerous for them to be out on a night like tonight."

"Tessa's out in this?"

As she turned on the light, Craig frowned from where he stood in the corner, pressed against the barrier. The look on his face confirmed he had heard the mind-spoken conversation. Using her mind connection, Macha replayed the scene in the barn between Ewan and Rachael.

Craig beat his fist against the barrier.

Macha's voice trembled. "I know, Death Walker...you have never trusted him."

Connor flicked on the switch of the bed lamp; soft light filled the room. "Christ! I knew Ewan hated Rudiobus, but I never dreamed he'd do anything to hurt Tessa like this." She threw back the linens. "You know what Tessa's doing, don't you? She's trying to hide him. Jesus, she must be terrified. She regards that horse as her connection to you."

Macha was miserable. "My husband is much changed since I passed. But, never mind that now."

Connor pulled on her jeans and a long-sleeved shirt before pulling on her boots. She paused only long enough to grab her oilskin coat from the hook near the front door and shrug it over her shoulders. Practiced fingers buttoned the coat from collar to mid-calf. When she opened the front door, wind gusted and rain saturated the exposed fabric of her jeans below the hem of the coat. She pulled the door closed behind her as she and Craig, in his incorporeal state, headed toward the bottom paddock.

Macha's voice rang in her mind. The urgency in her voice was unmistakeable. "Bring her home, Connor! Keep her safe! The future awaits her!"

"Tessa! Where are you?" Connor squinted as stinging rain beat into her eyes. Her feet and socks were soaked and her toes were numb. "Tessa!"

No other sounds could be heard over the constant drone of the rain, when, suddenly, a flash of lightning revealed a white shape at the bottom fence line. "Oh, thank God!" She pointed to the trees. "Craig, there's Rudiobus! Tessa won't be far away. Come on!" They were about twenty feet from where the stallion stood when the knot in her gut, began to loosen. Suddenly, her head shot up to a bone shuddering reverberation, like a jet taking off. From upstream, the second wave of floodwaters roared to life as the deluge thundered, taking with it, everything in its path. The swirling waters gnashed into the already flooded banks, eroding hundreds of tons of soil and grass. At the sudden shift in the landscape, the bottom fence groaned, then fell over, disappearing into the maelstrom.

Connor screamed as Tessa slid downward on the shifting soil. Tessa's shrieks of terror were smothered under the thunderous noise of the deluge. Rudiobus pulled backward, straining the leather of the reins, his God-Voice boomed over the din. "Hang on, child! Hang on! Do. Not. Let. Go!"

Horrified, Connor rushed forward just as Tessa sprawled face first onto the shifting muddy bank. Rudiobus roared and pulled backward as she kept her grip on the reins. Craig lunged toward her. The barrier contained him just feet from where Tessa lay. He screamed in frustration.

The ground gave way as Tessa slid toward the swollen river. She screamed, clutching the reins, until, finally, the force of gravity separated her fingers from the leather straps. Arms windmilling, she grabbed frantically, trying to get hold of something—anything.

Rudiobus screamed as he lunged forward. His front legs went out from underneath him as he lost his footing and crashed onto his side, sliding downward, careening toward Tessa and the flooded river.

Connor stood rooted to the spot, screaming in horror. "No! No! No! No! No!"

Before his weight could crush her, Rudiobus's God Voice boomed, *"Guardian! I summon thee."*

A golden flash lit up the storm clouds like a fireworks display. Macha appeared high above the river just as Tessa, engulfed by the dark, swirling torrent, disappeared beneath the surface.

Tessa screamed when the icy water engulfed her like a frozen shroud. She sucked in a big breath just as the water covered her head, flooding her mouth and nose. Arms flaying, she choked and spluttered as she struggled, sinking farther under the torrent. Her heart pounded like war drums in her ears.

Lub-dub, lub-dub, lub-dub, lub-dub, lub-dub, lub-dub, lub-dub, lub-dub…

Her lungs burned as her body, craved oxygen. Light-headed and dizzy, she was like a rag doll, punched and pushed by the undercurrents. Disoriented, she no longer knew which way it was to the surface. A thought popped into her oxygen-deprived brain: a television screen lit up where scuba divers followed a trail of bubbles to the surface. She opened her eyes. Claustrophobic, suffocating blackness greeted her.

Her long dressing gown tangled round her legs. The rhythm of her pounding heartbeat responded to her brain, which, compromised by the lack of oxygen, embraced the primal instinct to survive. Her heartbeat slowed in response to the call, as *brain-save* mode, redirected blood to her vital organs.

Lub.......dub....... lub.......dub....... lub.......dub....... lub.......dub.......

She was so tired.

A warm euphoria settled over her, so peaceful, so calming. She opened her eyes. Hundreds of pretty, coloured, pinpoint lights flashed off and on. She was weightless, as if floating on a cloud. Her mam's face popped into her mind. Flashes of memories were like a kaleidoscope. Lovely in the sunshine, mam sat in the paddock with Rudiobus cropping grass, while she read her book...

The smell of leather polish.

Mam cleaned tack out in the paddock while she talked to Rudiobus, they never ran out of things to talk about.

The tiny silver lights that danced among the other neon flashes were the same colour as the silverware mam took over to the paddock, where sat and polished and rubbed with a blue cloth. O'Dee had been very upset, something about... calling the police to notify them of the pilferin' of the family silver.

Grandda laughing made her happy.

An image of Andrew, newly born, filled her mind. He was a noisy boy with flailing arms and legs. She remembered her mam's laughter as he suckled at her breast. He made snuffling noises like grandda's Australian collie pups when they fed from their mam.

Laughter... Her mam's laughter... Gladness and peace filled her mind.

A blanket of calm soothed her.

No longer was she in the heart of a thunderous vortex. Buoyant and free, she was floating. Her heart still felt funny, but better now... It was quieter.

Lub..........dub.......... lub..........dub.......... lub..........dub...

An image of her father filled her mind. His strong arms around her waist and threw her into the air while they splashed and played in the river last summer. The sound of his laughter made her happy.

So sleepy now.So very, very, tired.

Time to...

Lub......................dub...................... lub......................dub...

Horrified, all Macha could do, was watch the scene unfolding before her. The Life Thread of Guardian she shared with Tessa, pulled taut, and, slowly, fibre by fibre the strands began to fray.

Connor stood on the bank, barely managing to stay upright as Craig screamed to her, signalling to her to move away from the river. Repeatedly, his fingers clawed at the barrier of his ghostly prison.

Macha jolted as if woken from a trance then thrust her arms above her head. Three bolts of white-hot energy exploded from her fingertips. Seconds later, shrouded in a golden glow, three celestial figures appeared, suspended in the sky.

Craig suddenly faded to invisibility.

"Why have you summoned us, Guardian?" Danu hovered with her arms crossed. The Goddesses Brighid and Morrigan floated beside her.

Screaming over the wind and rain, Macha pointed into the river. "My queen, I beg you. her. My daughter! The Successor! Save her!"

Looking down to the roiling water below, Danu's shoulders sagged as she shook her head. "The child is dying, Macha. Assume your place with us. There is nothing to be done. The Successor is lost to us."

Rudiobus burst from the shadows of the trees, screaming. "No! She cannot die! Restore my God form. Let me save her."

Morrigan, the old woman suspended to the right of the queen, cloaked in black raven feathers, flew backward, wings unfurled. Glaring at Rudiobus, she shrieked, eyes wide as she snarled, her God Voice boomed. "YOU!" A bolt of white energy exploded against the tree next to him, snapping it in half. "How dare you appear before me!" She threw her arms wide. A twenty-foot radius beneath her stilled to a tranquil millpond, as thousands of gallons of displaced water surged up the already flooded banks.

The surface of the water, like backlit glass, revealed Tessa, thirty feet down, slumped in the mud.

Rudiobus reared and struck out with his hooves. "Restore me! She is the daughter of the Guardian Protector. Would you forsake her? Will you doom the Successor to death, here on mortal Earth? She is of the Tuatha Dé Danann! Restore me, damn you!"

The Goddess on the right of the queen placed a hand on her arm. "Majesty! Save the child. She is our Successor! We have waited so very long. This has been a time of great comfort to us, to have both a Guardian and a Successor in the same lifetime." She pulled back the hood of her robe. The torrential rain didn't touch her. "You have the power to save her. To not do so, is to create imbalance and disturb creation. The Tuatha Dé Danann will suffer for such a crime."

Danu nodded. "You are right, Brighid."

Morrigan flew to the queen's side and blasted Brighid backward. The smooth surface of the river became a boiling maelstrom once more. "No! It is too late! The child is lost. Let me collect her soul and we can be gone."

Danu paused, then she nodded. All three Goddesses began to vaporise.

Macha screamed. "No! My queen, you cannot forsake my daughter."

Danu hovered; heartbreak lined her face. "Guardian, It is too late. This is a terrible moment for the Tuatha Dé Danann."

"No! Save her! It is not too late!"

"Guardian—"

"Save her, or I will never reveal my *son* to you."

Danu shrieked as she rematerialized. "You lie! There has never been a boy child born to a Guardian."

The black feathers of the raven shook with rage as Morrigan screeched. "Don't listen to her! She will say whatever it takes, to rob me of the soul of the Successor! Come, my queen. We must return to the Faery."

Macha arced her outstretched arm above her head. A replay of Andrew's birth flickered against the dark, stormy sky. Danu's eyes bulged as the scene unfolded then she raised her hand, summoned a bolt of golden light and hurled it towards Rudiobus.

It hit him square in the chest. He staggered backward as his four legs became two and his equine body took human form, just before he dived into the water.

Morrigan hovered, aghast. "My queen! The Guardian lies! What have you done? The Fates have played their hand! You must not interfere!"

Danu chopped her right hand, downward. "Silence! We do not know if what the Guardian has spoken is truth, or lie."

The queen flourished her hand and began to dematerialise. Her voice carried above the noise of the storm. "I hear your plea, Guardian. Until we meet again, all will return to how it was before this night. We will now take our leave. There is much to be considered."

An angry screech cut the air as the black raven feathers of Morrigan unfurled and she followed the other two Goddess of the Tuatha Dé Danann into the ether.

Connor slid on the mud and screamed as she crashed to the ground. Macha reappeared at her side, slid down beside her, then wrapped her in her arms. They gripped each other, staring at the river.

Suddenly, Rudiobus' God form head broke the surface. He rose upward until all seven feet of him, with long white hair, broad chest, and thick, muscled legs, hovered clear of the choppy water. He levitated with Tessa in his arms, uncaring of his nakedness. She lay like a white-faced, broken doll.

The Guardian held out her arms, took Tessa's limp body, and pressed her tightly against her chest.

Craig suddenly rematerialized.

He glared at Macha. "You knew! You knew that Death, the *thing* that tortured me in the Place of Shadows, is a Goddess of the Tuatha Dé Danann!"

She hung her head. "Yes."

Chapter Nineteen

ESSA'S SKIN WAS COLD – CADAVER COLD.

Connor screamed to Craig and Macha over the howling wind. "Not now! Macha! Turn Tessa onto her side!"

Macha lowered her to the ground, propped her daughter's still form against her knees, and angled her body forward. She gripped her chin and turned her head just as Tessa began coughing and retching, then vomited water.

A voice called out in the darkness. "Tessa, where are ye, lass?"

Hurrying down the paddock toward the river, Douglas and O'Dee came into view.

Craig watched helplessly. Connor sat forward as Macha gathered Tessa into her arms. "I must go. Please Connor, care for her." Shimmering light engulfed Rudiobus as he reassumed his horse form. Nodding to Connor, Macha faded from view.

Douglas helped O'Dee down the badly eroded bank. Connor sat in the mud with Tessa in her arms, her face pressed to the top of her head. Rudiobus stood beside them, his white coat smeared with dark sludge. When Douglas came within thirty feet of Connor with Tessa in her arms, a cry of anguish left his lips.

"Oh, sweet Jesus, no!" He tripped and fell, then slid the last twenty feet down the bank on his backside. O'Dee lurched and slid on the mud, swaying dangerously until she righted herself. Her voice was a constant drone of rapidly spoken words. "Our Father who art in Heaven, hallowed be Thy name…"

Douglas struggled to get to his feet. Rudiobus walked over to him and nudged him. Grabbing a handful of long white mane, he pulled himself upright. "My thanks to ye." When he turned toward Connor, his footing gave way. Rudiobus pulled backward, dragging Douglas with him to where Connor sat sobbing. Tessa was slumped in her arms.

The old man went down on one knee. "Tell me, she isna dead."

Connor shook her head. "No… No, Douglas, she isn't dead. Rudiobus saved her. If it weren't for him…"

"Oh, sweet Bride." O'Dee made the last few steps before sitting down on her bottom next to Connor. "Oh, my sweet child." She placed her hand on Tessa's head. "Blessed be to the Virgin Mother and God Almighty, for sparing her."

Tessa moaned, and then slipped back into unconsciousness.

"Christ and the saints," Douglas roared as water dripped off his nose. "What could have possessed the lass to come oot in this weather?"

Connor nodded to the white stallion. "She was just trying to protect *him*."

Douglas frowned. "What do ye mean, protect him? I *know* for a fact he was in his stall afore I went to bed."

Grimacing, she nodded. "Well…let's just say Tessa overheard something which convinced her that she needed to hide him."

"What? Why in the name of Jesus would she need to hide the horse? Ye are no' makin' any sense."

Connor grunted as she handed Tessa to Douglas and awkwardly got to her feet. Her legs zinged with pins and needles as the circulation returned to her lower limbs. "Let's get her home. It's freezing out here. We all need to get out of this bloody rai—"

Douglas held Tessa with one arm then snaked out his other hand and grabbed Connor's wrist. "We're no' goin' anywhere until ye tell me what the hell happened tonight to make Tessa come oot in this godforsaken rain."

Connor closed her eyes and sighed. "Oh Douglas, please, just let it be. Let's just get Tessa home. Then we can see to her and see how badly she's hurt."

His voice boomed the loudest she had ever heard. "TELL! ME! WHAT! THE! BLOODY! HELL! HAPPENED!—NOW!"

Connor spun on the mud and faced him. "Tessa was in the barn with Rudiobus when Ewan and Rachael showed up. She hid and overheard their conversation. It seems Ewan promised Rudiobus to Rachael. The plan was to load him with her horse and take him away from Glen Rowan before dawn this morning."

A flash of lightning illuminated Douglas's pale face. He walked over to Rudiobus then nodded his head in a gesture of respect and gratitude. His lips were set in a firm line as he spoke though gritted teeth. "Connor, get astride this horse. I canna believe after all the fuss aboot this animal and he was the one to save her life. I'll lift Tessa oop to ye, then ye can both ride back to the hoose. Christ knows, by now, the road oot of Glen Rowan will be well and truly underwater. We've no way to get her to the hospital."

Awkward in her movements, Connor's cold knees locked when she tried to walk. Her extremities and joints complained and groaned with every movement. "We'll manage. Between O'Dee and me, we'll keep a close eye on her. Fever and pneumonia will be the main concerns, that, and all the water in her lungs. We'll take shifts and make the best of it. Come on."

She hobbled over to the white stallion, then grabbed a handful of mane and lunged in an uncharacteristically, untidy mount, onto his back. She held out her arms to Douglas then manoeuvred Tessa in front of her, holding her close to her chest. Craig floated alongside; worry creased his brow. She leaned forward and pressed her knees against Rudiobus' belly, urging him forward. She turned to Douglas, who was helping O'Dee to her feet. "Walk alongside Rudiobus. Both of you hold onto his mane until we're clear of this paddock. After that, at least the ground will be relatively stable."

Douglas grunted as he held out his hand to O'Dee and helped her over to the white stallion. He placed her hand on top of the horse's neck and fisted a hank of mane into her palm. "Just walk with him, old woman. Trust him to keep ye on yer feet."

O'Dee nodded, unable to speak, stared at Tessa cradled in Connor's arms.

After they passed through the gate at the top of the paddock, Douglas lashed the chain around the post. Connor waited for him to catch up before she moved on. As they approached the stairs to the front porch of the big house, Douglas grabbed hold of the reins and pulled the horse to a halt. Arms outstretched, Connor leaned over and transferred Tessa into his embrace, then slid from Rudiobus' back, to the ground. The reins hung loose in her hand as she walked over to the barn, threw open the doors, and escorted him inside. She ran her hands up and down his muddy neck. "Thank you, Oh God, Rudiobus, thank you. Without you, she would've drowned."

"She is the child of the Guardian Protector, Daughter of the Highlands. I would give my life for her. She is destined for great things. Besides, it would have killed Macha had Tessa not survived."

Connor swung open the door to his stall and led him in, undid the bridle then hung it on the hook outside the stall. When she walked toward where the rugs were stacked on a shelf, he spoke. "Go now. See to the child."

Douglas walked up the front stairs with Tessa in his arms then kicked the door open with such force, the hinges ripped away from their moorings. The house shook when the solid oak panel hit the floor.

The sound of feet hitting the floor came from upstairs just before Angus and Marie appeared at the top of the staircase. The light from their bedroom threw a soft glow onto the front entryway. Marie gasped and started down the stairs. Angus caught up to her and grasped her hand. Connor and O'Dee stood, soaked to the skin, with Douglas standing just inside the threshold with Tessa in his arms. Marie's voice rasped. "Jesus, man, what has happened? Has there been an accident?"

Ewan appeared at the top of the stairs, dressed in unbuttoned jeans, naked from the waist up. Rachael came out of his bedroom wrapped in a crinkled sheet. His eyes bulged when Douglas shifted Tessa higher up onto his chest with one hand supporting her back. Ewan bolted down the stairs two at a time and took Tessa into his arms. Frantic hands swept the lank, wet hair from her pale face. "What's happened? Da! Tell me, what in the name of Jesus has happened?"

Douglas stood stone faced as he leaned forward and glared. "Just tell me one thing."

Ewan looked at him, confusion lined his face.

"Did ye tell yer bloody redheaded bed mate that she could have the lass's horse? Did ye tell her she could take him from Glen Rowan?"

"Yes, I did! What of it! You know how I feel about that horse." Menacingly, he leaned in toward Douglas. "I should never have listened to you! *Every day*, I regret listening to you! When Beth died, I should followed my instincts and shot the bastard!"

Douglas' voice became a gravelly baritone. "What ye didn't know, you bloody fool, was that Tessa was in the barn when ye and, " he flicked a cursory glance to Rachael at the head of the stairs, "*she* were doin' whatever it was ye were doin'. Damn you! The bairn heard ye give her horse away. I just pray to the good Lord that ye were no' engaging in yer pleasures when that conversation took place. Though I shouldn't be surprised. God knows ye kept the whole hoose awake tonight with the sounds of yer rutting."

Rachael giggled from the top of the stairs.

Ewan's stare was incredulous as he looked up at her, then back to his father. "Tessa was in the barn? That's why she took the horse out on a night like tonight? To hide him, from me?"

Douglas looked at him as if he were an imbecile. Suddenly, Tessa moaned and thrashed in his arms.

"No! No! Rudiobus! Rudiobus!"

Connor walked forward and put both of her palms on either side of her face. "Tessa. He's safe. He's over in the barn. I will see to..."

"No!" she screamed. "Take him away, don't leave him! She'll take him! Connor, please! Don't let her take him!"

"Shh, now, lass." Douglas smiled down at her. "No one's goin' to take yer horse, anywhere. Ye have my word." He looked up at Ewan, scowling, his lips a thin white line. "If it weren't for Rudiobus, we would've lost Tessa tonight. The river would have taken her, just like it's taken most of the bottom paddock. Do ye hear me, man? I doona pretend to understand the why of it, but that horse ye are so bloody keen to be rid of, saved yer daughter's life."

Angus cleared his throat as he grabbed Marie's hand, then turned and headed for the gap where the front door used to hang. He spoke over his shoulder. "We'll go see to the horse, man."

Douglas grunted his thanks.

A swishing noise came from the head of the landing as Rachael turned and walked back to Ewan's bedroom and closed the door. Within two minutes, she was back, fully dressed, descending the stairs. She walked over to Ewan. "Oh, dear, I think I've been given my cue to leave. Pity about the horse. You cannot imagine the things I would have let you do in exchange for him. I almost got away with it, too." She put a hand to his face and shrugged. "Never mind, I would have fucked you anyway. Well, I guess you were right about one thing, Ewan. I won't be coming to next year's school."

O'Dee sucked in a sharp breath.

Ewan stared at Rachael, shaking his head like an automaton.

She tossed her red hair and straightened her shoulders. "Never mind. All is not lost. I'll see next year at Nimerlin, Connor."

Connor looked up at her. "I don't think so. Save yourself the stamp and the paper, Rachael. I would've sent you packing on day one, if you'd been at my school at home. No, there'll never be a place for you at the next or any other school at Nimerlin. You don't have the discipline. Nor do you seem to have any insight into how your slutty behaviour demeans not only yourself, but everyone else involved with the school."

Rachael looked at her, disbelieving, then shrugged her shoulders. She hunched down into the neck of her blouse. With her head down and shoulders slumped, she walked into the rain, headed in the direction of the participants' quarters. No one in the room said a word. The constant hammering of rain on the roof emphasized the silence. Ewan turned to carry Tessa upstairs to her bedroom when O'Dee stood at the bottom of the stairs, blocking his way. "Leave the lass down here with me. I'll no' be able to sleep. I'll sit and watch her 'til the mornin' comes."

Ewan shook his head. "No, O'Dee, thanks. Tessa's my responsibility. I'll sit up and watch her."

Tessa opened her eyes and blinked slowly. "Da, if I go to sleep, will Rudiobus still be here when I wake up?"

Tears tracked down his cheeks as he pressed her face to his chest. "Oh, Tessa. What have I done? I promise you, he'll be here. Your mam's life was taken, but he gave yours back. I was wrong, Tessa. He's earned his place, here. He can stay."

She looked at him suspiciously. "Honest to God?"

He nodded.

"No Da! Say it! Say, honest to God. You can't lie, if you say, honest to God."

He kissed the top of her head and murmured, "Honest to God."

Connor walked down the stairs. Her damp clothes were well and truly soaked again before she reached the path to the barn. She pulled the door open and stepped inside, her da and mam sat on a couple of bales of hay. Rudiobus stood in his stall; a padded winter rug draped his huge body. Hades stuck his head over the gate of his stall and whickered. She walked over to him, put her forehead against his, and sighed.

Angus stood up, then walked over to her and closed his arms around her. "Christ almighty, it sounds like it was a verra near thing."

She turned in his arms and burst into tears. "Oh, Da! I thought she was dead!"

"Dear God." His big hand held her head to his chest as he whispered. "Is Craig here, lass?"

Nodding, she held him tighter.

He kissed the top of her head. "Good." He turned and looked at Marie with a question on his face. "Perhaps we should all find our beds?"

Marie stood up and brushed the back of her robe with her hand. "How can ye speak of sleep, man? My insides are still shaking. I swear, when I saw Douglas carryin' the wee lass in his arms…" She burst into loud, wracking sobs. "It was just like the night Yokami brought Connor home to us after…after…"

Angus held her in his arms. "Aye, lass, I know. I doona pretend to ken what really happened here tonight, but the Gods were merciful and spared the bairn's life, and for that we should all be verra grateful."

Marie sniffed, then spoke as if reminiscing. "Aye. The Gods giveth and the Gods taketh away."

A series of wracking coughs woke Tessa with a start. She gagged and wheezed; a rasping sound like wire dragged across metal then flopped back down on the lounge as the light of dawn filled the room.

"Da…grandda…oh, O'Dee, I'm so sorry."

Ewan got up and sat beside her on the lounge. "No, sweetheart, you've nothing to apologise for. I'm the one who owes everyone an apology. I forgot how like your mam you really are. Like her, you did what needed to be done, to protect the horse, and for that I'm very sorry." He picked up her hand and stared at it. "You and Andrew are everything to me." He started to cry in loud, gut-wrenching sobs. "I couldn't bear it if I'd lost you."

"Da…"

Douglas stood up slowly. The blanket that covered his legs slid to the floor. "Tessa, no harm will come to yer horse. You have my vow, and now yer da has given his. Rudiobus has earned his place here at Glen Rowan, and I defy any man to tell me, differently."

A loud creak came from the staircase just before Angus spoke." Hallo to the hoose."

Douglas called out from the lounge room. "We're in here, man." When Marie came round the corner, a big smile broke out on Douglas's face. "And mornin' to ye, Marie."

"And to yerself, Douglas."

When O'Dee went to stand up, Marie flapped her hands. "Stay there and doona trouble yourself. I'll manage well enough."

When Marie left the room, Douglas inclined his head to Angus. "I offer my apologies to ye and yer good wife. I'm truly sorry ye had to witness the events of last night."

Angus dragged his hand across his face. "Ye doona need to offer us any apology, man. What happens in a man's hoose is his own business. But I thank ye all the same for yer consideration."

Douglas nodded in gratitude, then shifted his gaze to his son, who sat white-faced and red-eyed, staring at Tessa. Her had was gripped tight in his.

She couldn't sleep.

As much as Connor tried, the events of last night kept going round and round in her brain, in an endless, torturous loop. Craig sat at his place by the sidewall with his back to her.

"Craig?"

When he turned toward her, his moss green, mirrored eyes, flashed with anger.

She frowned as she tucked a long strand of hair behind her ear. "What?"

He huffed, then blew out an exasperated breath. *"I was useless to her. Just like I'm useless to you."*

"What?" Fear crept into her voice. "What're you talking about?"

He stood and leaned his forehead against the barrier. *"I couldn't help her! I couldn't help her, Connor! Don't you see? I'm nothing more than an incorporeal memory. I'm of no use to anyone."*

She threw back the blankets and walked naked to where he was confined. "Where's this coming from?"

"Connor! You were there. I couldn't do anything to help Tessa. If not for Rudiobus — "

"Now hang on! Back up the bus for one damn minute. The only reason Tessa is alive is because the Queen of the Tuatha Dé Danann allowed Rudiobus to assume his God self. He couldn't have helped her, much less saved her, in his horse form." She frowned. For the first time, the true magnitude of his misery registered to her. "What's this really about?"

He bit the side of his lip before he mouthed the words. *"Do you ever wonder if our dreams are just that — dreams? That one day, I'll be able to walk alongside you again as your husband and that we'll be able to hold our son? Do you ever wonder if we're just kidding ourselves and that what we have now, is all that we'll ever have?"*

She snagged a blanket and a pillow and lay down beside his prison. He lay down and faced her, fingers pressed to the barrier.

"Do you, Connor?" His mouth moved slowly. *"Do you ever think the most you and I are going to have, is what we have now?"*

She shook her head. Her long blonde hair cascaded along the polished boards. "No. I will never accept that. I truly believe you, James and I are going to be a family again."

His voice was thick with tears as he whispered, *"I release you, Connor. I release you from your vow of marriage to me. If I can't be a real husband to you, I release you to go and find happiness with another man."*

She lifted her head from where she leaned on her elbow, pulled back her fist, and punched him hard in the belly. Her fist went straight through him. "Don't you dare ever say that to me again! Do you hear me! There's no one else for me, Craig. It's always been you. If what you and I have now, is what we end up with, then so be it! I'm grateful for every moment I have with you, be it in life or in death. I don't want anyone else! *You* are the only man for me."

A single tear tracked down his face. *"You'd give up the chance to have another baby? Another family?"*

The tracks of her tears matched his. *"You* are my husband and my family. James is our son. There will be no other men or their babies for me. You two are it."

He sat up suddenly; anxiety pulsated from him. *"Promise me you're saying this because you mean it. Not because you feel sorry for me or obliged to be with me in whatever bloody state this is".*

Hand over her heart, she gave him a tired smile. "I vow this to you, on the love I have for my da and my mam. You are my most beloved husband, my heart, my only true love. I will have you any way I can, be you changed or not. I love you. I will always love you."

Chapter Twenty

ANU RESTED IN THE THRONE ROOM DEEP WITHIN the Kingdom of the Tuatha Dé Danann. She clasped an ancient tome on her lap, almost hidden within the folds of her white robes. Brighid sat quietly beside two empty chairs while the Goddess raven, paced in front of them.

The air crackled with tension.

The queen glowered. "Morrigan, don't you dare to lecture me on what *we* know to be true."

Danu held up the heavy book with both hands. "*We*, the oldest surviving Goddesses of the Tuatha Dé Danann, are the only ones who know the true prophesy of our race. Our very name has been known throughout time as *The Children of the Goddesses*."

Morrigan ruffled her black raven feathers and snarled. "Lies, I tell you. The Guardian lied to save her child."

Danu frowned. "Death Harbinger, you know the tales of the Old Mothers. Are you willing to take the risk? Have you forgotten the words, or shall I remind you?"

The raven screeched. "Of course I have not forgotten the words. I, like you, cut my teeth on them." Suddenly, her demeanour completely changed. Theatrically, she mock-cleared her throat several times, then cupped her fingers, elbows wide, as if giving a recital.

"A passage from the Book of Prophesy of the Tuatha Dé Danann:

Child of the monarch, lost to the night.

Dark lifetimes of struggle, the way lost, to fight.

Pain and suffering, the price of arrogance paid.

From pure of heart, comes the rise of the king

Unseen by the Tuatha Dé Danann and its black wings.

"Whimsical, to say the least." Morrigan *tsked*. "The Gods are ever dramatic with their cryptic messages. Goddess knows, there are *soooo* many prophesies from the past. How do we know that these teachings are not just the fanciful words of some long-forgotten bard, who tried to please the Old Mothers with a dramatic song about prophesy and war and what could never be?"

Brighid sat up higher in her chair. "Majesty. What you did was right. Even if the Guardian," she glared at Morrigan, "did lie about there being a boy child and somehow *created* that vision we saw, it was still the right thing to save the life of the child—any child, be she Successor or not."

Still pacing, Morrigan flung her arms wide. Two black, shiny feathers floated to the marble floor. "Oh, yes—" She stopped and rolled her eyes. "The Tuatha Dé Danann's voice of reason. Our goddess of balance." She stuck two fingers in her mouth and pretended to gag. "Just because you are credited as being the midwife to Mary at the birthing of Jesus, does not give you the right to have a say in the life of *ev-ver-ry* child in the universe." Her voice became deliberately shrill, almost painful to hear. "You seem to have missed the point! *I* the collector of the souls of the newly dead am robbed of the soul of that child! I am telling you, my queen, a great mistake has been made this night."

"Listen not, Majesty." Brighid glared at Morrigan. "For centuries, we have lived our lives with the secret known only to us, a secret, deliberately kept from the rest of our race, for all eternity."

Cawing and bending back and forth like a crow picking the eyes out of a newborn lamb, Morrigan laughed. "You are deceived! There is no boy child! Just like there is no prophesy! Macha duped you both."

Danu stepped down from her throne to stand in front of Morrigan. "Take care, Dark One. Remember to whom it is that you speak." Danu raised her hand over the cloak of black feathers, and Morrigan crumpled to her knees. "Tell me this. Tonight, at the river of the mortals, what would you have done, Soul Stealer? Would you have sacrificed the Successor, without a second thought? Leaving us without a future Guardian to lead our army and protect our race?"

Black feathers shimmered as the raven shrugged her bony shoulders. "Well... It wouldn't be the first time the Tuatha Dé Danann has been left without a Guardian."

Danu's eyes widened just before she blasted the old woman with a whip of golden power. Morrigan hit the wall with such force the wooden structure shuddered on impact. A painting of an Ancient Mother crashed to the floor. "You would *dare* to speak to me of that time? Have you lived so long, that your brain is addled? Have you forgotten that terrible, dark age when the Tuatha Dé Danann was unprotected? You know the first part of this prophesy has already been proven when my Guardian daughter Dagda was taken by the dark Gods and was forever lost to us."

Holding out her hand, Danu helped Morrigan to her feet, then drew back her arm and slapped the Dark One hard across the face. "How dare you! The Tuatha Dé Danann was vulnerable, because we became complacent and ignored the teachings of the Old Mothers. My daughter most surely died because we, ignored the prophesy. That was a mistake, I will not repeat."

Danu gathered up her robe, turned, and stepped up to her huge throne of solid gold and gleaming marble. Her fingers smoothed the folds of her robe over her knees. Closing her eyes, she gripped the arms of the chair. When she looked up, she held her head high as her God Voice filled the hall. "Summon the Guardian!"

Macha stood beside her warriors, all astride their warhorses. The animals whinnied and stamped their hooves, nervous, sensing her anxiety. When the ceiling-high door to the Throne Room opened, she stood at attention and straightened her shoulders. A uniformed guard walked toward her, beat the left side of her chest three times, and bowed her head.

"Guardian, you are summoned." Not waiting for a reply, the sentry turned and walked back through the open doors.

Macha nodded once then followed the retreating guard. In the Throne Room, Brighid and Morrigan sat side-by-side. All conversation stopped when the doors opened and Macha entered the room. She stopped and bowed in deference to the queen and her counsel.

Danu spoke, her face an unreadable mask. "You are one of us, Guardian; chosen to protect the Tuatha Dé Danann. Yet it would seem that you may have deceived us. We celebrated when you bore a girl child, as was expected of you. This very night, you told us — nay, showed us — that you may have a very kept a very important secret. Explain yourself."

Macha looked at the queen. "There is nothing to explain."

"Treachery!" Morrigan turned to face the queen and Brighid. "See! It is just as I told you! Lies! All lies, to save her child! She's not even gracious enough, to be repentant for lying to us. You, Danu, may be queen, but you have the heart of a woman. Let us end this now as it should have ended." Black feathers rustled as she raised both hands above her head and replayed the scene where Tessa went under the water.

Danu and Brighid stood abruptly and screamed. "No!"

"You will not weave the Threads of Time!" Danu sent a bolt sizzling from her fingertips. Morrigan screeched as blood spurt from her nose and dripped down onto her ebony feathers. As the raven reached up, she painted her bony fingers with the red flow, then raised them to her mouth and licked them, one by one. An eerie screech filled the room as she launched into the air, elbows raised, fingers clawed in readiness to strike. "Danu," she snarled, "there is a price to be paid for spilling the blood of a Goddess."

"There is an even greater price for insulting your monarch. Now, stand down, before I really hurt you. As queen, I am bound by the laws and traditions of the Tuatha Dé Danann."

Morrigan returned to her chair, wings crossed in front of her.

Danu turned to face Macha. "I felt great power at the mortal river. There were God Threads that were not of our race. I will you ask you one last time, Guardian. What is your explanation?"

Macha's chin dropped to her chest. "My queen, I mean you no disrespect. You are right. Events have happened that involve other Gods. The Successor, my daughter Tessa—"

Brighid, who had yet to speak, raised a hand. "Perhaps we are all pawns in the Guardian's quest to save her child. But, isn't that what any mother would do—whatever it takes to spare the life of her offspring? When the Guardian spoke of her son—"

Slow clapping sounds bounced off the walls, like repeated strikes of metal against stone. Morrigan stepped down from her throne. She shot Brigid a look of contempt. "Well, thank the Goddess. Even *you* are finally seeing the truth." She stared at the queen. "You have been deceived, Danu. The Guardian is one of the very few who know of the prophesy. When she spoke of a son, it was an act of desperation." Unfurling her wings, she screeched. "She gambled that you would spare the girl child because of the prophesy. A gamble, which paid off, because that is exactly what you did. You have interfered with the Fates, and now the child who should be dead, lives."

The queen rose and the room suddenly darkened. Her face was unreadable. "You wish the Successor, dead? Remember, it is she, and she alone, who will protect us in the future. Do not forget your place, Goddess of Death and Souls. A Successor is born to the Tuatha Dé Danann but once, every three centuries." Turning to Macha, she glared, as a high-pitched hum filled the room. "Do you lie to me, Guardian? Have you invited your own death, to spare the Successor?"

Head held high, Macha stared at the queen. "I know the tenure of a Guardian, Majesty. I have served you, for a very long time. Everything I have told you is truth, although there are things, of which, you are not yet, aware."

Danu's eyes narrowed. "I hold the balance of your life, in my hand. It is only because you *have* served me well, for so many centuries, that I am prepared to be tolerant. Tell me of the boy, if, indeed, he does exist, and of the God Threads, I sensed at the mortal river. The truth is the only thing that will save you from a certain death, at my hand, Guardian."

"Rudiobus…"

Morrigan jumped to her feet. "Rudiobus, my arse! Gwydrion is his cursed name. May he suffer in life and in death." She spat on the floor. "He is exiled for eternity for his crimes against the Celtic Gods."

Danu screamed, "Twist the facts as you will, Banshee. Exile in his shifter form was the price he paid for *your* treachery! You were the one who broke with Tuatha Dé Danann tradition, when you mated with the king of the Celtic Gods. I have long questioned your motivation for deliberately conceiving with a God, not a mortal; as we have all done, since time began. Perhaps you thought to bear a son and create a liaison between the Celts and the Tuatha Dé Danann. No doubt, with you, standing beside the king, as his queen. Danu paused, then looked at Morrigan. "However, that plan did not quite work out quite as you had hoped, did it? You were a fool to trust the Gods. The price of that trust, was deceit. Your lover, the king, was never going to allow you to keep your child after she grew into a woman. He bragged that it was *your* blade he used to take your daughter's life and the life of your grandson!"

Black feathers vibrated with hatred. "Gwydrion violated her!"

Danu grasped the old Goddess's wrist. "He loved her. You did the king's bidding and promised her to the Druids; even though you knew, she had promised herself to him. The king seduced you into believing it was a powerful alliance with the Tuatha Dé Danann that he desired. It wasn't. The Druids are very powerful. What he wanted more than anything, was for them, to be allied with the Celts. But when he discovered Ayiel was with Gwydrion's child, she was of no further use to him…and neither were you."

Morrigan fell to her knees on the floor, keening the song of a woman with a broken heart while screeching the desolate caw of the raven.

The silence of the Throne Room, gave way to the agony of despair.

After several minutes, Macha took a step forward. "My queen, Rudiobus has been a loyal and faithful servant to me. Likewise, he has cared for my daughter. It only was because of your mercy that he was able to save Tessa from drowning. The Death Walker —"

Morrigan flew into the air and hurled a ball of black energy at Macha. "What Death Walker?"

A white-hot bolt of lightning flew from Danu's hand and exploding the black bolt in mid-air, then arced toward Brighid and Morrigan. "Leave us!"

The Goddesses stood stunned, hesitated, then dematerialised.

When Danu turned to Macha, she glared with the eyes of a raptor. "Last chance, Guardian. Tell me about this boy child and to whom do the Gods Threads I sensed, belong?."

Macha swallowed and nodded her head. Before she could speak, Danu gestured for her to sit on the throne closest to her. Macha hesitated.

Danu leaned forward. "Guardian, please, sit. Be warned, speak only truths, for I am not known for my patience."

"My queen, may I speak?"

Danu waved her hand in consent.

"I will speak plainly, for there is no more time, for deception or omission. As one of your Goddesses, of course I know of the prophesy. I also know of the ways of the Tuatha Dé Danann. If it had become known that I had given birth to a son, you would have taken him, in fulfilment of the second part of the prophesy of our race. I did not create him, for that purpose."

As Danu gripped the sides of her gold-and-marble throne, she leaned forward. "Are you telling me, that you made a conscious choice to birth a male child instead of a female? That you deliberately violated your matriarchal role and the spell of the first and only king?"

Macha held her head high and met the queen's eyes glare. "I did. I knew after the birth of my daughter, that sometime in the future, I would be required to surrender my mortal life and family and return to my role of Guardian of the Tuatha Dé Danann. I also know that one day, when the time comes, my daughter Tessa will receive the summons, to begin her training as my Successor. That would have left my husband, a man whom I love most dearly, completely alone. He would not have been able to stand the loss of his child, after he had already lost me. He is filled with bitterness and grief."

The queen leaned back in her chair, lips pursed, then abruptly sat forward. "I have seen countless Guardians mate with mortal males to produce girl children who have gone on to be their Successors. To date, I am not aware of the level of difficulty that you have described in any other of their joinings."

Macha whispered. "That is because to me, he was not just a source of the seed to produce a girl child. I love him. I truly love him. Every day of separation from him, hurts as much as when I first left my mortal self and returned to the Tuatha Dé Danann."

Hands clasped in her lap, Danu sat up straight. "I now see that this has been a difficult time for you, more difficult than I ever imagined. I also am hearing that you felt you could not come to me with— Wait!" She jolted in her chair. "The prophesy says, *From pure of heart, comes the rise of the king, Unseen by the Tuatha Dé Danann and its black wings.*" Fear crossed her face. "I don't know what that means, but if a boy child has been born, then, there is great change coming for us!"

Macha nodded as her eyes filled with tears. "That is why I hid his birth from you. Like me, he has the Sight for all creatures and beasts."

The queen stood and laced her fingers in front of her. "What you are saying is impossible." She took a step forward, then hissed. "You dare to lie to me? We are the People of the Sídhe. Our ancestors are all of the pure of blood of *Ériu. The prophesy states, He who will rule the Tuatha Dé Danann, will be of pure blood and shall create new order, whereby the matriarchal lineage will be led into balance and generations of the future, will no longer share mortal blood.*"

Standing before the queen, Macha hung her head and closed her eyes. "I know."

"Guardian, did you not hear what I said? Your child— If such a child exists, cannot be the one for which our race has waited millennia. The prophesised one must be of pure blood. *You* are a child of Ireland; however, your child was sired by a mortal."

"Yes, his father is indeed mortal, sired from a line of Scots that goes back hundreds of years to when the boundaries of Ireland and Scotland were blurred. Back then, the collective races were Celts. My husband, my love, is of pure Celtic blood."

Danu frowned and returned to her throne. Her knuckles blanched under her grip of the golden armrests. "If what you say is true, the Tuatha Dé Danann will claim the boy child and take him to the Faery."

Macha held her head high, hands by her sides. "To do that, you will first have to find him."

The queen started, disbelieving. "Have you lost your mind? We have powers beyond imagination."

Macha nodded. "Powers, which I also possess, and more. At the instant of his conception, I cloaked him in magic and shielded him from you and the rest of the Tuatha Dé Danann. As the first and only son of a Guardian, he is not part of the matriarchal line, so you have no connection with him."

Anger painted a flush on the queen's face. "You are a fool to underestimate me, Guardian. I can detect any child, born with the blood of the Tuatha Dé Danann."

Macha cocked her head in challenge. "Then find him!"

Danu stood, raised her arm above her head, and arced her hand across the space in front of her. "Show me the girl child of the Guardian."

An image appeared of Tessa lying on the lounge, covered in a blanket, with a dark-haired man sitting next to her. The queen made derisive sound of satisfaction as she again raised her hand and arced it above her head. "Show me the boy child of the Guardian."

The visual field in front of the queen remained unchanged. No images came into focus. No shimmer of colour or movement came into view. She dropped her hand and blew out a breath of frustration. "You know our ways, Guardian. You invite a death sentence for your actions. *I* should have known the minute *you* knew the child was a male. Never has there been a child that has been able to be shielded from me."

Macha's lips tightened. "And yet, you cannot perceive him. The magicks I wove are wards to shield him from detection, by the Tuatha Dé Danann."

The queen scoffed. "What are you saying? That neither the Goddesses of the Tuatha Dé Danann, nor I, will ever be able to detect the child of the prophesy?"

Macha nodded. "I have ensured my son will be safe from the Goddesses and their treachery, to allow him to grow up and know a mortal life with his father."

The queen went pale and slumped onto her throne. "What are your terms?"

Chapter Twenty-One

THE SILENCE WAS OPPRESSIVE IN THE THRONE ROOM. Danu looked at the individual portraits of the old Mothers, as if seeking inspiration. She struggled to control her temper before she returned her attention to the Guardian. "You deliberately chose to deceive me? I could end your life in the time it takes for your answer to cross your lips."

Macha stood rigid with her hands clasped in front of her. "I know, but I make no apology. It would be most unwise to kill me. Without me, you will have no means of training the Successor *and* you will never find my son. Remember the final sentence of the prophesy my lady; *Ignore him and war will destroy all.*"

The queen stood suddenly. Her robes fluttered around her legs. "I would never risk the boy child of a Guardian. I have lived all of my long life, in wait for such an event."

Macha straightened her shoulders, then walked over and stood beside her. "Like all words of the Gods, our prophesy, is open to interpretation. The word 'ignore' could mean to pay no attention to him. It could also mean that by virtue of the magicks I wove, you can do nothing else but ignore him, since you cannot sense him."

The nails of Danu's fingers bit into both palms as she clenched her hands at her sides. "Show him to me! I don't believe you! In my three thousand years of rule, nothing has ever been able to be shielded from me, magicks or not."

"My queen, there is more at stake here than the existence of my son, your king. There are others who have played important roles in his life, and in the lives of the Successor."

The queen flapped her hand and *tsked* in annoyance. "Yes, yes, Rudiobus. I saw him!"

Macha's lips tightened. "Rudiobus has offered me his fealty. I would bargain with you for restoration to his God status and immortality."

"Do you really think Balor, the king of the Celts, will allow him to resume his place? Unlikely. I am very fond of Rudiobus; he is loyal and strong, and now, thanks to you," sarcasm dripped from her voice, "very experienced in the ways of the Tuatha Dé Danann. In my vast lifetime, I have experienced firsthand, the shortcomings of the Gods and their retaliatory ways. I will not petition his case to Balor. To do so is to risk revenge against the Tuatha Dé Danann. I am sorry, Guardian. His days as a God and an immortal are over."

Macha pulled back her shoulders and jutted her chin. "My lady, you owe him a boon for saving—"

Golden bolts of power ricocheted off the walls. "What? How dare you!"

"I dare because, while you are queen, you do not know all there is to know. I beg you, please hold council with Rudiobus and the Daughter of the Highlands."

"What do the Ancient Horsemen have to do with this? Are these the Gods I sensed at the river?"

"Yes and no. Connor is a child of dual destiny to both the Ancient Horsemen and the Samurai."

Danu paused. "Powerful, then. I sense you speak the truth of this."

Macha knelt before the queen. "I tell you nothing but truths. Please, Majesty—"

"Enough! There is much for me to consider. Leave me. I will summon you when I have given due thought to your words."

Macha bowed her head. "My queen." She turned and walked out of the Throne Room.

Danu paced the floors of her chamber. Inside her head, the voices of the Old Mothers shrieked in fear. *"Hear the petitions of the Guardian. If she speaks the truth about the boy, you must not fail in bringing our prophesy to fruition. If you do not succeed, the Tuatha Dé Danann will fall into the hands of our enemies; Gods who would overthrow a race that has lost its future king."*

The hem of Danu's robes swished against the stone floor, making little sweeping noises with every step she took. She tapped her fist against the side her mouth as she walked. "What to do? What to do?" Confusion and fear roiled in her mind. Everything she had ever believed to be true was now in question. *The Guardian has admitted she has borne a son. Did she lie? Were the Goddesses right? Did she concoct this most unlikely story to save the daughter destined to be her Successor? Has the Guardian played me for a fool? Does this boy child actually exist? Surely not! I would have known the moment he was born, if he is indeed of Tuatha Dé Danann blood. Wouldn't I?*

She recalled the instant the Successor was born, even before the babe took her first breath. *Is it possible? Has the Guardian done as she has declared; cloaked a boy child in magicks so that he will remain forever hidden? Does the Guardian have the power to summon such a spell?* Her instincts told her the Guardian had lied. But, what if she was wrong? Could she take the risk of losing the boy child of the prophesy; if, indeed, this was part of their prophesy?

Dizziness overcame her as her mind became a kaleidoscope of colours and figures. The collective inherited memories handed down from the Old Mothers again flooded her brain.

Loud, excited voices shrieked over each other, as they all tried to speak at once.

Danu? Our queen! Is he come? The boy child of the prophesy! Is he come?'

She put her hands over her ears as the cacophony of voices became unbearable. "I don't know! I don't know!" Her feet stopped suddenly as the Guardian's words rang in her head. *"He has the Sight for all creatures and beasts."* The voice of one of the Old Mothers screamed above the rest. "Beware, Daughter, do nothing rash. By your own admission, you are not sure if the Guardian has spoken true. However, *if* the Guardian is strong enough to shield the child of prophesy from you, then she is indeed capable of great magic.

Beware, our queen. You do not want to be remembered as the ruler who robbed our race of its king."

Danu closed her eyes as a tremor of fear quaked through her. She drew in a deep breath and squared her shoulders.

She was queen.

She knew what she had to do.

Tessa slept for most of the day; at times waking, thrashing her arms and legs, calling out to Rudiobus. Each time she spoke his name, it was like the slash of a blade across Ewan's heart. The guilt he carried was fit to choke him. When Tessa threw back the blankets and put her feet on the floor, he stood up suddenly. "No, Tessa, you have to rest."

"Da! I've got to go and see Connor and Rudiobus. He'll be worried about me."

"No, Tessa, please... Just stay here for now."

Douglas walked into the room. "A-ha, ye are awake. What's goin' on?"

"Rudiobus. I need to see him! Please, Grandda. He'll be fretting."

Douglas looked over at Ewan and winced. "What say ye? Can I take her to the barn? I was just over there. Connor and I have dispatched the last of the participants and their horses. When I left, she was getting Hades tacked to go oot for a ride.

Tessa sat bolt upright. "Connor's going riding?"

Ewan stood between her and Douglas. "No, Tessa! No riding today! Jesus! At least let the sun set once on the day that you nearly drowned, before you get back on a horse again."

Her lips started to quiver. "Da, you promised..."

The five-o'clock shadow on his chin rasped as he rubbed his fingers back and forth on his face. "Yes, so I did."

Her face lit up like a beacon. "Grandda, will you take me over to the barn? I promise I won't ride," she looked at her father, "today. I just need to see Rudiobus. Please, Grandda, please. I promise I won't be any trouble."

Ewan looked at Douglas. After about thirty seconds, he gave one sharp nod.

Douglas took her by the hand. "Fair enough. But remember your promise, Tessa. Have a care, I doona think there is a person in this hoose who could survive another episode like last night."

Connor brushed Hades glossy black coat and mane until he shone like obsidian. When the barn door opened, she wiped sweat from her forehead with the back of her hand. "Douglas? Back so soon? Did you forget someth—? Tessa! Well, I didn't expect to see you today. It's good to see you up and about again, though."

Rudiobus stuck his head over his stall door and whickered. Tessa dropped Douglas' hand, ran across the hay-strewn floor, and threw open the stall door. She stood with her forehead against his. "Thank you, I know what you did. I know it was you that saved me. I saw you. You were beautiful then, too."

He whickered to her. "All is as it should be, Successor of the Guardian. The balance of all things would have been shattered, had you not survived."

A warm breeze caressed her face, and a sense of peace filled her senses.

She turned when Douglas spoke. "Are ye sure she's be all right here with ye, Connor? I can take her back to the hoose if you wish to go for a ride. I doona want to disturb ye any more than we already have."

Connor looked up with the brush still in her hand. "No worries, Douglas. Leave Tessa here. I'm sure she'll recover much more quickly if she and Rudiobus spend time together."

He went to turn, then stopped. "Well, if ye are sure, then."

"I'm sure, Douglas. Tell Ewan we'll be back over to the house in a while, after I finish up with Hades. I'll take him for a ride this afternoon."

When the door to the barn closed, Tessa walked back across the floor. "Thanks, Connor. I saw you on the riverbank. I'm so sorry I made you worry, but I had to do something. I couldn't—"

Connor smiled at her and shrugged. "Listen to me, I get it, Tessa. I'd do whatever it took if someone was going to try to take Hades from me or hurt him. I know how much you love Rudiobus. I completely understand why you did, what you did."

Tessa suddenly smiled and turned slightly to her left. "I'm sorry, Craig. I know you were with Connor last night, too." Tears tracked down her cheeks. "I'm sorry I made everyone so worried."

Craig held up the thumb on his right hand and mouthed. *"Just glad you're safe."*

An audible gasp filled the air as a warm breeze whipped around the barn. Then the air was still once more.

That night, as sleep shrouded everyone in the big house, Connor slept, dreamed and smiled. There! In the distance, the tall, blond-haired man with mirrored, moss green eyes walked toward her, silhouetted by the setting sun on the horizon. She ran to him with outstretched arms. He swept her off her feet as they laughed and cried together. A smile painted her lips when the feeling of being completely and utterly loved, flooded her body. Suddenly, the dream shattered, replaced by a creeping sense of being watched. Her eyes flew wide open as she scanned the darkness. The roar of the God Killer and the vibration of the Sword of War forced her to sit upright. The thunder of her heartbeat drowned out all other sounds.

Craig stood alert. *"What?"*

"I don't know. I was dreaming, then I felt something here in the room with us." She reached over to the bedside table, fumbling for the switch. When the room lit up with a soft glow, she threw back the covers.

"Come to me!" The God Killer landed in her hand, as she stood naked beside the bed.

She padded around the cottage, looking at the newly repaired kitchen window before checking the latch. Then she rattled the front door to check that the lock was in place. Shaking her head, she turned to Craig and shrugged her shoulders. "Guess I am just a bit jumpy after last night."

Hand extended, she bowed her head as she willed the God Killer to return to its scabbard. The hilt stayed lodged in her hand.

Frowning, she repeated her call for the sword to stand down. Again, it remained gripped in her fist. Just as she was about to speak, a warm breeze flew around the cottage. The sword in her hand began to hum as the Sword of War began to vibrate. The next instant, the warm air dissipated, replaced by the cool bite of early morning, when, suddenly, the God Killer returned to its resting place in the scabbard and the Sword of War became still under her tattoo. Connor climbed back into bed and turned off the light. Unable to sleep, she lay awake, listening for any clue as to what it was, the swords had sensed.

The clash of blades rang out at dawn as Connor and Tessa worked and practiced their katas. Craig sat to one side of the chalked area. After about twenty minutes, Tessa lowered the MacRobertson sword she gripped with both hands. Frowning, she looked at Connor, then whipped her head left then right. "You don't think there's any more wild dogs around, do you?"

Connor's brows knotted. "Dogs? No, I don't think so. Why? Did you hear something?"

Tessa frowned and bit her bottom lip. "Not exactly... It's just that last night, when I was almost asleep, I felt like someone was watching me. I thought it was Da or Grandda, but it wasn't. I got up and had a look around, but I couldn't see anything. I even looked under the bed. But..."

"But what, Tessa?"

"It felt like...like now, like someone is watching me."

Connor's blood ran cold as she looked over to Craig. "I don't think there's anything to worry about. You're probably still anxious from the stress of thinking you were going to lose Rudiobus. God Almighty Tessa, after what you have been through it is completely reasonable that you would be a bit rattled."

Tessa scuffed the toe of her right boot back and forth on the grass as she adjusted her grip on the handle of the sword. "You know Connor, at first I was really scared. Then, when I saw a man coming toward me, I knew it was Rudiobus. That was when I realised, I wasn't going to die. But last night, and now... I feel something. I feel like someone has been watching us ever since we came outside to practice." She arced the sword into the air just as Connor raised the katana and deflected the blow.

"Oh, I see, smarty-pants. So that's how it's going to be, is it? Trying to distract me, huh? You're getting pretty good with your sword. I can see I'm going to have to be more on my guard. She paused for a moment and put her arm around Tessa's shoulders. "You know Craig and I are really proud of you, don't you?"

Tessa smiled and nodded then suddenly lowered the sword and stood with a look of complete surprise on her face.

Connor recognised the look and immediately and spread her feet in a stance ready for battle; the katana gripped tight in her outstretched hand. "Tessa?"

Warm air eddied around them.

Chapter Twenty-Two

ANU SAT ON HER GILDED THRONE. MORRIGAN, Brighid and Macha sat in counsel. She was aware Morrigan was speaking, but her mind was racing with turbulent thoughts; she didn't hear what the raven was saying.

"My queen?"

Danu continued to stare ahead, not blinking, as if in a trance.

"My queen?"

"Hmm? What?"

"As I was saying, the situation with the Guardian must be addressed. We cannot tolerate disobedience or deceit. She is obviously the worst kind of liar; fabricating fanciful tales to trick you into saving her *whelp*."

Brighid gasped.

Unconsciously, Danu's fingertips began to tap on the arm of her throne, as if to distract her from the sound of Morrigan's whining. "Whelp? You would refer to the Successor as the offspring of a dog? Do you forget the countless millennia that we have been protected by the blessed children of our Guardians?"

Snorting, Morrigan waved her hand in dismissal. "I forget nothing. But, then again, how long has it actually been, since we needed to be protected from anything?"

"You are a fool, Morrigan. Your arrogance has already cost you the life of your child and grandchild. Did you learn nothing?

As queen, it is my role to ensure each Guardian produces a girl child that—"

Picking at a nail with her index finger, Morrigan shook her black feathers and then looked up with a droll look on her face. "And we all know how that turned out."

"Danu's face flushed. You dare to criticize me?"

"I am just saying that you interfered and saved the girl whom the Fates had decided would die. I fail to see why you let the Guardian manipulate you. She lies. It is obvious. It was an act of desperation, nothing more, nothing less."

The queen leapt to her feet. Her voice deafening, as it boomed with power. "Stay your tongue, Morrigan! I will hear no more! Both of you, get out! Get out!"

Danu sat back down on her throne and massaged her temples with the pads of her fingers, sighed, then closed her eyes. "Guardian, I summon thee."

Macha paced the floor of her quarters as anxiety knotted her bowels. Her mouth was so dry she could barely swallow. Dread and a sense of powerlessness overwhelmed her. The stress of waiting for the queen to consider the fate of both of her children was torture. *Was it a mistake to have confessed Andrew's birth and to have shielded him with magicks? Will the queen let Tessa live or will she allow Morrigan to wind back the Threads of Time and allow her drown? No! Oh sweet Goddess, no!* That didn't even bear thinking about. As she walked passed her bed, she picked up a pillow and clutched it to her chest. *What can I do? How can I convince the queen that I have spoken the truth? How can I do right by those who have helped me and my children?*

The queen's voice filled her brain, in summon to the Throne Room. Hot bile rose in the back of her throat. Anxiety and fear thrummed through her veins as her knees shook. Her legs were as heavy as lead. She hurled the pillow against the wall, squared her shoulders, and pulled open the door of her quarters.

She stood outside the Throne Room, gathering her courage, when the doors suddenly flew open. The queen, on her throne, wore her formal white robes. "Enter, Guardian."

Macha bowed her head in deference and continued to stare at the floor, putting one foot in front of the other until she stood before Danu.

"Your daughter, Tessa, that is what you named her? I have seen her. She is a warrior." Danu paused uncomfortably, then cleared her throat and for just a moment, warmth coated her voice. "It is a long time since the Tuatha Dé Danann had a Guardian that is a swordswoman; and Tessa, most definitely is a swordswoman. I am certain she will be a great asset to us."

"You have decided to let her live?" Macha sagged.

The queen stood then paced the Throne Room. Her voice carried as if she still sat on her chair. "I have made no decisions. There is much yet, for which I do not have answers. I have sensed true power and greatness, and not just from the Successor. I cannot make any decisions until I know what it is, that I am dealing with." She turned and faced Macha. "But know this, Guardian, although you have always had my favour, if you have lied to me or misled me in any way—"

Frowning, Macha took a step forward. "My queen, what is it that you are suggesting?"

"For me to make a correct ruling concerning whether anyone lives or dies, I, unknown to any of my Counsel, will meet with those whom you believe offer support for your petition. After that time, I will cast judgement. I agree to this, on the condition that you reveal to me, the child whom you claim is your son—the child who may fulfil our prophesy."

Macha stood, pale faced and trembling. "I will not let you take him. His father—"

"Enough! Be warned, Guardian, do not press me any more than you already have. I must be certain of your truths before offering consideration of the events of the future. This night, you will arrange a meeting, attended by all involved. I *will* have answers. Oh, and Guardian, *if* things are not as you said them to be, I will instruct Morrigan to sift time and allow your daughter to meet her death. And you, Guardian Protector, at my hand, will be dead before the come of the sun."

Macha frowned. "You would risk the lives of the Tuatha Dé Danann by leaving them without a Guardian?"

Danu stood with her head high. "A Guardian who cannot be trusted, is not a true Guardian. As a race, we are at risk from a Protector who would lie and deceive for her own end. I am hoping it does not come to that. You know how I suffered when *my* daughter…"

Macha bowed her head. "I know of your pain, my lady, and for that I am truly sorry. No harm will come to the Tuatha Dé Danann, while I am Guardian. This I vow."

The queen relaxed imperceptibly. "That is all. I will meet with all of the players this night. If, by the stroke of the witching hour, you have not revealed the boy to me, I will enact the death sentence for you and your daughter."

Connor sat on the floor, cup in hand. The warmth of the hot brew was soothing.

Pointing at her, Craig grimaced. *"You okay? What do you think happened last night? It's not as if you imagined it. The swords sensed it, and they're never wrong."*

She took a sip, then cradled the cup between her hands. "It wasn't that I felt threatened, exactly. But I did feel…*something*, and so did Tessa. But the swords sure as hell reacted like there was definitely some kind of threat. I can't really expl—"

Macha appeared in the centre of the room, her white robes translucent in the soft light.

Hot tea sloshed over the rim of the cup. Connor jumped. "Jesus, Macha! I'll never get used to you popping up like that."

"Sorry, Connor. I did not mean to alarm you. Well met, Craig." She held up her hand "And before you say anything, I know," she nodded to him as if in apology, "we have to talk, and we will. It is just that…"

Connor stood and put the cup on the table. "It's the queen, isn't it? I feel your fear."

Macha nodded. "Yes. She insists I reveal Andrew to her tonight, at a meeting. She sensed God Threads down at the river, for which she demands explanation. Also, she knows about Tessa and her ability with the sword."

"A-ha!" Connor looked toward Craig, her index finger pointed in the air. "Well, that would be the mystery solved, then. It would seem the queen has been spying on us. No wonder Tessa and I felt as though we were being watched! We were!"

A tear slid down the Guardian's face. "Connor, the queen leaves me no choice. The Tuatha Dé Danann can bend and weave time. She can return Tessa to the depths of the river. No one, mortal or God, will be permitted to intervene. Tessa will die."

Connor stood ramrod straight and scowled. "The hell she will! What does the queen want?"

Profound sadness painted Macha's face. "That is not all. If Danu proves that I betrayed her, Tessa will not be the only one to die."

Connor walked over to Macha, surrounded her with her arms, and held her as she cried. "Well, we'll just see about that!"

Macha pulled back a little. Worry lined her face. "I am so sorry, Connor. I cannot lose my children. I just cannot."

Connor wrapped her arms around her again. "When are you to meet with her?"

"Not me, *we*."

"What? Who else is attending this meeting?

Macha's voice quavered as she spoke. "Tessa, Andrew, you —"

Connor jolted. "Me? Why, me?" The distress on the Guardian's face silenced her rapid-fire questions. She waved her hand. "Never mind. I guess there is only one way to find out what she has in mind. When's the meeting?"

"Tonight."

"What time?"

Macha started sobbing again. "Before the stroke of midnight."

Craig's face was grim, lined with worry. Macha sat quietly and listened as Connor paced back and forth. "Okay, so, the queen wants to meet Andrew and get answers about the God Threads she sensed. Rudiobus needs to be part of this audience, and seeing as how he's returned to his horse form," she flourished her hand in front of her, "we can hardly meet here. So it looks like it has to be the barn."

Craig nodded.

Still pacing back and forward, Connor talked as if thinking out loud. "We'll have to wait until everyone's asleep if the kids are to come to the meeting. Oh, God, Macha, what the hell are we going to do if Ewan or Douglas discover them missing from their beds?"

A hint of a smile teased her lips. "I can manage that. I will cast a sleeping spell that will keep them in slumber until the rise of the sun."

"*You can do that?*" Craig mouthed.

"Yes, I have magicks, remember."

Connor chuckled. "You know, my da always says the best place to hide anything, is in plain sight. Let's just play this by ear, okay and see how we go? I don't want to do anything that'll betray Douglas or Ewan's trust. If I can't wrangle something, then you can always work your magic." She looked up and grimaced. "Sorry, no offense intended."

One side of Macha's lip pulled up in a sad smile. "None taken, my friend, none taken. Unless I hear from you Connor, we will meet in the barn, at the eleventh hour. Please know, after the stroke of midnight, the queen will deny any negotiations."

Connor frowned. "How will I contact you if there's a problem?"

"Just call me and I will hear you." As Macha rose from her seat, she smoothed the front of her robes. "I must speak to Rudiobus of the expected visit of the queen."

Then she was gone.

Connor put her cutlery down on either side of her plate and looked across the table to Tessa. "I'm going to do some sword work after tea, if you want to, come over. I thought we'd wait until it cools down a bit, though."

Tessa looked to Ewan, who nodded his consent.

"Me, too?" Andrew smiled his toothy smile. "Me, have the Pod?"

Connor quirked an eyebrow at Ewan and mouthed, *iPod*.

He winked and looked at Andrew. "Every time I see you lately Andrew, your ears are plugged with that contraption. I shouldn't be at all surprised if you're stone deaf, by the time you turn seven. All right, you can go with Connor too." He looked over at her. "That's if you can manage these two *and* a couple of swords."

"Tessa's no problem at all, and, well, once Pod Man gets settled, we don't hear much out of him, do we, Tessa? Let's just see how we go". A chill passed over her as she uttered the same words for a second time, in as many hours. "If he crashes, I'll keep the kids at the cottage and bring them back over in the morning."

Tessa, with the MacRobertson sword balanced on her shoulder, walked beside Connor, who held Andrew's hand. In the cottage, Connor retrieved the katana from the scabbard on the bracket on the wall.

Andrew's eyes lit up. The silver iPod sat on the table in the middle of the kitchen.

Connor laughed. "Go on, then, go and get it."

He dropped her hand like a hot potato, climbed up onto a chair, and reached over until he had the player in his hands and held it up to her.

She held the machine and scrolled through his newly down-loaded playlist, then plugged the buds in his ears. He sang out loud, as they walked outside to the practice area.

Connor walked Andrew over to the sidelines and sat him on his bottom while he kept on singing. Craig sat next to him, grinning.

After an hour, covered with sweat, they lowered their blades and bowed to the four points of the universe, then to their swords. Andrew lay on his back, looking up at the stars. He had one ankle on the opposite knee, and his foot tapped in time to the tune he was murdering.

Connor walked over and knelt down on the grass next to him, then pulled out one of the ear buds. "Time to go, mister."

He sat up, looking startled. "No. I stay at your house."

Relief flooded her veins. She checked her watch; it was a little after nine-thirty. They walked back into the cottage. Andrew parked himself on the lounge and promptly fell asleep with the music still playing in his ears. Connor crossed to the linen cupboard, dragged out a white cotton blanket, then snuggled it around him. When he was in a deep sleep, she returned to the kitchen and poured two glasses of juice She sat one in front of Tessa, the other, in front of herself.

"Tessa, honey. There's something I want to talk to you about."

She looked up from her drink. "What? You haven't changed your mind, have you? I'm still allowed to stay over tonight, yeah?"

Connor nodded and flapped her hand. "Yeah, yeah, of course. You and Andrew are always welcome here, silly, you know that. No, it's something else. Remember when Rudiobus told you about your mam and the Tuatha Dé Danann, and because you're her daughter, you are her Successor?"

Tessa nodded as the smile slid slowly from her face. "Connor, is something wrong?"

"No, sweetie. It's just that tonight we're going to meet a very special lady, the queen of the Tuatha Dé Danann."

Tessa's eyes, lit up like headlamps. "Why?"

"Your mam—"

Tessa stood abruptly. Juice spilled across the tablecloth. Will I get to see my mam?"

Connor handed both of the glasses to Tessa then bunched up the blue and white checked table covering and pitched it into the sink. She took back her glass, gulped a mouthful, and swallowed. Her mouth was dry; despite the cold, sweet fluid, she croaked. "It seems so."

A myriad of emotions flitted across Tessa's face. "Oh no! Rudiobus! He's a God—" Her eyes suddenly filled with tears as the colour drained from her face. "Will the queen take him away from me?"

Connor shook her head. "I have no idea what's going to happen." She reached across, took Tessa's small fingers in her hand, and gave them a squeeze. "Regardless, you're about the bravest kid I've ever met. Don't be afraid. We'll be with you."

Tessa jerked. "Oh, no! Craig! What will happen to him?"

With her head gripped between both hands and her elbows on the table, Connor sighed. "I honestly don't know."

The clock on the sideboard confirmed the time was ten to eleven. Tessa slept on the head to tail on the lounge with Andrew. Connor walked over and shook her shoulder gently. "Tessa, it's time."

Instantly awake, she threw aside the blanket. After she pulled on her shoes, she rubbed her eyes.

Connor reached over, and tucked the blankets around Andrew. He moaned then snuggled back down. She turned to Tessa, who was already standing close, and nodded to Craig. "Come on, then. Let's do this."

With Andrew cradled in her arms, Connor walked two paces, picked up the scabbard that contained the God Killer, and awkwardly swung the strap over her head. The scabbard thumped on her back as she shifted it into place. "Tessa, bring your sword."

They walked together to the front door and down the stairs. Moonlight illuminated the path to the barn. Tessa opened the doors and waited until everyone was inside, then pulled them closed. She bowed to the MacRobertson sword gripped in her hand and placed it reverently along a bale of hay, before she walked over to Rudiobus' stall and opened the door. She looped her arms around his neck.

Connor's heart clenched at the fearful look on Tessa's face and her whispered words.

"I'm scared.""Do not be afraid, child. The queen has lived a very long time. I have known her always to be fair and just. Come, let us all wait, together. Each of us here tonight, is here for a reason. Believe in the rightness of providence, Tessa. I will let no-one harm you."

Everyone walked over to the hay bales lined up on the side of the barn, sat down, and waited. Rudiobus stood beside Tessa, his muzzle just above her right shoulder. They talked quietly between themselves. Craig's outline shimmered along the back wall.

Everyone jumped when Tessa leapt to her feet. "Mam!"

"Oh, Tessa! Blessed daughter! I am so very pleased to see you again."

Tessa broke down into hacking sobs as she gripped her mother around the waist. They sobbed in each other's arms.

Macha looked at Connor, who still cradled Andrew. Her eyes bulged. "Quickly! We must conceal him. The queen will be here any minute." The instant Macha she raised her arm, bales of hay at the far end of the barn, moved like a mechanised prop on a movie set.

The solid rectangles, moved like automatons, stacking one on top of another, making a three-sided structure appear to be a solid stack of hay. Connor carried Andrew over to the shielded side of the barrier, snuggled the blanket around him and kissed him gently on top of his head, then returned to join the others.

Shaking, Macha held both hands in the air, as golden threads weaved into the newly stacked hay, shrouding the bales, fading them into invisibility.

Connor frowned as she watched.

"Fear not, Connor, I have reinforced Andrew's magicks. The queen will not detect him." She turned. "Tessa, Andrew is hidden. We do not want anyone to know that he is here."

Tessa nodded. Her face was pale and she trembled with anxiety.

Connor walked over to where the MacRobertson sword lay. "Tessa, trust your mam. Here, take up your sword."

Tessa crossed the floor, collected the sword then returned to her mother's side and stood with her feet splayed.

Connor sat on a bale of hay. The blade of the God Killer vibrated across her knees as the Sword of War sent white-hot bolts of energy through her.

Chapter Twenty-Three

A HIGH-PITCHED HUM FILLED THE BARN AS A GOLDEN shimmer appeared. Danu, dressed in the royal blue, formal, ceremonial robe of the Tuatha Dé Danann, materialised. Connor stood and lowered her head to the queen. She gripped the hilt of the katana and pointed the blade to the floor.

Danu cast a glance around the barn. A pulse of power surrounded her like an electromagnetic field. Rudiobus went down on one knee. "Well met, Majesty."

She nodded her head once. "And to you, old friend." Her gaze darted in all directions. "Guardian, I would meet the Successor."

Tessa gasped. Her knuckles shone white under her grip of the MacRobertson sword.

Macha turned and looked down. "It is all right dear one, the queen means you no harm."

She stepped forward, the broadsword gripped between both hands. "Hello. My name is Tessa."

Danu smiled as pleasure, for just an instant. When bright light reflected off the blade, her eyes lit up with red-hot rage. "Where did you get that sword!"

The blade in Tessa's hand, in response to the threat and suddenly roared the battle cry of the Tuatha Dé Danann. Tessa stood defensively, blade outstretched. "It was my grandmam's. It chose me, and now it is mine."

Danu's eyes, slitted with suspicion. "Your grandmam's?"

"Yes. She was of the MacRobertson clan."

Danu relaxed then smiled as spoke, as if to herself. "Loyal to the end, Finn of the MacRobertson. You upheld your promise and kept the blade safe since that terrible day when—" Danu gasped when she realised she had spoken out loud. As she regained her composure, she clasped her hands in front of her and nodded to Tessa. "Well met, Daughter of the Guardian. I am pleased to have witnessed your skill with the sword. You are quite remarkable for one so young; not unlike your mother. It would seem the blessed sword of the Guardian, has found its way home."

Tessa looked accusing. "That was *you* I felt, when Connor and I were practicing today!"

Danu nodded. "Yes. I apologise for spying, but I had to know more about you."

Rudiobus walked over to stand beside Tessa, the clip of his hooves was sharp against the stone floor. Tessa rested the sword over one shoulder and placed her hand on his back.

The queen laughed and shook her head at him. "You really have made a home for yourself here in this mortal world, haven't you?"

"She," he nodded his head toward Tessa, "has made a home for me, and for that I am truly grateful. But, my lady, it is time I returned to the Kingdom of the Celts."

Tessa gasped, and, as if to comfort herself, began vigorously rubbing her hand back and forth along his neck.

Macha stepped forward. "My queen, please, Gwydrion has redeemed himself by saving the Successor. Please consider his petition."

Danu shook her head, sadly. "Indeed, Guardian, he did retrieve the child and save her from the clutches of Death. However, you know well my terms. Before I make any decisions, I will see the boy."

Staring straight ahead, Macha stood, as if made of stone. "Majesty, no. Rudiobus is owed a debt of gratitude. He deserves the return of his God status. I beg you, hear my petitions this night." Looking at Tessa, Macha sighed. "It is because we all have everything to lose, that I dare provoke you, by begging your consideration. On my word, I will reveal my son to you, but only after you have heard from those who need your help."

Danu folded her arms across her chest. The audible hum in the barn suddenly escalated. Static energy crackled, sending blue sparks flying; her hair formed a halo around her face. "You test my patience Guardian! Yet, for some inexplicable reason, but I believe the words you have spoken are truth and that the boy does exist. As monarch, I cannot risk losing the child who may be our future king." Danu paused as if considering Macha's words. "Therefore, I agree to your demands. I will hear the petitions of those who seek the favour of the Tuatha Dé Danann."

"I thank you, my queen." Macha stepped backward and bowed.

Straightening her spine, Danu jutted her chin toward Rudiobus, when a tear tracked silently down Tessa's face. "What is he to you, child?"

A shuddering sob made her voice tremble. "He's everything. He's my teacher, he's my friend—" She hiccoughed as another sob escaped her lips.

"Guardian?"

Macha paused as she linked her fingers in front of her. "He is bonded to her through me. Rudiobus is mentor and protector to her, as well as being a very good friend. He has a vital role to play, in bringing Tessa to her destiny, her future."

The queen shook her head. "What you ask is impossible. Balor, Monarch of the Celtic Gods, will wreak havoc if Gwydrion returns in his immortal state. The king is extremely dangerous and remains eternally bitter over the loss of his daughter, even though she died by his own hand." Turning to Rudiobus, regret showed on her face.

His head drooped. The fine hairs on his muzzle almost touched the stone floor.

"I am not finished, old friend."

He lifted his head and looked at her.

"You saved the Successor." She raised her clenched fist. Golden light engulfed him. "I decree that you will remain in this mortal realm until the Successor ascends to her role as Guardian, Protector. If you agree, I offer you restoration to your God status, but only if you vow to become one with the Tuatha Dé Danann, to act as Advisor to Successor. You can never return to the kingdom of the Celts. War is guaranteed, if you do."

Rudiobus snorted and bowed down on one knee. "Of this I vow."

"You will live in your horse form, but I gift you with the power to assume your God status if and when it is necessary to protect and nurture the Successor. We almost lost her once. I will take no chances with her life in the future. On her ascension, you will also rise. Together, you both will become members of my council." As she lowered her fist, the golden light faded to invisibility. "It shall be so."

Still kneeling, his deep voice rumbled in his chest. "I thank you, *my* queen. Your gift is more than I could have hoped for." He lowered his head and assumed his human form, tall, blond, and strong. The white robe of the Gods of the Tuatha Dé Danann swept his ankles.

Tessa wiped a hand across her face and brushed away her tears as she spoke to the queen. "Really? He can stay with me? Oh, Rudiobus..." She reached out and accepted his outstretched hand. The blade of the sword still rested on her shoulder.

The queen stood tall and regal. "No, child, he is Rudiobus, no more. He is Gwydrion, Tuatha Dé Danann God and Advisor to the Successor."

Connor tightened her grip on the hilt of the katana when the queen turned to face her. Suddenly, Danu reared back then screamed. "Death Walker! Abomination!" She raised her hand and flung a bolt of power that knocked Craig high in the air; hurtling him against a grain shredder at the back of the barn. He lay slumped and still over the machinery.

"Craig!" Connor stood with the God Killer outstretched as the Sword of War flew from her left tribal tattoo to her hand. Tessa gripped the broadsword and held it likewise when suddenly there was a boom and a flash of light as Yokami Sukani and Tomoe Gazen appeared, katanas drawn, keening the Song of the Samurai.

The queen, momentarily flabbergasted, quickly regained her composure. "Ahh... Now it begins to make sense. The Successor wields a blade like a warrior." She inclined her head to the Samurai. "Well met, Gods of the Blade. It seems you have me at a disadvantage. I knew there were Gods at work here. However, I never dreamed the

Immortal Samurai would dare to interfere in the life of the Successor of the Guardian. Of what interest is she to the Holy Warriors?"

Yokami lowered his blade. He looked at Connor, then nodded. All present lowered their weapons at his signal. "It is not your Successor that is of concern to us. Although Tessa has natural ability with the blade, and, under Connor's tutelage, she has become a fine sword-swoman. It is Connor who is—"

A deafening clap of thunder shook the walls of the barn. A Highlander, resplendent in kilt, sporran, and white lace shirt, stood draped in a plaid bearing the colours of clan MacDonald. Two deep-set rubies in the hilt of his broadsword glistened like bright spots of blood.

The queen gasped. "What manner of magic is this?"

"I am Connor MacDonald, forebear and great grandsire of this young woman. Connor a child of my clan, of our prophesy; the one who is gifted in the ways of the Horsemen."

Tomoe Gazen stepped forward. "She is also connected to us. I have named her Daughter of the Sword, my Successor, as warrior woman to the Samurai."

The queen bowed her head to Connor. "Well met, child of the Ancient Horsemen and the Samurai. Dual destinies? You are, indeed, a very unusual young woman."

Looking from one person to the next, Danu spoke. "Why have the Gods of the Ancient Scottish Horsemen and the Samurai appeared before me tonight?"

The three Gods stood very still; blades gripped in their hands. Connor bowed her head to the queen, then pointed to where Craig lay at the back of the barn. "My husband and son died at the hand of an immortal." Looking at Tomoe Gazen, she paused. "In the accident, the Samurai protected me and saved my life. In so doing, my husband, Craig, was also somehow preserved. My son James, died in my belly a short time later. Craig has been—"

Danu snarled. "You would dare to offend me by seeking my help for a Death Walker? An obscene creature that is neither alive nor dead?" Her hair writhed around her head like the vipers of the Medusa.

All five swords were poised and pointed at the queen. Yokami stepped forward, his blade still extended. "Choose your words carefully, queen of the Tuatha Dé Danann. *The truth is clear only to those who have the courage for its witness."* The tip of his sword pressed a fine dent in the fabric of the robe that covered her heart.

At the touch, her eyes for an instant appeared unfocused. She gasped as she looked from him to Tomoe Gazen and back again. "It is true?"

Danu turned to face Connor, then arced her palm in front of her. Craig became airborne, then hung in the air like a broken marionette. He struggled to get to his feet when, suddenly, the queen screamed and pointed at him. "What is that?"

Confused, he shook his head and tried to speak.

"Do not dare lie to me, Death Walker! I will order you banished to the Shade, to suffer the Penance of Rogue Gods! One thousand lashes per day with the fiery whip of Ogmios." Her voice resonated like a percussion hammer. "I will ask you one more time. What is it that you try to conceal from me?" She flung her fingers in front of her. Craig crashed against the back wall of the containment barrier, held spread-eagle in mid-air, as if restrained by invisible chains. The fabric of his shirt disintegrated, slashed into a hundred ragged strips. The material fell from his body and fluttered to the floor. He hung naked, from the waist up.

The golden cuff glowed around his bicep.

The queen lunged toward him. "Where did you get that?" Her index finger trembled as she pointed to the amulet. "Tell me now, or so help me..."

He mouthed as he raised his head in defiance. *"From the Place of Shadows."*

Craig looked to Macha and mouthed. *"Tell her!"*

The queen vibrated with fury. The shimmer surrounding her flickered like licks of white hot metal. "Guardian! Tell me what it is that you know?"

"My queen, when Craig's heart gave its last beat, he was God Touched before he passed into the Place of Shadows. Morrigan, our Keeper of Souls, tortured him because he could not pass into the

Shade. I cannot explain how it is, that he returned to Connor in this state."

Staring at the golden cuff, Danu grimaced. "I will approach you, Death Walker. Do you give me permission to share your memories?"

He hesitated.

"I give you my word as ruler of the Tuatha Dé Danann and keeper of the voices and the memories of the Old Mothers, no harm will come to you at *this* time. Please allow me to—"

Craig held out his hand.

Mesmerised, she stared at the ornate golden band as she moved toward him. When her fingers made contact with his essence, she cried out, then snatched back her hand and cradled it as if a beast had gnawed it.

Macha rushed forward, "My queen!" Danu crumpled to the floor of the barn.

The Old Mothers screamed in a collective cacophony of rage. "Treachery!"

Connor tore off a piece of her shirt and dampened it with water from the inside tap. As she patted it across the face of the queen, Danu groaned. "Merciful Mothers." She sat up, then floated to her feet and looked at Craig. She was as pale as chalk. Hands shaking, she released his invisible bonds. "Tell me about the Place of Shadows."

The barn was so quiet, the creaking of the timbers sounded like branches snapping in a storm. For the next half hour, Craig mouthed the words that described his terrible time in limbo. He almost smiled when he spoke of the unnamed woman.

As he retold the story, the queen interrupted and spoke through gritted teeth. "*Death* threatened to destroy the woman's entire race if she revealed her identity, and to prevent that from ever happening, she cut out her own tongue?"

"*That was what she told me, and I believe her. She has suffered greatly. If it were not for the Phoenix—*"

Danu jolted. The colour drained out of her face as she started to say something. She clamped her lips shut, drew in a deep breath and composed herself. "Start from the beginning, tell me how it is, that you came to be *here*."

As he relayed the story of the woman who placed the feathers on the ground and spoke the chant, the queen appeared to age twenty years. "It is apparent that she trusted you. To send you from the Place of Shadows she took an enormous risk. Death does not take lightly to souls that go unaccounted for."

Craig rubbed his wrists, chaffed from the bonds. *"I know. Death came here. She broke into Connor's – "*

Suddenly agitated, Danu interrupted. "Did she see you, Death Walker? Were you discovered?"

He shook his head. *"No. I don't think so. The sword sensed her when she entered the cottage and chased her out."*

"Good. It is right that she remains unaware of your existence."

The lines on his face deepened. *"Why?"*

She paused, her mouth and chin trembled as she rose, to hover above the floor. Fury shone on her face. "Because, the woman you encountered in the Place of Shadows, your saviour, is the daughter I thought long dead. She is Dagda!"

Connor tilted her wrist; the numerals on her watch read 11:58. "Macha!"

The Guardian nodded, stiff with anxiety. "My queen, the witching hour approaches. Please make your pledges before the time is lost."

Danu straightened and looked first to Macha, then to Craig. "No, Guardian. As the Samurai have said, *the truth is clear only to those who have the courage for its witness.* I have seen with mine own eyes, the treachery that Death has brought upon me and upon the Tuatha Dé Danann. When I think of all those souls lost, and how Dagda, our chief Guardian Protector, was taken and we were left vulnerable for three centuries, until the next Successor, ascended."

When the numbers of Connor's watch ticked over to 11:59, the queen flung both of her hands in the air. Everything in the room, with the exception of the Gods, Connor, Tessa, and Craig, ceased moving. Even the spider spinning a huge web, dangled mid-spin, as time stopped.

The Samurai raised their swords and pointed them in the direction of the queen. Yokami flexed his fingers on the hilt of the blade. "For what purpose have you stopped time on mortal Earth?" He jutted his chin toward Connor. "You know how delicate the balance is for humans."

"I bear you no threat, Lord of the Blade. It was necessary for me to halt the passage of time. The witching hour for the Tuatha Dé Danann, is the moment when the portal to my realm closes. I cannot be left stranded in this world, separated from the Faery. If our enemies were to sense my absence, they would attack, and I would be stuck here, unable to protect my race."

She turned to Craig. "I thank you for your honesty. You have given me hope, where, for thousands of years, none has existed. Guardian, I accept the truths shared here tonight as *the* truth. The time for the final test has now come. Show me—"

Macha took Tessa's hand in hers and stepped forward. "Give me your word as queen of the Tuatha Dé Danann; keeper of the voices and memories of the Old Mothers, that you will agree to my terms. Honour my conditions and I will reveal to you, my son. However, he is to live a mortal life here on Earth until his father's passing." Suddenly she blurted, "Passes from old age that is. Then, and only then, will I agree to him taking up his place in the Faery."

The queen's lips flattened into a thin line. "You play a dangerous game, Guardian."

Macha straightened her shoulders. "These are risks I must take, to protect my children. I will have your vow."

The voices of the Old Mothers screamed in Danu's brain. *"Do not tarry, Daughter, meet the demands of the Guardian. The boy child is too important. Do this for the good of the Tuatha Dé Danann!"*

With one sharp nod of her head, she clasped her hands as if praying. "Reveal the boy to me."

Macha arced a hand in front of her and walked towards the back of the barn. The hay bales, suddenly lurched, then levitated to settle on the floor. She walked to the back of the barn then leaned forward. As she walked back towards the queen, her arms were extended and her elbows bent, as if she mimed carrying a load in her grasp.

Danu screeched. "Is this some kind of joke?"

"No, Majesty, merely a demonstration of the strength of the wards in place that protect my son. It is at my choosing that you will see him; just as I can again cloak him from you for eternity." The air around them shimmered, as a sleeping child, draped in a blanket appeared, snuggled in her arms. "My queen," she bowed her head. "May I present the king of the Tuatha Dé Danann."

Danu gasped! She dematerialised from where she stood, and abruptly reappeared next to Macha. She placed her hand on the boy's silky blond hair. "Sweet Goddess, it is true! This child is of pure blood, as pure as *my* blood. Blessed be." She dropped to the floor on bended knee. "My king, I welcome you to the Kingdom of the Tuatha Dé Danann." She rose slowly with a quizzical look on her face. "You have indeed spoken the truth, Guardian. You could have bargained for anything, and I would have agreed to it, yet you ask nothing for yourself?"

Shaking her head, Macha sighed. "No, my queen. It is for my children that I petition."

Danu sighed. "Your suffering has been great since you left mortal Earth. I feel your pain and grief from the separation from your chosen mate. A look of regret passed over Danu's face. "I cannot release you from your role as Guardian." Holding out her hand, a shimmer of light settled over Macha. "As mother to the awaited one, I hereby give you the power to dream-walk with the boy's sire and with both of your children. I hope this will soothe some of your pain."

Holding her sleeping son in her arms, Macha stroked his cheek. "I thank you. You have given me a great gift." She shuffled Andrew into a more comfortable position. "My queen... I have told you my truths. Now you must live up to yours."

The screaming and shouting of the ancient Mothers almost drowned out Danu's words, so great was their excitement. "It shall be so."

A blinding flash of light filled the barn.

"No! Oh, Jesus, no!" Connor screamed as the outline of Craig's body began to flicker, then...

He was gone.

And so was the queen.

Chapter Twenty-Four

*L*ATER THAT NIGHT, BACK AT THE COTTAGE, MACHA waved her hands over the children who lay head to toe under blankets on the lounge. Their little bodies suddenly relaxed and curled into sleep. Her heart clenched at the sound of Connor's sobs coming from the bedroom. Anxiety overwhelmed her. *What did it mean? Why had Craig disappeared? Was it the doing of Death, or the queen? Surely, the monarch would not have betrayed her.* Her heart sank when the sobbing started anew.

She walked to the bedroom. "I am so sorry."

Connor sniffed and looked up with eyes red and swollen. "Why Macha? Is he...? Are they both gone from me forever? What the hell am I going to do? I don't understand. What happened? The queen said she believed him, then the next thing, he's gone."

Macha sat on the mattress and stroked Connor's face. "Such is the way of the Gods, my friend. Forever duplicitous, always unpredictable. I do not know what has become of him. Unfortunately, I do not have the Sight with the dead. Connor, the queen has always been trustworthy. Now, I don't know what to think."

Raising her hand, Macha invoked a sleeping spell and Connor immediately relaxed and closed her eyes. Her breathing settled to a steady rhythm.

In the early hours of the morning, before the rise of the sun, Macha disappeared and returned to the Kingdom of the Tuatha Dé Danann.

Suddenly awakened when Tessa slid between the sheets, Connor started crying again. Tessa sobbed alongside her. "Is he gone? Is he really gone?"

Sobbing, Connor curled herself into a tight ball. Words would not come to her.

Later, she hugged Tessa and got up to find Andrew trying to put the ear buds in his ears. "Come on. I'll take you over to your da."

He put his hands in the air just before she swung him onto her hip. Tessa walked quietly behind her, in silence.

Over at the house, O'Dee's face crumpled with concern when Connor walked into the dining room looking dishevelled and unwell. "Oh, lass, do ye have the fever?" She slapped a fleshy hand on Connor's forehead.

She shook her head and sighed. "No, O'Dee, I don't think so, but just the same, I think I'll spend today over at the cottage."

O'Dee took Andrew into her arms and ushered Tessa to her place at the table. "Aye, that sounds like a verra good idea. Are ye up for some breakfast?"

Connor shook her head. "No, thanks, I think I'm just going to go back to bed." She nodded to Tessa, who looked bereft, and then to Andrew, who was chewing a mouthful of buttered toast. "I'll see you all, later."

Tessa nodded and lowered her eyes.

O'Dee frowned. "Doona tell me ye are comin' down with summat, too?"

The last thing Connor heard as she walked toward the front door was O'Dee fussing about hot water bottles and that bed was the best place for bairns who were feelin' poorly.

Over at the cottage, she gripped the rail she dragged herself up the front stairs, her legs were like two blocks of lead. As she threw open the front door, Danu appeared in the middle of the room.

"I owe you an explanation."

Connor slammed the door, crossed the room and stood toe to toe with her. "Explanation! Do you fucking think! My husband, whom I lost over a year ago, thanks for you, is lost to me, again! Without him, I have no way of ever being able to give my God Touched son the chance of rebirth. You've lost a child, you heartless bitch! How can you be so cruel? You got what you wanted. Macha kept her word! She revealed Andrew to you!" Agitated, Connor paced the floor. Her voice got louder with every sentence she spoke. "Do you not feel one shred of responsibility? Have you no heart? She's *your* Goddess, Morrigan, *your* bloody Death God, after all! She's responsible for torturing Craig and for his suffering. You know this! He told you the truth as you demanded!"

The queen made a sound like a growl. "Not only *his* suffering."

Connor glared at her. "What do you mean?"

"Eons ago, my daughter Dagda was taken. We have always held the Dark Gods responsible. However, we were wrong. Your mate, through his memories, revealed to me that she too, is a prisoner inside the Place of Shadows. I have many questions. Who took my daughter? Why take her? Why has she spent all of this time in darkness?"

Connor stopped pacing and returned to stand in front of her, arms folded over her chest. "How do you propose to get those answers?" Menacingly, she leaned into the queen. "And what the hell does this have to do with *my* husband?"

Macha materialised inside Connor's cottage. "I just came to check on how you —" She stopped abruptly, faltered, them bowed to Danu. "My queen?"

"The look on your face accuses me, Guardian. Before you ask, no, I have betrayed no one. It is important that you both understand that I need to plan and move carefully. I require answers before I take my revenge on the being that exiled my child to the Place of Shadows. I *will* know the truth."

Connor moved closer to the queen. "Well fuck! A God who denies betrayal! That's hardly a first! Because, you know, this feels very like betrayal to me! Now, tell me! What has happened to Craig? Where is he?"

"He is returned to the Place of Shadows. I reversed Dagda's spell to protect them, and I cloaked the cuff before I returned him. She knew him to be a man of worth." Danu nodded her head in respect." Which is why she took such a terrible risk to find you." The look on her face was one of hope. "So that he might be able to get word to me, that she still lives. I pray Death did not discover Craig's absence; I cannot bear to consider the consequences... Danu frowned. "I am perplexed though, as to how it was that Dagda did manage to find you."

Out of habit, Connor, unconsciously reached into her shirt and pulled out the gold chain with the rearing Friesian gold ingot and her two wedders. She opened her mouth to speak, but was interrupted.

"Ahh, of course." The queen stepped back and appeared to relax. Her demeanour changed, as though she had just discovered the answer to the puzzle of the universe.

"Care to share?" Connor snapped as she returned the jewellery to its resting place inside her shirt.

Danu looked out the kitchen window, staring, as if remembering. "At the beginning of time, after the death of the one and only king of the Tuatha Dé Danann, I had a forbidden...er...*brief* liaison and became pregnant. It was after this secret event, that I was crowned queen."

Connor shrugged impatiently as she looked across to Macha, who shrugged in return. "Can you just get to the bloody point? I'm fed up with bloody Gods and their riddles. Now, what hell has this got to do with Craig and how Dagda found me?"

A look of pride passed over Danu's face. "Your rings are made of fine spun gold, are they not?"

Connor nodded as she tapped her booted foot in irritation.

", The scabbard on the wall vibrated as Connor crossed her arms and spoke through gritted teeth. "Oh course he does! We are...were married! Craig said something about that Dagda was able to find me because of the connection between our rings; given that they were made from the same nugget of gold." Connor leaned forward and frowned. "How does that work or is it some deep dark secret only shared between the Gods?" Sarcasm and fury dripped from her voice.

"Is you daughter all powerful with metals or something?" The lines around the queen's eyes softened. "No…not metals, per se. Gold."

Wrinkling her nose in confusion, Connor cocked her head to the side. "Gold?"

"Yes, gold." Danu paused. The only sound in the room was from the clock ticking on the rosewood sideboard.

"Her sire is Midas."

Morrigan stood in the shadows inside the palace of the Tuatha Dé Danann. Anxiety vibrated off her. *Why is the queen not at court? What could this mean?* A sense of foreboding settled over her as she unfurled her wings and dematerialised into an ominous, black shadow.

She began scrying the moment she arrived at the Place of Shadows. Joy lit up her heart as relief flooded her. There, in the corner, sat the spawn of the queen, rocking back and forth with that pathetic bird on her lap. The Shadow twisted on itself as she launched in the opposite direction. The Death Walker lay curled on his side, staring into the gloom. She cawed before she screamed. "Abomination! You are unworthy of this place; the gateway of the Gods unto the Shade! You offend me and the Gods that have gone before you." A black protrusion struck out from the roiling shadow as she raked the claws of a raven down his back and viciously pecked him with her beak.

Blood dripped onto the cold, hard floor.

He kept screaming.

Yokami and Tomoe Gazen stood under the moonlight on the balcony of the Imperial Kingdom of the Samurai. She leaned with her forehead pressed against his. "Each one of her tears is a knife blade to my heart. No longer can I bear this guilt, my love. I must…"

"*You* could not have known that by trying to protect our Daughter, Craig would become a pawn of the Gods." His arms held her close, but the warmth of his body, for once, did not calm her.

As she took a step backward, she gripped the marble railing and looked down on mortal Earth. "No, beat of my heart, what have *we* done? When you saved Angus and Marie from certain death in the aftermath of the battle of Culloden and brought them to Australia, destiny was put into motion." Sorrow replaced anxiety on her face and hung there. "You and I have both contributed to Connor's incredible sadness." She placed a hand over her heart. "Husband mine, you know I regard her as my own child! I cannot think straight when she suffers and—"

An ear-splitting roar and the stench of sulphur preceded a burst of red-blue flames half a mile long. The enormous golden serpentine dragon of the Samurai Kingdom landed with a thud that rumbled the foundations, causing the marble columns wobble precariously. The bright green scales along her tail, shone iridescent in the moonlight.

"Rye?" Yokami bowed "You have returned. We have not seen you since—"

The long tail swished back and forth in agitation as a puff of acrid smoke escaped her nostrils. "Your love for the child blinds you. You forget what she is capable of! You fail to recall, what she did!"

"Speak your truths, ancient one. Help us!" Tomoe Gazen bowed her head.

"The girl child triumphed over Bishamon! She slay the Samurai's God of War. Now, she carries *his* sword as testament to the kill. The God Killer, the very sword that ended that bloodthirsty, evil bastard's life, the only weapon that can kill a God, *also* belongs to her."

The Samurai stood side by side. Both frowned. Yokami took Tomoe Gazen's hand in his. "I do not understand."

The dragon rolled her eyes. "Mortals are tedious, but Gods are worse. Do you not see what lies before you?"

The Samurai spoke in unison. "No."

"Your Daughter must discover the lost Rites of Redemption. If she is to restore Dagda, daughter of the queen, and the male she chose as her mate, she must kill Morrigan. Be warned, Lords of the Blade, you must seek the help and counsel of Danu. Else wise, if your daughter kills the Death Weaver, the Tuatha Dé Danann will make war against the Samurai."

Connor pushed away the plate in front of her; the food had long since gone cold. As she laid her napkin on the tablecloth, a tongue-clicking noise from the other side of the table, made her look up.

O'Dee shook her head as she *tsked*. "Are ye well, Connor? You've eaten barely enough to feed a wee gnat. I swear ye are fadin' away afore my verra eyes. Can I get ye summat else? I doona like anyone to leave this table, hungry."

Connor gave her a weak smile. "I'm good, thanks, O'Dee. I just haven't got much of an app—"

Thunder boomed over the house and the walls shook. O'Dee got up from the table and went to the window. As she pulled back the curtains, she frowned as she looked up. "Well, now, that's verra odd. There's nary a cloud in the sky. What do ye make of that, Connor?"

She turned back toward the table. "Connor?"

The room was empty.

When repeated claps of thunder boomed overhead, Connor jumped in her seat as much from being startled, as from the herald of her ancestors. She slipped out of the room while O'Dee was looking out the window. When she opened the door to the cottage, Yokami, Tomoe Gazen, Connor the clan chieftain, Epona and Danu stood grouped together in the centre of the room. The clan chieftain walked forward and wrapped Connor in his arms. "Ban-ogha, *my grand-daughter*, we have summoned ye, and I am verra sorry for it. I ken ye are sad aboot what has happened to your man." He inclined his head to Danu. "We have come together to discuss how we might help ye come to terms with—"

Connor pulled out of his arms and stood apart from the group, hands fisted at her side. "Come to terms? With what?" Bitterness laced her words. "That my husband is gone and that I'll never have the opportunity to meet my son?" She glared at them. "You know... I hated it when he died, when *they* died, but I understood the finality of it. But, now that I know he's out there, suffering, how do you expect me to reconcile myself to that? Or, greater still, how will I ever forgive, for what has happened to him?"

Yokami stepped forward. "Daughter, there may be a way—"

She held up one hand. "No disrespect, Mr Sukani, but I'm tired of the words of the Gods that say one thing but mean another. Even solid vows," she sneered at the queen, "mean nothing. They are just words spoken, to gain advantage."

Epona and Tomoe Gazen stepped forward. The soft lilt of the Scottish Goddess tinkled like a bell.

"As ye have discovered, dear one, the ways of the Gods are lined with lies and fraught with danger. Please listen with an open heart to the words spoken here today. Together, we will lay map to the future."

The Samurai woman bowed. "My Daughter, it is my greatest wish to help you. The actions and reactions that have brought us to this point in time represent a turning point in history. Let not hate, blacken your heart and blind you to the possibilities of the future."

Danu spoke from where she stood. "I do not blame you, child, for hating me. You are correct. I did give my vow to your husband that I would not harm him. I have kept my word. If Death had discovered his absence, she would have come looking for him and wreaked havoc on every living soul in her path."

Incredulous, Connor crossed her arms. "You expect me to be grateful to you for sending Craig back to that terrible place where he is forced to live in perpetual darkness and be tortured? Trust me, hell will freeze over, before I ever forgive you."

The queen arced her hand in front of her. An image of Dagda crouched in a corner, ragged and beaten came into view. When a sob escaped Danu's lips, the image flickered. Suddenly, the vision changed, to reveal Craig, sitting on the ground with his back turned. Blood painted his shirt.

A guttural sob escaped Connor before she lunged for Danu. "You sadistic bitch!" The katana roared just before the God Killer launched into her hand. The bright light of madness ignited in Connor's eyes, as she spoke with deliberate inflection. "No. One. Ever. Touches. That. Which. Is. Mine." Blade outstretched, she stepped forward. "I will do whatever it takes to see my husband and son returned—even commit murder."

The queen jolted, eyes wide; the image flickered, then returned.

As grief and battle lust burned bright, Connor closed in on the queen. The God Killer screamed in anticipation.

Yokami grabbed Tomoe Gazen as she lunged forward, restraining her as he whispered something in her ear. She stood beside him, white-faced and trembling. The clan chieftain took Epona's hand in his. Silent communication passed between them. She nodded and gripped his hand tighter.

Connor moved like a predator about to strike. The God Killer sang as it arced through the air. "Do you recognise this weapon?" The blade listed toward Danu, its keening for blood, terrifying. "*This* is the only weapon that can kill a God. I could strike you down right here, just like when I took the head of Bishamon—"

The queen dropped her hand. The image faded and disappeared. "That was you?"

"Yes. I killed the Samurai God of War." Suddenly, the Sword of War launched from beneath her tribal ink and landed in her left hand. Déjà vu consumed her. Connor was in the barn at Nimerlin, eighteen months, past. Jo Bruce, possessed by Bishamon, stood before her, sneering and taunting. Both swords then, as now, screamed as they swung in concentric circles, the death strike imminent.

Danu snarled at the Samurai. "How is this possible? She is mortal!"

Yokami roared "Daughter! Hear me!"

Like an automaton Connor turned, swords still making the *whup-whup* sound as they cut through the air. She blinked rapidly, then stared at him, eyes unfocused for barely a second then she nodded once.

Tomoe Gazen struggled in Yokami's arms and screamed at the queen. "You know Connor to be the prophesised one, of the Samurai and the ancient Horsemen."

Epona stepped forward. "Yes! Hear us! Our daughter has both our blessings and is under our protections. She is God Touched."

Both swords simultaneously stopped mid-swing. Silence filled the room as realisation shone on Connor's face. "If I am God-Touched and from the Celts, then the Place of Shadows, is the place I will go, when I pass. Is that correct?"

Danu nodded. "Yes, that is the way of the Gods of the Celts."

Connor squared her shoulders as she bowed her head. The God Killer disappeared under her right tattoo, the Sword of War under the left. She looked at the queen. "Your daughter is a God and she's in the Place of Shadows. Craig is God Touched and he, too, is there. Why are they still there? Why have they not passed into the Shade, as is the way of the Celts?"

Danu looked miserable. "I do not know."

"Well, I guess there is only one way to find out." Connor lunged.

Horror froze on Tomoe Gazen's face. "No!"

Connor snatched the katana from the Samurai's woman's hand, raised it high above her blonde head, then drove the blade deep into her belly.

Chapter Twenty-Five

HE FREEZING, HARD GROUND BENEATH CONNOR leached the heat from her body. Darkness surrounded her. The smell of moss and dirt was as cloying as it was claustrophobic. The sense of being buried alive engulfed her, as she stood inside what she presumed to be the Place of Shadows. Her hand flew to her belly.

"That's weird," she said out loud. The shirt she wore was intact. There was no tear, no blood and no wound from the blade on which she had deliberately ended her life. She frowned, remembering when Craig *returned*. He had no evidence of the mortal injuries sustained in the accident, either. He was as whole as he had ever been, in an incorporeal kind of way.

Looking around, she stood and listened, taking small careful steps, deeper into the shadows. Her fingers became her eyes, seeking, as they inched along the wall. After what seemed like hours, she encountered the junction where two walls came together at right angles. She dropped to the floor, pressed into the corner, and rested her head against the damp, moss-covered stones. An uneasy sleep settled upon her, just below the surface of consciousness. The katanas vibrated as they stood on watch.

With a start, she woke, her gaze immediately darting in all directions.

Darkness, nothing but darkness.

Awkwardly, she tried to stand on her numb feet when a sound, not close, but nearby, almost made her lose her footing. Silent and still, she listened when she heard the barely audible noise again. She cocked her head. Was that someone crying? Shuffling her feet, she moved slowly across the floor. The shadows were so dense she couldn't see her feet, let alone the floor in front of her.

Suddenly, the sound got louder.

"Hallo. Is someone there?"

A gasp came from the darkness.

Connor stood still, trying to get a sense of where the sound came from. "Where are you?"

The vibration of the swords increased. "I'm not going to hurt you. I can help—"

In the gloom, a woman sat on the floor. Her long, matted hair hung down, covering her face. She didn't get up when Connor approached. Instead, she turned her back.

"Dagda?"

The woman turned suddenly, lunged, eyes wide with terror as she slapped her hand over Connor's mouth and shoved her downward. As she pinned her to the stone floor, she frantically shook her head. A golden torque with a huge red stone hung from her neck.

Suddenly, the Sword of War flew from Connor's left tattoo and morphed into the enormous red dog, teeth bared and hackles on end.

The woman slowly sat forward, rigid with fear.

Connor peeled the dirty fingers from across her mouth and whispered. "I'm sorry. I forgot. No one can say your name. I won't hurt you."

The woman closed her eyes as she reached for the gold chain around Connor's neck. She grasped the ingot, then slid it along the chain. Next, she held the engagement ring and slid it farther up the chain where it clinked against the ingot. Finally, she held the wedding ring in her hand. Her eyes flew wide. She dropped the ring and grasped Connor's hands in hers. A flicker of hope shone on her dirt smeared face.

A deep growl reverberated from the shadows. "Come to me." The dog morphed back into the Sword of War and returned to rest under her left tribal tattoo when the shrill *aahh-aahh* of a raven vibrated across the gloom.

Morrigan's sharp, black beak snapped open and closed as she muttered to herself. Her obsidian feathers vibrated with anxiety. The queen had not in the past ten thousand years, left her court unaccompanied. Yet, this day, Danu had taken her leave without a word to her guards or Goddesses as to her whereabouts. Frustration rose like a wave. As Morrigan descended toward the portal, worry exploded into rage. The God Threads at the threshold to the Place of Shadows, designed to keep out all but the Celts, lay shredded on the stone floor.

"What?" Her glossy black head shifted left and right as her white eyes searched for the intruder. With a loud screech, she flapped her wings and flew deeper into the shadows.

The abomination leaned against the wall, staring ahead. She crept into the room, unfurled both wings, then flayed him with her immortal feathers. He dropped to the stones on his knees. Blood gushed from his head and arms. He listed, then fell forward. His skull crunched against the floor. She laughed as she beat his unconscious body one more time, in exaggerated, theatrical movements, then shook the blood and flesh from her feathers. Droplets unseen became part of the darkness. Scrying the room, she didn't detect any fresh Celtic God souls. Endless corridor after endless corridor, she searched for any sign of the newly dead.

Dagda stood and held out her palm, watchful for the reappearance of the red dog.

Connor reached up and took her hand. "Thanks. I'm Connor. My husband Craig, is here somewhere. I need to find him."

The gurgling sound of the ruined tongue at the back of Dagda's throat matched her lip movements. *"Yes, he is here."* She put her index finger vertical on her lips before she mouthed, *"How do you know my name?"*

"Your mother—"

Her lips moved impossibly fast; the gurgling sound was wet and guttural. She gripped both of Connor's forearms.

"Sshh, stop!" Connor raised her hand. "Slow down! I can't understand you."

Closing her eyes, Dagda breathed deep. *"My mother knows I am here?"*

"Yes."

Dagda dropped to her knees. Her shoulders shook as she sobbed and curled in on herself.

Connor dropped to the floor and went to put her arms around her, when she suddenly jerked backward. A red and gold bird appeared on Dagda's lap. The golden torque had disappeared.

"I don't know what just happened, but is that a Phoenix? Jesus! How can that be?" She was unable to tear her gaze away from the bird. "I've come to help you return to the Faery. Then, hopefully, my husband and I will be able to try to find some way back to the lives we left behind."

The Phoenix stretched her neck and brushed Connor's cheek with the tips of her feathers, then lowered her head.

Dagda put her hand on the feathery breast then gasped as the bird began to nod its head. She reached out to Connor. *"There is much you need to know."* The Phoenix suddenly vanished and the golden torque reappeared around her neck. Dagda stood and held out her hand. *"Come, I will take you to your man."*

Craig groaned as the fabric of his shirt, deep within his wounds, tugged every time he moved. His blood-soaked clothes added to the chill. Every part of his body was a pyre of pain. He didn't have the energy to open his eyes. The pull of the shroud of final rest, began to settle over him. When he finally registered the sound of footsteps behind him, whoever was there, was already close. Instinctively, he tried and failed to cover his face with his battered arms. Screaming in pain, he braced for the attack when the pace of the footsteps, increased to a run.

"Craig!"

Connor! He never thought to hear her voice again. Now he knew for sure that he was dying. He willed himself to keep her beautiful face in his memory. His Life Thread, already taut, slowly began to unravel.

"Craig!" Connor's mouth went dry as she realised the extent of his injuries. She dropped to the space on the floor beside him and began to sob.

Slowly, he turned his head, his voice, no longer wracked with pain, but soft and dreamy. The split of his lips, through to his chin, made his words almost incomprehensible. "Connor... I will always love you."

The blond hair on his head fell backward as he slumped while trying to reach for her.

"No!" She leapt to her feet. "Come to me!" The God Killer launched into her right hand and howled with grief. The Sword of War landed in her left palm. She held both blades in the air and then drew the tips toward each other. When they almost touched, she screamed. "Power of the Immortal Samurai, I, Daughter of the Sword, summon thee. Hear me. Share with this male the essence that is mine. This I command!"

The tip of the blade of good, met the point of evil, engulfing her and Craig in a brilliant green, luminous glow. The swords screamed in anguish as an almighty explosion rocked the Place of Shadows. Then, suddenly, it was quiet. The swords roared in protest as they returned to the tribal bands.

Connor staggered then slumped to the floor.

Craig lurched as power channelled through him. He gasped as he rolled over and pulled her into his arms. With his hand, he held the back of her head and pressed her cheek against his chest. "No! Connor! No! Please..."

She groaned as she looked up at him, eyes unfocussed.

He wrapped her in his arms. "You're alive! Oh, thank God, you're alive!"

He gripped her tighter. "How did you get here?" He held her forward so he could see her face. "Sweet Jesus, tell me you aren't dead."

Her hand caressed his face, no longer bloodied and torn. After he kissed her on the lips, she smiled. "As dead as you are, I'm afraid."

"Why? Oh, Christ, Connor, why?"

She sat up and swayed as she held out her hand toward Dagda.

He jolted in surprise.

Connor groaned. "Oh, crap, I feel like I've been hit with a bus. Here, help me up."

He lifted her to stand next to him. She swayed slightly then leaned on him. "*This,*" she waved her hands in front of her, "and you two. It just doesn't add up. The passage of the Celtic Gods from life to the Shade is an expected journey, not a punishment. So why are you two still here?" She held up two fingers and ticked them off as she spoke. "First of all, we know that this place is exclusively for Gods; or, as in your case," she leaned over and kissed him, "for those who are God-Touched. Secondly, those who pass through here must be of Celtic Blood, which you both are." She looked down her nose like a professor addressing a student. "So? What is the unknown factor here? Whatever it is that has prevented you from passing into the Shade, must be here. *Something* is keeping you here, which," she kissed him again, "is lucky for me. Otherwise, I would never have seen you, again."

Rolling her shoulders, she massaged her tattoos then looked over to him. "I get that Tomoe Gazen bound you to her, at the time of the accident. So, for you, it's been a tug-o'-war scenario between life and death."

At the mention of death, Dagda began to sob again. The Phoenix once more appeared in her arms. Connor reached out. "But you, Dag—"

The Phoenix flapped its wings and let out a loud chirrup. Dagda jerked and stood wide-eyed with fear.

"Sorry, sorry, I forgot. All right, I'll call you D, okay? Promise."

A frown passed over Dagda's features, before she nodded. The Phoenix stroked her face back and forth, drying her tears. She leaned into the feathery caress when a guttural, gurgling sound broke the silence as her lips moved. *"Not something!.Someone!"*

Connor squeezed her hand. "I know about Dea—er, Morrigan."

D, scrambled backward, a look of horror on her face. *"No! Please! You cannot be one of her minions! No!"*

Craig leapt to his feet. The cuts that had criss-crossed his flesh, the peck holes and bruises, were all gone. He took Connor into his arms, then snaked a steadying arm around her back as he faced D.

"No. Connor isn't one of that bitch's minions. She's my wife. Didn't you just see her save my life?"

D, frowned and looked at Craig. At his nod, she slowly walked over to Connor. *"I am sorry. I did not know others knew of Mor—the raven. Sit, let us talk, there are things you should know."*

The katana on her back screamed in frustration as Tomoe Gazen paced the floor of her chambers. "Yokami! What if Connor failed to reach the Place of Shadows? How can we be sure such a place even exists? What if she has sacrificed herself for nothing? What of the Samurai? History has taught us that millennia can pass before such a woman crosses our path, again."

Yokami rose from where he sat on a chair in front of a warded window. "I have confidence that Connor will succeed in her journey. We must have patience. The answers will come to us, wife of my—"

A deafening boom rocked the walls of the Immortal Kingdom. Katanas launched into the air and landed in their palms. Back-to-back, they turned, swords outstretched, waiting to face the threat.

"Yokami?"

When silence ensured, the swords whined as they returned to their scabbards. He grabbed Tomoe Gazen around the waist, lifted her off her feet, and spun her in a circle. "She has done it! Praise the Masters! Connor is in the Place of Shadows."

With her palms pressed against the front of his robes, she pushed backward. When he lowered her to the floor, she frowned and she crossed her arms. "How do you know this? I have *no* sense of this place, nor of her."

Guiltily, he ducked his chin. "She has enacted Samurai magicks."

A wary look passed over her face. "Husband—!"

He stood silent.

"Yokami!" Grabbing his forearms, she shook him. "Tell me!"

His face was unreadable. "These magicks will only succeed if she has united the power of the God Killer *and* the Sword of War to share her essence with Craig."

Tomoe Gazen's hand flew to her throat. "You know well our magicks are sacred to the Samurai."

His God Voice boomed. "Is she not master to the two most powerful weapons that history has ever known? Is she not the child you named as your successor? *SHE. IS. SAMAURI!*"

Realisation replaced shock on her face. "*You* did this! *You* gave her the magicks! Just before she fell on my sword, you called to her!"

His black hair moved as he nodded. "Yes. It is so. I foresaw what was to come. I could not stand by and do nothing."

She glared at him in disbelief before she turned to the wall of books behind her and scanned the shelves.

"I am sorry I did not share this with you." He walked over and circled his arms around her, his chin resting on her shoulder as his belly pressed against her back. "I did not wish to add to your burden, something that may not have ever, come to pass." After he kissed her cheek, he released her. Her fingers moved silently across the spines of the books.

He caught her hand in his. "What book is it that you seek?"

Turning, she faced him. "The tome of Samurai Magicks. However, I suspect the answer I seek, exists in no book in history." Her face, hardened. "Tell me, husband mine, now that you have *again* interfered in the life of our daughter, what will be the consequence? What of Craig, who is already God Touched; when Connor, my God Touched progeny, combines her essence with the combined power of the God Killer and the Sword of War?" She gasped, as her hand flew to her cheek. "What of the unbor—" Her eyes suddenly flew wide in terror then her chin dropped to her chest.

Yokami jolted then hung his head. "I do not know."

Fear paled her face. "*If* Connor is successful, and *if* she finds Craig and Danu's daughter, how will we know? How will we find her?"

Yokami returned to the chair and stared out the window. "What is done, is done; the magicks are enacted. If Connor finds the daughter of the queen, I am praying that, with Craig, they will return to the Faery. The portal is heavily guarded and there is but one entrance. All arrivals are met by the queen." He paused and took both of Tome Gazen's hands in his. "If Connor does not succeed, wife of my heart, I will have failed you and we will never see her again."

D, stroked the feathers of the Phoenix. The bird closed her eyes in pleasure as she purred. Slowly, Connor leaned forward and held out her hand, palm up. Gold and red feathers ruffled as the ancient bird closely regarded the digits. After a few seconds, the Phoenix leaned forward and rubbed her face on the fingertips, allowing the gentle stroke back and forth under her feathery chin. Connor chuckled. "You are seriously cool. Do you know that, bird?"

Guttural noises made her look up. D mouthed, "*Ainneamhag.*"

"What?"

"*Ainneamhag is her name, from the language of my race. She has been my companion for eons.*"

"God, she's beautiful." Connor continued to stroke the lush red and gold breast feathers. "I thought the Phoenix to be a creature of myth. She is incredibly beautiful. Has she always been with you?"

D, nodded. "*Since birth.*"

Connor chuckled, again. "Well, she'd be a hard baby-shower present, to top."

D, drew her parchment-dry lips, together. "*My father is not one to be upstaged.*"

"Midas? Ainneamhag was a gift from your father?"

Shock painted D's face. "*How could you know the name of my sire?*"

Digging into the front of her shirt, Connor flashed the rings that hung from the chain around her neck. "Remember how you found me? Your mother worked it out. She realised that you had used your father's abilities."

"*My mother must be much changed, since I last saw her.*"

Flapping her hand, Connor dismissed the statement. "I don't know about that. Now, tell me, why did your father give you a Phoenix?"

Sadness passed over her face. "*To gift me with his affinity for gold, so I would always have wealth. Also, to protect me. You know that the Phoenix can rebirth that which has been destroyed?*"

Connor froze as D's words hit her like a sledgehammer. "The Phoenix is the Rite of Redemption?"

"*Yes. My father hated the Gods. He gave me the means to always find my way back to my mother and to the Tuatha Dé Danann.*"

Connor got to her feet and stumbled. "I don't understand! What am I missing here? All this time, you've had the means to be restored, yet you didn't use it? Why? Or, at the very least, why the hell didn't you fully restore Craig, instead of sending him to me barely visible and imprisoned so that I could never hear him or touch him."

D, stood. "*I am sorry, Connor, there is much you do not understand. It is true, I could have returned to the Tuatha Dé Danann by using my father's gift. But at what price? The Dark One, when she discovered me missing, would have lived out her threat and slaughtered my whole race. Why would I choose to replace eternal loneliness for eternal loneliness? As for Craig, my sire's gift, acts solely through me. The torque is useless to anyone else. The red stone is a pool of my birth blood; that is Ainneamhag's connection to me. To restore Craig fully, it would have been necessary for me also to make the journey. As much as I wanted that for him, I could not offer it. I will never risk my people. As for why he returned to you as he was, the cuff he wears not only allows me to mind-speak with him, it allows him to exist in two worlds. He is God Touched. I hoped and prayed one of the Gods might heed him and help him.*"

Ainneamhag jolted and silently morphed into the torque and settled around D's neck.

"Aahh-aahh!" Feathers ruffled. Morrigan's beak clicked on each word. "Now, what do we have here? A little friend has come to play... How nice!"

Connor, Craig, and D, stood side by side.

The raven took a step toward them, then looked at Connor. "This must indeed be my lucky day. Welcome, " her white eyes glowed in the dark. "to the one who instructs the spawn of the Guardian to wield the wretched sword of the Celts, I greet you." She suddenly flapped her unfurled wings up and down; the updraft scattered a wall of dirt and debris that forced them to step backward and shield their eyes with their hands. "It would have been so much simpler if the brat had died when she fell from her horse. Tsk, tsk, tsk, I must be losing my touch! She is proving so much harder to kill than her mother."

Chapter Twenty-Six

THE GOD KILLER SCREAMED AS IT CAME TO CONNOR'S hand, vibrating in its lust for blood. She held the sword in front of her. "D, run! Hide! I will find you!"

Tears dripped down D's chin as she turned and ran into the darkness.

"Take one step closer, you fucking bitch, and I'll rip your head off!" Craig moved forward as he tried to push Connor behind him.

"Aahh-aahh," Morrigan drawled. "abomination, it seems you have forgotten our previous little *get-togethers*. I do so enjoy your pain. It soothes me. I hunger for the morsels of flesh that I gouge from your body — *sooo* tasty!" The razor-sharp tips of her feathers ground against each other like a knife blade on a whetstone. Suddenly, she lurched forward and knocked him to the ground, clawing his body with her talons while she raked him with her wings. Morrigan screamed in delight as he writhed, when a vicious gash from her talons, split the length of his torso. Standing beside him, she lifted one wing, plucked a loose, bloody feather, and ran it between her lips. "Aahh-aahh, an aperitif of things to —"

Craig sprang to his feet. His belly wound undulated as the edges of the gaping injury inched toward each other. Closer, closer, until the flesh closed into a thin red line that became a silver scar, then disappeared.

"What manner of magicks is this?" Morrigan shrieked as she lunged for him.

The God Killer swung wide, severing the tips of the flight feathers of the raven's right wing. "Craig!" Connor stumbled. "We have to split up! You're unarmed! Go! I'll find you! Go!" Suddenly, she thrust out her hands, as vertigo from the essence sharing unbalanced her. She stumbled and fell to the ground.

"No!" Craig lunged for her as a wall of black feathers beat him to the ground.

Morrigan flapped her wings then became airborne, awkward with her uneven flight feathers.

Craig leapt up from the stone floor, ran to Connor and gathered her into his arms. "Sweet Jesus, Connor! Are you all right?"

As her head lolled backward, she thrust out her left hand and slurred. "Come to me." The Sword of War landed in her hand. Connor's voice was barely a whisper. "H...h...hunt!" The sword morphed into the huge, red, Australian dingo. The dog threw back her head and howled before she turned and disappeared into the darkness.

Danu paced back and forth in her chambers. Brighid and Macha searched through dusty tomes stacked high on the table. Books littered the furniture and the floor around them.

"Well? Have you found anything yet?" Danu scanned the litter of invaluable books. "Surely, somewhere in history, someone made a record of enactment of the Rites of Redemption! How can I be so close to reunion with my daughter, yet the means to restore her, eludes me? We must keep searching!"

Brighid stepped forward, eyes moist. "I am sorry, my queen, we have not yet found any reference to that which you —"

The room vibrated, bathed in a bright green glow. Macha, sensing the disturbance summoned her security force. They materialised in the room. Brilliant spheres of magicks burned bright in Macha's hands.

Yokami and Tomoe Gazen stood side by side.

"Samurai! It is forbidden to enter the Faery, uninvited." Danu, after several long seconds, nodded to Macha and the guards stood down.

Yokami bowed. "I bear news."

"Of my daughter? What news?" Power pulsed from the queen as she gripped his forearm.

"Connor has reached the Place of Shadows."

"How can you know this? I sense nothing." As Danu searched his face for signs of untruth, she increased the pressure of her grip. "I pray you are not foolish enough to have—"

The walls of the Kingdom of the Tuatha Dé Danann rocked under the percussion of thunder and the stamping hooves of warhorses, as Connor, Clan Chieftain, and Epona, materialised. "Our child is weakened. I feel it."

A pall of silence fell upon the room. The energy field around the queen began to flicker as rage sprang up in her belly. The iridescent shimmer became red and yellow tongues of flame.

"MORRIGAN! I summon you!"

The raven flew drunkenly. The uneven tips of her feathers gouged long, thin tracks along the wet stone, when the summons of the queen blasted in her mind. Her tone dripped with sarcasm. "What? Now? Just a little busy, you useless bitch!"

Scrying before she landed, Morrigan sensed no other souls. She screeched and swerved as she almost flew into a solid wall; blood dripped from her feathers. "Fuck! What to do? What to do?" She landed awkwardly, and then began pacing the length of the corridor. "It will be useless to assume glamour, to hide this little mishap," she inspected the severed flight tips of her right wing, "the queen will know immediately. I will never be able to explain such an injury." She began pacing again. "What to do? What to do?"

In the shadows, the red dog flattened to the floor and crawled silently on her belly. Unblinking, her eyes, the colour of molten steel, fixed on Morrigan. Closer…closer…the target was almost in range, when, suddenly, she lunged, grabbed the raven by the throat, and dragged her down to the ground. The dingo's massive, powerful jaws closed as the bones in the slender avian neck popped, bone fragments shattering.

"Stop!" Connor called from where she lay draped in Craig's arms.

He lowered her to the ground, keeping his arm around her waist. "Easy, now." His breathing was even, despite carrying her through a myriad of corridors.

She held onto him, unsteady on her feet. "Do not kill her!"

The dog's jaws opened as she released the raven, then lay her great body across the black feathered form. White teeth snapped, just missing the long black beak. The raven wheezed; her torn throat bleeding onto her breast feathers.

Limping, Connor leaned heavily on Craig's shoulder as she shuffled over to where Morrigan lay pinned to the floor.

"To me!" Connor tapped the side of her leg with her fingers. The red dog stood, then leaned down. The slavering gob of drool that hung from her mouth dripped down onto the face of the raven. The dog sat on her haunches, waiting...Connor swayed again. "Get up you evil bitch!"

Craig tightened his grip as she moved forward, the God Killer pointed at the heart of the raven.

Morrigan thrashed. Damaged feathers flew in all directions as she cackled. "You will pay for this! I am the Harbinger of Death. I relish the moment when you die beneath my —"

Craig turned when guttural noises filled the room. D, rushed forward and supported Connor on the other side, helping to keep her upright.

The red dog nodded her welcome. Connor leaned toward the dog then pointed down the corridor. "Lead us home. If she tries to escape, then feast upon the bones of Death!" She jabbed the point of the sword into the prone body before her. "I said, GET UP!"

Struggling, Morrigan got to her feet just as Connor raised the God Killer against her ruined throat. The keening for the kill in the dark was eerie. "Move!"

A terrible cackle escaped her beak. "Fool! There is no going back! No one goes back! I will keep you here for all eternity! My pretty play —"

D, took a step to one side. The golden torque started to vibrate as Ainneamhag appeared, floating in front of her. The Phoenix shimmered as she took the human form of Midas.

"My daughter. For you, I sacrifice the chance for return to a life where my food doesn't change into gold and those I love don't harden into statues for all eternity. I, Midas, King of Lydia, do bestow the blessing of Dionysus upon you, my daughter, for Redemption is not mine. No, gold is my choice, my mistress. Let this be so." As he slowly disappeared, his voice boomed. "To those who are God Touched, who have brought this prophesy to pass, prepare to receive your reward." A hint of sadness, laced his voice as he smiled at D.

"A crossroads. A time of reckoning.

The price paid for a debt, not owed

Redemption for deliverance from evil

Death in exchange for life, undone.

Incite the Rites of Redemption!"

For the first time in history, a brilliant flash lit up the Place of Shadows. As it faded, the raven screeched as they all disappeared into the ether.

The red dog appeared in the middle of the Throne Room. She snarled, hackles raised, as Connor and Craig appeared beside her. Morrigan stood rigid with the blade of the God Killer jammed across her throat.

As one, the Gods descended upon them. Yokami nodded to Connor. "Daughter!" Hand outstretched, he added, "Craig! Thank the mercy of the Masters!"

Tomoe Gazen, Connor, the clan chieftain, and Epona stood alongside him. "Bless the Holy Lords, you have both returned to us."

D, stepped out from where she stood behind Craig. Danu gasped and vanished from her throne and reappeared at her side. Her fingers pushed back the long, lank hair as she explored her daughter's face. "Oh, Goddess! Dagda!" They gripped each other in a hug and sobbed on each other's shoulders.

Standing with the God Killer still against her throat, Connor shouldered Morrigan forward. "Danu, I believe *this* belongs to you?"

The queen clutched D, to her. Staring across her daughter's shoulder, she hissed, "Speak now, carrion eater!"

Ruffling her feathers, Morrigan tested her wings. Guards held her where she stood. "Thank the Goddess you are here, my queen! These two God Touched abominations attacked me. Your dear daughter and I, barely escaped with our lives."

D, leapt at her, beating her with her fists, when, suddenly, the guttural sounds escalated into a loud scream. Her jaws moved as if tasting something, then she smiled. "Thank you, Father!" She stood in front of Morrigan, her unused voice, broke and cracked as she spoke. "You have been my captor and tormentor for eternity!"

The shimmering field around Danu began to pulse. Fear flashed over the faces of some of the guards. "Why? Why would you let me believe my daughter to be dead for millennia?"

The raven cackled. "Even *you* can't be that stupid, surely." Her bony shoulders shook as she laughed. "I have loathed you for as long as I have known you." Her throaty cackle, laced with venom, dripped with hatred. "I tried to send your Guardian into the Shade, but I failed. I relished the death of the Successor as revenge for the death of my daughter — a fair trade. I should have been queen! Balor, the lying dog, tricked me! He coveted the Tuatha Dé Danann for his own, but he underestimated our strength. It was never me, he wanted! It was always you! He knew he would never conquer this kingdom while protected by a Guardian. It was indeed fortuitous when he sought my help to dispose of the Guardian; your only child. Your destruction has been my life's work. When I banished Dagda to the Place of Shadows, I rejoiced in your tears as the Tuatha Dé Danann slowly weakened. Then," she glared at Macha, "you arrived and interfered with my plans. I laughed that day when I smote you down, while you and that white bastard were out riding." Her maniacal stare was unblinking at the queen. "It brought joy to my heart to make one of *yours* suffer, even though Balor cast me aside, in favour of easier conquests. As for the Successor; the pallor of death will become her."

The pulsation around Danu grew louder as furniture flew into the air and artwork on the walls crashed to the floor.

"Silence! For your treachery against the Tuatha Dé Danann—"

"Oh, spare me the drama! Has it slipped your mind, you stupid bitch, that I am a Goddess? You cannot kill me!" Her evil cackle was an ear-splitting screech

Connor stepped in front of Danu. "No, you're right. Your queen can't end your miserable existence."

Suddenly, there was a loud *whup* as the God Killer swung in a circle to the right of Connor's body. The blade keened loud in summon, as the red dog morphed into the Sword of War and landed in Connor's left hand. Both blades swung in circles at her sides. The *whup-whup* of the ancient weapons was drowned out by the dual call for the kill. Suddenly, Connor arced the blades and brought them to rest on either side of Morrigan's neck. Feather shavings fluttered to the floor.

"Oh, be gone, God Threads! You are really starting to annoy me. It is a true twist of Fate that you discovered the means of recovery for those destined to spend eternity in the Place of Shadows. Why do you think the Rites of Redemption were lost to history?" Morrigan cackled. "The Dark Ages was a time of incredible discovery; not the period of darkness, as thought today. At that time, there was way too much power to be had, so I wiped the whole period from history." She lifted her uninjured wing, then unfurled her fingers toward the blades. A moment of fear passed over her face when the swords didn't disintegrate onto dust. "Good trick, God Threads! Pity you are but God Touched and not immortal like me."

The blades pressed deeper into Morrigan's neck. "God Touched?" Connor suddenly became overwhelmed with rage. "You have no fucking idea!" Flashes of Craig's wounds, D's terror, and the great gaping maw of a tongueless mouth, changed her vision to red as her mind telescoped inward—only two beings existed: her and Morrigan. "You, Mistress of Death, broke my indissoluble rule! There is a consequence for all who break that rule." Connor's voice was icily calm as she plunged the Sword of War into the heart of the raven. "That is for James!"

Morrigan stood in front of her impaled on the sword and cackled sarcastically as she slid back and forth along the blade. "Again! Immortal!" Her laughter was shrill enough to flay skin when the battle cry of the Samurai filled the room.

Suddenly, the God Killer screamed, in flash of movement, it cut out both of the raven's eyes and severed the top of her skull. The brain tissue was incongruously white against the blood that oozed from the eye sockets. The God Killer launched the rounded top of the skull into the air. It thudded to the floor before coming to rest against the boot of one of the guards. The lifeless body of Morrigan, slumped to the floor.

Connor recalled the swords, then looked around the room. "No. One. Touches. That. Which. Is. Mine."

Epilogue

CONNOR JOLTED FROM SLEEP TO WAKEFULNESS. THE weight of the God Killer across her knees, where she sat on the lounge, was reassuring. Sunlight streamed in through the western window, as the afternoon shadows, lengthened.

"Oh, no. No! No! Please don't tell me I was dreaming!" The familiar bite of grief gnawed at her belly. Profound sadness settled over her, as she stood and went to the kitchen, poured a glass of water, and took a sip. She looked all around. Everything was where it should be. Everything, except for Craig, who no longer stood incorporeal along the sidewall. As she walked toward the front door, her gaze settled on the dark stains across the blade of the God Killer that lay across the cushions of the lounge.

As she opened the door and stepped out onto the front porch, she blew out a deep breath as she fought the panic rising in her chest. The setting sun was warm on her face, when a sense of beckoning filled her mind. With one hand shielding her eyes, she squinted, blinked, and froze. The glass slipped from her fingers and smashed onto the floor as she leapt down the stairs three at a time and started running. In the distance, a tall man silhouetted by the setting sun on the horizon walked toward her. She ran with outstretched arms. "Craig! Oh, my God, Craig! You're back! Oh, thank you, Midas! Thank you."

Craig swept her off her feet as they laughed and cried together. "Connor, oh, sweet Jesus, Connor. I love you." His moss green, mirrored eyes, shone bright.

They clung to each other in the middle of the paddock under the setting sun, exactly as they had a hundred times before, in her dreams. A rush of warmth filled her when the top button of her jeans popped. Grabbing his hand, she placed it on her rounded belly.

"Is that…? Is he…?"

She laughed and nodded. "Yes. It's him. Oh, God, I can feel him. Oh, Craig, you're back! You're both back! I'm so happy. I love you both so much. I wouldn't have cared how you came back. It wouldn't have mattered. I'll take you both, changed or not. Nothing could ever make me stop loving you."

A deep rumbling voice mind-spoke to her from deep within her womb, as blue-mirrored eyes flashed into her brain.

Be careful what you wish for, Mother mine.

The End

Meet the Author

As a career nurse/midwife, I have celebrated life and birthing. Study and research has always been my playground. After being awarded a PhD, I turned my attentions to my other great passion—writing. A love of the Scots and their history is a common thread in my works of fantasy.

I smell rain before clouds gather across the sky. I feel the dawn before the sun paints the world the colours of the earth. It is the flit of gossamer wings above my head as I walk through my garden that warms my soul and makes me glad that faeries exist. The universe is my mistress and my strength. Things that growl in the shadows or snap at my ankles in the night are my dark friends—the source of my creativity. I, am Kathrine Leannan

Coming Soon

To Baile Do Cailleach
A Home for Witches

Adrianna Randall, born of pure ancient blood, is a witch. She isn't exactly popular with her sisters of the Sydney Witches Coven, or insurance companies. While blessed with the blood of hanged witch Elizabeth Randall, she is healer to all beasts and restorer to Mother Earth; there is just one problem…

She has an affinity with fire and she has no idea how to control it.

Visit KathrineLeannan.com for book release and purchase information. While you're there, leave a comment for the author and sign up for news and updates.

www.ingramcontent.com/pod-product-compliance
Lightning Source LLC
Chambersburg PA
CBHW070853180626
46817CB00003B/755